Only when the darkness falls can you see the light of the stars.

THE SECRET
Irin Chronicles Book Three

For thousands of years, the scribes and singers of the Irin race have existed to protect humanity and guard the gifts of the Forgiven. They have lived in the shadows. They have kept their secrets.

But the Irin aren't the only race with secrets.

Ava and Malachi have survived the darkness, but will they ever discover the light? A powerful cabal of the Fallen may hold the answers, but to surrender them, it wants the Irin race to finally face their enemies. Both those coming from the outside and those raging within.

The Secret is the third book in the contemporary fantasy series, the *Irin Chronicles*, and the conclusion of Ava and Malachi's journey.

"The Secret is a beautiful, intelligent, captivating close to the Irin Chronicles series. Hunter's writing is richly sensual, and she proves yet again that she is a master of weaving together past and present, mythology and reality into a tale so enthralling you never quite want it to end."

—Colleen Vanderlinden, *author of the Hidden and Copper Falls series*

Praise for the Irin Chronicles

"THE SCRIBE is a perfect marriage of urban fantasy with tinges of romance. Creating a world in which ancient evil battles for turf and the heart, and the innocent are trapped in the crossfire, [Hunter] leads us on a riveting journey through the streets of Old Istanbul and old magic. An awesome ride!"
—Killian McRae, *author of 12.21.12*

4.5 out of 5 stars "I am in love with this new series."
—Karina, *Nocturnal Book Reviews*

"5 stars ...this may actually be THE best thing I have read this year."
Douglas Meeks, *Paranormal Romance Guild*

"Hunter's finest work to date.... This book is simply stunning."
—Leisha O'Quinn, *Rolopolo Book Blog*

"The Singer boasts a truly excellent blend of action, treachery and romance that ends with a startling plot twist. Hunter is an author to watch!" —RT Magazine

"Passionate, spellbinding, and heartbreaking -- "The Singer" is all this and so much more. Hunter is at the top of her game, drawing you into a story of love, loss, bravery, and redemption. If you loved "The Scribe," you will absolutely adore this sequel."
—Colleen Vanderlinden, *bestselling author of the Hidden series*

"Haunting, mysterious and passionate, THE SINGER will seduce you at the first page and knock you breathless by the last one.
—Grace Draven, *USA Today best-selling author of Radiance*

"Hunter has created a magnificent world of amazing characters, entangled in a web of deceit, danger, loss, power, politics, and love that will have your heart racing time and time again."
—Sandra Hoover, *Cross My Heart Reviews*

The Secret

Irin Chronicles Book Three

ELIZABETH HUNTER

THE SECRET
Copyright © 2015
Elizabeth Hunter
ISBN: 978-1508820802

This is a work of fiction. Names, characters, places, and incidents are the products of the author's imagination or are used fictitiously. Any resemblance to actual persons, living or dead, business establishments, events, or locales is entirely coincidental.

Cover art: Damonza
Edited: Victory Editing
Formatted: Elizabeth Hunter

For information, please visit:
ElizabethHunterWrites.com

For my mother and father

Thank you for showing me what love
Looks like
Sounds like
And acts like
Every day of my life.

ALSO BY ELIZABETH HUNTER

The Irin Chronicles

The Scribe
The Singer
The Secret

The Elemental Mysteries Series

A Hidden Fire
This Same Earth
The Force of Wind
A Fall of Water
Lost Letters & Christmas Lights

The Elemental World Series

Building From Ashes
Waterlocked
Blood and Sand
The Bronze Blade

The Elemental Legacy Series

Shadows and Gold

The Cambio Springs Series

Shifting Dreams
Desert Bound

Contemporary Romance

The Genius and the Muse

They took and brought me to a place in which those who were there
were like flaming fire,
and when they wished, they appeared as men.

They brought me to the place of darkness,
and to a mountain, the point of whose summit reached to heaven.
And I saw the places of the luminaries and the treasuries of the stars,

and of the thunder,
and of the uttermost depths.

The Book of Enoch

Chapter Seventeen

Prologue

SHE WALKED AS SHE always walked in these dreams. Slowly. With no thought of where she was going. She only knew that, within this forest, a dark angel walked on her right and her mate walked on her left. Sometimes she could smell the soft damp rot of the forest; sometimes she couldn't. Sometimes she could hear her footsteps as she walked over leaves. Often the birds chirped and called, but this night they were silent.

She might see his shape, but often the angel was only a presence lurking on the edges of her mind.

This night, her mate was beside her and the angel's dark form walked at her side, his presence tangible. His power muted.

"Why do you visit me like this?" she asked him.

"Because I want to."

"There is another reason."

"If I am here, then the other cannot be."

She glanced at the warrior beside her. "But *he* is here."

"He belongs here. The other does not."

A tendril of anger threaded through her dream. "I don't understand you."

"You will."

"Why can't he hear you? See you?" She glanced at the warrior. In the low light, his *talesm* glowed with a silver sheen. He didn't touch her, but she felt his presence as if the whole of him were wrapped around the ephemeral thought of her, anchoring her mind to her body.

She would drift away without him.

"Your mate is not mine as you are."

"I don't know what that means."

"You will."

"When?"

The dark angel paused. "Soon. You will know soon."

They walked, and the night grew darker. Colder. She shivered, and her *reshon* reached out, taking her hand in his. That was all he did, but the cold fled and she was drawn into his light. The mating marks on her arms lit. Her shoulders grew warm, and the fog that surrounded them grew thinner.

The angel stopped, so she did too. He stepped closer, until his face was lit by the light that glowed from her body. Her own marks. Before her, he grew. And he was not a man. He was more, but she was no longer frightened.

"This is how it should be," he said, one hand hovering over her rune-marked shoulder. "Thousands of years, and I finally understand."

She felt her mate draw closer, but the dark angel held up a hand. He was forced to retreat. The scribe said something she did not hear because her eyes were locked on the familiar gold gaze of a man who was not a man.

"I want you to remember now."

Remember what?

He sent an image to her, but it was not one of the visions that were familiar and frightening. It was a narrow room, and two men were there with a woman. With *her*. One sat next to her. The other in a corner.

This is a memory. This is mine.

"Remember, Ava."

"You are… Irin scribe house."

"Istanbul."

"What are you?"

"…angels."

Angels? Her eyes closed. Her mind focused. Angels.

"Did you think the angels—"

"Ava!"

THE SECRET

SHE woke with a sharp breath, sitting up as her eyes flew open. Malachi was beside her, his hand on her arm. It was early morning, and grey light shone around the corners of the curtains in the house by the sea. The room was cold, but she was covered in a sheen of sweat.

"Ava?"

"I'm awake." She cleared the rasp from her throat. "I'm okay."

"Was it Jaron again?"

"Yeah."

She took a soothing breath as he pulled her into his arms. She no longer had to ask. He no longer hesitated.

In the month since he'd come back to her, they'd grown more familiar, though they still handled each other with care. Malachi was cautious about certain topics. Their past in Istanbul was safe. Their months apart were not.

Part of Ava felt as if she'd woken from a nightmare when Malachi came back.

The other part waited in terror to wake from the dream of him being alive.

"Better?" he whispered into her hair.

"Yes." She breathed again, closing her eyes and listening to the steady surf in the background. "Yes, better."

He held her against the solid wall of his chest, anchoring her to his body, holding her in the circle of his arms.

Safe. Safe.

Some mornings Ava woke feeling as if she could drift away. She was smoke on those mornings. The thin fog that hung over the ocean in the moonlight. They clung to each other in sleep, no matter what had happened during the day or how distant she felt.

Sometimes she woke and he was watching her, frowning as if he was trying to remember.

On the best mornings, she woke and Malachi was the man he had been, light in his eyes and a teasing smile at the corner of his mouth. They made love on those mornings with playful passion. The joy of new lovers in familiar skin, hiding away in his grandparents' house on the edge of the sea.

On those mornings, they didn't speak of the other times he woke her. The hours when she cried in her sleep. Stifling screams. Weeping with remembered loss. In the bleak darkness of those nights, they held each other desperately.

"I'm here," he'd whisper. "Ava, I'm *here*."

Once, she bit his shoulder hard enough to break skin, and the taste of his blood had lingered in her mouth for days.

"I'm here." He said it over and over again.

And in the mornings, she believed him.

But the nights always came. The dark angel walked with Ava in her dreams, and she woke crying, seeing Malachi's face dissolve into gold dust that rose in the damp air of the cistern where he had died.

"HOW is she?"

"She grieves."

Rhys paused on the other end of the phone call. "But you're back."

"Her mind knows that. But there are moments when I think her heart forgets."

Malachi held the phone to his ear while he watched his mate take pictures near the shore. His grandparents' house sat on the ocean north of Hamburg, hugging the edge of the North Sea. It was bitterly cold in the middle of winter.

Malachi craved the warmth of southern waters, but Ava resisted a return to Istanbul no matter how Rhys and Leo reassured her.

His brothers called every week and asked the same questions.

How was Ava?

Had Malachi remembered more?

Had any more of his *talesm* returned?

Malachi continued to remember in scattered bits, but nothing like the full recovery they'd hoped for when he and Ava reunited. His *talesm* were stalled. They were nowhere near a scribe house where he could perform the rituals correctly, and none of his previous tattoos had reappeared as they had for a while during their dream-walks.

Ava refused to use her magic.

"Have you asked her about going to Vienna?"

"She keeps saying 'later.' She'll go later. We were going to go when her father performed there, but she changed her mind at the last minute. Said she wanted to have more time with just the two of us."

"That's understandable."

Malachi shook his head. "That's not the reason, Rhys."

"No?"

He took a deep breath and debated confiding in the scribe who had once been his closest friend. Though he couldn't remember all of it, moments came to Malachi when he remembered how close he and Rhys had been. Years of history tied them together. He'd had to learn to trust the man he had been, even if he couldn't remember the whole of himself. Even if it was possible he'd never remember it.

He watched Ava as she looked out to sea. She hadn't moved in minutes. She was letting the icy surf lap her feet as the wind picked up. It whipped her hair into a cloud of black waves. But even as the cold crawled up her legs, she didn't break her gaze on the horizon.

"She won't use her magic."

"What do you—?"

"She's reading a lot. Has me help her with translations sometimes. She's read through everything Orsala sent at least twice."

"But she's not practicing spells?"

"No. She mouths the words, but she won't say anything aloud."

"Do you ever see her marks glowing?" Rhys's voice was concerned. "Any sign?"

"Dreams. Only in our dreams."

"And the visions?"

"Nothing like what happened to her in Norway. She dreams, but she doesn't remember it clearly."

Both men paused in the conversation, and Malachi looked up and down the beach as Ava continued to walk and take pictures. Scanning for threats. Always scanning. She was his to protect and always would be, even now that she had her own power.

Ava looked up and smiled at him once before she went back to taking pictures of something in the water.

5

Other than when she was reading, she was rarely without her camera, and he often glanced up to see her taking a picture of him with a shy smile.

He loved it when she did.

"Do you think she's feeling unsure of using her magic?"

"I think she's terrified."

"Of what? You're more than capable of shielding her at this point, even with your *talesm* diminished. Your bond with her—"

"She's terrified of what she can do. She hasn't said anything, but you know she feels different."

Rhys was silent.

"She's not like the others, Rhys. Even Sari and Orsala know. They don't say anything, but her magic feels… different."

"We've never understood where it comes from. That has to be disconcerting."

He squeezed his eyes closed for a moment. "Disconcerting" didn't even touch the surface of it.

"Is there any sign of her grandmother?"

"If the older Ava is still alive, Jasper Reed has hidden her so completely that not even I can suss out her location. We've torn through his financial records. Other than being ridiculously wealthy and spending money on enough drugs to intoxicate a small country, everything lines up."

"He's that much of a junkie?" Malachi curled his lip. He'd spoken to Ava's mother on the phone, even spoken briefly to her stepfather. They were polite. Her mother was warm but cautious. Her stepfather, disinterested. But it was difficult to imagine them allowing an addict—even a rich one—into Ava's life.

"I don't know that I'd call him a junkie," Rhys said. "He has many of the signs of bipolar disorder. The drugs he takes could be a form of self-medicating. He's mostly functional, other than the typical artistic excesses."

Ava's father was a world-famous musician and composer, but his off-stage antics were legendary. He'd been a peripheral part of her life when she was a child, but they'd developed an affectionate, if distant, relationship as Ava had become an adult. Malachi knew they e-mailed regularly and were planning to meet when her father was on tour in Europe.

"Any word from Vienna?"

"Nothing since last week."

Orsala and Sari were in the city with Damien, quietly taking stock of the fallout from their confrontation with Volund's Grigori in Oslo. The rumbles of discontent from the watchers over Europe had grown, and the Scribe Council in Vienna had been forced to take notice. But for the almost-immortal elder scribes on the council, change did not come swiftly. It would take more than the concern from soldiers in charge of the scribe houses to make the politicians take action.

The stated policy of the Irin Council had not changed.

Protect humans from the Grigori, but do not engage further.

Do *not* provoke the attention of the Fallen.

Defense, not offense.

But though the Irin Council remained silent, formerly hidden Irina around the world had been roused by the attack on Sarihöfn.

Irina who had hidden themselves since the Rending were making their way to scribe houses around the world.

And the Irina weren't interested in defense.

SHE watched him as he ate, marveling at even his simplest gestures. The way his full lips closed around the tines of a fork. The movement of his throat when he swallowed. The shadow of stubble that grew every day, only to disappear each morning when he shaved. It would rasp against her lips when she kissed him at night, an edge of coarseness against the soft strength of his mouth.

He looked at her, the corner of his lips turning up. "What are you thinking?"

She smiled back and took another bite of the stew he'd made. Ava was pleased to discover that Malachi was a very good cook. He'd never cooked for her in the scribe house in Istanbul. The quiet routine they'd fallen into when they came to the sea was nothing like what they'd ever had before. There had been the tumult and the ecstasy of their time in

Turkey. The agony of their separation. The uncertainty of their reunion in Oslo.

They had never just *been*.

"You know what I'm thinking," she said. "What are you thinking?"

"I'm thinking we should finish dinner and clear the table."

"We could leave the dishes until later."

"We could, but I have other plans for the table." He patted a hand on the edge of the sturdy table where he'd eaten as a boy.

Ava smiled. "Your grandmother would be scandalized."

He laughed, and the rich sound of it filled one of the cracks that still riddled the tentative foundation they were building.

"If you knew her and my grandfather," he said, "you'd know how false that is."

"What were they like? Do you remember much?"

He nodded. "I've remembered a lot since we've been here. Stepping through the door. Hearing the ocean… I remember much more about my childhood with the anchors here."

Malachi never said it, but she knew he wanted to go back to Turkey. Wanted to try to jog his memory where they had first met.

According to Leo, it was safe. He and Rhys had been put in charge of rebuilding the Istanbul scribe house, and with so many of Volund's Grigori dead from the attack in Norway, there was little supernatural activity in the city.

It was quiet, but Ava sensed it was the stillness before a violent storm. Jaron's visits had not lessened, and the darkness she sensed around the edges of her dreams only grew deeper.

"Tell me," she said. "About your grandparents. What were they like? They were married—mated?"

"Yes, but not as we are."

"How?"

He took a sip of red wine and refilled her glass from the bottle on the table. "They were mated, but they were not *reshon*."

"What?"

He smiled. "I told you not every Irin couple has that connection. They met when they were both young. They fell in love and took mating marks, even though they knew they might meet their soul mate later."

"What would happen if they did?"

He shrugged. "Nothing. They were bonded. They had shared their magic. They loved each other very deeply and were committed for life."

Ava blinked. "Did they dream-walk?"

"I imagine so. That's a consequence of mating, not because a scribe and a singer are *reshon*."

"But…"

Malachi hooked his ankle around her leg. "What?"

"I guess I can't imagine it. To *not* have that connection… You make everything weird about me make sense."

"I'm glad." His eyes warmed. "Even though I don't think you're all that weird."

"I am. You just don't remember."

He smiled, even as his eyes drifted to the fire they'd started earlier. It crackled and popped in the cold air. "Are we more than soul mates, Ava?" His voice was pensive. "I wonder sometimes. If you are here—with me— from only that obligation."

"I'm not with you out of obligation."

"Are you sure?"

"I'm positive." She blinked the tears away. She was done crying, and he deserved more than her doubt. He deserved his life back. His memories. His mate. "I love you."

"I love you too." He waited for her to speak, but she said nothing. "Come here."

Ava stood and slid into his lap as he pushed away from the dinner table. His arms came around her, and she laid her head on his shoulder, pressing her cheek to his neck. Skin to skin. The comfort was instant. The voices swirling at the edges of her mind were silent. The terrible energy that crawled under her skin calmed.

"Do you want to go back to Istanbul?" she asked.

"I want to be where you feel safe. And happy."

9

She opened her mouth but paused before she gave him an automatic answer.

He deserved honesty too.

"Happy may still be a ways off. But… I'm content with you. I feel complete."

"You're still frightened."

"Yes. But being with you makes me feel safer. It's going to take time."

"Do you want to go to Istanbul?"

"I want you to find yourself again. To get back to your life. With me in it, of course. But you need to have a purpose again. To help your brothers. I know you're restless here. And I can take pictures anywhere."

"I'm fine."

"You have chopped enough wood in the past month to heat a castle for a year."

"I have not." He ran a hand through her hair. "I've worked off energy in other ways too."

"And I'm a fan of those ways." She kissed his neck. "We can go back. If you want to."

He held her tighter. "Are you sure?"

No.

She took a deep breath and said, "I will be."

Chapter One

MALACHI WATCHED THE TRAFFIC crawl by as they eased onto Atatürk Bridge before crossing the Golden Horn in the taxi Ava had flagged down outside the airport. She'd resisted telling anyone they were returning to the city, still wary of any communication that could put them at risk. They'd flown from Frankfurt to Istanbul during the night, arriving just as the sun was rising. It was rush hour, and the familiar shouts of drivers and vendors filled the air along with the smell of the water.

He glanced at his mate, who was sitting quietly next to him in the back of the car. Her phone was out and her fingers danced over the small keyboard, but her leg rested against his.

Touch. Connection. He suspected in the tumult of the busy city she needed as much as possible.

"What are you doing?" he asked.

"Answering e-mails." She tapped faster. "Checking… stuff."

"Anything interesting?" Malachi might have lived longer, but in some ways, he was far more ignorant of the world at large. Ava was independent. She managed her own finances. Ran a business. He knew she had a home in California, but he didn't think she'd been back for over a year.

"A few things from my mom. Two from my agent. One from my dad's manager. A couple from… from my financial adviser."

"Are you still ridiculously rich?"

"Yes." She looked up. "Are you still okay with having a rich wife… mate? Whatever I am?"

"Yes." He smiled. "It's good that one of us knows something about money."

Ava shook her head. "What did you do without me?"

"I don't know." His smile turned into a grin. "Honestly, don't remember a thing."

She shoved his arm. "Don't joke about that."

"Why not? There's nothing else to do."

"You'll remember," she said. "Eventually."

"I have you back." He reached over and squeezed her knee. "There are worse places to start."

She grew silent, but he could see the shadow of worry fall on her.

"What about work?" he asked. "You said there was something from your agent. Is there anything interesting? Any new jobs?"

Ava hadn't worked a proper photography job since the one in Cyprus a few weeks before they'd met.

Through scattered conversations in the past month, Malachi had been able to put together a timeline of what had happened to him and his mate, even though he only remembered pieces. Only a year had passed, and Malachi's world had taken over Ava's with no end in sight. She'd been running from Grigori. Hiding from fallen angels. Learning who and what she was in the world, as much as any of them knew.

A human job might seem like a vacation.

Ava shrugged. "There's an offer from a magazine, but nothing tempting."

"Where is it? Would it be possible for us to go? I can go with you."

"No." She curled her lip. "I mean, it'd be possible. I just don't want to do it."

Malachi frowned. It bothered him that her life had been so disrupted. He couldn't remember what they had planned before they'd been separated, but he knew that she had a life outside of him, and he didn't want her to lose it.

"What would you be doing now?" he asked. "If you'd never met me? If all this hadn't happened."

Ava shut off her phone and looked at him. "I don't know. Traveling. Taking pictures. Going to more doctors? Hiding somewhere remote so I wouldn't go crazy."

His voice dropped, not that he thought the driver was eavesdropping over the pulsing pop music blasting on the speakers. "Is it better than last time?"

"The voices?" she asked softly, reaching for his hand. "Yes. Much better."

"Good."

At least she was using her magic to shield herself. It hadn't been an issue in Germany, but they'd been in the country. He'd worried about her being back among humans, especially in a crowded city like Istanbul. Her refusal to use magic could be a liability to her safety, and no matter how much he could protect her body, there was only so much he could do to help her mind.

"Being with you has always helped. Any kind of contact…" She threaded their fingers together and picked up her phone again. "It makes life much more bearable."

Malachi tugged her toward him, and she rested her head against his shoulder. It was a small thing for him to do. A small thing for her to give him. But she let herself lean on him, and he was content. She continued scrolling through her inbox, reading and deleting things as he turned back to watch the city inch by.

Istanbul was achingly familiar. In the puzzle of his mind, he still had more blanks than complete pictures.

A few things were clear. Summer holidays as a child. Portions of his schooling. Running with his father in the evenings. His remembered that his father had loved to run.

But so much was still empty. He occasionally caught pieces when Ava would say something or he recognized something familiar, but he hoped being back in Istanbul would jog more memories. Especially those of when he and Ava had first met.

"How does it feel?" she asked. "Being back."

"Good." He smiled. "And warmer."

"No complaints about that."

They'd spent the Christmas holidays in Germany. The Irin didn't celebrate Christmas as the humans did, but he'd bought Ava a tree and hung some lights. The Irin *did* celebrate midwinter holidays, but Malachi had little memory of what to do. They were supposed to sing songs, but he didn't remember them. They were supposed to hang lights too. There should have been candles and laughter. But all those memories peeked into his mind before running away.

So they'd celebrated Christmas, and he'd made her a dish that he thought his mother had made, though he'd had to look the recipe up online. It hadn't tasted right, but it was better than nothing.

Heavy clouds hung over the city, and he was glad that Leo had told him the roof of the scribe house was already repaired.

"Jasper sent me an e-mail," she said. "Or his manager did."

"Oh?" Malachi honed in on any mention of her father. They still needed to talk about Jasper Reed. He had been reluctant to bring the subject up, but he knew Rhys wanted Ava to get in contact with Reed to ask about the grandmother she'd been named after.

Her bloodlines were still a mystery.

Irin tradition told that magical ability passed through the mother's line. Only an Irina could give birth to someone with Ava's power. And from what the Irina of Sarihöfn said, Ava had plenty of raw power.

But her mother wasn't Irina. Not in any sense. Rhys had even asked a friend in Los Angeles to trail Lena Matheson in order to confirm what Ava had told them. Malachi hadn't told her yet, but the scribe in California was certain Lena didn't have even a hint of angelic blood.

Ava's paternal line was the only option.

"What did your father say?"

"I talked to his manager. Luis said the usual. Jasper's really busy. Blah blah blah. Crazy tour schedule. He'll call when he can. You know."

"No." He frowned. "I don't. I thought you said you hadn't seen your father in a year and a half."

"I haven't," she muttered, still scrolling through her phone. "We probably should have gone to that concert in Vienna, but…"

"Forget Vienna. Your father is still in Europe?"

"For the next few months. He'll be in Italy, I think. Then France. There may be a concert or two in Spain. I'm not sure. Then he'll go back to his recording studio in LA."

"But right now, he is in Europe?"

"Yeah."

"And you are here."

"Obviously."

Malachi still didn't understand. "But Istanbul is not far. He is traveling anyway. Why doesn't he simply fly to see you?"

She only shrugged.

It baffled Malachi. Irin children were rare and treasured because of it. Fathers and mothers both doted on them, especially when they were young. Scribes were expected to stay close to their families when a child was small, even if they were warriors, as Malachi's father had been. The few memories he'd recovered of his parents were precious.

But though Ava had a close relationship with her mother, her father and stepfather were both distant.

It was something he would never understand. Should they have children, Malachi couldn't envision being disinterested. The thought of Ava bearing his children brought only feelings of excitement.

"Did we speak of having children?"

She looked up from her phone. "Not... specifically. You told me Irin children were rare."

"They are. But most couples are able to have one or sometimes even two."

He saw her color rise. "Are you saying you want children with me?"

"Of course." He had the privilege of a mate when few other Irin males did. Of course he wanted a family as well. "Do you not want children?"

"I..." She glanced at the driver. "Could we talk about it another time?"

"If we must." His stomach felt like lead. He'd never considered that Ava might not want children, though he knew many human women chose not to have them.

"Hey." Her voice softened. "It's not something I thought about. Before, I mean. When I thought... you know."

When she thought she'd been mentally ill. Malachi nodded. Ava probably would not have considered herself a suitable mother then.

He put an arm around her. "We have time."

"I know."

They had centuries if they wanted them. A thousand years to be together. Maybe longer. Many Irin mates broke up the centuries of life by spending significant time apart. It only made reunions sweeter, and they always had their time together in dream-walks.

Malachi didn't want to be apart from Ava. He guessed he could have centuries and still hunger for her.

If they managed to survive.

As if thinking the same thing, she asked, "Still no sign of Grigori in the city?"

"None. Volund depleted his forces in Oslo, and there don't seem to be any rushing to fill the void. Have you had any more visions?"

"Still the same."

Jaron walked with her at night. He could sense the fallen angel's presence but not see him. Not hear him as Ava did. Malachi had never said anything to Ava, but it infuriated him that he was powerless to stop the intrusion of the Fallen into her mind. He could protect her body—would protect it with his life—but he could do nothing to guard her mind.

In that, she was completely alone.

THEY pulled up to the house in Beyoğlu fifteen minutes later. Leo was standing at the front step, enjoying the morning sun with coffee in hand. He grinned when he spotted them turn the corner in the cab. The old house stood in the background, scarred from the fire Volund's Grigori had started, but slowly coming back to life.

"Sister!" Leo held out his arms as Malachi helped Ava out of the taxi. She ran to him, and the big man enfolded her in his embrace. Malachi felt no twinge of jealousy at their contact. His brothers had been the ones to take care of his mate when he'd been gone.

But he did envy their familiarity.

"I can't believe it!" Ava said. "You've gotten taller."

"I have not. I promise."

"No, you have. I know it."

Leo smiled at Malachi. "You've just been spending too much time with this midget."

Malachi chuckled. He was above average height for most Turks due to his mother's German heritage, but Leo and his cousin Maxim were from Northern blood. They towered over all the other scribes in the house at well over six and a half feet.

Rhys appeared at the door, and Malachi walked over to him after paying the driver and grabbing their bags.

"We didn't know you were coming," Rhys said.

"She worries." Malachi stopped and set down their bags before he spoke a question that popped into his mind, as familiar as please and thank you. "Does the fire still burn in this house?"

"It does." Rhys's mouth spread into a grin. His eyes darted between Malachi and Ava, who had come to stand at his side. "And you are welcome to its light. You and your own."

"Rhys!" Ava held out her arms, and Malachi let her go and watched as the dark-haired scholar embraced her.

"Welcome home, sister."

"I missed you guys."

"We kept the fire burning."

The fire that burned in the ritual room of each scribe house was sacred. The fire of Istanbul had burned continually since the house had been founded during the Byzantine era. The scribe house had been torn down. Moved. Rebuilt. But the fire remained the same. Combined with magic, Irin fire could heal, and it was necessary to the scribes who tended it. Rhys had risked his life to save coals from the hearth when the wooden house had burned the year before, knowing the human firefighters would extinguish it with their modern equipment.

The fire still burned. The history was intact. And Malachi felt another key turn in the vault of his mind.

Visions of shadows and light. Candles flickering against carved walls. The tight burning pain as the needle hit his skin. He hissed, looking down at the intricate *talesm* that rose on his right forearm.

"Malachi?" Ava turned to him and noticed it. "Your arm. What—?"

"I just remembered writing it," he said quietly. "In the ritual room here. It was right after I'd met you. I'd been tempted, and I still thought you were human. I wanted to touch you, but…"

Rhys looked down, his scholar's eyes keen on the mark. "It's a spell of focus. To enhance self-control. Very well done, brother."

"Thank you."

"Is it painful?"

He nodded. "Like I've just tattooed it."

"Hmm." Rhys cocked his head and pulled Malachi and Ava into the foyer of the house. Leo followed them until they were away from prying eyes. "It's very likely that your *talesm* will reappear with your memories. They may be tied to specific places. You had the memory here, and the spell reappeared. It seems to be complete, though I don't know if you'll be able to access this magic since it is not connected to your *talesm prim.*"

Malachi's newly scribed *talesm prim* was on his left wrist. The original it replaced had been the first spell he'd ever tattooed on himself, the one that tapped into his natural magic and let him control it better. As he'd grown older, more spells had been added. But when he'd died, they'd died with him. When he'd returned, it was as if he'd been reborn.

To date, he'd only recovered a portion of the magic on his left forearm; the recovered spell was on his right.

"There are these as well." He pushed up his sleeve and showed Rhys the spells that had first reappeared during his dream-walks with Ava. Shadows of his former magic, lurking like smudges beneath his skin. They were sporadic. Patchy.

Leo's eyes narrowed. "You didn't show us these? When did this happen?"

Malachi glanced at Ava. "When she sang to me," he said. "In our dreams."

She bit the corner of her lip. "But I'm not singing to you anymore."

He pushed Rhys and Leo away from examining his arm and pulled Ava to the side. Speaking quietly, he said, "When you are ready, you will sing to me."

"But—"

"There is no rush, *reshon*. We are protected here. My strength is returning on its own. Your magic is *yours*. You must make the decision to use it when you feel safe."

She nodded, but her mouth was still downturned.

"Smile, Ava." He touched her chin. "We are home."

"Don't tell me to smile when you're still not whole."

He swallowed the pain. He wasn't whole. He wasn't the man she'd once loved. He was different. Damaged.

"Do you love me?" he asked.

"Yes."

"Then I'm whole."

A wound doesn't heal just because it stops bleeding.

They were both still wounded, but her love had stopped the bleeding. Malachi knew everything else would come in time.

HE walked next to her in the forest, the trees towering over them and the moon high and full. He could hear the birds. Feel the grass beneath bare feet.

She walked with the dark angel at her side, but he could not hear them. As much as he strained, no voices reached his ears. It was as if the dark one had wrapped Malachi's mate in a fog, shielding her from him. From the forest around them. From the night.

From everything.

For a heartbeat, his grey eyes met the golden gaze of the Fallen, and a whisper came to his mind.

Thousands of you, Scribe. One of her.

The warrior scanned the forest with newly woken senses. No longer did he reach for his mate wrapped in the fog; he reached outward.

Darkness surrounded them. And though the light from the full moon shone overhead, it did not illuminate the forest, save for the path they walked. A heavy presence pressed against his skin, and at once he perceived the truth.

Do not fear the darkness.

The dark angel was shielding his mate as she dreamed. Hiding her.

But from what?

MALACHI woke when her lips met his. The black night was a cloak around them as she moved over him, covering his body with her own. His magic reached for her but only brushed against the cool of her skin. Whatever barriers fell in the nighttime, she still held her soul back. His *talesm* glowed in the cocoon of their bedclothes, lighting their skin as they moved together.

She was silent as they made love. Their bodies spoke for them.

Kiss me. Hold me. Mend me.

Make me whole.

He felt his soul reach out, straining for hers. Ava sighed as he entered her. His breath became hers.

Again.

More.

Again.

Tighter. Higher. Faster.

When they came, it was together; he felt her pleasure as his own.

She held him over her, her arm wrapped around his neck so their cheeks pressed together. He panted into her neck.

"Ava, let me—"

"No," she whispered. "Stay. Just like this. Need you. Need this."

"Too heavy."

"No." He was still buried in her. She wrapped her legs around his hips and held him tighter. "Stay. I need to feel you."

He said nothing more. Only held her. Kissed her. Over and over. Soft lips brushing her cheeks. Her lips. Her eyelids. Her neck.

"I'm here," he murmured.

"Not a dream." Her voice had become frantic again.

"It's not a dream. I'm here."

"Okay."

"Ava."

"Hmm?"

He pulled away just far enough that their eyes could meet. "Let me in, *reshon*."

Her eyes darted to the moon shining high through the narrow window of their bedroom. "What are you talking about?"

He looked at her for a moment, then he reached up, bracing his arm at her side so that his other hand was free to trail up her body.

Over the curve of her hip. The dip of her waist. The rise of her breast.

His finger settled over her heart and he wrote there, scribing the ancient words she had used to call him back. Dips and swirls of angelic runes over her skin. The incantation glowed gold under his hand.

Vashama canem.

"Malachi?"

Come back to me, reshon.

HOURS later, Ava still wouldn't rest. He wondered if she was afraid to dream.

Malachi only dreamed of her.

He could see the dawn begin to break. Birds sang in the small garden below them.

"I need to find out who I am," she said, her voice barely audible in the quiet room.

"What do you mean?"

The first crackle of the muezzin's call to prayer echoed through the air as Malachi rolled to his side and traced a hand over her shoulder, letting his magic flow over her. Her skin flushed gold as her mating marks came alive. She shivered at the contact.

"Stop," she said. "Don't distract me."

He smiled. "But I'm so good at it."

She turned toward him, capturing his hand between her own. She laid them beneath her cheek, and he was content.

"I need to find out who I am," she said again. "*What* I am."

Jaron. Hiding her in dreams. The Fallen protecting her from… something.

Do not fear the darkness.

"You want to find your father."

"Yes."

Chapter Two

"I'M BEING STRAIGHT with you, Ava. Your dad—"

"When are you ever straight with me, Luis?" Ava paced in the living room.

Her coffee sat cold on the end table, and Malachi read the newspaper silently in the corner, keeping one eye on her and the other on the subtitles at the bottom of the television screen. The paper he was reading was Arabic. The news was in French.

She'd once thought herself fairly adept at languages. She had nothing on an Irin scribe.

"Do I need to remind you that I don't work for you?" Luis was starting to get pissy. "I work for your father. And his interests—"

"Are your only interests. I get it. I'm not asking for much. I just want to know where he is because I need to ask him a question."

"Is it something I can help you with?"

She clenched her fist so hard her fingernails dug into her palm. "Is there a reason why you're blocking me from him?"

"I'm not blocking you. Who said I was blocking you? Don't you have his mobile number?"

"He's not answering it."

"What about e-mail?"

"Not answering those, either."

Luis was silent. Her father's manager wasn't usually this big an asshole. He *was* an ass—he worked in the music industry, after all—but it wasn't usually this bad. Which meant something was going on with her dad.

She still had a hard time thinking of Jasper that way, but when she learned the news as a teenager, she hadn't been all that shocked, either. He'd been a part of her life since she was a kid. She just didn't realize he was her father. Jasper and her mother had remained close, despite their past relationship. In fact, Ava had always suspected that Jasper still held a torch for Lena. She was one of the few constants in his life.

The other was Luis.

"Luis…" She rubbed her eyes. "Tell me what's going on."

"Nothing is going on. Your dad is in the middle of a tour, and you know how stressed he gets about that."

"Bullshit. He loves performing. The bigger the venue, the better."

"It's tiring, Ava. I imagine he's exhausted."

"You imagine *nothing* with him," she bit out, her patience at an end. "You are in his business every single day. That's why you have very nice houses in LA *and* Maui. So you know where he is. You know why he's avoiding me. And you know what he's been doing."

Luis said nothing, because there was nothing to say. Ava had paced over close to Malachi, and he put out a hand, absently hooking a finger in her waistband and running his thumb across her skin. The small contact soothed her, and she took a deep breath.

"Ava—"

"Is he using again, Luis?"

"You know he—"

"Dumb question. He's always using. Is he *crashing*?"

Luis was silent again. Ava took another deep breath and sat down on the couch. Malachi reached out and took her hand. She clutched it and could think again.

"Okay, I'm taking that silence as a yes. Where is he?"

"I can't tell you that, honey."

Luis only called her honey when he'd taken off his manager hat. Just like her and Jasper, she and Luis were still figuring out the boundaries of their relationship. He was her father's right hand, but according to Lena, Luis had been the one to discourage Jasper from having a relationship with Ava when she was a child. For her sake or for Jasper's? It could be argued either way.

The man had no life outside her father's career. And Jasper would say he'd be useless without Luis herding him. He respected Ava. Respected her role in Jasper's life. But her father was still the man's first priority, and nothing she said would budge that.

"Has he hurt anyone?" Her voice was rough. She wished she didn't care so much, but she did. She'd always loved him. Even before she knew he was her dad. It was like her mother always said—*There was just something about Jasper.*

"Has he hurt himself?"

"No. Nothing like that. Just… a little worse than normal. He'll be fine."

"I need to talk to him."

"Not the best thing right now, Ava."

"It's important. It's about…" She racked her brain. "It's a health thing. I have some questions about family stuff on that side."

Luis paused. "He's not going to be able to give you much. You know that, Ava. Besides, your father's healthy as a horse."

"Other than the drugs?"

"Despite them." Luis's voice dropped. "Listen, I don't know what deal he made with what devil, but the man has never been sick a day in his life, other than the shit he ingests himself. I've seen guys do… a *tenth* of the shit he's done and ruin their bodies. What's going on with your health? Lena said you were staying in Turkey with friends the last time I talked to her. Are you sick?"

Malachi must have heard the question. She kept forgetting that his *talesm* gave him enhanced senses when he activated them. No doubt he'd been listening the whole time.

He frowned and shook his head.

Luis hadn't earned their trust.

Ava decided to go with attitude because being reasonable wasn't working. "Like I'm going to tell you what's going on with my health when you're not even willing to tell me where my own father is."

"Don't be like this, Ava. If he hears that you're sick—"

"He'll be pissed. We both know it. So why are you keeping me from him?"

More silence.

"He's going to hear one way or another, Luis. And I don't think you want to be the one standing between him and his only kid. Do I need to call my mom?"

It was her one trump card, and Luis still wasn't budging.

"Yeah, why don't you have Lena call me, Ava?" His voice was frosty. "She's not an immature little girl throwing a tantrum. Your mother knows what Jasper's limits are."

"His limits?"

"I'm done with this conversation. I'll call you next week."

Ava hung up her phone when Luis's end went silent and resisted throwing it against the opposite wall.

"So," Malachi said, "that went well."

"Asshole."

He raised a single eyebrow. "Is he always like that? I do not like the way he talks to you, and I'd be more than happy to make that clear."

"Luis?" She huffed out a breath. "He's usually pretty cool. But he's in protective mode right now, which tells me my dad is holed up, trying to see just how many drugs he can ingest without killing himself."

Malachi folded up the paper and pressed his lips to her knuckles. "I'm sorry."

"It's the way he is. The way he's always been."

"But you don't know where he is?"

"No."

"Where was he last seen?"

Ava turned on her phone and pulled up the app she used to keep track of her father. The mobile application was fan-created and borderline creepy, but it had become a convenient way to keep track of Jasper and his schedule. "He had that concert in Vienna on the twentieth of last month.

Then another in… Budapest. Then it looks like he went under." She scrolled back up the page and mentally counted down. Four weeks. Six…

"Yeah," she finally said. "He was due."

"Due?"

"It's just the way he is. Every eight weeks or so, when he's touring, he'll crash. Luis works it into his schedule. His next show isn't for three weeks."

"He takes a three-week vacation to get high?"

"Among other things. It's better when he's recording. Seems to work some of the energy out for him to be creative. I can relate," she muttered. "I was kind of the same way before we met. Not with the drugs, but…" She shook her head. "He'll be fine for a while. Using but functioning. Then every now and then he'll go off and get really wasted. It varies how bad it is."

"How bad does this seem?"

"If he's not answering my calls or e-mails? Pretty bad."

"Drugs?"

"Drugs. Vodka. Lots and lots of women."

He narrowed his eyes. "Really?"

She shrugged. "It's sad, but it really is typical music-industry stuff. A lot of these guys are like that. You wouldn't believe the excess. Probably one of the reasons he allowed my mom and Carl to raise me without much interference."

"Hmmm." He was rubbing a hand over his chin, scratching at the thick stubble that had already appeared. It was his usual sign that he was mulling things over.

"What are you thinking?"

"I'm thinking…" He pulled out his own phone. "We should call Max."

That hadn't been what he was thinking about, but she let it pass. "Where is Max?"

"I don't know. But he *is* answering his phone, and if you want to find someone, I think he'd be the one to ask."

"You think?"

"I do."

It wasn't a bad idea. Malachi was clearly remembering more about his brothers after being back in the scribe house. He was easier with Leo and Rhys. Seemed more comfortable in his own skin every day that passed. And Ava knew Max was the one the others turned to when they needed information.

"You think Max could find my father? He won't be at any of his usual houses. Probably won't even be using his name."

Malachi shook his head. "Not a problem. He's human."

"What does that mean?"

"It means he has only human methods of concealment. Which means that Max's finding him will not be a problem."

THAT night, Leo and Ava were practicing with knives when Rhys walked in with the phone. Malachi rose from the weight bench in the corner, but Rhys held up a hand.

"Damien," he said into the phone. "I'm with the others. I'm putting you on speaker."

"—long as you've swept for bugs recently," the voice came from the mobile phone that Rhys set on the counter in the large bedroom on the second floor where the workout room had been set up.

"I swept yesterday," Leo said, then he flipped two knives in quick succession. One hit the bull's-eye right next to Ava's last throw.

"Good. I'm looking in the corners here, so expect surveillance from the council. Be wary of any scribes who turn up unexpectedly."

"Why?" Ava asked as she threw another. It was a new set that Leo had found for her. Perfectly balanced.

"Ava?"

She could hear the smile in Damien's voice.

"Hey, Damien! Is Sari there?"

"Here," a woman's voice said. "How are you, sister?"

"I'm good." She smiled at Malachi, who was watching her with a smile of his own. He wiped his forehead with the shirt he'd stripped off earlier. "We're both good. Happy to be back."

"Good. I'll let Damien update his men. Then we should talk."

"Got it."

Ava turned back to the target she was sharing with Leo. It felt good to practice. Malachi was more of a dagger-fighting fan. Throwing knives wasn't something he enjoyed as much as Ava did.

"As I was saying, be wary of any unknown scribes."

Rhys asked, "Are we declining hospitality?"

"No. We can't do that."

Ava knew that would be a serious breach of Irin etiquette. Scribes were always welcomed by other scribes. No matter what. To go against that would raise alarms in Vienna and create enemies out of those who should be friends.

"Officially, I'm still here petitioning on the part of the watchers. I have letters from the houses in Berlin, Oslo, Budapest, and Paris. I'm warning the council about the rising threat, but I'm not having much success. They're loosening funds for repairs and rebuilding our house and other houses, but other than that, they're much more occupied with the Irina question."

Malachi asked, "The Irina question?"

It was Sari who responded. "The threat against Sarihöfn and the attacks in Oslo have finally spurred a response. I've been in contact with other havens. The leaders there are mostly of the same mind as I am."

"Which is?" Rhys was perched on the edge of his chair.

Sari paused. Ava held her breath.

"It's time," Sari said. "We can't ignore those calling for compulsion. If we're going to come out of hiding, it will be on our own terms, not the result of politicians threatening us. It has already started."

"I've heard," Rhys said quietly. "There are Irina showing up at scribe houses all over the world. The children and many of the others are still concealed, but more and more Irina are stepping forward and demanding a place at the scribe houses."

"The council must love that," Malachi said.

Ava put her knives down, no longer able to concentrate. "What can they do, though? They can't force Irina into retreats. Not when they've been hiding for so long. What right do they have? What—"

"No right, Ava." Leo put a hand on her shoulder. "But there are those who could make life difficult if they chose to."

"How?"

Sari answered again. "Most of us have mates who are active in Irin society. Soldiers. Watchers. Teachers. Right now, if a scribe has a mate and family, it is accepted that he might be gone for a time. Sometimes for a very long time. But if those in authority over them wanted to, they could make it impossible for those scribes to see their mates and children."

"They would break up families?" Ava asked.

Damien said, "They would make it sound like they are only thinking of the safety of those families. The problem is, the Irin council members who take the Grigori threat seriously are the ones most adamant that the Irina must be forced into retreats. And those who believe the Grigori are no threat are those who would allow the Irina to step forward on their own. In their own time."

It was Malachi who asked the question. "Sari, what do the Irina you speak to want?"

She walked over and kissed him on the mouth. "Yes, Sari, what do the *Irina* want?"

Leo and Rhys laughed, but Malachi just smiled and pulled her down to sit next to him.

Sari said, "Right now, we're trying to decide who should come to Vienna. We haven't had a ruling council for over two hundred years. My grandmother is adamant that it must be reformed if anything is to be accomplished."

Rhys asked, "And what does the Irin Council think about that?"

"They're old men not used to sharing power," Leo said. "What do you think?"

Damien said, "They know it is inevitable. With Irina raising their voices again, they cannot ignore it. They're positioning singers who believe in compulsion to take positions of power."

"There are Irina who believe in compulsion?" Ava asked.

"Yes," Sari answered. "We are not of one mind. Nor do we have to be. But we've changed in the years since the Rending. There are too many who lost everything to the Grigori and the Fallen. They won't be compliant again."

They spoke of specifics for some time. Which council members were sympathetic. Which were hostile. Sari was passionate. Damien was fed up and clearly wanted to kill someone or something as soon as possible.

It was a full hour later before she and Sari could speak privately.

"You're not using your magic," Sari said.

"Sari, I—"

"I don't want to hear excuses. I want to know why."

Ava pursed her lips. "You're not my mother or my boss."

"I care about you, Ava. And your mate is one of Damien's closest friends. Your power is substantial, and whatever we may be facing, we need you to be able to control it."

She said nothing. How could she explain the threat she felt inside? It came from within. There was a darkness that lived in her. Ava had never sensed the same in Sari or Orsala or any of the Irina she'd met at the haven.

"I'm different, Sari."

"Do you think I don't know that?"

"Did Orsala—"

"My grandmother knows your power is not like the others. That doesn't make it dangerous unless you don't learn control. Are you shielding at least?"

"Yes."

"How about offensive spells? Have you practiced those? Malachi and Rhys can help you."

She clammed up.

Sari huffed out a breath. "You have to use your magic."

"I'm using it."

"Not the way you need to be."

She picked at the edge of the blanket in their bedroom. She could hear Malachi waiting in the hall, trying to give her privacy. She wished he would just come in.

"I have other stuff on my mind, Sari."

"What is more important than learning how to harness your power?"

"I don't know. Learning where it came from, maybe?"

The other woman was quiet, and Ava heard Malachi pacing. Frustrated, she sent out a tentative brush of power. It was hard to describe. A little like blowing air in his direction, but with her mind. A second later, she felt an answering brush of awareness, and he cracked the door open with a grin.

"You *called* me," he whispered, smiling.

She shrugged one shoulder and said, "I need to go, Sari. Malachi is here."

"How is he?"

"He's a pain in the ass sometimes. Right now he's very smug." Her mate kept smiling and lay down on the bed, putting his head in her lap. "But he's mine."

"You sound content."

She brushed a hand through his hair. "I am."

Malachi let out a rumble of pleasure and turned his face to her belly, putting an arm around her waist.

"I'm going to send Orsala to you."

Her fingers tightened in his hair. "What?"

"Ouch," he said. "Ava, really… ow."

"I just decided. This will be good! You were going to come here, but Vienna is unstable right now. I don't know how you'd be received. Instead, Orsala can go to you. Mala is here and restless. I'll send them both to you in Istanbul. Damien says Rhys is one scribe short for the house. Mala will more than make up for that."

"And she'll torture me."

"You're probably out of shape."

"Sari!"

"Let go," Malachi said with a grunt. "It's not my fault she's sending them."

"Tell Malachi I heard that," Sari said. "What are you doing to him?"

Ava was panicking. "Sari, I really don't think—"

"Damien is nodding. He agrees with me. I'll talk to her tonight, and we'll let you know when they will arrive."

Malachi untangled her frozen hand and sat up next to her.

"But I need to go find my—"

"Whatever it is, my grandmother can help. She needs something to do anyway, and that way she'll be able to continue your lessons like she was going to after Oslo. This is an excellent plan. Damien agrees."

"Sari!"

"I need to go. I'll e-mail with details later."

The phone was silent a second later, and Ava sat with her mouth hanging open. "I was ambushed."

"I was injured," he said, rubbing his scalp. "Sari's wrong. I don't think you're out of shape at all."

THE phone rang late that night. She was in Malachi's arms, and she reached across his chest to grab it before he could wake, putting it on silent as she checked the number. She didn't recognize it, so she answered cautiously.

"Hello?"

"Ava?"

"Max?"

"Your father is in Genoa. Well, a little town in that region. Not far from Portofino."

"Portofino?"

"He has a house there. An old castle he's renting."

She blinked, trying to clear her mind. "You've seen him?"

"Renata found him. He's not in good shape, sister."

She was still only half awake when Malachi took the phone from her.

"Send us the details," he said, rubbing her shoulders, which had gone stiff at Max's tone. "We'll leave tomorrow."

Chapter Three

MALACHI OPENED HIS EYES, knowing he was no longer in Istanbul.

He dreamed, but Ava was not with him.

He was no longer in the forest of his mate's walks, but a room that resembled the ritual room of a scribe house. Wax candles dripped on the center table where coals from the sacred fire forced tendrils of heat through the room. Etchings marked the walls, ancient spells protecting the children of the Forgiven from harm.

And the black presence that stalked his mate lurked at the edge of his dreaming.

An epicene figure rose in the corner of the room. "I cannot reach her, but I can reach you."

Malachi turned, recognizing the voice that laughed in some shadowed corner of his lost memory. "Volund."

"Yes."

Malachi scanned the room, reassuring himself that Ava was nowhere near.

"She is not here," the angel said. "I have tried. He has shielded her from my sight. He excels in such things."

Malachi stepped closer. "Show yourself."

The slim figure rose and grew, abandoning the sculptural facade he showed the human world. Here, Malachi realized—in dreams—he could see the angel's true face. All traces of human flaw fled from Volund's visage. Blue eyes bled to gold. His skin, pale before, grew luminous as the moon. His hair, a sandy brown that would blend with the human masses, became true amber, translucent in the glow of the candles flickering in the center of the room.

He was utterly beautiful. A god to human sight.

Malachi was transfixed.

The angel's eyes glowed with barely restrained power, like the sun hiding behind a morning fog.

"Do you love me?" Volund stared into Malachi's eyes.

"No," Malachi said. "You do not want to be loved."

Volund smiled with closed lips. "No, I do not."

"What do you want?"

"I want to be feared. Worshipped."

"You were not meant to be worshipped."

Volund laughed, the cynical smirk marring the angel's handsome face, which melted back into a more human appearance. Stunning, but less otherworldly. And yet it was as if his power had simply condensed. Black energy licked along Malachi's skin.

This is a dream.

"If you think I have no power over your dreams," Volund said, "you are mistaken, Scribe."

"I am protected."

"By whom? Jaron guards your mate, though you know not his reasons." Volund's blue eyes danced. "You are nothing."

Malachi took a deep breath and closed his eyes, breaking the connection with the monster who taunted him and willing himself to return to waking.

"You are nothing." The voice was different.

Malachi opened his eyes, and the angel had departed. Left in his place, the phantom of the Grigori soldier he'd killed on the rooftop in Oslo.

Brage's expression held nothing of the arrogance he'd exhibited in life. His blue eyes were blank and hollow. His face was as beautiful as the day Malachi had slain him.

"We are nothing," Brage said. "Nothing."

"You are an illusion."

Then the corner of the Grigori's mouth turned up, and Malachi saw the wicked edge.

"Since when have dreams ever been illusion for those of our kind?"

"I am nothing like you."

Brage only laughed.

Volund appeared over his shoulder, his human face now a mirror of his son's. He embraced his child, stroking the hair back from his forehead and closing his eyes in sensual pleasure.

"I can be patient," he whispered. "Now that I have found you, I will find you again."

"Go away," Malachi said, stepping closer to the sacred fire.

"For now."

A spark of recognition showed terror on Brage's face, as if illusion had passed from his mind and stark reality intruded. The Grigori's eyes widened in horror. His mouth opened in a scream.

Volund pulled his child into the darkness and was gone.

Malachi bolted up in bed, a harsh gasp ripping from his lungs. He looked around the room, but there was nothing. No trace remained of the ritual room or the angel's darkness. He looked down.

Ava slept beside him, and she did not wake.

HE didn't tell Ava about his dream. Malachi didn't know if it was a nightmare or a vision, and his mate had too many other things on her mind.

The train that took them along the coast of Liguria chugged steadily, stopping at the small towns along the route, exchanging a mix of humans for other humans varied in age and shape. Grandmothers going for a visit. Tourists with cameras. Hikers with backpacks. They came and went, and Malachi wished that he and Ava had reserved a private car. If that was even possible. She was firm in her belief that their best concealment was the routine of the mundane, so he indulged her.

Currently, he could not fault her reasoning. She managed to fit in with the humans with ease. She was the native, the tourist, the anonymous traveler with a small satchel and a camera. Unless he had the preternatural senses to feel her power, he never would have noticed her.

"Hmm," he mused, watching her as she snapped pictures out the window.

"What are you thinking?"

He was thinking about Volund's unexpected ability to invade his unconscious, but he didn't want to bring it up. Luckily, his mind could turn to pleasant things very quickly when he was with her.

"Do you really want to know?"

"Yes. I wouldn't have asked if I didn't."

It was true. Ava wasn't a woman who felt the need to fill the air with chatter. He wondered if years of traveling alone had trained it out of her or if the constant voices that had once plagued her were company enough.

"I am thinking… you're very beautiful."

He loved the slight flush she gave him when he complimented her. It made the offer of his praise all the more satisfying.

"You're the only one who's ever said that."

He was surprised, but not overly. Humans could be very superficial, and Ava's physical features were not the most astonishing thing about her. Pretty, but not uncommonly so. Clear skin. Dark hair. Her eyes were the most arresting part of her face, but only other Irin would recognize the unusual shade of gold as anything more than light brown or amber.

No, it wasn't her physical features that were remarkable. And Malachi loved that only he saw the secret of his mate.

Her beauty lay in her mind and her heart. Quiet strength and resilient humor were not things valued enough by the world.

"Hmm."

She gave him a quiet smile. "You always did that," she said. "Before. 'Hmm.' You'd be thinking something you didn't want to say, but I knew it was about me when you would say 'Hmm.'"

"I often think about you."

"That's probably a good thing."

They were sitting across from each other in the compartment. He put his foot on the edge of the bench beside her, enclosing them. Doing his best to block out the world. Ava set down her camera and slid a hand up his pant leg, her fingers playing along his skin.

"I think about you too," she said. "Some would say I'm obsessed."

"And you take pictures of me when I sleep. I hear the clicking in my dreams. It's borderline stalker behavior, really."

"It's settled then. We're both certifiable." She smiled and closed her eyes, sliding down in her seat and tilting her face toward the sun as it shone through the window. The weather was cool, but it was still sunny.

"So beautiful," he whispered.

"So handsome."

"Hmm." He nudged her hip with his foot when she laughed. "You just like my tattoos."

He'd seen a few humans on the train eyeing his arms when they sat down. He'd shoved up his sleeves because the compartment was warm, and his *talesm* were visible. It was a relief, living in a time when body modification was not as unusual as it had once been. Humans did all sorts of things to mark themselves now, so the intricate lettering on his arms was noticed but rarely remarked upon.

"Only yours," Ava said. "I was never a tattoo girl before I met you."

"No?"

She shrugged. "I never thought much about them."

"And you don't have any yourself."

"Only the ones you gave me." Her eyes sparkled with humor. "And those aren't for everyone's eyes."

Malachi supposed a more evolved scribe would try to suppress the surge of possessive satisfaction.

He wasn't that evolved.

Forcing back a smile, he glanced around the compartment. Since no one was paying attention to them, he decided to broach a subject he knew she'd been avoiding.

"Your shields," he said and felt the immediate tension in her fingers where they lay on his calf.

"Why are we talking about this?"

"Because we need to. I know you're still shielding yourself from the voices, but—"

"I thought you said that I could go at my own pace."

"You can. But I need to know what's happening in your dreams."

"Then what are you talking about?"

So it wasn't something she was doing. He hadn't thought so, but he wanted to be sure.

He glanced around again, then turned his eyes back to her. He'd suspected Ava had protection, but Volund's words confirmed it.

"During our dreams," Malachi said. "Do you sense it?"

"What?"

"The layer he's placed over you."

"Who? Jaron?"

"Yes."

She frowned. "I've sensed… something. But it's not something I've thought about much."

"He's shielding you," Malachi said. "I'm sure of it."

"From you?"

"No." From another, darker threat. "He's an angel. Jaron would probably be able to shove me out of your dreams completely if he wanted to. Or maybe not. I don't really know. As far as I've read, the Fallen do not enter our dreams. I don't know why Jaron can walk in yours, but I'm fairly sure he's shielding you."

He wished she would share what had happened on the rooftop in Oslo. There had been a break in time for him. Looking back, he knew that Ava and Jaron had some exchange, but he didn't know what had passed between them. As much as Ava shared with him, there were fears she hid. Malachi didn't even know if Ava realized she was hiding.

"If Jaron is shielding me from something, I don't know what it is," she finally admitted. "He's as confusing to me as he is to everyone."

I cannot reach her, but I can reach you.

Was he right to conceal Volund's intentions toward her? Malachi didn't know, but he didn't want to bring it up. It was one more problem for which he had no solution to offer.

Malachi shrugged. "The Fallen have never shown any interest in protecting humans as far as I can remember. I have no idea why Jaron is doing it."

"Not even their human lovers?"

"Humans are disposable to them. All humans."

"But he protects me." She frowned. "Maybe there's more to the angels than what you've been taught."

"I doubt it, Ava."

"But…" She frowned. "The Fallen and the Forgiven? They're all angels, right?"

"Yes."

"So what's the difference? Why were the Forgiven capable of compassion and not the Fallen?"

"I don't think you could call the Forgiven compassionate. They were just…"

"What?"

He shook his head. Some lessons were still crystal clear, even if he couldn't remember when or where he'd learned them. "The Forgiven gave up their place on earth—their offspring, their human lovers—but it was because they were cut off from heaven. They wanted to go back. It was for our sakes, but more for their own."

"So they were selfish to leave? Not sacrificing?"

"It was both. There had to be an element of sacrifice, because they were allowed to gift their children with magic. The Fallen were not."

"Don't the Grigori have magic?"

"Only the natural magic that comes from angelic blood. Which shouldn't be underestimated. But they don't know the Old Language as we do. So their magic is limited. It is our main advantage."

She was still frowning. "I don't get it, though."

"What?"

"Why don't the Fallen teach the Grigori the same magic? Wouldn't it make them more powerful?"

"I don't know if the Fallen want their children to be that powerful. Or even if they are able to teach it to them. They might not be able."

"You don't know?"

He shook his head. "They're Grigori. We don't engage them in conversation. We kill them."

Ava snorted. "For a race you've been at war with for millennia, you guys don't know much about your enemy, do you?"

"They're a predatory race. We know enough."

"Do you?"

He sat up straighter and lowered his leg. "What does that mean?"

She was looking out the window. "You know I'm no fan of the Grigori. But part of me wonders if the Irin don't choose to be ignorant about them. About their world. It's easier to dehumanize something you don't understand. Easier to kill someone you don't see as a person."

"There's a problem with your reasoning, Ava."

"Oh?"

"The *Grigori* are not human."

"No?" Her eyes swung back to his. "Think about it, Malachi. They're half human. Half angel. The Grigori are as human as you."

MALACHI stewed silently for the rest of the trip.

The Grigori as human as he was?

Hardly.

The monsters who had tracked Ava like an animal? Seduced and killed countless human women? Taken his own life? Flashes of memory haunted him, flipping through his mind in a litany of accusation.

Knives and blood. Knives were the only way to kill them and release their souls for judgment. And knives were messy, bloody weapons for fighting. Slices across his arms. His chest. He'd almost lost an ear once.

Knives and blood and dead, lifeless eyes. Not the Grigori. No, their bodies dissolved like so much dust, leaving the remains of their prey for others to find. Dead eyes, often open in surprise or rolled back in ecstasy. The Grigori were beings who made a mockery of love, the human women they hunted never suspecting that the glorious creature who touched them was actually sucking the life out of them.

A small, inconvenient voice in the back of his mind whispered, *You would too.*

His touch would be deadly too.

So the Irin didn't touch any but their own.

That was the point. It was what made them different. Made them the protectors, not the hunters. They were nothing like the Grigori.

He could hear Ava's voice. *But…*

The Grigori had no fathers or mothers as they did. Had no families. No training in magic. They had no Irina.

They had no Irina.

So what hope did they have?

And what monsters would the Irin have become with no hope?

He was silent when they arrived at the hotel. Silent when they made their way to their room. Silent even as Ava stoically put their things away, unpacking from the single bag they had brought, carefully arranging the room with the long practice of years living in hotel after hotel.

"I know you're mad at me," she said as he walked up behind her. She was standing at a small dresser, arranging their clothes. "It wasn't my intention, I'm just saying—"

"Shh." He bent down, wrapping his arms around her waist and kissing her cheek. "Ava."

"What?"

Her shoulders had been tense, but she relaxed as he held her and kissed her cheek. Her neck. They had few fights because they were still uneasy around each other. Both of them often retreated into polite silence, and he knew it wasn't right.

"I love you," he said, drawing her away from the bureau and into his chest. His hands traveled up her torso, slipping underneath the thin sweater she wore. He hungered for her skin. "You are my hope."

"Malachi—"

"You are. It is easy to forget"—he kissed the curve where her neck met her shoulder—"what I would be without you. There was a time when I was as hopeless as they were. I don't think the Irin are like the Grigori, but I will think about what you said."

"I'm not saying I want to be friends with them," she said, turning in his arms. "I just think there are things we could learn. Me, mostly. But maybe you too."

"You're right."

A teasing light came to her eyes. "You're so sexy when you agree with me."

"Am I?" He bit her lower lip as his hands ran back down to cup her bottom. "How about now?" he murmured against her lips.

"Say it again."

"You're right."

"Oooooh," she said. "Even sexier."

He grinned as he kissed her. He loved it when she teased him. When she laughed. It was happening more and more as time passed.

"You're my hope too, you know."

He paused. "What?"

"What was I before I met you?" she asked. "Lonely. Lost. Never fitting in anywhere. Ruining any relationship I tried to have."

"Human men would never have been good for you." A sudden spike of jealousy. No other man would touch her. Not as he did. His mate belonged to him alone. He picked her up and carried her to the bed.

"I know that now."

She let him roll over her, strip her clothing off so that he could feast on her. Breasts. Knees. Thighs. He bit the soft swell of flesh on her belly. No inch of her body was safe from his ravening mouth.

And she coaxed him with her words.

"I love your mouth," she whispered. "Love what you do to me. No one has ever made me feel like you do."

"Ava—"

"I was so lost without you." Her voice choked on the words. "So lost, Malachi. Only my dreams kept me sane."

He groaned and pressed his mouth to her breast, turning his head to listen to her pounding heart. To her, he had been gone. A painful memory. But to him, she had been a siren. His only touchstone in a world that made no sense. And he could only hold her in dreams.

Now she was real. With him. Not a dream. Not a memory.

Ava was everything.

"Come here." She pulled at his clothes, as hungry as he was. "I need you."

And when they made love, she dug her fingers into his shoulders. Anchoring him in their joined flesh, even as his magic flared. Reached for hers. He could see the glowing silver *talesm* on his arms.

"Sing to me," he whispered in her ear as they moved together. "Sing for me, Ava."

She remained silent, but he felt the curl of her magic wake, and her mating marks flickered in awareness.

"*Canım*," he said.

"Malachi." Her hands tightened in his hair.

"My hope, Ava. You are my hope."

THEY rented a scooter the next day, climbing up the hills of the Italian Riviera where Jasper Reed had rented a secluded house. They told no one they were coming, and Malachi only hoped that the man who had disappointed Ava so many times would not do so again. It would pain his mate, and Malachi would be hard-pressed not to vent his anger on the human.

Ava leaned against his back, her cheek pressed against his shoulder as they drove over the twisting roads. The sun shone down on them, despite the bite of cold in the air. It was Italy, but it was still winter, and clouds were gathered on the horizon. But Ava had wanted to rent a scooter instead of a car, and he had indulged her.

The address Max had given them led them past a small village and up another steep hill. They came to a gate on the road with the number of the house. He could see it at the top of the hill. Ava opened an unlocked gate and began to climb. A steep fall of stairs cut into the hillside brought them to another gate, this one guarded by a solid man Malachi guessed was American. His stance said professional; his bearing spoke of experience. He was younger than Malachi but would be a reasonably skilled opponent if he were not human.

"Hey, Ruben," she said, her voice a little breathless from the climb.

"Ava." The guard's tone offered surprise, even if his eyes were invisible behind dark sunglasses. "I didn't know—"

44

"Yeah, I know I'm a surprise. You gonna let me in, or do I have to call him?"

"I…" Ruben hesitated, but then his shoulders relaxed a fraction and he opened the door. He glanced at Malachi, gave him a little nod, then turned back to Ava and took off his glasses. "He's not expecting company."

Malachi noted that he'd been assessed and filed away as Ava's bodyguard. It was incredibly strange to be among humans who just expected to have armed men following them around for security.

"Really?" Ava raised an eyebrow. "He's not expecting company?"

Ruben sighed. "Okay, he's not expecting his daughter. You know how he is. Ava, I wish…"

Malachi realized, quite suddenly, that this bodyguard was more than familiar with Ava. That he actually cared about her.

The guard had probably known her for years. He might even live in her father's household. Did she consider him a friend? They might have traveled together. Eaten together. How strange to live and travel with people you employed. Were they friends? Was true friendship possible when one was employer and the other employee? The thought added a new layer of loneliness to Ava's history.

"I know how he is, Ruben." She brushed a hand along the human's arm. "It's fine. Is Luis here?"

"Not right now. Went into town to do some stuff. There's no Internet up here."

"I bet he loves that," she muttered. "Do me a favor and don't call Luis, okay?"

Ruben's tone was pleading. "Ava…"

"Fine." She sighed. "Call your boss so you don't get fired. Is Jasper alone?"

"Right now? Yeah."

"No girls expected?"

Ruben shook his head. "Not until later."

"Got it." She took his hand. "This is Malachi. He's with me."

Ruben examined him with newly suspicious eyes.

That's right, human. I am much more than her bodyguard.

"Hey." He held out a hand. "I'm Ruben."

"Malachi." They shook hands, and Malachi was relieved the human didn't do the idiot measuring hand squeeze. That never ended well for humans. He did, however, make a point of meeting Malachi's eyes. The threat was unspoken but clear. The man considered Ava his responsibility.

They stared at each other until Ava said, "And it appears we all have plenty of testosterone. Ruben, let go. Malachi's my... boyfriend."

"Boyfriend?" Ruben was definitely surprised. He dropped Malachi's hand and stepped back.

"I really don't like that word," Malachi said.

"What should I call you? My lover? Husband? Ma—"

"Boyfriend is fine." He squeezed her hand, glanced at Ruben, then nudged her toward the door. "Don't you need to see your father?"

"You're so cute when you're annoyed," Ava said lightly, and he could read the tension in her voice. She was nervous and trying to hide it.

"Come on." He let go of her hand and put a steadying arm around her waist. "Ruben, where can we find Jasper?"

The guard's keen eyes flipped between them, but he said, "Probably out in the gardens."

"Thanks."

"Anytime."

Malachi let her guide them up another set of stairs, this one shorter than the last. When they walked through the last gate, the garden opened up to a graveled walkway lined with olive trees interspersed with flower-filled urns. Ava didn't stop to admire the view but went straight up the path, heading for the large house he could see towering over the gardens.

They passed the front door and the covered patio beside it, still following the path to the side of the house where he could hear the faint sounds of a guitar and the recognizable voice of one the most celebrated human musicians.

Jasper Reed was known for performing rock and roll, blues, and American folk music, but he'd collaborated with classical musicians and even written scores for movies. He was, without a doubt, one of the most gifted human musicians of his age. And when they finally rounded the corner and came upon him, Malachi knew his talent wasn't merely rumor.

THE SECRET

The man sat on a low bench, guitar in his lap, several empty coffee cups on the table in front of him along with an overflowing ashtray. Several of the domestic staff watched him from a shaded doorway, one smoking, two whispering, but all of them with rapt eyes on the man.

Reed appeared to be in his forties, but Malachi knew he had to be older in human years. Dark hair like Ava's. A classically handsome, unlined face. And a soft voice laden with a practiced breathy rasp.

The music was pure in its simplicity. Seductive in its tone. His voice was quiet but seemed to suffuse the air around him until every human within its hearing was held in thrall. Even Malachi was entranced.

Ava stopped in the shade of a spreading oak, watching her father. And he was, undoubtedly, her father. She'd said she looked like her mother—and she did—but there was a quality of expression she shared with Reed. So much that Malachi wondered how anyone could have been ignorant of her parentage. Her face was yearning. Her power flared.

And was answered when the music stopped and her father turned toward her.

A crooked smile. "Ava? Baby girl, what are you doing here?"

Then Reed's eyes fell on Malachi, and the scribe knew without a doubt where his mate's power had come from.

Talented musician. Wasted drug addict. Delinquent father. Jasper Reed might have been many things.

But he wasn't human.

Chapter Four

"HEY, JASPER."

Her father put his guitar down and held out his arms. "Come here! What are you doing here, Ava?"

She could lie to herself all she wanted, but when Jasper opened his arms, the little girl in Ava leaped with joy. The girl who'd never belonged stepped forward and embraced the man who had fathered her.

"Came to say hi."

"Why didn't you call?"

His arms were warm, and he smelled like sunshine and coffee and soap. He'd probably smell like cigarette smoke soon enough, but in that moment, she took a deep breath and enjoyed the feeling of his stubbled cheek against hers.

"Wanted to surprise you."

Jasper wasn't stupid. He pulled back and raised an eyebrow. "Since when?"

"Since Luis was being closemouthed about where you were. Why weren't you answering my e-mails?"

He scratched his cheek, the dark stubble hinting at some Mediterranean heritage he'd never confirmed. He didn't know much about his family, he'd always told her. But was it the truth? Or did he just not want to share?

"No Internet up here, baby girl. And I'm not sure where that phone is." He looked around, and Ava could see his eyes were bloodshot. Hard nights. He'd been having hard nights. She was surprised he was up and playing early with eyes like that.

THE SECRET

Jasper had called her "baby girl" as long as she could remember. When Ava was a child, it had seemed a sweet endearment from a man she thought of as an uncle. It was only later, when she'd learned he was her biological father, that it had become the poignant reminder of how much he'd missed by being absent for so much of her life.

He'd stayed as close to her as Lena would allow and often crashed at their house in LA when she was growing up. It was to her stepfather's credit that the man hardly batted an eye. Then again, when it came to running the house, what Lena Matheson said was law. And she never gave Carl any reason to doubt that Jasper and Lena's romantic relationship was firmly in the past.

She patted his cheek. "You gotta keep your phone on, Jasper."

He winked at her and pulled out the pack of cigarettes he kept in his pocket. "But then everyone would call me. Maybe I need to get a phone only you have the number to."

"Might not be a bad idea," Malachi said behind her.

She turned to see Malachi watching them with wary eyes. She stood up and held out a hand for his.

"Jasper, this is Malachi. He's not a bodyguard."

"He's not? You brought your guy to meet me, Ava?" Her father looked strangely touched. "Really?"

"Yeah." She knit her hands with Malachi's, but his fingers were tense. Odd. Maybe he was worried. "Malachi's my—"

"Fiancé," he said. "Ava and I are getting married."

She turned to him and mouthed, *We are?*

He shrugged and turned his eyes back to her father.

"Damn, Ava." Jasper blinked, and Ava saw his eyes were wet. "Really? You're getting married? Your mom didn't tell me."

"We just decided a little while ago." Ava decided to go with it. It was probably the easiest way for her mom and Jasper to understand what role Malachi would play in her life. She didn't care about getting married, but her mom would. "Mom doesn't know yet."

Jasper cackled. "You better tell her. She'll be pissed if you don't. I'll wait to call her. Malachi, huh?" He stood and offered a hand. "Nice to meet you, man. Cool name."

ELIZABETH HUNTER

"Thank you." Malachi shook his hand. "Nice to meet you too. Ava has spoken of you."

"I'd say it's all lies, but she's too honest, so I'll just offer a general apology for all past behavior." He sat down and looked around the garden. "Where'd they go?"

Ava thought he looked pretty good for being on a bender. But then, there was a reason she'd chosen to visit in the morning.

"Jasper, I wanted to ask—"

"Sit down!" He waved to the chairs across from him and craned his neck toward the house. "Sit. Those girls were just here. Gotta get you guys some coffee. Where'd you two meet? Malachi, you drink coffee?"

Ava sat. "We met in Istanbul. I was there on a job and Malachi—"

"You're Turkish, man?" Jasper drew on the cigarette again and nodded. "I can see it. Cool. Yeah. So what do you do, Malachi-with-the-cool-name?"

Ava barely caught the edge of suspicion in Jasper's eyes. It was odd for him to be protective, but then, she'd never brought a boyfriend to meet him. Never really had a boyfriend stick around long enough to matter.

"I'm in private security," Malachi said smoothly. It was a practiced lie; he'd implied the same thing to her when they first met. She supposed, in a way, it was true.

"Fuck," Jasper said with a snort. "I thought you said he wasn't a bodyguard, Ava?"

"Maybe I should have said he wasn't *just* a bodyguard."

Jasper laughed.

"Hey, they're the only guys who ever stick around," she said wryly.

"Carl didn't hire him, did he?"

"No."

"Good. All the guys Carl ever hired had a stick up their ass. Of course, Carl does too. So that's not really a surprise."

"Jasper…"

"Kidding. Kinda." He grinned at Malachi, who still sat silently, his expression a careful blank.

Malachi said, "I work for a private international firm based in Vienna. But I take my own assignments."

"So Ava's your assignment now?" Jasper's eyes were keen on Malachi.

"Yes."

"Good. Too many sick fuckers in the world." He lit another cigarette and looked toward the kitchen where one of the maids was bringing out another French press filled with coffee and two more cups. "Ah, there she is. And Ava, I never liked you hoppin' around all over the place."

"Yeah, you're one to talk."

"I speak from experience." He nodded toward Malachi. "I guess if you're gonna do it, good you have someone with you."

"Thanks. Jasper—"

"Hey." He interrupted her again while he waved the maid away and poured the coffee. "I wanted to talk to you about the Malibu house."

"You mean *your* house?"

"No. It's your house. It's been in your name for over a year now."

"Jasper, I already have—"

"Move your stuff from Lena's place. Live there when you're in LA. You can consider it my wedding present, if you want. But you need your own base, baby girl. Not a crash pad."

He refused to meet her eyes. It was an old argument, and one Ava didn't feel like having again. Jasper had already given her too much. The trust fund alone was in the multimillions. He had more money than God and was constantly trying to give her things. Cars. Jewelry. Houses. She didn't want that stuff. Didn't need it.

"I don't need a big house. I can stay with Mom when I'm in California."

He gave her his worried look. "This place—have you even been there?"

"Luis sent me pictures."

"It's quiet, Ava. I picked it myself. Secluded. Lots of acreage. Overlooks the ocean. You know…" He glanced away again. "Quiet. I know you need that."

And there it was. The knowledge she'd been skirting around ever since she'd found the Irin. Found the real reason she heard those voices in her head. Jasper had been one of the few she'd never had to hide around. She'd known, even as a child, that the man who heard beautiful music in his head—was tormented by it at times—would understand the isolated girl she'd been.

Jasper had known all along. Somehow, he'd known.

"Jasper."

His hand shook as he lifted the cigarette. He was getting worse before her eyes. The demons were waking up despite the warm Italian sun and the peaceful garden.

"Just take the house, Ava. I want to give it to you."

"Dad—"

"I told you"—his eyes flared as they met hers, a flash of gold behind the brown—"you don't have to call me that. I mean, you can, but… you don't have to. I never expected that. I know I wasn't…"

There was something going on. She felt Malachi's hand tighten on hers. "Jasper, I need to ask about your family. *My* family."

His face went out of focus for a second. When she blinked, it was back to normal. A trick of light and shadow. For a second, his skin had appeared luminous.

Jasper's voice was harder when he answered. "I told you I don't know much about them. Foster care, remember?"

He was lying. Ava knew it. She opened her senses to listen to his soul's voice.

Jasper's voice was the other reason Ava had always trusted him, even as a child. Though not as pure as Malachi's, it nonetheless had a resonance that had been soothing to her as a child. Jasper's voice had always made her feel safe. She'd put it down to him being an artist. He created beautiful music; why wouldn't it resonate from his mind?

Now that voice sounded broken. Halting.

"Malachi," Jasper asked the man at her side. "You have family?"

"I did. My parents are both dead now."

A hollow longing tone rang in his mind. "Sorry to hear that. My mom died when I was young."

A lie. Ava was positive.

Jasper continued, "That's why I don't know much about my family, you know? She was alone." He glanced at Ava. "On her own. Glad… I'm glad Ava met you."

Ava leaned forward. "Jasper, I wanted to know—"

"Nothing to know." He leaned toward her and cupped her face in his hands. "Beautiful girl. Beautiful Ava." His thumb brushed across her cheek. His fingers, thickly callused from years of playing, were warm. "You got a good guy now. I know he is. Because you'd never settle for less. And you're gonna get married. Maybe even have kids someday. And you'll be a kick-ass mama, 'cause that's what you had. A kick-ass mama. I haven't done a lot right in my life, but the one thing was picking a hell of a good woman to have my kid. So don't worry about the past. Look to the future, baby girl. Don't look for ghosts."

He knew. He knew something, but he wouldn't tell her. Maybe he thought she was prying, but she knew there was something; otherwise, why would he lie about it?

"Dad, why won't you tell me?"

He closed his eyes, and his voice was hoarse. "About what?"

"About your mother." She took a deep breath. "About Ava."

He drew back as if he'd been burned. "Who told you that?"

"I did," Malachi said. "We know your mother was named Ava, Mr. Reed. And we know that you made the records of her disappear. Why did you do that?"

A trick of the light again, and the scent of sandalwood and ash on the breeze. Ava sucked in a breath and it was gone. What was going on? Her father looked angry. Jasper was never angry with her. At himself? Often. But never with her.

"Jasper?"

"You had your man check up on me? Who's the 'we' he's talking about, huh?" He shook out another cigarette. "What the hell, Ava?"

"It was… I was curious—"

"You don't need to be curious about that shit. You don't need to know about my *maman*."

She saw Malachi tilt his head at the word.

Ava asked again, "Your mother? *Maman*? Is that French? Was she French, Jasper?"

He lit the cigarette with shaking hands. "I'm done. I'm not talking about this. Will you move into that damn house or not?"

"Jasper, I need to know."

"No, you don't. And I'm not talking about her." He lit the cigarette, and when his eyes met hers again, he was totally shut down. She knew she'd get nothing out of him.

"Dad—"

"I fucking hate," he whispered, "that you call me dad when you want something from me, Ava. Fucking hate that. I'd rather you call me Jasper. Rather you call me dickhead or bastard or one of the million names you probably thought over the years. I'd rather you call me any of that shit than call me dad just to… to get something from me."

The anger was always there, though she pushed it down. Forced it back. Chose to treasure what they had and what they could become. But it was always there. The lack of him simmered in her blood.

"I never wanted money," she said from behind clenched teeth. "Or houses. Or cars. Or anything, *Jasper*. I never wanted any of that stuff. But this? The one thing I've ever asked you. This you won't give me?"

He fingered the cigarette in his hand and reached for his coffee. Put it down.

"Ruben!" he yelled.

"Jasper, please."

Malachi stood up and moved behind her, but Ava stayed sitting, staring at her father, begging him to meet her eyes.

Ruben walked around the side of the house. "Yeah, boss?"

"Please, Dad."

Jasper ignored her. "Ava and her fiancé need to go. And find me a bottle of Grey Goose."

She shook her head.

"Unbelievable," Malachi said.

"Congratulations," Jasper said, lifting his eyes to her mate. "I'm fucking thrilled for her. And I can see how much you love her just by looking at you. I can see shit like that. I love her too. I know she's pissed at me right now, but she's the best thing in my life, and I'd do anything to protect her."

Malachi squeezed her shoulder and said, "Maybe the way to protect her is by telling her whatever you're trying to hide."

"She may think that, but she'd be wrong."

Her father's eyes finally met hers, and the haunted look was back. It was the look he wore sometimes when he looked at her mother. At her. The tormented part of Jasper Reed knew how much he'd lost by not being a good man. It was the same part that locked himself away from the world for months at a time and wrote some of the most achingly beautiful music Ava had ever heard.

"Love you, baby girl," he said to her. "Gonna work on your song when I get back to the studio. Promise."

As if she hadn't heard that promise a million times. There must be a dozen different versions at this point. She had never heard a single one.

"Sure. Right." She stood and took Malachi's hand. "Bye, Jasper. Take care of yourself."

Ava walked away from the man who had fathered her without looking back. She held Malachi's hand the whole time.

HE'D spent the hour since her unsuccessful meeting with Jasper holding her on the small couch in their hotel room. He hadn't said anything. Hadn't offered any words of comfort or anger or frustration, though she could tell he was worried.

Her concentration was strained, her emotions were strung out, and Ava was exhausted. Malachi's voice slipped through. Before she'd been able to shield herself, his voice sat in the back of her mind constantly. But like her father's, it was more like a steady background music than a jarring intrusion.

Reshon.

Soul mate.

"Imagine a person created for you. Another being so in tune with you that their voice was the clearest you've ever heard in your mind."

It was a voice that had come to mean everything to her.

And then it was gone.

Silence.

And for the first time, silence had made her scream.

For a time after he'd come back, Ava worried she wouldn't be able to hear Malachi as she had before.

She thought she'd lost him forever. Lost that connection forever.

Bit by bit, she was taking down the wall she erected around her heart *and* her mind. His voice slipped through more and more often.

In that moment, his voice hummed with concern. With love. But there was a dark thread that kept coming back over and over again.

Grigori.

"Why are you thinking about the Grigori?"

"Hmm?"

"Your head keeps whispering it. Over and over. *Grigori.*"

"I didn't realize. I'm sorry. Have your shields grown weak?" He put a hand on her shoulder, drew something there, and she immediately felt the surge of energy.

"Don't do that without warning me," she said, blinking as her heart sped.

"Sorry."

"They were a little weak, but—"

"Your father, Ava. I was thinking about your father. I don't understand him."

"I know. He's not much of a dad, but I knew that already."

"No, I mean, he's something…"

She turned when he stopped speaking. "What?"

"Don't pull away. I need to feel you." He slid his hand over her forearm to clasp her fingers. "He's other, Ava. He's not human. Not one hundred percent, anyway."

"But…" She frowned. "What do you mean? I mean, we figured he had some Irin blood, so why were you thinking Grigori? He's not… you're not thinking—"

"Your father is not Grigori. He doesn't smell it. Doesn't look it. But he's not human either."

She paused. "It's hard to wrap my brain around that when he's always just been Jasper."

"There is nothing 'just' about Jasper."

"Why do you say—"

"Think about it. He's in remarkable health, despite his lifestyle. He looks extremely young for his age."

"And he's a musical genius," she said. "Rhys said a lot of Grigori off-spring are gifted in music. But he's not Grigori. You said so."

"No." Malachi sighed. "Rhys suspected bipolar disorder, and I'm tempted to think the same thing."

"And my mom would agree with you. To be fair, that might have nothing to do with Irin blood. A lot of artists have the same problems he does with depression and addiction. Hell, the whole world thought *I* was crazy for years."

"And you're Irina. So what does that make him?"

"Malachi, I don't—"

"He's not Irin," Malachi said, turning her so that she faced him but still holding on to her arm. "He's not... anything I've ever encountered. How long were he and your mother together?"

"Awhile. Not a long while, but long for him." Ava searched her memory. "Months, I think. A few months." Which fit with her pattern of relationships before she'd met Malachi. Her longest relationship had been in the three-month range.

"An Irin scribe could never be with a human for that long."

"But he's not human, either." She thought about the odd flashes she'd had of him. The strange scent in the air. The gold in his eyes.

"There was something," she said. "Something new. I've never noticed it before, but—"

"You never knew what you were before."

She turned to him. "Do you think my dad has magic?"

"I think so, but it's not obvious." He frowned at the wall. "It's... covered."

"What?"

"It's like his power was covered. That's the way it felt to be near him. Sort of like you in your dreams."

"The same as my dreams?" She sat up straight. "*Exactly* the same?"

Malachi narrowed his eyes. "Yes."

"Do you think Jaron is shielding me *and* my dad?"

Malachi paused in thought. She could hear his inner voice going crazy. Words tumbled through his mind in a rush.

"If that shielding is a mark of angelic protection," he said, "then yes. Jaron or another one of the Fallen must be protecting your father."

"Could it be one of the Forgiven?" Her hope lasted for a moment until Malachi squashed it.

"It's not possible, *reshon*. The Forgiven are gone from this world."

"Are you sure?"

He nodded. "Unless one has chosen to fall again, they cannot come back here. Jaron has already shown a connection to you. It's possible he has one to your father as well. It is the most likely possibility."

"But why?" Ava asked. "Why would Jaron do that? My father has never… he's not involved in your world."

She felt his arms tighten around her. "*Our* world, Ava."

She nodded. "Our world. And he's not involved."

"How do we know that?" He turned her so he could look in her eyes. "Ava, he knows you're different. The way he talked about that house he bought for you. The *quiet*. The seclusion. If his mother was Irina—"

"How could she be Irina and have a child with a human?"

"I don't know. It might be possible. So many went into hiding after the Rending, Ava. If your grandmother was Irina and had a child with a human, it would be the first to my knowledge."

She rolled her eyes. "Yeah, well I discovered at Sarihöfn that there's a lot the Irin don't know about the Irina anymore."

"You may be correct. It could be possible—even likely—considering you exist."

"Would a quarter Irin blood be enough to let me touch you?"

He ran a hand up her arm. "I think that answers itself. It has to be."

She settled back against him. The sun had reached its zenith in the sky, and Ava felt drowsy. The room was warm and her mate stretched out on the couch, cushioning her body with his own. As upset as she'd been with her father, his refusal wasn't a surprise. It was easy to deal with disappointment when that was all he'd ever given her.

"What are you thinking, *reshon*?"

"I'm thinking… I like the thought of us getting married. It'll be easier to explain you to my mother if we marry."

"You know, you will not grow older now. With our magic combined, there will come a time—"

"Shhh." She pressed a finger to his lips. "I know. Someday, we'll have to disappear. For now, let me be happy."

He fell silent again and pressed a kiss to her hair. "Be happy," he whispered. "Despite everything happening around us, I am."

She watched the sun track across the room, dozing every now and then as she rested against him.

"I don't think she's dead." Her eyes felt heavy. "My grandmother. There was something about the way he spoke about her."

"If she's alive, *canum*, we will find her. I promise."

I promise.

Ava realized as she drifted off to sleep that to Malachi, those words meant something.

7.

JARON WATCHED FROM ACROSS the crowded street. He had taken the face of an old man and was holding a newspaper and watching the humans pass in front of him as they strolled the ocean promenade with family and friends. The winter wind gusted on the Italian coast, but it did not bother the angel, only flapped the threadbare overcoat that covered his narrow shoulders.

Another old man came to sit beside him, holding a bag of warm chestnuts.

"Does she know yet?"

"She's intelligent. She'll find the answers soon enough. And the scribe is keener than I expected."

Barak lifted the steaming bag of chestnuts to his nose and inhaled but did not reach for one. "Mikhael's offspring are often underestimated," he said. "Seen more for their physical prowess than their strategy. This is a mistake."

Jaron nodded. "Mikhael is a great strategist. His prowess rivals Yun's."

"Only when Yun is not working with you." Barak tugged on the grey beard that covered his face. "I prefer the human eras that favor facial hair."

Jaron lifted an eyebrow at his friend. "Do you? I detest them."

"You detest every human era anymore."

"Why do you think I'm doing all this?"

The corner of the old man's mouth lifted behind his beard. "Why, indeed?"

"Have you heard what your son is doing?"

"I hear everything." Barak's face wore a look of annoyance. "Which one?"

"You know of whom I speak. Have you traveled to Sofia lately?"

"No. Kostas is my brightest child in centuries. There is a chance he would sense me if I came close. I have others watching him."

"And do you approve of what he is doing, my friend?" Jaron was amused. "He would remake the world here, even as we seek to remake the heavens."

Barak watched a clutch of giggling female children pass by. They shouted and shoved each other, bumping into the knees of the two old men and shouting embarrassed apologies before they ran off.

Both of the Fallen watched them.

"Balance," Barak finally said. "In our arrogance, we have forgotten how the universe loves it. No world can exist for so long without balance."

"You're saying change is inevitable."

"Is that not what you're striving for as well?"

Jaron shrugged and the old coat slipped off one thin shoulder. "My goals are for myself. And my friends, if they desire it."

The other angel sat back, lifting the bag of cooling chestnuts again. "I have not yet decided."

"Decide soon, brother."

"Vasu will go his own way."

"I have seen it."

"And me? What have you seen for me?"

"I see nothing, because there is nothing yet to see."

"Hmm." The bearded man stood and reached over the bench, tossing the untouched bag of chestnuts in a bin.

Jaron caught Barak's hand, closing the wrinkled palm in his own. "This time, my old friend, we do not have millennia."

"I know this."

"You must decide soon."

"I know this as well." Barak squeezed Jaron's hand and blinked out of sight as the humans rushed by with unseeing eyes.

It was the way of things. Human sight was so very limited.

Though Barak had shifted away, Jaron's eyes were trained on the balcony where Ava and her scribe sat, drinking wine and watching the street musician who played below them. The musician was… not good. But Ava seemed to enjoy the performance anyway.

The scribe's eyes watched her but more often swept up and down the street, surveying the crowd, watching for threats. Jaron could tell the scribe did not care for his mate being out on the balcony, exposed to possible danger.

The angel approved of this. Perhaps Ava's unexpected call to heaven had manifested a boon for him. He still didn't fully understand why the Creator had allowed the scribe's body and soul to return, but that didn't mean he wouldn't take advantage. More than his own eyes would be trained on the woman if he weren't protecting her.

It wasn't time. There were still pieces to move into place.

Soon, time would run out.

Chapter Five

THEIR RETURN TO ISTANBUL was easier the second time. Ava seemed less cautious and more relieved to be heading back to Turkey. They caught a morning flight and were driving to the scribe house by lunch time. To Malachi, it almost seemed as if she'd left her melancholy in Italy with Jasper. She was lighter. Smiling more.

"You're happy to be back," he said.

"Yeah." She smiled. "It feels like… coming home. With you. I missed it." She rolled down the window and took a deep breath of the air, only to wrinkle her nose at the smell of fish as they crossed the bridge. "Okay, I didn't miss that."

Malachi laughed and reached over her to roll the window up. "So no fish for lunch?"

"No," she said. "I want lamb and salad. Maybe some of those fried potatoes you make."

"Now *I'm* hungry." But happy. He enjoyed cooking for her, and her mood was infectious.

They reached Beyoğlu just a few minutes later, and when they walked into the house, Malachi heard fighting.

Immediately on alert, he held up a hand and put a finger to his lips. Ava dropped her bags and went to the closet, searching for the cache of weapons Leo and Rhys kept ready.

"Who?" she whispered.

He shook his head and held out his hand, catching the sheathed dagger she tossed him. Ava stuffed a throwing knife in her waistband and grabbed a short staff, falling in step behind him.

Malachi crept down the hallway, past the living room, and toward the closed door. The sounds were coming from the practice room, but there were none of the usual shouts and cheerful taunts of his brothers. Strained breathing and grunts. The clash of wood and bodies hitting the floor.

"Wait." Ava put a hand on his lower back. "I think…"

He turned and put a finger to his lips. "Wait here," he mouthed, tracing his *talesm prim*. He felt the wash of magic over his skin. His eyes grew sharper. His ears keener.

"But I think—"

In one movement, Malachi shoved the door open and rolled in, staying low as his eyes swept the room. Leo was on the floor in the corner, a woman straddling him with a staff across his neck. The big man was trying to throw her off, but she only pressed down harder, the muscles rippling in her lean brown arms. Leo scissored his legs in an attempt to flip her, but the woman pushed into it, angling the staff even harder against his throat.

Malachi heard his brother choking. He charged the woman, ignoring his mate's shouts from the doorway. With a bent shoulder, he tackled her to the ground, only to have her twist away before he could put her in a choke hold. Her staff came up and struck his temple, but he shook his head and brought up his dagger to attack.

"No!" Leo jumped between Malachi and the woman. "Malachi! Don't you remember Mala?"

Mala?

A faint memory from Oslo. Mala was one of Sari's Irina. A fierce warrior who'd lost her mate during the Rending and almost lost her own life in a battle near Lagos.

He shook his head. "Mala?"

"We were only sparring." Leo was panting. But grinning too. "She's amazing. Such skill with the short staff! I've never fought an Irina before. Are they all like this?"

Leo sounded as excited as a child at his Naming Day celebration.

"Mala!" Ava ran over, laughing as she embraced the dark-eyed warrior. "Please don't kill my mate. We just got home. We weren't expecting you."

The corner of the woman's full lips turned up. She embraced Ava with one arm, then pulled back, using her hands to sign.

"Slowly," Ava said. "I'm out of practice."

Mala signed again. Ava nodded, still grinning. "I'll tell him. She says you have a strong tackle, but you should work on your balance. Strength is no substitute for grace."

Malachi glowered.

"Hey." Ava held up her hands. "Don't kill the messenger."

His eyes shifted to Mala, who only looked amused. It was a welcome expression on an otherwise fearsome face. The Irina had been beautiful once. Was still beautiful. But her jawline was marred by horrible scars that looked like an animal had attempted to rip out her throat. That was why she did not speak. The Grigori had taken her voice.

Malachi held out his hand. "Well met, sister. You are a fierce opponent."

Mala bowed slightly, then turned to Leo. Ava translated when she started signing.

"I think… she says you rely too much on your size. A smaller opponent is often more… flexible?" Ava paused, watching Mala. "Nimble?" Mala nodded and continued. "She says you should practice dancing." Ava frowned. "Really? Dancing?"

Mala nodded vigorously.

"I can do that," Leo said with a grin. "But I'd need an Irina partner."

Mala picked up her staff and walked out of the room.

Leo said, "I guess that means she doesn't volunteer."

"I'll dance with you, Leo."

"Are you any good?"

"Not really. But at least you won't make me pass out, which is an improvement over most partners you're going to find around here."

"True."

Malachi sheathed the knife and tried to calm a heart that still raced. "Leo, do you still want to spar?" he asked. "I've been on a plane all morning and I'd love to stretch my legs."

"Of course." The big man picked up the second staff that was lying on the mat of the training room. "Ava, Orsala arrived with Mala."

Ava groaned and covered her eyes. "No."

Malachi went to her and kissed her temple. "She's probably with Rhys in the library, devising more magical torture for you. The longer you delay, the worse it will be."

"Save me," she said.

"I will battle Grigori for you, *canim*," he said gallantly. "I'll abandon heaven and cross continents."

"My hero!"

"But I will not interfere with that old singer's plans. Do you think I want to die again?"

She slapped his backside and walked toward the door. "Leo, kick his ass for me. He's getting way too cocky."

Malachi only laughed. "I love you, Ava."

Leo said, "I love you too, Ava. Good luck with Orsala."

"Both of you—useless!"

"MALACHI?"

He looked up from his drawing pad. "Orsala?"

The old woman smiled tentatively when she walked into the room. She wore the silver hair and lined face of an Irina who had stopped her longevity spells. Malachi had heard her mate had been killed years ago, so allowing herself to age and pass away was not unexpected.

"Am I interrupting?" she asked.

"Not at all." He pushed the sketches to the side. He had several *talesm* he'd been planning to scribe once they were back in Istanbul, and he needed to practice the characters. But sketching could wait. Malachi had a feeling she wanted to talk about his mate. "Is Ava—"

"She's fine. Resting, I think. She went to your room with a headache. I believe she was becoming frustrated."

He rose to go to her, but Orsala put a hand on his shoulder. "If I could have a moment…"

Malachi paused. "What is it?"

"She is very resistant."

"To using her magic?"

"Yes."

"I know." He took a deep breath. "She's afraid of what she can do."

She smiled, and warm creases formed around her silver-blue eyes. "I do not want to interfere. Or ask you to break her confidence. I want to help her."

"Let me talk to her again."

"Thank you."

"I warn you, though." He gathered his papers and turned to leave. "I will not pressure her to use her magic if she's not ready. My loyalty is to her, not any cause."

"As it should be," Orsala said. "You remind me much of my own mate. He was highly protective, even when I was at my strongest."

"It is when we are strongest that we often don't protect ourselves," he said. "Whatever her destiny is in this life, it is my job to defend her."

"For the Irina, I think the time has come for offense, not defense."

He shook his head. "I'm not talking about the Irina. I'm talking about Ava. I will not let her be dragged into a war of your making, Orsala. However much I may support your cause, her part in it will be of her choosing."

"She has not chosen this," the old woman countered, "but Jaron has. The Fallen has targeted her."

"And protected her."

"I know." Orsala stepped closer. "We need to know why. There is a darkness in her. A darkness to her magic that I have never seen before."

"I do not fear her darkness."

"Nor should you. But we need to understand it so we may understand her. She needs to understand herself, Malachi. If you do not fear the darkness, then do not shield your mate from it, either. Sometimes we must do exactly the thing that terrifies us most in order that we may live the life we were meant to have."

WHEN he reached their bedroom, he knocked. It was their shared room, but if she was exhausted—

"Come in, Malachi."

He pushed the door open. Ava was lying on the bed in a beam of sunlight, the sun catching red strands in her hair. Her eyes were closed. Her forehead smooth.

"Orsala said your head was hurting."

"I lied. Kind of."

He toed off his shoes and lay down next to her. "What's wrong?"

Ava rolled over to make room for him. "You know, I think this was what I missed the most when you were gone."

He said nothing. The fact that she was talking about her grief was extraordinary enough. He didn't want to interrupt her.

"I missed lying next to you. Just… that. Not sex. Not even your touch. I missed all those things, but it was just… you. Being here. Knowing that someone gave a shit about me other than my mom. Knowing you were beside me at night." She moved her leg over to hook it around his knee. "I could reach out for you if I needed you. Or just wanted you. When I had that… I'd never had that before."

He took a deep breath. "Sometimes I feel as if I'm a second mate. As if you grieved for someone entirely different. That you still grieve."

"I'm sorry."

"Don't." He rolled over and watched her face in profile. Her eyes were still closed. But now there were lines of tension on her forehead. He took a finger and smoothed them away. "Don't be sorry. You lost me, but I never lost you. I think I would go quite mad if our roles had been reversed. The man I am now has always had you. My memories began with you, so I never felt the pain you did. You were where I began, Ava. I was the lucky one."

She choked out a laugh even as the tears leaked from the corner of her eye. "You were the one who died."

"But that pain only lasted a heartbeat. Yours lasted for months. Please, don't hide your grief from me."

"I'm afraid," she whispered. "At night I wake up, and for a second, you're gone again."

"Reach out. You'll find me."

"I'm afraid if I reach for you, I'll find out this is a dream. That I'm caught in some kind of delusion. I don't know what's real in the dark."

He rolled over and drew her back to his chest, wrapping his arm around her waist. He called up the ancient magic that lived in his skin, allowing his *talesm* to glow. "Look, Ava."

She opened her eyes.

"When the darkness comes, reach for me."

She said nothing, but he could feel her fear.

"What are you afraid of? It's not just losing me again."

"I don't—"

"Don't lie." He tapped a finger against her temple. "I can tell."

"I think…" She put her hands over his and gripped them tightly. "I think my magic is evil, Malachi."

"It's not evil. I've felt it. It's beautiful."

"It's dark."

"Dark does not equal evil." He took a deep breath and felt her match him. They lay together, quietly enjoying the afternoon sun. "Is this because of what happened on the roof with Jaron?"

"It's more than that."

"Tell me."

Ava said nothing for a long while.

"I saw a black angel once," she whispered. "There was a Grigori attacking me in Norway. He'd broken into the room with another who'd gone after Mala. They were trying… I don't know what they were trying to do. Kill us? Capture us for Volund, maybe? But he was on me, and I'd made him angry by fighting back. His hand was on my throat."

Malachi forced his body to remain calm as he held her, but the rage bubbled beneath his skin.

"What happened?"

"I couldn't remember the spells, and I was so mad. I was *furious*. I'd lost you. Lost so much. And he was trying to take more. I felt this darkness well up inside me. It poured out of me. I opened my mouth, but I couldn't speak. It didn't matter. I could hear… wind. And then it was like the shadows in the room came to life. There was a figure. It felt like Jaron, but more. Darker. Heavier. There was no substance to it. Like a vacuum. And the closer I looked, the more it drew me in."

He couldn't help it. His arms tightened around her. "Ava—"

"Feathers," she whispered. "It sounded like feathers."

His stomach dropped, and his heart pounded. "What happened?"

She stared at the ceiling, lost in the memory. "I heard screaming, but it wasn't me. I think I passed out from his hand on my throat. By the time I came back, it was the Grigori screaming. His eyes were open. He was staring into nothing as if he'd seen it too. But it had captured him. It wasn't letting go."

Ava's voice dropped to barely a whisper. "He was so terrified. And I knew… He'd seen what I saw. But the shadow took him. I wanted him to see it, and he did."

"Ava, this was not…"

…*your fault.* Malachi couldn't say it. Because it might have been a lie. No one knew what she was capable of.

Thousands of you, Scribe. One of her.

"What was it?" She rolled over to face him. "That shadow? You know, don't you?"

He didn't want to tell her what he thought. But this was his mate. She'd know if he tried to lie or avoid the question.

"Death," he said. "You saw Death."

"How do you know?" she asked. "Maybe it was one of the Fallen. There are probably—"

"He is not one of the Fallen. He is Death."

She shook her head, dread marking her face. "No."

"Ava, I've probably seen him, even though I don't remember."

"Don't…" She sat up in the bed. "So, there really is an angel of death?"

He nodded. "Our books say he is neither Fallen nor Forgiven. He is Death. Some scriptures call him Azril. He comes for any with angelic blood. He is neither good nor evil. His job is to gather souls that have been released."

"And I called him?"

"No," he murmured. "I don't know. He serves no one but the Creator. But you saw him."

"But so did the Grigori. And I was the one dying, not him."

"Yes, he saw…" Malachi sat up next to her. "He saw what you saw."

"Yeah, I said that."

He took her hand. "Think about what you've done in the past, Ava. When you allow your magic to work."

She paused. "I see things."

"You see things," he murmured. "Why does your photography strike a chord with so many? Because they're not just pictures to you. Your camera is a lens into your mind. Your heart. You *show* things. I think your magic carries the same gift. What you see, you manifest in others' minds. When Jaron gave you a vision and you sang about it in Oslo, we *saw* it. Not just imagined it, we saw your vision in our own minds. You saw Death. And when you did, the Grigori did as well. And Death terrified him."

"How?" she whispered. "Who does that? Is that…" She frowned. "Is that Leoc? Leoc's gift? Orsala called me a daughter of Leoc."

"Leoc is a seer. He gave his daughters the gift of foresight." Malachi shook his head. "What you do is different."

"So where does it come from?" She pounded her fist on the bed. "Where do *I* come from?"

"Ava, it's not—"

"Dammit, Malachi! I need my dad to be honest with me."

"Ava—"

"No, really. I'm pissed. The more I think about my dad, the angrier I get. At first I was the sad, disappointed daughter I've been for years, but now? I'm just pissed."

"Your father—"

"My father *knew*. If his mother was the same as me, he's known for years that I heard voices. Maybe he knows about soul voices, maybe he doesn't. But he knew what was wrong with me, and he said nothing. Even just telling me he understood would have made me feel like less of a freak. But he was too selfish to do that for his own daughter."

He took her fist, spreading her fingers until he could thread them through his own. "We don't know—"

"He knew why I ran away from life. Knew why I could never have any real relationships. No home. No friends. No boyfriends."

"He might have been trying—"

"My dad *knew* what all the hovering and the bodyguards and the endless, *endless* psychological exams must have done to me. And he knew they wouldn't do anything to help. And he still said nothing."

"It's possible—"

"He. Said. Nothing."

Malachi stopped trying to calm her.

"And I know his mother is alive! I know it. And you know what? I bet he *knows* that I know it. And he's still lying to me. He's still keeping all these secrets."

She swung her legs off the bed and started pacing their room like an angry cat.

"I'm sick of secrets!" she said. "I'm sick of my dad keeping them and Jaron playing with me like I'm a pawn in his little games. I'm sick of being chased and hunted. I'm sick of acting calm when I really want to scream."

"I know." Deep down, Malachi was relieved that Ava was showing this much emotion about anything. She'd been too calm for far too long. She had a right to her anger. It was long overdue, and resignation did not suit her.

"I'm sick of it."

"I can see that." He tried to stop the smile, but she caught the edge of it.

"Are you laughing at me?"

"Absolutely not."

She stopped pacing. Her mouth hung open. Her hands were on her hips. Malachi felt the smile spread across his face.

"You are," she said.

"I'm not laughing. I'm thrilled."

"About what?"

He stood and faced her, putting his hands on her small shoulders. "I'm glad you're angry. Ava, I *love* it. You have every right to be. Take it. Use it. Force your father to be honest with you. Don't let him ignore you. The next time you see Jaron in a dream, question him. I can't, but you *can*. If he can reach you, then you can reach *him*. Don't let him ignore you. You want to find answers?"

"Yes!"

"Then what can I do to help?"

Chapter Six

"I DON'T TELL YOU often enough," Ava said, love for him filling her up, balancing the anger. "I love you. You're strong and protective, smart and kind. You're just a... a very *good man.*"

"Thank you."

"I fell in love with the man I met in Istanbul. The mysterious one who touched me and made me feel like I was magic. And I grieved for the hero who sacrificed himself to protect me. But the man you are now? The man you're becoming? He's all those things. And he's more."

His eyes had lost all their humor. He reached up to cup her cheek. "Ava."

"You're a good man. And maybe I don't know who I am, but I know I'm grateful that you're mine. That I can find out who I am with you. And maybe help you find yourself too."

She stood on her toes and kissed him. Malachi reached down and lifted her up, swinging her around until they sat on the edge of the bed again, lips still locked. She pulled back and peppered his face with kisses until he was smiling. Until his dimple couldn't be hidden. Until he laughed. And Ava thought she might become addicted to the sound of Malachi's laughter. If she could find the answers she needed and live a thousand years with this man, she would never grow tired of hearing him laugh.

Then she was the one smiling when he threaded his fingers through her hair and kissed her deeply, teasing her tongue with his. He tasted spicy, like the peppers and sumac she had smelled from the kitchen during lunch. His shoulders were firm beneath her hands. His body commanding hers to give more. Deeper. His soul voice rang in her head, tuning her mind and body. She felt her magic rise up and settle against his.

He let out a gasp and pulled back. "Ava, it feels so good."

"More?"

"More."

She kissed him again. Heard the words in her mind. Pulled away to whisper in his ear.

"*Hanama*." She recited the simple spell, picturing what she wanted in her mind as she spoke. "*Da'adanama*."

Take of me, the magic whispered. *Give to me*.

His magic shot through her, and she could feel her mating marks burn as his arms tightened at the small of her back. Malachi's own skin was hot beneath her hands. Like a circuit sparked by her passion, their magic joined and fed them both, opening them to each other. No insulation. No barriers.

She could see his *talesm* glowing on his forearms. Could feel the ghost of them under her palms. Once, they'd covered his body, marking the territory of him like a map. She'd told him once that the lack of them didn't matter to her, but it did. Because they were part of him. Each spell carefully chosen and written. Not simply words a scribe had written to protect himself, but a guide to the man he'd chosen to become.

She wanted them back.

Cautiously, she bent to his ear again.

"*Ya davarda*," she whispered, the spell slipping from her lips. It should have been easy after all the times she'd recited it in her mind, but she was so afraid.

Remember.

It was a command she imbued with the deepest longing of her heart. For Malachi to remember who he was. And who he'd made himself to be.

"*Ya davarda, reshon*," she said it again, a little louder.

She felt the energy leave her fingertips and enter him. A slip of silk brushing against her skin. There for a heartbeat, then gone. Away from her. Into him.

"Ava!"

THE SECRET

Malachi pulled back, his hands clenched on her hips so hard Ava knew they would bruise. His eyes were closed. The marks on his forearms glowed like fire fed from a sudden gust of wind.

She kept her hands on his shoulders, pressing down as if to keep them both from flying away. His face was clenched, but it was not in pain. His eyes darted back and forth beneath his lids. She felt a burning beneath her right palm and looked down.

Like living vines, his *talesm* crawled up his left forearm, joining and sometimes overwriting the spells he'd added after his return. The glowing quicksilver lines moved up his arm as she watched, twisting and turning. Traveling across and around his wrist, his forearm, his elbow, and bicep. His skin burned as from a fever.

The lines disappeared under his shirt. In their wake, his skin swelled and reddened, leaving ash-black ink embedded in his flesh.

Malachi's chest heaved for a few deep breaths and then fell still. His head fell. The magic seemed to leave him and retreat back into her.

"Malachi?" She squeezed his shoulders and he winced. Ava quickly pulled her hands away, but he did not open his eyes. She had felt him, shoulders rock hard under her hands. But she could also see the lines of red blood seeping through the white cotton of his shirt.

She tried not to panic. "Malachi?"

He opened his eyes, and Ava could see a gold fire ringing his irises. Then he leaned back and tore off his shirt. Fine wells of blood stained his entire left arm, crawling up to his collarbone.

"You," he panted, "did this."

"Are you okay?" Ava was trying not to freak out. She'd wanted him to remember, but though he didn't look angry, there was a violent expression in his eyes.

"Hurts."

"I'm sorry." She willed herself not to cry. She'd wanted him to remember, but his skin looked raw and wounded. She'd done this to him. Some of his *talesm* were back, but it must have been incredibly painful. "I'm so sorry."

"No," he grunted.

75

She tried to scramble off his lap, but he only held tighter, his hands digging into her hips. "Let me—"

"Not sorry," he said. His forehead was gleaming with sweat. The burning in his skin hadn't stopped. "Don't be sorry." He reached up and grabbed the back of her neck, forcing her mouth to his in a bruising kiss. Ava leaned into him. Relieved. Excited. She could feel the raw energy rolling off him in waves.

Adrenaline. Endorphins. Her mate's body had been hit with a massive cocktail of magic and hormones in the space of a few minutes.

She pulled away, gasping as his hands began to tear at her clothes. "Oh. Not angry."

"No."

MALACHI made love to her with furious focus, ignoring what had to be brutal pain on his left side. Ava just held on and let him vent the surge of power into her body. Over and over. He asked if she was okay. If he was hurting her. He wasn't. She was more afraid of hurting him, but he was insatiable and seemed to find as much satisfaction in her pleasure as in his own.

They took a break when the sun set, and someone—who wasn't brave enough to speak—knocked on their door, reminding Ava they weren't alone.

Malachi reached down, threw one of his boots at the door, and the footsteps hurried away.

Ava laughed into the shoulder that wasn't sore. His arm had already healed over, but it was an angry red.

"You're quite the beast today, aren't you?"

"It's your fault," he said, rolling onto his right side. "Do you know how much magic you woke in me?"

She tentatively touched his left arm. "A lot?"

"Yes. And Rhys was right."

"About?"

"I remember, Ava."

She paused, stunned that it had worked. "How much?"

"Most of my childhood. The earliest things." His eyes shone with tears. "I miss my parents again."

"I'm sorry," she said, stroking his cheek. He'd shaved that morning, but he was Malachi, so half a beard had already grown.

"Don't be sorry," he said. "I'm glad I miss them." He brushed the wet away from his cheek. "They deserve to be missed."

"How… What is it like?"

"You told me to remember, and it was like… a key unlocked in my mind. This door opened. And then inside that door, another door. And then another. I kept passing through each one, and it was as if the rooms they unlocked were infinite. Eventually, my brain just shut down. I remember everything through my school years. Rhys was there." Malachi frowned. "He may be my best friend, but by heaven, he can be an ass."

Ava burst into laughter. "He likes tormenting you."

"Still does." A reluctant smile crossed his face. "I suppose it was mutual."

"And your *talesm* grew."

He lifted an arm. "Apparently."

"That looks really painful."

"It is."

She winced. "I'm so sorry."

"Don't be. I wanted them back." He stretched his arm out and she could see the skin already healing around the tattooed flesh. "I feel stronger already."

"Then I'm glad."

"Good." He touched her chin until she looked at his face. The gold fire had retreated and his eyes were a beautiful, cloudy grey again.

"What is it?"

"I adore you, Ava. Your mind is fascinating. Your spirit humbles me. And your body feels as if it was made to fit my own. Even now that I have more of my memories back, my thoughts continue to circle you on a level that's borderline obsessive."

She blinked. "Wow."

"Know that. Understand it, because I'm going to say something that will likely make you angry."

She frowned. "Oh."

"You need to stop fooling around and work on your magic."

"What?" Her mouth dropped open. "But you said—"

"I know what I said. 'Go at your own pace. No pressure.' That was me being supportive and protective."

"I like you being supportive and protective."

"I don't think you need me to be supportive and protective right now. I think you need a kick in the ass. Because the magic I just felt has nothing dark or evil about it. You're scared of something that doesn't exist."

Yeah, okay. That made her a little mad. More than a little. He didn't know what she saw. Had no idea the shadows she felt lurking on the edge of her mind anytime the magic drew near.

"Until we know where my power comes from—"

"Ava, we may never know." He sat up and she followed him, facing each other on the rumpled bed. "We could search the world, question your father, wring answers from a fallen angel, and there is no guarantee we'll ever know why you were able to call me down from heaven. Or why you can show others things like the face of Death itself. We may not know any of it. Ever."

She had nothing to say, because he was right. She hated it, but he was right.

"What we do know," he continued, "is that your power is unique. It could be an incredibly potent weapon against those who want to hurt you. And you need to learn how to wield it like you just did with me."

She raised an eyebrow and glanced down at his naked body.

"Okay, maybe not *just* the way you did with me. You know what I mean."

She swung her legs over the edge of the bed and stared at the wall, unnerved by his honesty.

He was right. She'd felt the power when it left her. Felt the echo of it come back when they made love. It wasn't the dark shadow she'd felt in the past. The dark edge was still there, but it hadn't hurt Malachi, so she knew it wasn't inherently bad.

Could she use it to hurt?

Undoubtedly.

But she could also use it to heal. Her mate was in temporary pain, but his magic had been given a huge boost with the restoration of part of his *talesm*. The Old Language Orsala had taught her bent to her will, taking on her magic before she spoke it into life and power.

She had done this.

And she knew she could do it again.

Ya davarda, reshon.

It was a command. She'd told him to remember and he'd remembered.

How did Irina not become intoxicated by this power?

ORSALA examined Malachi's arm, lifting it to search every inch of the *talesm* that had reappeared.

"And these are what you remember?"

"As much as I can remember, yes. They feel right. If that makes sense."

"It does. These are your original marks. I can see the progression in expertise." She touched the skin that had already healed at his wrist. "A young man's marks here, for certain." Her finger passed over his forearm and elbow as Ava watched anxiously from her chair in the library. Rhys sat next to Ava as Orsala inspected Malachi in the full light of the window. "And then as we go up the shoulder… Yes, an obvious progression. You could be rather dramatic when you were young, yes?" She smiled at him, amusement twinkling in her eyes.

A faint flush stained his cheeks. "I was not always the most rational when choosing my marks."

Rhys said, "Still aren't."

"Shut up, Rhys."

"I can see a hotheaded boy in this arm," Orsala said, patting it. "But also the beginnings of a passionate, protective young man."

"Thank you."

Orsala turned to Ava, smiling. "You did this."

"I did."

Rhys nudged her arm, catching her eye with his mischievous smile. "And then they celebrated after. Loudly."

Malachi sent his friend a smug smile as he pulled on a shirt. "Jealous."

"Obviously."

He crooked his head and Rhys abandoned his seat next to Ava to go lean on his desk.

Orsala said, "I'd caution you to go slowly. When you unleash that level of magic, you're going to exhaust yourself. And each other."

Rhys couldn't smother the laugh.

Orsala narrowed her eyes at him, unable to hide her own smile. "While I'm sure some might find it amusing," she said, "I'd warn you to take your time. And also accept that one spell might not continue to be effective in the same way. It may be that a simple command to remember no longer works at some point. But you've taken the first step. You've started to heal each other."

Orsala reached down and took Ava's hand. "You are more open, I can feel it." She turned to Malachi and took his. "And you've regained some of your past. I can see your confidence returning. Your strength. I can feel…" She closed her eyes and drew in a deep breath, holding both their hands. "Your connection is almost tangible. I think your mating will be unlike anything our world has seen."

"I concur," Rhys said with a wistful smile.

"Be cautious," Orsala warned. "I want to work with you, Ava. Far more than we have been. Mala's physical training can wait for now. I do not think physical combat is your gift. I want to work on your magic."

Ava felt Malachi nudging her knee with his own. "I know. I will."

"And no holding back as you have been."

"I already promised this guy," Ava said, looking at her mate. "No holding back."

"I'll join you," Malachi said. "If she needs to practice spells, I'll be happy to help."

Orsala said, "I'd prefer to do this in Vienna with Sari, but we'll do what we can. When can you two go to the city?"

Ava exchanged a look with Malachi. "I need to get some information from my father before I go anywhere."

"Why?"

Malachi frowned. "To find her origins, of course."

Orsala looked at Rhys. "Isn't that something you can do while she's in Vienna?"

Rhys said, "I think Ava's father is the only one who knows the truth. My searches have come up with nothing."

"And my dad's currently in the middle of his mid-tour binge," Ava said. "He's not really all that coherent most of the time. Is there such a thing as a magical truth serum?"

"We can work on that if you think it will help," Orsala said. "But remember, truth is relative. He might tell you something he believes to be true, but there's no guarantee that his own perceptions are accurate, particularly if he's damaged his mind with drugs or alcohol."

"I'll take my chances. His memory has never been damaged, no matter how much he takes. Luis is right. How that man has managed to keep in perfect health is beyond me."

"Really?" The old woman stepped back and frowned.

"As far as I know. The drinking and drugs seem to work for him."

Orsala's eyes had lost focus. "I wonder…"

Ava waited for her to continue, but she seemed to have lost track of her thoughts. The singer wandered over to a stack of books on the library table and began to page through them. Rhys smiled at Orsala and came to stand in her place.

"I'll continue to search, but I don't know what other avenues to check."

Ava had a thought. "Rhys, speaking of Luis…"

"Luis Martin? I've checked him out. He's aboveboard. No criminal record. No links to our world that I can find."

"How about his personal property? Investments. That kind of thing."

"What about them?" Rhys frowned. "He's been a good financial manager for your father and seems very honest. There's no evidence of embezzlement or anything of the sort."

"Ah, but what about his own money?" Malachi smiled. "I know what she's thinking. We were looking for properties or payments in Jasper Reed's financial life that might indicate something about his mother. But did we check Luis Martin? If Reed truly wanted someone hidden, would he put it in his name or hide it behind someone he trusted implicitly?"

Rhys nodded. "It makes sense if he truly trusts Martin that much."

Ava said, "He does."

"Then I'll look into Luis Martin's financial life. I'll let you know if anything looks interesting."

"Thanks, Rhys."

Orsala called from the other side of the room. "Rhys, do you have a copy of *Gabriel's Old Tales*?"

"Which version?"

"The Hofstra translation is what I prefer, but any will do. Even one in the Old Language."

"I know I have at least one. Don't know about Hofstra…" Rhys led Orsala to the shelves, the two of them scanning the rows of books and muttering quietly back and forth.

"What are *Gabriel's Old Tales*?" Ava asked.

"Hmm? Oh. Children's stories." Malachi frowned. "Somewhat frightening ones, as a matter of fact. I'm trying to think of a human equivalent."

"*Grimm's Fairy Tales*?"

"Perhaps."

"Fair maiden does something stupid and ends up eaten by a wolf or losing body parts and wandering hopelessly alone for the rest of her life? That kind of thing?"

"Yes," he said. "That kind of thing. My grandmother read some of *Gabriel's Old Tales* to me when I was a child, and I don't think I slept for a week."

"Nice."

"Now that I think about it, let's agree to never tell our children those kinds of stories, shall we?"

"We never finished the kid conversation, you know."

He reached over and put his arm around her shoulder, nuzzling his face into her neck. "You want my babies."

Ava felt herself melting. "You are confident, aren't you?"

"I'm confident because I know you want my babies. And you're a fierce woman who will make a tremendous mother."

"Mine was pretty great, even though my dad and stepdad were kind of useless."

"As our children will have the benefit of a superb father, you should have no concerns."

"What was Orsala saying about your confidence coming back?"

HER eyes opened in the darkness. She could sense her mate. He was by her side, unaware they were no longer alone.

Was she dreaming? She didn't quite know. All she knew was darkness and quiet. Peace filled her heart.

Darkness materialized from the shadows, but it wasn't Jaron. The rustle of feathers whispered in the air as the beautiful man leaned forward. His face emerged from the void of his hood, pale as the moon and holding an ancient, delicate beauty.

Ava felt no fear.

His eyes weren't the rich gold of Jaron's, but a silvery grey outlined by deep ebony lashes. His hair was the blue-black of a raven's wing; his face spoke peace.

Beautiful, immutable peace.

She put a hand on Malachi's shoulder and was surprised to feel the heat of his skin under her fingers. This was a dream, but it wasn't.

"I've seen you before," she said.

Death nodded, but he did not speak.

"You're not like the others."

He shook his head, a small smile playing across his lips.

"Am I going to die? Is he?" Her hand pressed into her mate's back, and Death's eyes followed her hand, resting on Malachi as he slept.

"No," Ava whispered, fear clutching her chest. "Please no."

Death flew to her side, pressing a warm finger to her lips. He drew her to his chest, and when he embraced her, a still, quiet voice whispered in her mind.

I am not here for you. Or him. I only see you together, and it fills me with a rare joy.

"You took him," she whispered.

I take them all. It is not often I am allowed to bring them back.

A sense of laughter in her mind.

Come with me, daughter. And I will show you secrets.

Death spread his arms and enfolded her in the night. His cloak was a blanket of stars, wrapping her in its depths as he surrounded her. She was weightless. Formless. And yet she still felt Malachi's strong shoulder under her hand as her soul flew with the black angel.

Come.

He opened his cloak and revealed a dark room. Three beings met there, cold and frightening in power. And though she stood in the center of them, Death held her shoulders, turning her around the chamber, and Ava knew they did not see her.

Listen.

The whispers came to her from behind a veil. Thoughts and voices tangled together. Ava knew they were speaking in the Old Language, but she had no trouble understanding.

"…troublesome child."

"Barak should have killed him."

"You killed Barak. Why… son still alive?"

They were indistinguishable by feature. She could only sense two beings with bright, glowing power and another clinging to one as a parasite to a host, feeding from the greater, though he did not know it. The Fallen were veiled, cloaking their power from the world and each other.

"…not long now."

"Watching. We must…"

"Scattered." Another voice drifted in and out. "…act now or they will discover them."

"There is no danger."

"There is every danger."

"If they find them—"

"If they find them, they will be reborn. The silent must remain hidden…"

84

Ava strained, but she couldn't hear more.

"…Irin will wake."

"A sleeping enemy does not trouble me."

"And Jaron?"

A pause. "Our brother does not have the strength to oppose us."

Something in the mocking tone of his voice reminded Ava of Brage, and she knew the speaker was Volund.

"He will make their army his own."

A growing sense of urgency. Wariness. Alarm?

Ava felt the black arms embrace her again just as Volund turned to stare into the void where she listened.

"Quiet, brothers." A long pause. "Azril, do you come among us?"

She dissolved, only to merge with her body again, her fingers still resting on her mate's back.

Warm hands clasped her face, though she could not see them. A check pressed against her own.

I cannot go to her, the angel whispered in her mind. *Though she calls me by my true name, I cannot reach her.*

The longing in his voice almost broke her.

"Who?"

Tell her I have not forgotten.

He was melting back into the shadows, and Ava still wasn't sure what was a dream and what had been real.

"Who are you talking about?" She crawled toward the darkness, desperate to understand. "Please! Who?"

Ava.

And he was gone.

Chapter Seven

DESPITE THEIR INITIAL HOPE, searching through Luis Martin's financial information proved to be just as successful as searching Jasper Reed's.

"If anything," Rhys griped, "this is even more frustrating."

"Yes, he's a bit paranoid about privacy, isn't he?"

Malachi and Rhys were in the library. Malachi was waiting for Orsala to call him. She was doing meditation exercises with Ava in the sparring room. Then he would join them and they were going to practice defensive spellwork.

"It seems wrong to call him paranoid when we're hacking into his e-mail, doesn't it?"

Malachi shrugged. "Slightly."

"Oh well."

They continued to work, Rhys trying every keyword search he could think of to look for any mention of Ava's grandmother. Unfortunately, she was also named Ava, meaning that any search for her name hit on correspondence related to Jasper Reed's daughter and not his mother.

"He and Luis talk about her often," Rhys said. "I think her father thinks of her more than she realizes."

"Thinking of her and actually acting like a father are two very different things."

"Have you and Ava talked about children?"

"Briefly." Which wasn't something he wanted to discuss with Rhys. "What is that? He just mentioned a transfer to a Swiss bank."

"Shite." Rhys groaned. "Not that one. Their systems are archaic."

"But secure," Malachi said. "There's a reason why they're still as popular as they are. If Luis was making payments there, we need to determine what for."

"We're not going to be able to find out. Not from the bank. They still use paper. But let me…" Rhys tapped the keys rapidly. Screens popped up and disappeared faster than Malachi could read them.

"What are you doing?"

"I'm searching the exact dollar amount within his financial records. It wasn't a flat amount. $41,569.14 is not a random number. That's payment for something…" He tapped a few more keys and smiled. "Something specific. And monthly. Aha." Rhys sat back, a smile of satisfaction on his face. "I believe he pays that amount every month."

"How do you know?"

"Because he's transferred five hundred thousand dollars into that Swiss account every year for the past five years. Divide that by twelve and you have—"

"A little over $41,569? But why the single payment then? There must have been something unexpected that came up."

"Maybe it was just timing. That first payment was in December five years ago. A single month's payment before a monthly fee was set up? Automatically paid from the Swiss account probably."

Malachi sat back. "What costs that much for one person?"

"I think Reed—through his manager—is paying to keep his mother somewhere. A private institution, perhaps. Remember what Ava thought when we first met her? She thought she was insane. If Jasper Reed's mother was like Ava and living among humans, they might lock her up for hearing voices. That amount would fit with a private mental institution."

"And he'd hide her so thoroughly because he thought she was mentally ill?" Malachi was skeptical. "Wipe her from the public records? Hide her behind his manager and a Swiss bank account? That seems excessive."

"Unless she's violent. Dangerous. Or *in* danger from someone else."

It was possible.

"We need to search private mental institutions in Europe and the US." He turned and saw Orsala standing at the door. "Search for any that cost that much on a monthly basis."

"Already on it," Rhys said. "See to your mate."

MALACHI shook his head. "No."

Ava's eyes were pleading. "But I can't practice defensive spells unless someone is attacking me." She spread her legs shoulder width apart and squared her body to his. "Go on. I've rehearsed this a million times, but I don't know what I'll do in the middle of the actual spell. Orsala is here to stop me in case anything goes wrong."

Malachi crossed his arms over his chest. "While I'm duly terrified of your defensive abilities, *canim*, I'm more reluctant to attack you because you're my mate and I don't wish to hurt you. You may proceed without the attack from me."

Ava's jaw dropped. "Wow. Really? How old did you sound just then?"

Orsala said, "About four hundred years old. Ava, what did you expect? I told you it would be better to ask Rhys or Leo."

Malachi glared. "Absolutely not."

"Your friends would have no problem helping Ava practice."

"They would if they wanted to avoid injuries from me."

"Stubborn man!"

"I don't need an old woman's approval to protect my mate."

Ava held up both hands and stepped between them. "We're not doing this. I need to practice. This isn't a battle of the sexes. Malachi, you're my husband. Mate. Whatever. And I expect you to help me become stronger. I've tried unprovoked defensive spells, and they just don't work. I'm not getting that gut reaction I need to make them effective. So if you aren't willing or able to help me—"

"If there is no other option, then fine." Her matter-of-fact attitude convinced him. She was correct. To not help her become stronger would be to fail in his duties as her mate. "And we're getting married as soon as possible. If you prefer not to call me your mate, then I'll at least be your husband."

"Technically," Orsala said as she moved back to the wall, "she's not your mate either."

Ava's mouth dropped open, and Malachi said, "Yes, she is. Why in heaven would you say that?"

Orsala frowned. "Has she completed the mating ritual? I thought only you had performed it. Your magic doesn't reflect a mated couple."

Ava looked horrified. "I haven't." She turned to him. "What does that mean? What do I need to do?"

According to what he'd been told, Orsala was technically correct. Malachi had marked Ava before his death, but she'd never completed her side of the ritual, and he hadn't tattooed the mark that would make her claim permanent.

Ava was upset. "But we're dream-walking. And I... I feel you. I thought I was your mate. What we have—"

"Of course you're my mate," he said, soothing her. "We are *reshon*. Nothing can negate that. It's fine, *canim*."

"It's not," Orsala said. "He gave you his power, but you have not given him yours. Your mate will not heal fully until you do."

"But what do I do?"

Malachi marched over to the old woman. "She will not be pressured into this. This is between Ava and me."

"I'm not pressuring her. But you do her no favors. Mates carry each other's burdens. Do you think she is not able to carry yours?"

"That has nothing to do with it." And everything to do with Ava being as strong as possible. If she gave him her power, as so many Irina had before the Rending, then it was possible she would be weakened at a point when she might be vulnerable.

He turned to Ava. "We will complete the ritual in our own time. When things are safer for you."

Ava stepped to him. "Is she right?"

He was unable to lie to her. "I'm strong enough without borrowing your power."

Malachi saw Orsala shaking her head from the corner of his eye.

"It's not about strength or weakness," she said. "It's about sharing a burden."

The old woman strode over and, without warning, pushed Malachi over. Surprised by the old woman's move, Malachi lost his footing, falling backward on the mat. His shoulders bounced off the practice mat, his hands slapped down. He was up as quickly as he'd fallen, his fists clenched and his shoulders squared.

"What was that?"

"A point," Orsala said, circling the angry scribe. "I'm not stronger than you. Magically, perhaps, but I didn't use magic." She stepped closer and lowered her voice. "Trust me. You'd know if did."

Malachi felt the press of her influence in his mind, but he refused to look away from her testing eyes.

The corner of her mouth lifted in reluctant approval. "You have the will of an ox."

"What is your point, old woman?"

"I'm not stronger than you, but you were not expecting an attack. You were unbalanced. Balance can be more important than strength, depending on the situation. If you and Ava are out of balance, then both of you are weaker. You are mates. Two halves of a whole. Learn from the foolishness of your fathers, Malachi of Sakarya, and do not make the same mistakes. Don't underestimate your other half."

Malachi looked at Ava. "I don't want—"

"I'm offering." Ava stepped forward. "I want this, Malachi. I've always wanted it. I didn't like you giving me your power to begin with."

"It was necessary." According to Rhys, she wouldn't have survived the battle in the cistern without his strength. Malachi had no regrets, even if it had cost him his life and his memories.

Ava turned away from him. "Teach me what to do."

Malachi crossed his arms again. "Not at the expense of your defensive spellwork."

"I can teach her both," Orsala said. "Have no fear, Scribe. Your woman will be protected from all sides. And now can we depend on your help to finish this lesson?"

Malachi looked between Ava and Orsala, knowing that at some point he'd lost the upper hand. He just couldn't figure out when. "Fine."

"Cool!" Ava said.

She grinned and Malachi couldn't be annoyed anymore. She looked too happy. He'd promised to attack her during her lesson, and she was thrilled.

"Gabriel's bloody fist," he muttered, bracing himself for the lesson ahead.

"I'M sorry!" She knelt over him, his hand clutched between hers. She might have said she was sorry, but she didn't look it. She looked thrilled.

Malachi wiped the trickle of blood from his lip and grinned. "Very good, Ava."

Without warning, he grabbed her by the shoulders and hooked his ankle around her knee, rolling them over so he was straddling her.

"*Vashahuul*," she whispered, freezing him for a split second. In that moment, she lifted her knees up between his legs and pressed up, throwing him off-balance. "*Vashaman!*" she shouted, amplifying the spell. He froze again. It didn't last long, but the split second he was paralyzed gave her an edge.

"Don't forget '*fasham*,' Ava!" Orsala shouted from the side of the room.

"*Ya fasham*," she hissed, and Malachi felt the wave of dizziness hit him immediately. The ground tilted between his feet.

Fasham. A simple word in the Old Language meaning "to tilt or un-balance" but in the mouth of an Irina, *ya fasham* was the command to fall.

He fell. Flat on his back, the wind knocked out of him.

"Now the staff. And remember, any spell can be amplified with *man*."

"Got it," Ava said, panting. She rolled to the side and grabbed the short staff that all Irina trained with. Malachi could remember his mother's. Always propped in a corner of the kitchen, it looked more like a broom handle than a weapon. But in the hands of a trained Irina—

"Ha!" It came down at the side of his head.

Narrowing his eyes, he reached out and snatched the staff from beside his head, giving it a swift tug and kicking his foot out to catch her ankle.

"Shit!" Ava yelled, losing her grip on the staff. Malachi spun it around and used it to vault himself to his feet.

"Did you mean to give this to me?" he said, taunting her. "Thank you so much. My mother had one of these. I felt it on my backside more than once."

She narrowed her eyes. "So you're used to taking a beating? Good. I won't feel too bad then."

"Ha!" He didn't try to stop her when she ran for the row of weapons on the wall. She grabbed another staff and pounced, wasting no time before raining down a flurry of blows. She'd been taught well—by Mala, he was guessing—but her inexperience showed. He easily parried her blows, pushing just hard enough to challenge her without frustrating her. He allowed her to land a few blows before he took control.

"I thought we were practicing your defensive spells," he said.

"Seems a little unfair since I was beating you every time."

He laughed and brought the staff down, tapping her ankle and forcing her to the corner of the mat. She feinted right, and the end of his staff bounced up, striking her right in the stomach. She went down with a sharp groan.

"*Oof.*" She rolled on the ground, clutching her belly.

"Ava!" He tossed his weapon to the side and fell to his knees. "Ava, I'm so sorry. I didn't expect—"

"*Vashahuulman,*" she whispered, tensing under his hand. "*Ya fashaman. Aman!*"

The wave of dizziness swamped him, and when his eyes cleared, Ava was the one straddling him, a staff held over his neck and a smile on her lips.

"Did I ever tell you I went to acting camp?" she said. "We spent a whole week on how to take a fake punch."

Malachi grinned. "You are evil, and I am very proud of you."

"Thanks!"

THEY shared a shower later that afternoon before they went down to dinner. Ava was drying her hair and chattering about another spell Orsala had introduced to her that was supposed to cause instant nausea in any attacker. Messy, but effective. Malachi was listening with one ear but was distracted by examining the recovered *talesm* on his left arm.

"—for the spell. But that depends on me getting stronger, because that spell can only be used once I develop the ability to fly. Know what I mean?"

"Mmmhmm," he muttered.

She snapped her fingers in front of his face. "Hey, handsome."

He looked up. "Yes?"

"So you're cool with that, right? You can help me learn how to fly?"

He frowned. "What are you talking about? The myths about angels having wings are simply that. Myths. Ancient people had to rationalize angelic abilities somehow, thus the artistic depiction of… What are you smiling about?"

She tousled his hair. "You're so cute when you're being a nerd. But you should really listen to me instead of staring at your pretty tattoos."

"I don't remember writing them," he muttered, "but I seem to have been somewhat obsessed in my early years with sexual potency."

Ava burst into laughter. "Really? So that's all magically enhanced, huh?"

He closed his eyes and gave into laughter. "Apparently so. I apologize if you thought it was natural. I hate to disappoint you."

She was still laughing when she shoved him back and straddled his lap.

"Not disappointed, babe. Not even close."

He lay back and let her lean over him, tracing the line of her shoulder with one finger. She'd been softer in his isolated memories of her before he'd been killed. Her arms hadn't been lean with muscle. Her legs hadn't been quite as thick. Part of him missed the soft give of her flesh under his hand, but the other part was satisfied that his mate was more formidable now.

"Talk to me about the mating ritual," he said. "Are you sure you want it?"

"Why wouldn't I want it?"

He shrugged.

"A shrug is not an answer."

"I don't know," he said. "I worry. It's a permanent thing. Far more permanent than marriage."

"But you've marked me, right? I'll wear your mating marks forever."

"Yes."

"What did you write? What was your vow?"

He didn't remember the ritual they had shared, but he had examined her body when the magic held her, had seen the marks he'd written with his power. They glowed gold when they were intimate.

He felt the heat in his face. "There are many passages from Irin poetry we write during the ritual. Just like there will be many passages you will have to memorize to sing to me. You know—"

"But there's part that's just yours, right? The part that goes up my back and then over my shoulder to my heart? That's what Sari said."

"Yes." He traced the line of her back, seeing the words in his mind. He'd seen them countless times since. His own vow on her skin. A reminder of who she was and what he needed to be for her.

"What was it?"

"It was simple," he said, suddenly feeling inadequate. The words he'd written weren't enough. It wasn't often that he wished he was less of a warrior and more of a poet. "I must not have had much time. If I'd had more time—"

"What did you write, Malachi?"

"'I am for Ava,'" he said quietly. "'For her… my hand and voice. For her, my body and mind. Her strength in weakness. Her sword in battle. Her balm in pain. I am hers. Hers to cherish. Hers to hold. Hers to command.' That's what I wrote."

Malachi tried not to hear disappointment in her silence.

"I know it's simple—"

"You see that, *read* that, every time my marks glow?" Her voice was hoarse with emotion.

He traced a finger over her heart, following the words he'd written there. "Yes."

"So every time we make love, you are reminded of that vow. Every time you touch me"—she swallowed hard—"that promise is on my skin."

"It is Irin tradition. It's the way it has always been."

94

"And you don't want the same thing from me?"

Malachi dreamed of wearing her mating mark across his chest. It would be centered over his heart. And while the singer decided what words to include in her vow, it was up to the scribe to embellish those words and make them his own. His father's mating mark had been an elaborate illumination from his mother's German heritage. Scrolled flowers and birds marked the edges of her vow. He'd even broken tradition and added color.

And every time Ava faced him, her own promise would be written in his flesh.

"I want to wear your vow more than anything," he said with a pounding heart. "But I worry. Everything seems so precarious right now."

She sat up. "So you want me wearing your vow, but I shouldn't make any promises to you?"

"That's not… I don't mean it that way. You don't need to. I know you're my mate."

"Then you can take my mark, Malachi. You deserve my promise too."

"Don't you understand?" he asked. "You'll be surrendering some of your power. To me. But it's *you* that Jaron is tracking. It's you whom Volund has attacked. Ava, I don't want—"

"We're in this together." She spoke softly, but her voice was firm. "You heard what Orsala said. We work in balance or we don't work at all. We survive together, or we *don't* survive."

"If we'd been mated when I was killed, it could have killed you. It likely would have."

"You don't know that. Plus I'm stronger now. And you're not dying again."

"Ava—"

"Stop." She put a hand over his mouth and took a deep breath. "I'm serious. I don't really know how I brought you back the last time. I think it was beginner's luck. So don't even think about trying it again, because you'll probably just have to stay dead. And that's not acceptable, not even an option, okay?"

He saw that despite her attempt at humor, she was fighting off tears. Her strength humbled him again. Malachi peeled her hand away and said, "Okay."

"All right." She sniffed and wiped her eyes. "Discussion over. Let's talk about what kind of mating mark I have in mind. I'm thinking maybe some Nickelback lyrics. What do you think?"

He couldn't fight the smile. "Very funny."

"Maybe Beyoncé, if we want to go the more epic route." She traced something over his chest. "As for art, I'm cool with you just doing a little butterfly if you're worried about the pain."

He growled and flipped her over when she started to laugh.

"You are in so much trouble."

Chapter Eight

"HOW CAN WE PRACTICE like this and not…" Ava waved her hands at Orsala. "You know."

The old woman smiled. "Why are we able to practice spells without actually working them?"

"Yes."

They were going over the mating ritual in the library of the scribe house, taking advantage of the collection Rhys had been building. So much of the old library had burned in the fire the Grigori had set, but not all of it. Rhys was supplementing it with some of his own books and others that the scribes in Cappadocia had sent.

Most of the books had more information on written spellwork than spoken, but that was to be expected. Orsala and Ava could read and practice the poems she'd need to memorize for her mating ritual. Those were universal. But most of Orsala's teaching was verbal in nature.

"We're able to practice spells without actively casting them because…" The old singer frowned. "How to explain… Don't you feel the difference? You've worked various spells now."

"I have. I'm super careful about saying any words in the Old Language, though. The last time I did that, I brought my dead mate back to life, so… yeah, kind of makes me nervous."

"I suppose it would." Orsala paused. "There has to be… intention. Purpose. I suppose a spell only works when you believe it will work. What words, exactly, did you say when you called him back?"

Ava took a deep breath. "*Vashama canem, reshon.*"

"Hmm." Orsala drew her hands together in front of her. "Not a command, then. A plea. To your *reshon*, specifically. A mourning cry."

"I'd heard it so many times."

"It's something we all hear if we're listening, isn't it?" Orsala's eyes filled with sorrow. "The soul cry at the loss of a beloved. A mate. A child. Irin and human alike. It's not a spell. Not exactly. Though I suppose any words spoken with enough power could be. That was our bargain with the Forgiven. They gave their daughters their voice. Their songs."

"What did they give their sons?"

"Glyphs." Orsala ran her hands down her arms. "Their *talesm*. But angels are not tattooed as our males are; their glyphs are part of their skin."

"So why did my words, which aren't even a spell, bring Malachi back from the dead?"

"I don't know," she said. "Perhaps because it wasn't a spell. It was a plea. To Malachi? To the Creator? Maybe it was simply an answered prayer."

Ava paused. "It wasn't because my power is different?"

"Your power is different and it isn't," Orsala said, leaning her elbows on the table. "It feels the same as all Irina power but… condensed. Your eyes are so gold. Your power so raw. Even untrained, you worked incredibly powerful magic. Your bloodlines must be very potent, whatever they are." There was a flicker of concern in Orsala's eyes, but then the old woman blinked and it was gone. "We should get back to—"

She broke off at the commotion near the doorway. There was a slam. A shuffle of coats and shoes. Low, urgent voices. Ava and Orsala rose to their feet just as the door burst open.

Maxim strode into the room.

Leo followed him. "But I don't understand—"

"Ava," Max said. He came to her, put his hands on her shoulders, and stared. "*Ava*."

"Max, what is it? Why are you here?"

Orsala looked past them to the door. "Renata? What are you doing here?"

Ava put her hands over Max's and ignored the other voices in the room. She almost felt as if she were the one holding the massive man up. His eyes were focused on her as they had been the first time they'd met in the old scribe house, when Malachi had drawn the ancient words over her skin, marking her as one of their lost Irina. Max had stared then as he stared now.

Wonder. Confusion. Awe.

"Max, what's going on?"

"I can't…" His eyes pleaded with her. "I can't explain. You have to see."

"See? See what? What are you talking about?"

She turned when the door from the kitchen opened and Malachi walked in.

"Maxim," he said. "What has happened?"

Max just shook his head, still staring at Ava.

Renata walked further into the room and said, "We've just come from Bulgaria. The two of you—"

"He said nothing about Malachi," Max said.

"He is her mate," Renata said. "She's not going without him."

Rhys walked in on the commotion. "What in heaven's name—"

"You need to come with us," Max said. "There's something you have to see."

"In Bulgaria?" Malachi asked.

Max shook his head again. "I can't explain. You have to see. I didn't believe… didn't know. But now… It changes everything, Malachi." He squeezed Ava's shoulders. "Trust me?"

She nodded. Max had been instrumental in spiriting her away from Istanbul after Malachi had been killed. She knew he had dubious contacts in the outside world, but she trusted him implicitly.

"Malachi?"

Her mate said, "If you want to go to Bulgaria, we'll go to Bulgaria. Did you two drive here?"

Renata said, "Yes."

Orsala asked, "What's going on?"

"I want Mala to take you to the city," Renata said. "I want you with Sari and Damien. We'll send Ava and Malachi to you after we travel to Sofia."

Orsala narrowed her eyes but said nothing else.

Ava exchanged a look with her mate. Malachi shook his head, looking as confused as she felt.

Ava didn't know what was happening, but for the second time in her life, she had a feeling that everything had just changed.

"TELL me again," Renata said. "What did your father say about his mother when you confronted him?"

"Not much," Ava confessed as she sat next to Renata in the back of the car, talking about Jasper. "He called her '*maman.*' Claimed she died, but I know he was lying. I could hear it."

"Hmmm."

"And not much else. There were a couple of times he looked..."

"What?"

"I don't know."

"What did you see?"

Her voice dropped. "He looked... different. I can't say exactly. Just different than he used to."

"Hmm." Renata sat back and folded her hands on her lap. "Interesting. We don't know enough, but it could fit."

"I really hate you guys keeping me in the dark on this."

"I know that, but if I tell you what I suspect, then I'll have to tell you everything." Renata waved her hand in a cutting gesture. "And if I tell you everything, you won't believe me."

"You realize that makes absolutely no sense, right?"

"It will after we get there."

"And where are we going?"

"To meet a man named Kostas."

"Does he know where my grandmother is?"

Renata shook her head. "I doubt it. But you might get some answers about *what* she is."

"MAX." Malachi's voice was a low growl in the front seat. "What is this? I thought we were going to the scribe house."

"You have to trust me, brother."

Ava had never been to Sofia, the capitol and largest city in Bulgaria. It was only six hours from Istanbul but seemed farther when you climbed the mountains. Snow dusted the sides of the road in places, and the temperature had dropped from the damp and mild weather along the Bosphorus.

Ava asked, "Who's Kostas?"

"Someone I've known for a long time," Max said.

Malachi said, "The name sounds familiar, but I can't place it."

Max said nothing as Malachi carefully scanned the outskirts of the city where industrial areas sprawled. Wherever they were going, it didn't look close to the heart of the historic city. Commercial trucks and trailers seemed more common than cars.

"Tell me where we're going," Malachi said.

"To see Kostas."

"Damn it, Max!"

"You're going to have to trust me," he said, gritting his teeth. "I am limited on what I can say. I gave my word."

"Your withholding information makes me want to grab Ava and walk back to Istanbul right now."

Ava looked at the whipping wind outside the vehicle grabbing flurries of snow. "Maybe we shouldn't walk. I do know how to hot-wire a car."

Renata bit back a smile. "You are always full of surprises, my friend."

"Rebellious kid with lots of money and an overprotective mother. I had interesting friends as a teenager."

"I suppose so."

They turned onto a small road that led between a group of warehouses. Some of them were open, but most were closed. It was nearing midnight, and Ava rubbed her eyes to fend off the worst of the exhaustion.

Malachi must have caught the gesture, because he said, "We should find a place to rest. Do this tomorrow."

"It was difficult to get him to agree to meet with us. I don't want to delay."

They turned into a small parking lot in front of an older warehouse that looked more like a barn. It was freestanding. Not connected to any others, but still had the anonymous grey paneling they'd seen everywhere else.

"I'm so tired," Ava said with a yawn.

"I don't like this," Malachi said.

"Trust us." Renata grabbed her hand as they came to a stop. "Stay with me and Malachi, Ava. Let Max do the talking right now."

They walked toward the door where a small window was glowing. It was the only light in the darkness. Not even a star appeared above them. The clouds had rolled in during their drive, and the night was pitch-black. Ava fell in step between Malachi and Renata.

Ten feet from the door, Malachi halted. "What the hell?"

Max turned and held up both hands. "I know what you're thinking, but you have to trust me. I would never lead Ava and Renata—"

"*What the hell?*" Malachi's voice echoed between the metal corridor of buildings and Ava heard the door open.

She looked beyond her mate and Max.

"Ava, get back in the car. Now!"

Renata held tighter to her hand. "Malachi, calm down. No one is going to hurt her."

There was a silhouette in the doorway. The man stepped forward, his lithe body moving with preternatural grace. As he stepped closer, Ava saw him and her heart almost stopped.

Pale, luminous skin set off eyes the color of the winter sea. Dark, curling hair fell over his forehead, touched by hints of the snow that had started to fall.

Beautiful.

Ethereal.

Grigori.

Malachi roared and reached for his knives as Ava stepped back.

Her mate rushed the soldier, who immediately countered with his own weapons. Malachi fought in a fury of knives and kicks, slashing the Grigori who fended him off with a short staff and a machete.

"Malachi, no!" Max was yelling.

Renata held Ava in an iron grip, keeping her from running to the safety of the car or joining her mate in battle. "Stay here and keep out of it."

"Stop," Max shouted. "Please!"

They didn't stop. Malachi had a deep gash across his cheek, but the Grigori looked worse. Still, the soldier fought with grim determination and focus. He winced and rolled away when Malachi knocked him to the ground.

Max, Ava noticed, was not helping. He was only shouting at the two men to stop.

"You have to listen to him," Renata shouted. "Malachi, stop!"

Four more men appeared in the doorway, hands clenched on their own daggers. One held up a gun.

"No!" Max yelled, rushing toward them. "He doesn't know!"

Renata left Ava and ran to Malachi, spinning him around and pulling him away from the Grigori. "Stop, you idiot, and listen!"

Malachi bared his teeth at Renata and lunged at the Grigori again, though the man was curled on the ground, barely moving.

Renata pulled him back and punched Malachi across the jaw.

"Hey!" Ava shouted, rushing forward. "What are you—"

"Don't you lose your head too," Renata said, swinging Ava around and holding her arms behind her back. "Look at them."

"Malachi—"

"Look at them!"

She looked.

Another Grigori stood in front of Max, his hands in his pockets. She could smell the sandalwood on his skin. His eyes surveyed the scene clinically as the soldiers rushed from the doorway and rolled their brother to his back to examine his wounds. Malachi was stirring, his hand reaching for his dagger, but Renata stepped on it and bared her teeth.

"Let. Max. Talk."

"Kostas said to bring the girl," the soldier in charge said to Max. "Not an Irin assassin."

Max said, "The scribe is her mate. She doesn't go anywhere without him. And you didn't leave me time to explain. I told Kostas to wait for my signal."

"Kostas does not answer to you." The Grigori's eyes narrowed. "And the butcher of Berlin isn't known for his understanding."

"Let me talk to him, Pietro."

"Fine. But get him under control. Or Kostas will refuse to allow any of you in." His lazy eyes flicked to Ava. "Maybe her."

Calm. Slight interest. But none of the grasping hunger she'd felt from the Grigori in the past.

There was something different in his gaze.

"Calm your mate, sister," the Grigori named Pietro said to Ava. "Then come inside."

Ava froze.

Pietro turned and followed the other Grigori, who had not attacked but only carried their fallen comrade into the dimly lit warehouse. Malachi stopped growling and rose to his feet, suddenly aware of the change in the air.

"Ava, what's going on?"

Sister?

He reached for her frozen hand as Ava's heart had begun to pound.

"Ava—"

"I want to go in," she whispered. "I need to go in there."

She followed the strange Grigori without thought. Malachi fell in step behind her, still grasping her hand. She felt the blood sticky on his palm, but she couldn't seem to stop. Ava could feel the tension ratcheting up his arm.

As the Grigori led them through the building, various doors cracked open, but no one attacked them. No one even showed their face.

They made it into the cavern of the warehouse, a living area lit within the darkness. Low conversation flowed around the small group of men. No more than ten or fifteen were there. As they approached, they passed tables and chairs set up, old pallets and broken-down crates.

A man rose from the couch, his hands fisted on his hips.

His hair was long and pulled back to reveal another stunningly handsome face. Rich brown eyes and coffee-colored hair. Aquiline features that bore a hint of nobility, despite the grime and wreckage around him.

Max stepped forward and held up a hand. "Kostas."

"I said you could bring her. Not a scribe. He injured one of my best men."

"She is his mate. I told you she wouldn't come without him. And I saw him. No permanent damage was done. Please excuse me. This is my fault. I didn't prepare Malachi to meet you. I thought... I didn't know how much to say. It would be better to see."

Kostas's eyes flicked to Malachi, assessing him. "He is the one who returned?"

"Yes."

"Who are you?" Ava asked.

The Grigori's eyes shuttered. For a long moment, Ava waited to see what he would say, half of her tugging forward and the other half wanting to run. She lifted her shields and listened to the voices around her. Unlike the scratched voices she was expecting, these Grigori voices were touched with a resonance that reminded her of the Irin. But it was a jumble; her own mind was too scrambled to make sense of anything. She could only hear emotion.

Longing.

Anger.

Fear.

Ava looked around. She was surrounded by at least fifteen Grigori, but no one was coming after her. No one even approached. The normally seductive stares were wary. Cautious.

"As long as my people come to no harm, he may stay," Kostas said, then he narrowed his eyes at Ava.

Malachi stepped forward, blocking his gaze. "What is this place?"

Kostas smiled and, despite the knot in Ava's stomach, she reacted. He was so beautiful it was as if the sun had broken through clouds.

"Welcome to the heretics' house," Kostas said, giving them a deep bow. "The children of the Fallen your brethren have killed surround you."

"Oh shit," Ava said as Malachi tensed.

Kostas continued. "Allow me to officially extend my appreciation for your service." The gleam in his eyes was lethal. "We *very* much appreciate it."

"What the hell is going on?" Malachi asked Max.

"Wait."

The Grigori named Pietro stepped toward Kostas. "Boris and Roman checked the perimeter. They're alone."

"Good." Kostas looked toward a corner blocked off by crates. "Kyra, you may come out now."

A woman stepped from the shadows as Ava moved forward. She felt Malachi's hand on the small of her back; he stood steady and protective behind her.

She was tall and dark-haired; her long brunette mane was streaked with ebony. She turned her gaze, and Ava met eyes a mirror of her own. Glowing gold behind thick black lashes. She heard Malachi suck in a breath. The woman was beautiful. Incandescently beautiful.

Inhumanly beautiful.

Like the Grigori she stood beside.

"Ava." Kostas took the woman's hand. "I'd like you to meet my sister. Kyra."

Of course.

Of course.

Sister.

The memory of a dark angel's voice in her mind.

"Soon. You will know soon."

It was a startling, beautiful clarity, fresh as the sky after rain.

Kyra smiled at Ava. Her gold eyes were shining. "Did you think the angels only had sons?"

77,

JARON STOOD ON THE ROOF of a warehouse near Barak's son, watching Ava in his mind's eye.

Of course.

"Did you think the angels only had sons?"

No.

There had always been others.

Barak appeared a second later. Vasu followed.

"She knows," they said together.

"Soon she will go to their city," he said. "And I will remove my protection."

"Volund will be drawn out?" Vasu asked.

"He will come," Barak said. "He has his own interest in the woman."

Vasu curled his lip slightly. "I still do not understand your fascination."

"Not fascination," Jaron said. "She will draw him as nothing else can."

Jaron opened his eyes to them as they watched the scene play out among the sons and daughters of angels below them.

The Irin. Children of the Forgiven, their power glowing not with the wild raw fury of Fallen children but the low, controlled burn of a well-tended fire. Their magic had been honed. Trained. Tested. Their blood farther from the angels, they had used the knowledge the Forgiven had given them to become more powerful than those they fought. Male and female. They were a balanced race.

The Grigori. Raw fury and terrible hunger. Slaves to the Fallen. Abandoned to ignorance, their children raged against the human world with the fury of a child denied. Their sons, predators. Their daughters, a secret.

Born in fear. Terrible with untrained power. Forgotten. Disposed of. They called themselves *kareshta*. The silent ones.

Their fathers called them nothing. Those who allowed their daughters to live usually abandoned them to the madness of the human world. After all, female offspring were rare.

He'd never turned his mind to them, because for Jaron, there had only ever been sons.

Until there hadn't been.

"I sing sometimes when you're not here."

Broken.

His only daughter was so terribly broken.

"Your son, Barak," Vasu said with dark amusement in his eyes. "Kostas would remake the world we have built. There is power in that one. Are you sure he thinks you are dead?"

"Yes." Barak cocked his head. "He won't hear me. Whatever magic Jaron has laid over the woman protects me as much as it does her."

"Kostas is perceptive," Jaron said, "But he is not more powerful than me."

"Why do you shield her?" Vasu asked.

"I have my reasons."

Reasons only Barak knew. And his oldest friend only knew because he'd found Jaron in a killing rage sixty years before. A rage that would have swallowed the world unless Barak intervened.

Jaron had not taken a human lover since, and his line was dying.

He wanted it to.

Vasu, the most terrestrial of them, crouched down, clearly intrigued by the scene that Jaron showed them.

"I have never understood the fear of them."

"That is because you have never raised your daughters," Barak said.

Vasu shrugged. "If they run to the humans, the humans may have them."

"The humans consider them mad."

"What is madness but a form of wisdom?" Vasu murmured, his eyes still locked on the warehouse. "Once they were called seers. Holy women. They were revered in my territory. But Volund fears them. Hates them. Galal butchers them in the name of progress. Why?"

"They are of us," Jaron said, "but unlike us."

Barak said, "When the first Fallen daughters were born, they were killed immediately. Considered defective human offspring."

"Many still view them as such," Jaron said.

He remembered when Barak had stopped killing his female children. It was when the first pair of twins had been born. The two children grew to be some of his most powerful, though the daughter was always kept hidden from any he did not trust absolutely. Jaron was the only angel who knew Barak no longer killed or abandoned his daughters. Not that many didn't escape his control. Those, he left to the human world. Or he had, before betrayal had rent their world. Barak had also ceased siring children sixty years ago, for many of the same reasons Jaron had.

Yet Vasu knew nothing. He still stared at the warehouse, watching the scene as if it were performed on a human stage.

"Vasu," Jaron said.

Gold eyes looked up. Vasu's dark skin was colorless in the night, but his gold and black hair whipped in the wind. The gold reflecting the starlight, the black swallowing the darkness.

"What do you want of me?" he asked. "I do not want the same thing you do. I have decided."

"You will remain here?"

"Yes."

Barak stepped forward. "Are you certain?"

"Are you?"

Barak's eyes narrowed. "I am. If you remain, you will be alone."

"If we succeed, I will not be. There will be no more reason to hide, and my people will return to me."

Jaron said, "Killing Volund will not erase all your enemies, brother."

"It will erase enough of them," Vasu said. "Galal will be nothing without Volund's support. You have your vengeance, and I have mine."

"Enough," Jaron said quietly. "We are decided."

"We are decided," the three Fallen said, turning their eyes back to the cold warehouse on the edge of the mountains where the earthly realm had changed in the space of a single word.

Chapter Nine

SISTER.

Malachi's mind rebelled.

No.

It wasn't possible.

They would have known.

They *had* to have known.

How could they not have known?

He reached for Ava's hand, but she was already walking toward the woman called Kyra. Renata was at her side.

"Ava, don't!"

The Grigori around them had been calm, almost eerily so. But at his protest, they turned furious eyes toward Malachi, as if they were enraged at the interference. Max put a hand on his arm and he calmed.

"Renata is with her. She'll be fine. Kostas would never attack Ava, especially not in front of his sister."

Sister.

A sister.

"How—"

"They are Barak's children. Twins. Both their sire and mother are dead." Max lowered his voice. "Malachi, *surely* you can see."

He knew Max was telling the truth. It was the eyes. The woman's gold eyes were exactly like his mate's. She had luminous skin. Ethereal beauty. She was Grigori in female form.

Not Grigori.

Grigora.

"Max, it's not…"

"It is."

"But we would have known," he said. "There was never any—"

"Why would you have known, Scribe?" Kostas's eyes pierced him from across the room. "When does *your* kind stop to ask questions?"

Malachi ignored the Grigori and watched Ava. She was holding Renata's hand but reaching for Kyra. She looked over her shoulder, searching for him.

"Malachi?"

"I'm here."

"I…" Ava looked between Malachi and Kyra. Kyra and Kostas. "This is real?" she whispered, her eyes revealing her deepest fear.

He forgot the angry Grigori and walked over to her, bending to whisper in her ear. "This is real, *canim*. You're not dreaming. Does this feel like a dream or a vision?"

"No."

He squeezed her hand. "See?"

"Interesting," Kostas mused. "I wondered what she could do."

Malachi's head whipped around. He left Ava with Renata and Kyra as he stalked toward Kostas. "My mate is none of your concern."

Kostas looked amused, but Malachi said nothing else. He had no wish to confirm or deny anything about Ava until he knew more about whatever was going on. He glanced over his shoulder, but the women were locked in intense conversation in the corner of the room. The males around them had withdrawn, keeping watch but not interfering.

Malachi drew Max to the side. "How did you discover this?"

"I've known Kostas for years," he said. "We've traded information. Favors, at times. I knew there were others like him—Grigori free of their sires—but they're very secretive."

"And the women? Why did we never see them? Hundreds of years—thousands! How could a secret like this remain hidden?"

"How do we remain hidden?" Max said. "Human see what they want to see. And sometimes Irin do as well."

Malachi couldn't argue with that. He looked at the protective Grigori soldier who stood near them. Watching his sister. Watching them.

The man was different than the others. All these Grigori were. There was none of the desperate hunger he associated with his mortal enemies. The men around him looked like Grigori. Smelled like Grigori. But… they did not act it. And Malachi wondered how it was possible. Was the presence of only one female so powerful to them?

"Your sister." Malachi walked toward Kostas. "There are others like her?"

"Yes. Though there have never been many," Kostas said. "If you're truly interested, I'll explain, though it probably won't improve your opinion of our race."

Malachi asked Max, "Do you trust him?"

"I wouldn't be here if I didn't."

Malachi crossed his arms and stared at Kostas. "Maybe you're different. But don't try to tell me most of your kind aren't murderers and rapists. I've witnessed the aftermath of too many attacks."

"I'd never claim to be anything but what I am," Kostas said. "But if it helps, the same angels trying to kill you would love to kill me as well."

"Why?"

"I'm an abomination," he said with a grim smile. "I should have died years ago when my father was killed, but I didn't. Volund, especially, hates that I even exist."

"Volund killed your father?"

Kostas nodded. "He wanted his territory. Barak used to control most of Northern Europe."

"That's all Volund's land now," Max said. "He was successful."

"How much do you know about us?" Kostas asked Malachi. "Other than what you've learned in your efforts to kill us, what do you know?"

"You have magic, but not like us."

"True." Kostas motioned them toward a number of ragged chairs. The Grigori who were sitting there moved away immediately. It was obvious who was in charge. "The average son of the Fallen lives for around one hundred sixty to one hundred eighty years. Nothing close to the Irin lifespan."

"But there are some who are much older."

Brage, the Grigori who'd killed Malachi in the cistern—who'd tried to take Ava from him—had been present during the Rending. He'd been at least two hundred and fifty years old.

"Our lives can be prolonged by magic—as the Irin's can—but only at the will of the Fallen. We exist for them. An angel who finds a particular child useful can extend his life indefinitely."

"Do they?"

"Rarely." Kostas leaned forward, his elbows on his knees. "Do you know what the Grigori are, Scribe?"

"You're sons of the Fallen. Half angel and half—"

"We're slaves," Kostas said with a bitter smile. "The Irin forefathers left, giving their children knowledge and freedom. The Fallen stayed and kept their children under their thumbs. We exist to serve them. We have no will other than theirs. No life beyond what they give us. If they call us, we come. If they command us, we obey. To do otherwise is unthinkable. We feed…" Kostas drew in a ragged breath. "We feed on humans because our touch hunger is voracious and most Grigori have no outlet other than the humans we're presented with when we are mere children. No mothers. No sisters. No mates."

"So you kill like monsters?" Malachi asked.

"We are never taught to care. We take what we want because we can. Cruelty is rewarded. Mercy or conscience is not."

"So why should I trust you?" Malachi asked. "How many women have you killed?"

Kostas's eyes froze. "Too many."

Malachi leaned forward. "And why should I not execute you here?"

"Because my men surround you," Kostas said. "They owe me their loyalty. And I cannot allow you to take my protection away from those who need it."

"How do I even begin to trust you?" Malachi said. "You could lie—"

"I love my sister." Kostas's eyes softened as he looked to Kyra. "I have always protected her. Even when my father was alive. I am far from guiltless, but she is the reason I've never surrendered to the total rage most Grigori feel. Her touch. Her life. Our father allowed us to stay together because I was useful to him, and I'm stronger with Kyra near me."

ELIZABETH HUNTER

"Barak did not have an overly cruel reputation."

"Some angels are more lenient than others," Kostas said, turning back to them. "Some are negligent and don't care. But all of us exist at the whim of the Fallen. Free will only came to me once my father was dead."

Malachi checked on Ava again, but his mate was still huddled in the corner with the other two women, speaking in low voices. "Why have we never seen a female of your race before?"

"How do you know you haven't?" Kostas asked.

Malachi had no answer.

"Kyra and I were fortunate," he continued. "Barak doesn't kill his daughters at birth like most of the Fallen do."

A knot tightened in his gut. "Killed at birth?"

A hollow look came to Kostas's eyes. "The females have always been harder to control. Most angels consider their daughters too dangerous to live."

"Why?" Malachi asked.

"Think about it," Max said. "If we draw the Irin and Grigori parallel out, Grigori would be able to work magic if they could write as we do. If they were taught the spells."

"But the Fallen do not teach them," Malachi said, still profoundly grateful for that fact. Kostas the heretic might be controlling himself, but that hadn't changed his opinion of Grigori as a whole.

"Nor should it," Kostas said, looking at Malachi.

He tensed, realizing the man had heard his thoughts. "You're telepathic?"

Kostas shook his head. "Not truly. I hear whispers of thoughts every now and then. Barak's children sometimes do. If I'd had training from my father, I might know more."

"They offer you no teaching at all?" Malachi could hardly believe it. Knowledge was revered in Irin culture. Training started before children could speak. It was given in playful verses and songs from the time they were born. The teaching of magic was an Irin parent's primary responsibility.

"They do not teach us, or they cannot," Kostas said. "We don't know. I'm certain they wouldn't, even if they could. It would make us more powerful. And if we were more powerful—"

"You might be harder to control," Malachi said. "But why are your sisters considered more dangerous than their brothers?"

"They hear things," Kostas said, his voice low. "Sometimes they say things. Dangerous things they have no idea how to control. Many are unwell in their minds. Tormented by—"

"Voices," Malachi said, glancing at Ava. "If they are like our women, they hear the soul voices of humanity."

"Obviously your women have a way to control it. Ours do not. My sister... I try to keep her as isolated as I can. She wanted to come and meet your mate, though I advised against it."

"Ava was the same." Malachi offered that one comfort. "Before we found her. She survived."

Kostas took a deep breath. "I love my sister. I cannot remember a time when I did not. Even when my father was alive. Barak was... negligent. He didn't kill his daughters, but they were sent away. He had places that were mostly prisons. Those who escaped were left alone, but then they were at the mercy of the humans. Yet his negligence was still better than most of the Fallen. Many infant daughters, even if they aren't killed, die of neglect when their mothers give birth to male children."

"Why?"

"Because we kill our mothers," Kostas said. "Simply by existing."

Malachi tasted acid at the back of his throat.

"Don't you understand?" Kostas continued. "Your ancestors were forgiven because they recognized the truth: Angels don't belong here. Their children—all of us—never should have existed. We are abominations. They left because they knew that, so the Creator had mercy on the Irin. My people?" Kostas leaned back. "We received no mercy. We don't deserve it. We're all murderers before we can speak."

The man's self-loathing was so evident Malachi had a difficult time condemning him further.

Max leaned forward and said, "You fight to make things better, my friend."

Kostas gave him a rueful smile. "I would call you my friend, Maxim, but for your willful ignorance of the truth."

"It's not ignorance. I simply don't judge you as harshly as you judge yourself."

"I saved Kyra," Kostas said to Malachi. "I have been able to save a few others. I protect them. That is my penance for the lives I've taken. The harm I've done."

"How many women?" Malachi asked. "How many do you protect?"

"I don't trust you that much, Scribe. No matter who you are mated to."

"When I finally discovered it," Max said, "I knew I had to tell you. For Ava."

Malachi narrowed his eyes at Max. "You think Ava is Grigori?"

"No. Yes?" Max said. "I don't know. I see more in common than different."

Malachi's eyes turned to Ava and Kyra. He could see it, see the similarities, but he could also see profound differences. Ava didn't look inhuman, as Kyra did. Her skin wasn't as pale or as luminous. Her eyes were the same, but she was no ethereal creature. His mate had a delicate, yet earthy, beauty.

"I don't think she is, Max."

"There's something…," Kostas said. "Her eyes drew me at first. But I agree. Your mate does not look like our women."

"She's at least half human. Her mother is fully human, but her father is not. That may be the connection."

"Is her father Grigori?" Kostas asked. "Some of us are able to father children with human women. Some have enough control."

"He doesn't smell it. Or look it. Though there is something different about him."

"Reed's mother," Max said. "That has to be the connection. Ava's grandmother must have Grigori blood."

Malachi said, "We've been trying to find her, but we haven't had much success. Could she be one of yours?"

Kostas took a deep breath and frowned. "If she is, I'd have no way of knowing without meeting her. No records are kept in our world, particularly for females. The ones who survive are mostly in the human population because they're safer there."

"Safer?" Malachi asked. "Among humans who think they're insane?"

"They can't hurt humans as the males do, so they can often blend in. It's better than what faces them among the Fallen."

"Do you have any idea how many might be out there?" Malachi asked. "How many… Grigora?"

"The Fallen call them Grigora. They call themselves *kareshta*. The silent ones."

"Silent ones?"

"Those who make it through childhood learn to be silent. Not to use their voices. It's their only chance of surviving in our world."

Kareshta.

Kostas continued, "I would estimate only two—maybe three births in ten are female. The Fallen tend to create male children. Some have no daughters at all. Whatever genetics are in play, women are rare."

"Only four in ten Irin children are female," Max said. "We have no idea why. It's always been that way."

Kostas said, "Of that twenty percent, more than half are probably killed at birth. There could be hundreds. Thousands, counting all the minor angels. We have no way of knowing. Most of them are in the human world. Free Grigori like us who shelter the *kareshta* will only shelter those whose fathers are dead."

"What?" Malachi asked. "Why?"

"Security," Kostas said with a grimace. "If our sires are alive, they can find us. It doesn't matter where we go. Only those whose sires are confirmed dead are allowed. Almost all the women I shelter are my sisters. I cannot risk them. Too many of the Fallen are trying to kill me."

"Why?" Malachi asked. "Barak is dead. Why do they care what you do?"

"My mere existence is heresy. I'm the one telling the Grigori they can live without reducing themselves to murderous animals. That there *is* another way."

"But not a way the Fallen are happy about."

"How could they be?" Kostas asked. "In order for the Grigori to be free, the Fallen *must* die."

"I'M not *kareshta*," Ava said later as they lay in bed. "I thought at first that I was, but I'm not."

They'd avoided the scribe house in Sofia, not wanting to explain their presence if it might compromise Max's promise of secrecy to Kostas and Kyra. Instead, they'd found a small hotel near the highway and taken two rooms. They were threadbare, but clean.

"You're not *kareshta*, but…?"

"There is something. Kyra feels familiar. Her voice sounds right, if that makes any sense."

"Her magic feels the same as yours."

"Yes, I think that's it."

Malachi hadn't said anything, but he'd sensed the same thing. More, Kostas's sister gave off the same nervous energy that Ava had been drowning in before she'd learned to shield herself from the soul voices of the humans around her.

He wrapped her in his arms, shaken by the truths they'd discovered that night.

For Malachi, it changed everything.

He was forced to see the Grigori in a new light. Yes, most or all of them were still victimizing humans, but they were also victims themselves. And some, like Kostas, appeared to be trying to change things. His black-and-white world had been thoroughly washed in grey. But in the confusion, his scattered mind focused on a kernel of hope.

If Ava had Grigori blood, how different could they be?

"You're not *kareshta*," Malachi agreed. "But it wouldn't matter to me if you were. You know that, don't you?"

"Yes." She snuggled deeper into his side. "I can hear you."

There was a dark edge to her magic. The visions that came to her were unlike anything Irina experienced. But Ava was good. Not perfect, but *good*. Her heart was warm and generous. She was protective. Courageous.

His.

She reached out with her magic, and it was as if small hands stroked him from head to toe. He shivered with wanting her, but Ava was too deep in thought.

"I think my grandmother must have been one of them. That might be why my father locked her away. Tried to hide her. Kyra said that many of the *kareshta* end up in mental institutions because people think they're crazy."

"That makes sense." He'd come to the same conclusion, but he knew she needed to work it out in her own mind.

"Yeah, it makes sense."

He felt her shoulders shaking before he heard her cry. "Shhh, Ava." He stroked her back, pulling her so tight to his chest that he was worried she would bruise. Her pain was a stab in the heart.

"They're out there," she said. "Others like me. Those are the stars in Jaron's vision. Out in the darkness, Malachi. So many of them. And so horribly alone."

"I know, Ava."

"We have to find them."

Could finding the *kareshta* be a way out of this never-ending war? Could Grigori society turn into something like the Irin? Kostas had said that those Grigori who had contact with their sisters were more stable. Had more control. If they could find more of the female Grigori—teach them to protect their minds—would it change their enemies as Kostas hoped?

What was the alternative? Endless, blood-soaked war? Generation after generation caught in the same vicious cycle? His own son continuing the slaughter of a people Malachi was starting to believe were more like his own than he wanted to admit?

The Irin Council's policy had remained unchanged for thousands of years. Scribes protected the human population from the Grigori, killing them any time they attacked. But with a few exceptions, the Fallen themselves were never targeted. Why? Malachi had always assumed they were simply too hard to kill. But could there be another motive for tacitly allowing them to exist?

What power would the council have without an enemy to fight?

"We need to go back to Italy," Ava said. "We have to find my grand-mother. I refuse to let Jasper stonewall me. If she's like me, she's been liv-ing with voices her whole life, Malachi. There must be something I can do."

Ava's conscience would never allow her to let another live in the tor-ment she'd faced for over twenty years.

"We'll go to Italy," Malachi said. "We'll find a flight to Genoa in the morning. I think it's only six hours or so with connections. We can be there by tomorrow night."

It was a good thing Max's forger was competent. Their fake passports were getting more than a little mileage.

"Do you think my grandmother is in Italy?"

"Honestly? No. Italian hospitals are the first Rhys checked because your father tends to take his holidays there. None of them match the in-formation we have. But we are going to Italy, and we are going to find her."

"How—?"

"We tried getting information from Jasper and got nothing." Malachi smiled in the darkness. "I think it's time to talk to the man who holds his keys."

Chapter Ten

THEY TOOK A FLIGHT to Genoa the next morning and were driving by late afternoon. Ava had a hard time sleeping. Part of her wanted to find her grandmother, but another part wanted to be back in Bulgaria. Only Kyra's urging had allowed her to leave.

"Go. Find your grandmother. You know who and what she is now. You can help her."

Ava had wanted to start lessons immediately. She'd wanted to find the old monastery Kyra had spoken of where thirty Grigori women hid from the world and the madness that lurked on the edges of their lives.

Kostas and Malachi had refused. Kostas, out of distrust; Malachi, out of concern.

It was too soon, her mate said. They needed to think. Needed to plan. How could they risk putting Irin knowledge into Grigori hands? Ava knew Max and Renata agreed, even though they clearly trusted Kostas and Kyra more than Malachi did.

Her brain knew he was right, but her heart had other ideas.

For Ava, meeting Kyra had been like looking in a mirror. It wasn't her looks, because the woman's angelic beauty was nothing like her own. In fact, Ava was almost resentful she'd gotten all the mental anguish of Grigori blood without the excellent skin tone.

Oh well.

It was her eyes. Kyra said all the female Grigori had gold eyes like their angelic fathers, but it was more than that. The pain was the same. The constant stress of hearing. The ache of being *other*. Kyra, like Ava, had lived most of her life alone, though she'd been lucky enough to have a brother. She spoke of Kostas with a fierce and protective admiration, as if daring anyone to think badly of him.

Ava didn't think badly of the renegade Grigori. She didn't know what to think.

It was hard not to be wary.

While Kostas's men didn't exude the voracious hunger of the Grigori that had stalked her and killed Malachi, they were still clearly the sons of the Fallen. The seductive features were there. The scent of sandalwood that lured her. Their hunger was in their eyes, even though it wasn't layered with blind rage.

But they were also different from their brethren. Did they exude tension? Yes. But it was controlled.

"Ava?"

"Hmm?" She glanced at Malachi as he drove them toward Portofino.

"Why don't you try to sleep?"

"I'm too wound up."

"Try, *canim*. We don't know what this day will be like."

"More warrior lessons?"

He smiled, fine wrinkles appearing around his eyes. "Yes, like they taught us in school. Eat when you can. Sleep when you can. Fu—"

"I get it." She reached over and slapped a hand over his mouth. "Bad man. They didn't teach you that in school."

"The professors might not have, but the older boys did," he said as he peeled her hand away and kissed her palm. The smile fell from his face.

"What is it?"

"The Grigori have all this power—all this natural magic—and they have no control over it. I think it would be better to be human."

"Do you have to make it sound like that's the worst thing in the world? Being human? I was one, you know."

He gave her a raised eyebrow. Oh, those eloquent raised eyebrows her man offered.

"You know what I mean," he said. "If they were human, they'd have no magic, but at least they'd live a normal life."

She squeezed his hand.

"No mates," he continued. "No children, except those they sire by accident, and what kind of relationship would they be able to have with them? They've had thousands of years to be hungry with no relief. I'd never thought about that before. I cannot imagine the rage they must feel. To have so much power and no control. To live only to be a slave for the Fallen."

"They're no innocents, Malachi. They hunted me. They killed you. They've killed thousands of humans. They seduce them, rape them, and—more often than not—kill them."

"I know."

"And you feel sorry for them?"

"No." He paused. "Yes. Some. I feel sorry for some of them. Those who are trying to live peacefully but are caught on the other side of a battle they don't want. I feel sorry for the children."

"Do you think we can make the council see that?"

"I don't know."

They both fell silent.

When Malachi spoke again, his voice was low. "How will we make them see when I have trouble accepting it myself? Grigori killed my parents. Slaughtered our women and children. I cannot forgive that."

"Bitterness only hurts you," she said, echoing a lesson her mother taught her after she'd learned the truth about her father. "You can forgive without forgetting."

He reached over and played with a curl of her hair. "My wise woman. What would I do without you?"

"Have a peaceful, normal life?"

Malachi grinned. "Now why would I want that?"

SHE caught him strapping two knives to his torso a few hours later. "What do you need those for?"

They'd settled into their hotel in Portofino and searched online to find directions to Luis Martin's house.

She knew going after Luis was a good idea. Her father's manager knew everything about Jasper's life and didn't trip her emotional wires.

Rhys had found he was staying at a villa outside the harbor town a few towns over from Jasper. Malachi was confident. Ava was… unsure, but had agreed to follow Malachi's lead.

According to Rhys's research, Luis Martin used his credit card almost every night at a small tavern in the town. The card was swiped around eleven o'clock every time it was used. It matched what Ava knew about Luis's habits. He was a very predictable man.

"Malachi?"

"Hmm?"

"The knives? Why are you taking knives?"

Malachi ignored her. He finished settling the straps around his shoulders before he came to kiss her forehead.

"*Reshon*, how many times have you asked Luis for his help getting information?"

"Between the phone calls and e-mails? A lot."

"And has he given it to you?"

"You know he hasn't, but I don't want you to hurt him."

He chucked her under the chin. "Don't be silly. I won't need to hurt him."

"So why—"

"I just need to scare him a little." He reached into his suitcase and took out another knife, flipping it in his fingers before he tucked it in his waistband.

She walked to him, putting a hand on his forearm. "Babe, I really don't think—"

He stopped her mouth with a hard kiss. "Enough. He has information you need. Information you have a right to. You can reveal your power by using the spell Ursala taught you—"

She stepped back. Ava hadn't realized Malachi knew about the spell.

"Yes, I know about the spell. You can use that, but it risks Martin knowing you're not a normal human. That leaves me with the option of playing the brute."

"You're not a brute!"

He gave her a wicked grin. "I can be when I want." He put a finger to her lips when she went to object again. "Enough. We're doing this my way.

We're getting the information. And I promise you, all Luis Martin will have is some soiled sheets and a bit of embarrassment. Happy?"

She probably should have objected harder to terrorizing Luis....

But it wasn't as if the man couldn't be a huge asshole when it suited him. He was Jasper's manager. Ava figured he probably had it coming.

AVA watched Malachi—dressed completely in black—as he stood at Luis's door. It was a villa he'd rented for the month, but it appeared to have top-notch security. Ava recognized the logo on the keypad Malachi was fiddling with. Her stepfather used the same company for his homes.

"Babe, you realize this system—"

"Mmhmm."

"So I know you cut the landline, but—"

Malachi muttered something in Turkish, and Ava frowned. Leaning forward, she noticed the small wireless earbud he must have slipped in during their walk to the villa.

He was talking to someone on the other end. Probably Rhys.

"Yes. Tell me when," he said in a low voice. A few more seconds, then Malachi pushed a seven-digit code into the keypad, and Ava heard a small whooshing sound that sounded like a seal being released. He turned the knob and the door opened quietly.

"Dogs?" he asked her.

"He's allergic."

He walked into the house, holding her hand but moving ahead of her as he scanned each room.

"How did you get past the retina scan?" she asked.

"Rhys was able to override with an emergency password. We have five minutes before they call to confirm his safety."

"How did Rhys get his password?"

"Because Luis Martin had a folder on his home server labeled Passwords."

Okay, he was just asking to get robbed. Ava felt slightly less guilty.

They started up the stairs. Ava could hear someone snoring loudly.

"I feel like it should bother me more that you're so good at breaking and entering."

"Why?" Apparently, Malachi was no longer concerned with security. His voice was louder. He pulled out the earbud and tucked it in a small pocket of the vest he was wearing. "I've been doing this kind of thing for three hundred years. Trust me, it's a lot less messy than it used to be. I don't break and enter for personal gain. It's just a useful life skill."

"Useful life skills are starting a campfire, or… knowing how to tie really good knots."

"I know how to do those things too." He tugged her close and leaned down to her ear. "Give me one weekend without a world-changing revelation," he whispered, "and I'll show you my knot-tying skills."

The color rushed to her face. "Bad man. Very bad man."

He chuckled. "You wouldn't be saying that by the end of the weekend."

The snoring stopped and they both froze. There was a rustling sound before it started up again.

"Come on," Malachi said. "Let's get this over with."

The first doorway in the hall at the top of the stairs was cracked open. A shoe was lying right in front of it. Malachi pushed the door open while Ava kept her eyes closed, hoping Luis wasn't a nude sleeper.

"He's fine," he said, tugging her into the room. "And alone."

The hard-nosed negotiator looked far less like her father's pet pit bull and more like a normal guy when he was sleeping. His mouth hung open slightly. His hair was mussed from tossing and turning.

Ava sighed. "Okay. Time to scare the shit out of him. He's never going to return my calls again."

"Oh yes, he will." Malachi put one knee on the edge of the bed and leaned over Luis. Pulling out a long hunting knife, he put it under the edge of Luis's jaw.

"Luis Martin," Malachi said in a loud voice. "Wake up."

The snoring stopped, then the man's eyes slowly blinked open.

"The hell?" he muttered. His eyes widened when he saw Malachi, and he jerked up in bed, only to catch the edge of the blade and cry out in pain. A line of blood welled up from his skin and dripped down his neck.

Just then, the phone rang.

Oh shit.

Malachi was totally calm. "Do you recognize me?"

Luis's eyes darted between Ava and Malachi. "Ava, what—?"

"Eyes on me." The phone was still ringing. "You're going to answer the phone and tell them you're just fine. Otherwise, I'm going to hurt you."

"No fucking—"

"Yes, you will." Malachi reached up and wrote something across Luis's forehead with a finger. "Luis?"

"Yeah?" The man sounded dazed.

"Answer the phone."

"Okay."

Ava watched as her father's fierce manager followed Malachi's order like a well-trained dog.

"Yeah…" He was muttering into the phone. "Just tired. I don't know." Another pause. "Nah, I'm fine. Maybe kind of… drunk."

A few moments later, the phone was in the cradle and Luis's eyes were clearing.

"What was that? What did you do to me?"

"As you can feel, you should not attempt to move. Do you know who I am?"

Luis tried to nod but winced when the blade bit into his skin again.

"Answer verbally."

"Yes, I know you."

"Good. That will make this easier."

Ava was watching Malachi. He was very careful not to move the knife. As long as Luis didn't move, the edge wouldn't touch his skin. But the wily little man had always had a hard time sitting still for anything.

She started to warn him how jittery Luis could get. "Malachi—"

"Ava has questions for you," her mate said. "You're going to answer them. If you don't, I'm going to hurt you."

Ava could smell the scent of urine in the room.

"I see that you believe me," Malachi said. "That's good. I'm going to sit here while Ava asks her questions. Are you going answer her?"

"Yes," Luis whispered, his terrified eyes flying to hers.

"Louder. So she can hear you."

"Yes."

"Are you going to take her calls from now on?"

"Holy fuck," Luis whispered.

The knife moved. "Answer the question, Luis."

"Yes. I won't avoid her calls." His voice was higher than Ava had ever heard.

"One missed call is fine. Two is not acceptable. Do you understand?"

"Yes."

"Are you going to block her access to her father?"

"Who are you?"

Malachi didn't move the knife—he moved. He leaned down closer. "You don't need to think about me," he said. "Are you going to interfere with Ava?"

"No."

"Good." He finally looked up and met her wide-eyed stare. "Ask now."

Ava stepped closer. "Luis, I'm so—"

She stopped when she heard a low growl. Malachi was glaring at her and shaking his head slowly.

Okay, no apologies.

She took a deep breath. "Is my grandmother alive?"

"Y…yes."

"Did you help my father erase her records?"

"No." He sucked in a breath when Malachi brought the knife higher. "I put him in contact with someone who did. But I didn't do it myself."

Ava took a deep breath and tried not to panic. Malachi was totally calm, but Ava was battling a nervous breakdown. It was one thing to fight through an army of Grigori soldiers who were trying to kill you. It was entirely different threatening the life of someone you'd had over for holiday dinners.

"Ava?"

"Okay, okay. Um… Luis, why did my dad hide her? My grandmother, I mean."

"I don't know." The knife moved a little bit up and Luis attempted to raise his hands. "I'm serious. I didn't ask. Jasper was always secretive about her. There's something wrong with her."

Malachi grunted and Luis backtracked, clearly free from the earlier compliant fog Malachi had put him under. "I mean, she's mentally ill! Or… something. I don't know. I think she's been violent in the past because I had to find a place that had housing for high-risk patients."

"Where?" Malachi asked.

Luis swallowed and looked at Ava, his eyes begging. "Ava."

"I need to know, Luis."

"He wanted to protect you. He didn't want you to think… I know there's some stuff about you he hides. Even from me. From everyone."

Malachi pressed the knife closer and the man whimpered. "I want a location. Where is she being kept?"

"It's in France. There's a hospital outside Albi. Catholic. Saint… Saint Cecelia's."

Malachi leaned down to the man, whispered in his ear, then stood. "Do you understand?"

"Yes." Luis's face was pale, the line of red blood dripping into the silk sheets that were rumpled around him. "Ava, I'm sorry."

How exactly did you say good-bye to the man whose life you just threatened, knowing you'd probably see him again?

"Um… It's fine, Luis. Take care of my dad."

"Jasper loves you, you know?"

"No, I don't know. I never did. Not from him." She walked over and took Malachi's hand. "Good-bye. And… sorry about the sheets."

Chapter Eleven

VOLUND PACED THE RITUAL room where Malachi dreamed.

Angry, Malachi thought. The angel was very angry.

Frustrated.

The Fallen muttered words in the Old Language that Malachi couldn't catch. Bit out curses under his breath.

He didn't know what had happened to make the angel so enraged, but he couldn't help feeling satisfied.

Just as the feeling threatened to bring a smile to his face, Volund spun and forced Malachi's eyes to his.

Volund roared, and the rage rolled over him, searing his skin, stealing his breath.

"You cannot," Malachi choked out, "hurt me."

He gasped for breath. His mind knew this was illusion, though the dream state felt real. Ava was still nowhere in sight. He stood naked and stripped of every shield while the angel continued to rage.

Ash and cinders whirled around the ritual room, burning and scraping his skin until he could smell his own blood in the wind.

"You cannot hurt me," he said again.

Malachi opened his eyes and Volund was there, gold eyes wide with madness.

"She is mine!" the angel screamed.

In the next breath, Volund plunged the black dagger into his heart, and Malachi woke, gasping for breath, a hand pressed to his chest.

THE SECRET

HE didn't speak of his nightmare. She had too much on her mind. Too many worries creased her forehead. He longed for a time when it could just be the two of them again.

Malachi wanted answers, but he also wondered whether Martin had sent them on another leg of an endless wild-goose chase. A mental hospital in France? Even if they found Ava's grandmother, what would they discover? Kostas hadn't painted a pleasant picture of female Grigori in the human world.

But Jasper Reed's money had provided an escape for his daughter. Perhaps it had sheltered his mother in a similar manner.

In the end, it was easier to drive to Saint Cecelia's than fly. They stayed one more night in Portofino before heading to France in the same rented car they'd picked up in Genoa. Nine hours of driving to reach an uncertain reception. Nine hours farther away from Vienna.

The converted chateau fifteen minutes out of Albi in the Tarn region of France could have been a luxurious country home or even an exclusive hotel. Rhys's search confirmed that it was neither of the two, but rather a very exclusive, very secure mental health facility run privately with a live-in staff and only fifteen to twenty permanent residents.

As far as caring for the mentally or emotionally troubled, it didn't get more comfortable than Saint Cecilia's.

Malachi turned into the drive, approaching the house through an allée of stately trimmed linden trees, their branches winter bare. They'd stayed the night in Albi before coming to the hospital that morning. Malachi called Max after they left Italy and told him their plans. They would leave the rented car in Marseilles and from there catch a flight to Vienna.

He was edgy. Mala had already taken Orsala to the city. Rhys and Leo had closed up the scribe house in Istanbul and joined them. Renata and Max were flying to Prague to check on an Irina safe house there before they joined Damien and Sari. All the former scribes of Istanbul were crisscrossing the continent with one destination in mind.

Vienna.

Kostas might have wanted his existence to remain a secret, but the Irin Council needed to know of the existence of Grigori females. The whole Irin world—especially the Irina—needed to know.

Because along with the inevitable dread of facing the council, Malachi also carried a mad hope.

The Irin race was dying.

Yet Ava had Grigori blood, and they had mated. More than that, he and Ava were *reshon*. Bound. Destined for each other by the Creator. And if he and Ava had a future together, anything was possible.

The Grigori had decimated the Irina, while the Fallen had thrown their own daughters to the chaos and darkness of the human world. If those women, the silent ones, could be found, it was possible they could be saved. Grigori and Irin alike. The very women the Fallen had shunned could be the salvation of the Irin race.

But what condition would they be in? Kyra had been fiercely protected by a devoted brother. Ava had never known she was anything but human. Malachi hoped that finding Ava's grandmother would give them a larger picture, especially regarding why she'd been targeted by two fallen archangels.

"You ready?" he asked her.

"Yes."

Luis Martin had called ahead and given the hospital permission to allow Ava and Malachi to visit. He'd also warned them that, from all reports, Ava Rezai was uncommunicative.

"Rezai," Ava mused as they parked in the gravel-lined oval in front of the house. "Persian?"

"I believe so."

"Jasper's Persian?"

Malachi shrugged. "His coloring is ambiguous. And we don't know. He could have taken after his father."

"Who is a complete mystery." She took a deep breath and unbuckled her seatbelt. "Shall we go visit Grandma?"

He took her hand, seeing through the bravado immediately. "You realize she might not speak. We might get nothing from her. And if we don't, we will continue on."

"We'll confirm she's *kareshta*, though. We'll be able to tell, don't you think?"

132

"I do." Her hand was so small in his. Such energy, such life in so small a person. "I love you. I'm very proud of you."

She squeezed his palm with her fingers. "Say that after I've made it out of here without embarrassing myself with tears."

And without another word, she opened the door.

Cold wind whipped around them as they walked up the path. Gravel crunched under their feet and Malachi could smell snow in the air. Before they reached the large wooden doors, one swung open and a woman dressed in a sage-green uniform waved them in.

"Ms. Matheson, yes?"

"Thank you," Ava said, stepping through the doorway and brushing her hair back where it had tangled around her face. "Yes, I'm here to see Ava Rezai."

"Of course. We were expecting you. This is good! Ms. Rezai doesn't receive many visitors."

Malachi followed them, touching Ava's arm as the woman—who looked like a nurse of some kind—led them farther into the entryway. There was a fire burning in a massive stone hearth, and two women sat near it, one in a soft white robe, the other in another of the green uniforms. Both were knitting and speaking softly. Past the large living area, a sunroom looked out over a clear blue pool and manicured grounds. Two men were sitting at a small table playing chess, one a patient, another an orderly or nurse of some kind.

Ava's eyes swept the room, searching for a sign of her grandmother.

"Ms. Matheson?"

"Please, call me Ava."

The nurse motioned down a wood-paneled hallway. "Ms. Rezai is not in the common area. Can I show you to the doctor's office? He wanted to speak to you before you see her."

Ava nodded. "Of course." She held out her hand and Malachi took it. Her skin was ice-cold.

They walked down the hall following the nurse, but Malachi didn't let his guard drop. There was something foreign in this place. Some energy teased his senses. Perhaps it was the echo of Ava's grandmother, but he didn't think so.

The nurse left them alone in a large office.

"It's nice," Ava said. "The house, I mean. It's beautiful here."

"It is."

"I guess if he was going to lock her up, it's good he put her someplace nice."

Malachi tucked a curl of hair behind her ear as they took seats in front of a large oak desk. "Don't think of it that way. It's possible she's been too damaged by the world. This place is quiet. Do you hear much?"

"No." She shook her head. "I listened when we first walked in, and I was worried the people here would be so sick their voices would freak me out, but it's not bad. Pretty quiet, really."

"See? This might be a restful place for her. Think of it as another kind of haven like Sarihöfn."

"Do you think—" She turned when the door opened and froze.

Malachi followed her eyes.

The unobtrusive form of Dr. Sadik stood in the doorway.

"Hello, Ava."

Malachi was on his feet in an instant, only to be pinned to the wall by the power of the Fallen.

Ava said, "Put him down, Jaron."

"Tell your mate not to try to attack me. It is annoying."

"You could have given us a bit of a warning. What did you do to the human doctor?"

"He is resting in another office," Jaron said, still wearing the appearance of the psychologist Ava had been seeing in Istanbul. He waved a hand toward Malachi.

He slumped down the wall at once, the pressure at his throat gone in an instant.

Jaron sat behind the human doctor's desk and spread his hands. "So you know."

Ava sat in the chair in front of the desk, glaring at the Fallen who'd been shadowing her for months.

"Yeah, I know. So that was the big secret? That the Fallen have daughters?"

"Trust me, it is a secret we have endeavored to hide for thousands of years."

Malachi stood behind Ava. He had no interest in sitting with the angel.

"Why?" Ava asked.

"They're uncontrollable. Unbalanced. Most do not have the physical strength of their brothers, so they're not useful. They've always been a problem for us, and they're considered a weakness."

Malachi was disgusted, yet hardly surprised.

"You act completely disinterested, but if that's the case, why are you here?" Malachi asked. "What's so special about Ava Rezai?"

For once, he sensed a reaction in the inhuman eyes of the Fallen before him. Jaron might have morphed his form into the shape of the harmless, middle-aged academic before them, but his eyes were the same. Frozen gold that shone with neither fear nor joy. But for an instant, there was a hint of something else. Had he imagined it?

Jaron ignored him and turned to Ava. "Why are *you* here?"

Her mouth dropped. "Because she's my grandmother."

"You already know the magic in your blood comes from your father through her. And you probably guessed she has Grigori blood. What more do you hope to learn?"

"I… I don't know. I just want to meet her."

Jaron slid forward, put his chin in the palm of his hand as he rested an elbow on the edge of the desk. "She might not speak. Would you leave here even more confused than you came? Will this ease your mind or torment it?"

"I don't know," his mate whispered, "but at least I'll know the truth."

"The truth…?" Jaron stood. "An interesting concept. You seek the truth, but will her truth be one you can accept?"

"I want to try."

"And you?"

Malachi looked up, realizing Jaron was talking to him. "What about me?"

"Why do you want to meet her? What do you hope to gain?"

"This is not about me, Jaron. It's about Ava."

"Yes." Jaron's eyes bored into his, and Malachi felt his body sway under the power of the angel's stare. "I have spent much of the past sixty years concerning myself with Ava."

He drifted off for a moment, his eyes lifting to the high windows that covered one wall in the doctor's office.

"Come," he finally said. "Let us meet her."

WHEN they stepped out of the office, Malachi noticed the quiet immediately.

There was no one in the house.

No chattering nurses near the large oak reception desk. No men playing chess. The fire crackled, but no one took up the knitting needles lying forlornly on the sofa.

"Where is everyone?"

"They're here and they're not."

Ava stepped forward and looked across the now-empty room. "Is this a dream?"

"In a sense," Jaron said. "More accurately, *they* are in a dream. A simple twist of time. When I call them back, they will have no memory that they didn't spend this time in the living area, going about their tasks."

Malachi felt his skin prickle. "You can just… make everyone disappear?"

"Not humans with angelic blood. But pure humans?" Jaron shrugged. "It's not without effort on my part, but I hardly consider either one of you a threat."

Malachi had never heard of such a thing. Never even conceived of it. Why was Jaron revealing this power now? He eyed the man with suspicion but followed him down one hallway and up a wide set of stairs. As Jaron walked, he grew, morphing into the form he'd taken the previous times he'd revealed himself to Ava. Close to seven feet tall, dark hair falling around a clearly inhuman face. He was an ancient god. An artist's mad dream.

And Malachi sensed he was still seeing only a fraction of the angel's presence.

THE SECRET

It was on the third floor of the massive house that he stopped and turned to Ava. A long corridor stretched before them, empty like the rest of the house.

"Is your mind shielded?" he asked Ava.

"Yes."

Jaron cocked his head, clearly curious. "How?"

"It's like… a door. I can keep it shut or open it."

"Interesting. I always wondered. That door?" he said. "Keep it locked."

Malachi became aware of a growing power. It called him. He could hear the seductive voice in his mind. Twisted whispers of longing. Need.

Anger.

Whatever called to him was hungry.

Malachi heard a high girlish hum drift down the corridor. It was beautiful. He needed to find the voice. Hold it. Touch—

"Enough!" Jaron lost any human facade when he shouted, startling Malachi out of the trance. "Silence, Ava!"

Without another word, the angel strode toward down the hall. He raised a hand and a paneled door swung open. Malachi followed cautiously, holding Ava behind him.

"Do you feel it?" she whispered.

He nodded but didn't speak. He felt it. Like coals glowing under long-dead ashes, the voice waited. He hesitated at the threshold but felt Ava's hand at his back, urging him through.

When Malachi turned the corner, he saw something his years of training could never have prepared him for.

Blinding color filled the institutional room. It was as if he walked in an impressionist painting. Swirling seas and mountain crests. An achingly brilliant sunset covered one entire wall. On the opposite side, a blood-red eclipse hung, surrounded by black night and whorls of stars. Flowers filled one corner. Bones filled another. Twisted roots and looming trees. Layer after layer, the paintings filled the space, even crawling up the ceiling.

And in the corner, a woman sat, huddled on Jaron's lap.

Beautiful was too soft a word.

Her eyes were closed, and her cheek was pressed to Jaron's chest. When her breath stirred, the raised glyphs on the angel's skin glowed with a bronze light. Her hair was streaked with red and gold, her skin a dusky echo of the angel who held her. And on Jaron's face, an expression of such familiar tenderness that Malachi knew immediately why Jaron had been shadowing his mate her entire life.

"Come in," Jaron said in a voice touched with despair. "Come, Ava, and meet my daughter."

Chapter Twelve

"DAUGHTER," AVA WHISPERED, knowing immediately it was true. It had been there all along. Jaron's strange protectiveness. Watching her. Guarding her in his own way. And Ava's magic, far too powerful for someone completely untrained.

Of course she was strong. Her great-grandfather was an archangel.

She stepped closer, reaching for Malachi's hand to anchor her in the beautiful, frightening room. "She's my grandmother. But… she's too—"

"She stopped aging soon after she bore your father," Jaron said, stroking the hair of the woman on his lap. "Like our sons, our daughters do not age as humans do."

Ava stepped past Malachi, no fear in her heart. The frightening intensity that had bombarded her in the hall had leveled off the moment Jaron entered the room. "She's so beautiful."

"Once, she was the most beautiful creature to walk the earth. Her beauty rivaled the children of heaven."

A wave of longing washed over her. She wanted to touch. Wanted to hug. She was drawn to this strange woman her father had named her after, but she was also afraid. And Jaron showed no sign of letting his child go.

"Ava?" she whispered, crouching down across from her.

There was no furniture in the room except a bed bolted to one wall and a small table attached to the opposite wall. No mirrors. No windows. Plastic pots of vivid paint were lined on the table in precise color order.

Ava looked up and wondered how she had reached the tops of the walls and ceiling.

"I have no idea," Jaron said, guessing her question. "I've wondered that myself."

Ava looked back to him, surprised by the gentle amusement in his voice. "Does she know I'm here?"

Jaron pressed a palm over his daughter's temple. "She's aware, but she's resting right now. The only real peace she has is when I am able to visit her. Otherwise, she's quite mad."

"Why?" Malachi asked. "Is it because she has your blood? The woman we met in Sofia—Kostas's sister—wasn't like this."

"Why do you care, Scribe? She's the daughter of your enemy."

Malachi ignored the taunt and knelt down next to Ava, his eyes on the trembling woman in Jaron's arms.

"I have seen trauma like this before, Jaron, usually on the faces of Grigori victims. Who hurt this woman?"

Ava reached for his hand, strangely comforted by the anger in her mate's voice. The thought of someone hurting a stranger might not have roused another man's protective instincts, but Malachi wasn't other men. Even the daughter of a Fallen angel was someone to be protected.

He brushed a kiss over her temple and waited for Jaron to answer.

Jaron said, "Yes, she has been hurt. In ways you cannot imagine."

Her grandmother—it was hard to think of her as a grandmother when she looked the same age as Ava—twisted in her father's arms. Her mouth opened in a wordless groan.

"Who hurt her?" Malachi asked.

Jaron raised his eyes to meet hers, and Ava saw the truth in the rage and betrayal in his gaze.

"It was one of the Fallen," she said. "One of the others. Who else would be able to hurt your daughter?"

The angel nodded and let out a heavy breath, more human in that moment than Ava had ever seen him. "Unlike my brothers, I doted on my daughter with no thought of hiding it. I'd only ever had sons, then after she was born… I indulged her. She was quite spoiled."

Her grandmother's features twisted in pain before Jaron put a hand on her forehead and she settled again.

THE SECRET

"Her mother was a lover I held in some regard. Atefah was descended from royalty. Beautiful. Spirited. A worthy lover for me. She survived the birth, mostly because I forced her to let my older sons care for their new sister. No princess was ever more pampered. Unfortunately, Ava's mother did not survive a second child. She died giving birth to a son."

"Did you love her?" Ava asked.

"Love?" Jaron frowned. "No. The Fallen are not capable of love. Atefah loved *me*. Quite desperately. I should have sent her away, but Ava was attached to her mother. So she stayed and died, along with the child. She was the last human lover I took and the only one who gave me a daughter."

"And that's why you care about Ava," Malachi said. "You may not call it love, Fallen, but I can see your regard."

"As others did," Jaron said grimly. "It was my own failing. Ava was the first being in thousands of years I held some… affection for. She amused me. If I have a personality in this realm, she reflected it. Perhaps that is why I care for her still." He looked up with sardonic eyes. "Everything is vanity, after all."

Vanity, maybe, but Jaron appeared to be fiercely protective. What idiot would have risked his wrath to hurt her?

"Volund," Jaron said, reading her frown.

Ava's eyes grew wide. "Volund?"

Jaron's daughter jerked in his arms.

Malachi picked up the connection immediately. "This is because of your damned rivalry? That was why he targeted *my* Ava. Why he killed me."

"It's about power." The gold fire in Jaron's eyes was a banked rage. "Everything is about power in our world. Volund was expanding his territory. He had eliminated his competition in Northern Europe. My allies. He had ambitions to hurt me, though I was a far more difficult target. He hurt my daughter to make a point. She was nothing more to him than a political maneuver."

"I don't believe you." Malachi's voice was low. "This was more than political."

141

"Perhaps it is more correct to say it *began* as a political move." Jaron's hand tightened on his daughter's back. "But he became… curious."

A knot formed at the pit of Ava's stomach.

Malachi asked, "About?"

"It was the Irin who gave him the idea."

"What idea?"

Jaron shook his head. "Volund—"

"*Nooooo!*" A shriek from the formerly silent woman startled them all. Even Jaron.

She shouted and scrambled away from her father, huddling in a corner, her eyes sweeping the room. She was frantic. Ava wasn't sure her grandmother saw anything more than the demons in her mind.

"Stop!" she shrieked. "Stop it. Don't speak his name." The words poured out of her, a river of tormented pleas. "Please, *Bâbâ*, no!"

"Ava—"

"*Bâbâ, Bâbâ*, no." A torrent of what sounded like Farsi poured from her lips. Ava wasn't fluent enough to decipher it. But the strange energy pouring from her grandmother was familiar. Ava knew she could reach her if she could only catch her attention.

Ava crawled forward, ignoring Jaron's warning to crack open the door in her mind.

"Grandmother?" she said. "*Ava.*"

Their eyes connected.

Jaron's daughter held a trembling finger over blood-red lips. "Shhhh."

Ava listened, but the only thing she heard was a twisted cacophony of pain.

Her grandmother stared at her, gold eyes transfixed on Ava's face.

"It's a secret," she whispered. "Like me. You can't tell a secret."

"You can tell me."

The tormented woman tore at the shining hair that fell over her face and shook her head. "Demons play tricks," she muttered. "Don't. Can't hide. Not even in my mind." A haunting singsong voice. "My mind, my mind." A bitter laugh. "If I lose myself, not even he can find me. Hide in the woods—don't dream! Don't sleep. He can't see the visions I keep." A high, keening laugh. "*Bâbâ…*"

"I'm here, Ava." But Jaron stayed in place, as if touching his child might hurt her. A low hum filled the air, and Ava's grandmother rocked back and forth, hitting her head against the wall.

Ava moved closer.

Malachi said, "*Canım*, be careful."

"She's hurting herself."

The woman stopped rocking. Her eyes rose to Ava's.

She stared at her, and for a brief moment, Ava knew her grandmother was completely sane.

"Be careful," she said, her voice low and calm. "I cannot force him out. Do you understand?"

"I have your blood," Ava said. "Don't tell me. *Show* me."

Ava caught the dark flicker in her grandmother's eyes a moment before her vision went black. Her body froze and her muscles locked as her mind raced through the vision Ava sent her.

A lively street market in Beirut. A boy with seductive eyes.
Temptation.
"Just for the night. My father…"
Ropes. He had tied her. Why had he—?
Bâbâ!
Gone.
Where were her brothers? They were gone. Her father…
Why couldn't she feel her father? She could always feel her father.
"Let me see her."
A darker, deeper power hovered over her, blocking her from the light.
"Beautiful child…"
Such darkness.
Anger.
Pain.
"Mine."
NO!
It ripped through her. The tearing of innocence and hope and light and nothing—
Nothing would be light again.
He was in her.

In her body. Her mind.

The darkness trampled over the flowers of her soul and crushed them with his power and everything…

"Everything is dark."

"Ava."

No.

Violation was only the beginning.

"Ava."

Her dreams a torment. She ran but could not escape.

"Ava."

Hissing laughter bruised her mind.

The dark angel had marked her.

His laugher twisted as he called her mate.

He came again when she closed her eyes. Every night. Every day. Even when her body was taken back to her brothers, he was there. When the child was born, he was there.

His power lived in the child who bore the face of her nightmare.

Love and hate and light and darkness.

"You'll hurt him, Ava."

Take him away…

"Ava."

There was no escape.

Ava rocked back, gasping. Hoarse cries broke from her throat. She could feel Malachi's arms around her, holding her steady as she trembled.

"Ava!"

The sound of her name only made her sob.

"Oh God!" She clung to Malachi. "It can't… she can't…"

Jaron pulled his daughter's shaking body into his arms. Her eyes were closed again, her mind shut down to anything but her sire's touch. And Ava knew from looking into her grandmother's mind that Jaron's presence was the only thing that gave her any kind of peace.

Because her dreams were nightmares she couldn't escape.

"Ava, what was that?" Malachi held her tightly, his arms almost crushing her ribs. "I couldn't see. You have to tell me."

"Mate," she whispered. A connection so deep and profound that had been utterly twisted by pure evil. "Volund didn't just attack her, Malachi. He took her. He wanted to know... He raped her. And he *marked* her."

His hands froze. "No."

"He wanted to know if it was possible for an angel to mate with one of the *kareshta*. He was curious. So he marked her with his power and bound her to him." Ava choked. "He's in her dreams, Malachi."

"She dream-walks with the Fallen who raped her?" he whispered.

"She can't escape. He's there every time she closes her eyes."

There was dread in Malachi's voice when he asked, "Your father?"

"He's Volund's child. She tried, but she couldn't bear it. Jasper looks like Volund did when he took her."

The room had grown deathly quiet. Ava could only watch her grandmother, a woman locked in the torment of her own mind. She had sensed the darkness there as well. Volund's touch had marked her in more ways than one. There was violence and a burgeoning rage belied by the woman's still form. Jaron, she knew, could sense it. His eyes met hers as he held his child. He bent down to whisper something in her ear and Ava relaxed completely.

"She needs sleep," Jaron said. "She only truly rests when I am here."

"Why can't you help her?" Ava asked. "Heal her? Keep Volund from torturing her every time she closes her eyes!"

"I do not know how." He took a deep breath. "In thousands of years, no angel has violated his brothers' children the way that Volund did mine. She has even begged Death to come for her, but Azril will not. I do not know why."

"Why didn't Volund kill her?" Malachi said. "After he'd attacked her, why didn't he—"

"Whether he likes it or not, Ava *is* his mate. When Volund bound himself to my daughter, he didn't realize it would affect him too," Jaron said. "Perhaps it is her only power now, but she became his curse. He would kill her if he could do it without harming himself. But he cannot."

"You hate my father." Her instincts were screaming at her. "Because he's Volund's son."

"Yes."

"But you protect him."

"Yes."

"Why?"

"He's her son as well. She did not hate him. And… he has my blood."

"What is my father? Half Grigori. Half angel. How can he even exist?"

"How do any of our children exist?" Jaron asked. "They are the will of the Creator. Though if my master has a purpose for your father, I have not discovered it yet. Perhaps Jasper's only purpose was fathering you."

Ava tried to wrap her mind around it. "And Volund? Would he hurt my dad?"

"At first, Volund was interested in your father. I had to hide them both. He thought the child of an angel and a *kareshta* would be even greater than the Irin. But the child was far too unstable. He had power, but no control. More damning, Jasper has free will. I cannot control him, just like I cannot control you. Volund lost interest when he found out he could not control Ava's child."

"But he knows who I am."

"He learned when you came to Istanbul. He was watching me and found you. When you attacked his men in the cistern—"

"All I did was scream."

Jaron gave her a look that made Ava feel like an ignorant child.

"You unleashed power the Grigori had never experienced before," he said. "Our children live in fear of their sisters, because their voices hold power the Grigori don't understand. Volund's sons didn't know what you were. Your magic was dark like the children of the Fallen, but you were in the company of Irin scribes and they treated you as one of their own."

"So?"

"You attracted his attention, Ava. It was easy enough for him to discover the connection when he started to look. You have his blood, after all."

She shivered, and Malachi's hands soothed the goose bumps from her skin. "That's why he wants me."

"Yes."

"Why?"

"I honestly don't know. Nor do I care. He has become erratic." Jaron stroked Ava's temple. "Perhaps she torments him in his sleep as well. I can hope, but it does not matter. He cannot have you. Volund has taken enough of what is mine."

Malachi broke in. "Unbelievable. This is like two dogs fighting over a bone. Ava doesn't belong to either of you."

"Why?" Jaron asked. "Because she belongs to you?"

"She belongs to herself!"

"Enough." Ava stood and started pacing. "You can find me anywhere because I have your blood, can't you?"

"Yes."

"Can Volund? He's disgusting, but I am his granddaughter."

Jaron hesitated. "Unless I'm shielding you and you're shielding yourself, Volund can find you. The Irina magic you learned has helped immeasurably."

"That's why he couldn't find me in Norway."

Jaron nodded. "Your magic and mine, combined with the old singer's, made the haven the safest place for you."

"Until I left."

"The minute his Grigori spotted you, Sarihöfn became useless. I was the one who violated the wards there. You needed to leave."

She shook her head. "You've been playing me all along. And Malachi?"

Jaron waved a careless hand. "I owe your Irin mate no protection. He is not mine."

"Do you know how—"

"I have no idea how you were able to call him back. It was unexpected. But your blood holds the power of two archangels, and through your bond with this scribe, you were given the power of Mikhael's line as well." Jaron stared at her. "You *are* utterly unique, Ava. There are thousands of him, and only one of you. I do not care about him, but as long as his purpose helps mine, we are in accord."

Malachi said, "I would say the same of you, Fallen."

"Then we understand each other."

Ava rested against a flower-covered wall. "What *is* your purpose? What are you after?"

Jaron said nothing.

"I know," Malachi said, leaning against the bed, his arms crossed over his knees. "He wants to kill Volund."

"Yes," Jaron said.

"And he needs our help."

The angel's face was blank.

Ava asked, "Why should we help you?"

"Volund masterminded the Rending," Jaron said.

A vein pulsed in Malachi's forehead. "And you had nothing to do with it?"

Jaron smoothed the hair back from his daughter's face. "I didn't stop it, but I refused to use my sons to participate. I knew the Irin would kill many of our children, even in a surprise attack. Volund and his allies didn't agree. I suspect they had some deal with whatever Councilors had power at the time, though I hardly think the Irin knew the extent of his plans."

"You lie."

"Do I?" Jaron asked. "Are your elder scribes so incorruptible, son of Mikhael? Are they not hungry for power?"

"We are not Fallen," Malachi said.

Jaron only smiled.

"You didn't participate in the Rending," Ava said. "But you found me. You were looking for Fallen daughters in the human world. Why?"

"After the Rending, I began to see a way I could use the loss of the Irina to usurp Volund's power," Jaron said. "He had grown *very* powerful."

Malachi said, "It wasn't revenge for your daughter?"

"I didn't have a daughter then. I simply saw the females as an asset."

"How?"

"The Irin had lost most of their women. The Fallen had women it didn't want, some of whom still clung to their fathers out of loyalty. How better to gain power over our only adversaries in this world than by giving them the females they so desperately wanted? Females we could track. That we had influence over."

Ava's stomach turned. "You were going to use them like cattle. Pawns for your political games."

"Yes." Jaron's expression was unapologetic. "I was well on the way to putting my plan in place—ferreting out the Grigora who had filtered into the human world—when my daughter was born."

"Did you change your mind about using them?"

Jaron blinked. "No. I had no plans to use *my* daughter. She was to be protected."

Ava shook her head. Typical.

"What about me?" she asked. "Did you plan to use me when I came to see you in Istanbul?"

"You were unexpected. I had connections all over the world searching for women with Grigori traits, but I didn't expect my own granddaughter to be one of them."

"Why not?"

"Your human guardians had always seemed quite protective. The fact that they let you travel surprised me."

"I used Jasper's money. They really couldn't control me after I got that."

"Ah." A slight smile lifted the corner of the angel's mouth. "And we come full circle. Volund's son draws you into the game, no matter how much I try to avoid it."

"He's your grandson too."

Jaron's face grew cold. "He is an abomination. No one like him should exist. My daughter's torment will not be repeated."

"Of course not," Malachi said. "Because if you convince the Irin to take in the daughters of the Fallen, you know we'll protect them. We may not be perfect, but we value our women. And we won't let even the daughters of our enemies become victims."

Jaron cocked his head. "You're very predictable. It's useful."

"And to protect them, we'll even help you kill Volund."

"He did mastermind the slaughter of your innocents."

"Volund needs to die," Ava said, her eyes glued to the sleeping form in Jaron's arms. "He *has* to. Not only for killing you and masterminding the Rending. When Volund dies, your daughter might finally live."

777.

"WHAT NOW?" VASU WORE the face of a petulant child. Thin and black-haired, he kicked at the post that stood innocently on the sidewalk.

Barak was walking along a curb, his arms held out for balance. That morning, he wore the face of a French schoolboy, waiting at the bus stop. "He's told them everything."

"What will they do?"

Barak shrugged his small shoulders. "They're flying to Vienna now."

Vasu scowled impatiently and a car traveling the road near them swerved on the icy road.

"Well, what can we make them do?"

"Nothing," Barak said. "They are not our children. They have free will."

"That was the Creator's mistake, giving the Forgiven's children free will. What was he thinking?"

Drifts of snow began to fall on the dirty sidewalk. Barak lifted his head to the sky and opened his mouth to catch one.

"Gifts given freely are more precious," Barak said, staring into the cloudy winter sky. "And our children are capable of love."

Vasu watched a girl walking along the sidewalk across the street. She hurried, perhaps late for school. Her breath fogged in the morning air.

"What are we capable of?" Vasu said.

"Watching," Barak answered him as he stopped his movements to follow the girl with his eyes. "Waiting."

The car took the corner too fast. Barak heard the driver's panicked thoughts when he spotted the little girl in the bright green coat. She wasn't looking at the road. Hadn't noticed the ice. She was a child. She was thinking about her mathematics test.

The two boys watched impassively as the car spun in the road and jumped the sidewalk, crushing the little girl beneath its wheels in a sickeningly quiet thump. Shopkeepers rushed out of their buildings, crying and screaming. One wrenched the driver's door open. The human was pale and shaking.

"We watch and wait," Barak said.

Silently, Vasu crossed the street, stepping between the cars that had halted in the road. His hands were shoved in his pockets. Nobody noticed the solemn-faced boy in the grey coat as he crouched down next to the wheels of the car and reached out.

The little girl in the green coat smiled at him and took his hand. Standing next to Vasu, she watched the crowd with a small worried frown until the dark-haired boy tugged her hand. Then the two children walked up the sidewalk, Vasu holding her hand as old women cried over the dead child's body and sirens started to wail.

"And some of us still serve," Barak whispered as his eyes followed the archangel wearing the face of a child.

Chapter Thirteen

MALACHI CLOSED HIS EYES and dreamed of Constantinople.

Cobbled walkways under his feet as he strode the paths his ancestors had followed. Sun-warmed stone and the smell of the river in his nose. The familiar streets were a comforting respite from the tumult of his waking hours.

Ava reached out and took his hand.

"Where are we?"

"When," he said, taking a deep breath and pulling her to his side. The heady scent of the spice market teased his senses. "*When* are we? These are my memories, *canim*. This is Constantinople when I was young."

Malachi heard the echo of horses clopping on the streets and vendors calling to bargain, but they were alone in the streets of the city he'd loved as a young man. The city where he'd met her.

"We're dreaming," Ava said, her face spreading into a smile. "We're in your dream instead of mine."

"I suppose so."

"I like it." She ran her fingers along the carvings of a wall as they passed, and Malachi could see the ancient words rise beneath her fingers like shadows reaching for long-dead eyes. "No, I love it. Your dreams are so much clearer than mine."

"I don't feel him here."

"Jaron? No." She turned and brushed a kiss on his cheek. "I like the privacy."

"So do I."

They walked for a while longer, enjoying the empty streets where the voices of long-dead residents clamored. He hadn't known dreams could be like this. It felt lighter. Brighter. Like a pleasant memory they could enjoy together.

"When this is finished," she said, "I want to come back here."

"To Constantinople?"

"Istanbul, remember? They changed the name a while ago, old man."

"So they did." He pinched her side and felt her squirm as she laughed, her body as real to his hands as if they were awake on the plane heading to Vienna.

"Why do you think we're in your dream and not mine?"

"Maybe because I'm remembering more."

"Are you?" She pulled him to a park bench along the Hippodrome, and Malachi heard the echo of wings as pigeons took flight. She pushed him down, then straddled his lap and faced him.

"What do you have in mind, *reshon*?"

Her words came shyly. "I want to sing to you again."

"Yes, please."

He waited, eyes closed in the sunlight as his mate put her hands on his cheeks and began a tentative song. It was an old poem he remembered his mother singing when she wanted to center herself. A focusing ritual before more complicated magic was sung.

"Relax," she whispered in English before she began the halting words.

Malachi resisted the impulse to correct her pronunciation as she sung the spell. He wouldn't interfere until something became dangerous.

Before, Ava had commanded him, a heady, forceful magic intoxicating to the senses. This time she coaxed. The words were lighter, more playful. A sunny, teasing spell that made him want to smile. Even the burn of the *talesm* on his shoulder and collarbone felt more like a tickle than a knife.

"Ava." He hummed her name when her lips tickled his ear. His hands smoothed over the curve of her hips, up her sides, and wrapped around her shoulders, drawing her body into his. Overhead, he heard the flap of bird wings again, but nothing in the sunny dream could distract him from the desire that coursed under his skin.

"Sir."

"Don't stop," he whispered into Ava's ear as her song died down.

"Sir, I'm afraid you have to stop."

That wasn't his mate's voice.

He came awake with a start, the disapproving flight attendant staring down at him and trying to block the view of the other passengers.

"Really, sir, if I wasn't sure you were sleeping…"

Malachi realized his hand was up Ava's shirt, her body splayed over his as they reclined in the airplane seats. Ava was still asleep, her hand heading in a southern direction as his headed north under her sweater. Though they had a blanket thrown over them, he realized they must have been giving the other passengers quite a show.

Slowly, he drew his hand away and nudged Ava over into her seat, ignoring her sleepy protests.

"I do apologize," he muttered.

The flight attendant took an impatient breath and opened her mouth—no doubt to offer some other warning—when her eyes widened in alarm. "Are you well?"

"I'm sorry?"

"Your chest. What happened?" She pointed down and Malachi caught the edge of blood welling up through the fabric of his collared shirt. "Do you need a doctor?"

"I'm fine." He reached for the scarf he'd shoved in Ava's purse. "I apologize. It is an old cut that must have opened as I moved. I'm quite all right."

"Malachi?" Ava blinked her eyes open. "Where are—" She saw the bleeding. "Oh, babe. I'm so sorry. Does it hurt?"

She sat up, and then Malachi had to deal with two females fussing over him.

"I'm fine," he protested. "It's nothing."

Luckily, the bleeding from his reformed *talesm* distracted the formerly annoyed attendant. She rushed away to retrieve some first aid supplies while Malachi tried to calm his body's natural reaction to the rush of magic and endorphins his mate had produced.

THE SECRET

Ava must have caught the tent in his pants, because he saw her hiding a smile.

"You are in so much trouble when we land," he muttered.

"I'd apologize, but—"

"Don't." His command was hoarse. "Never apologize for that."

Her smile was wicked. "You may come to regret telling me that."

"Just as long as I come."

Her eyes widened. "Someone's in a mood."

Malachi growled and grabbed a handful of her hair, pulling her in for a brief kiss. "I want to disappear somewhere with you, not go to Vienna."

Her smile fell. "Me too."

"If we go back to sleep, do you think we can avoid the whole mess?"

"Probably not. And we might get in trouble with the flight attendant."

"Damn."

THEY landed in the early evening; the sun had already set. Luckily, taxis weren't difficult to find. Rhys had e-mailed Ava an address near Judenplatz, within the Innere Stadt, the oldest part of the city. They would be within walking distance of the Library that served as the council chambers, but far enough away to afford privacy. They'd also be near St. Rupert's Church, one of the few places in Vienna Malachi felt didn't drip with ostentation.

"Has Damien told anyone about me yet?" she asked as they waited in the taxi queue. "Or about us?"

Malachi shook his head. "He's been trying to meet with different elders every day but isn't having much success. While Sari's presence in the city has caused some speculation, the Irina question is still being debated. The council is still treating the battle in Oslo as an isolated incident. And since so many of Volund's Grigori were killed, they consider it a victory."

Ava's mouth dropped open, but a car was pulling up. Malachi grabbed her hand and walked toward it.

He helped her into the taxi and loaded their luggage in back, happy that his mate packed with the economy of a seasoned traveler.

She'd already given the driver the address by the time he closed the door and settled into the cab.

"Volund wasn't even in Oslo," she whispered, well aware that most taxi drivers in the city would speak English.

"I know that," he said just as quietly. "But Brage was. And he was taken out. As Volund's oldest and most feared child, the council considers that a victory. Remember, they don't target the Fallen. In all my time as a soldier, I only remember hunting one angel. Grigori? Hundreds. But the Fallen are out of our reach. Of course, I don't remember everything, so don't take that as a complete picture."

"That's just…" She sputtered and shook her head.

Malachi could hardly argue with her. Underestimating the Grigori threat was ridiculous. And yet he was unsurprised that Damien hadn't found success. Watchers had been pleading for years to take a more aggressive stance against the Fallen, but it was a difficult argument in a city that hadn't seen a Grigori attack in centuries.

Now Jaron wanted Irin help to take out Volund. How he expected Malachi and Ava to convince the council of that was still a mystery.

Malachi was desperate for his memories. Without them, he was playing this game in the dark. He tried not to take his frustration out on Ava. It wasn't her fault he couldn't remember. And he still worried about pressuring her into the mating ritual. Though it would make him stronger, it could weaken her, and that was the last thing he wanted.

The fear of losing her was his biggest weakness.

Ava fell asleep on his shoulder just as they reached the Ringstraße. The days of scattershot travel around the continent had worn her out. He was tired as well, but he'd not be able to relax until he had his mate safe and was reassured that no harm would come to him while he rested. Their unpredictable travel had allowed them to remain anonymous for weeks. But now they were in Vienna. It was a spiderweb of politics, and a man only had to touch one wrong thread to attract dangerous attention from the wrong eyes.

THE SECRET

THE next morning, they were lying in bed and Malachi was dozing in the grey dawn. The flat Rhys had let for them was small and tucked into a quiet corner of the neighborhood, away from the more lively restaurants and bars. He'd heard the crowds when he helped Ava to bed the night before, but the noise died down quickly. That morning, the only sounds that met his ears were the street sweepers and dog walkers below. The smell of coffee and bread drifted on the air, and his mate was curled safely into his side.

He was as content as he could be. Malachi had no idea whether Ava had traveled to Vienna before. She seemed to speak of more rural locations than urban, which would make sense with her previous inability to avoid the voices of the humans around her. As he lay there, smelling the bread and roasting beans from the *kaffeehaus* down the street, a few pleasant childhood memories intruded.

The first visit with his father to the Library where the elders met, the gallery above crowded as scribes clustered to observe the quiet work of their elders below. A tour of the archives that held the wealth of Irin history within its plain walls. Hearing his mother sing a story at the house of a friend, the walls echoing with laughter.

His mother had loved Vienna.

Perhaps they would have a few days to explore before Damien and Sari drew them into political maneuverings.

Probably not.

"Malachi?" Ava whispered.

"Hmmm?"

"Are you awake?"

"A little."

Ava's body didn't know what time it was. She'd woken after midnight, greedy for him. They'd made love with quiet intensity. She'd muffled her cries of pleasure in his shoulder, then fallen quickly back to sleep with his scent on her skin.

"I was thinking."

Malachi twisted a strand of hair around his finger. "Tell me, *canim*."

"I can't stop thinking about my grandmother."

It was the first time she'd mentioned it since France. Malachi had tried not to bring it up. He'd come to learn she needed her silence. She'd speak to him when she was ready.

"What are you thinking about?"

She took a deep breath. "Seeing her was like a vision of all my worst fears made real."

Her power still frightened her. Ava had spent the majority of her life fearing her own mind, constantly questioning her perceptions. If she was ever to fully access her power, she would have to accept it, but accepting it meant not hiding from the darkness inherent in her nature.

Malachi had to remind himself how young she was. When he was her age, he was still in the middle of his training, the reality of battle years away. Ava had been picked up and thrown into a war that had been raging for centuries, and she'd lost the first battle when her mate had been killed. Both of them were still recovering.

"Your grandmother's mind was broken by violence," he said. "And by a continued violation she has no way of stopping." He put a palm to her temple. "You never have to fear that. The only one allowed in your dreams is me."

"Volund could get in."

"I don't think he could."

She rolled toward him. "If Jaron wasn't shielding me—"

"But he is." He kissed her forehead and whispered, "We will find a way to free her, Ava. Volund is powerful, but so is Jaron. There must be a way. And we'll find it."

She blinked away the shine in her eyes. "But his evil is still in me. And it'll never go away. I have his blood."

He knew a lifetime of fear couldn't be washed clean in a single year or with a single revelation. They were both works in progress.

"Do you remember our dream on the plane?"

"Of Istanbul?"

He nodded.

"Yes."

"That was your magic touching mine. Healing me. And there was nothing evil about that. That was beautiful."

"But—"

"I'm not saying you're all sweetness and light." He smiled when she narrowed her eyes. "I wouldn't want you to be. And you *are* Jaron's grand-daughter."

He saw her shoulders tense, but he continued. "I do not fear it. Nor should you."

"Why not?"

"You hold power. And soon, you'll learn to claim it. Control it." The corner of his mouth turned up. "This city has not seen your like before."

A quiet knock came at the door.

Malachi brushed a hand along the *talesm* at his wrist and opened his senses. His ears recognized the familiar step. There was the scent of coffee and flour. And the irritated murmur when hot liquid spilled on skin.

"Get dressed. Rhys is here."

"Bossy." She rolled over and huddled under the covers. "I'm tired."

"That's because someone decided to be insatiable last night just when I was trying to get to sleep." He winked at her.

She threw a pillow at him and he laughed.

"Go back to sleep if you wish. We can go out for breakfast."

She peeked from under the covers. "You sure you don't mind? I just… don't feel like seeing anyone. Not yet."

"It's fine." He smiled. "We won't go far. Don't leave the apartment."

RHYS muttered the entire way to the coffeehouse a block away.

"Don't know why I bothered bringing you an espresso—"

"Rhys, you brought me Starbucks." Malachi shook his head disap-provingly. "What were you thinking?"

"It's perfectly good coffee, and there's one right downstairs from my flat?"

"We're in Vienna." He pulled open the wood-and-brass door and the happy scent of roasted coffee, sugar, and flour assaulted him. "If I have to put up with the politics, I should at least take advantage of the coffee."

"Anything is better than that mud you make at home."

The waiter looked up from his newspaper and nodded toward a table in the corner. Malachi and Rhys both unwrapped their scarves and coats to hang them by the door. Winter had come with a vengeance, and icy wind bit his cheeks. A few flurries of snow had dusted the sidewalk the night before, but he had a feeling they wouldn't last.

"Why did I leave Istanbul?" Rhys asked.

"If it's hot, you complain about that. If it's cold, you complain about that." Malachi settled onto the leather-wrapped bench and shook out a paper someone had left nearby. "Is there any weather you do like?"

"England."

Malachi frowned. "Really?"

"In the spring."

"When the flowers are blooming, or do those give you sneezing fits?"

"Ha-ha."

"I'd forgotten how amusing your snits could be."

"You've forgotten pretty much everything about me, old friend." Rhys's eyes were sharp on his face. "Has that changed?"

"Some." Malachi leaned forward, glancing around the wood-paneled restaurant. "Is this place—?"

"It's friendly." Rhys nodded at an older gentleman who sat across the room sipping a cup. "It's owned by one of us."

"The waiter is human."

"But discreet and lacking in curiosity. Excellent qualities in a human, I've always found."

Rhys paused to give his order to the man. Malachi did the same.

"Now," he continued, "what has changed?"

"My *talesm* have returned to"—he leaned back and motioned halfway across his right pectoral muscle—"about here. A few more are scattered down my arm. And as my *talesm* have returned, I've recovered more memory."

Rhys's face was pale. "So you know about—"

"The badger prank was your idea, not mine. I cannot believe you tried to let me take the blame."

Rhys was affronted. "It was not! And if you hadn't started laughing, we would have got away with it."

"We were right little demons at school, weren't we?"

Rhys burst into laughter, and Malachi couldn't help but grin.

"We were," Rhys said. "Our poor mothers."

"It's amazing we survived to adulthood."

His old friend paused. "Your family marks?"

"No."

"I'm sorry, brother."

The tattoos his father had given him when he reached the age of thirteen hadn't reappeared. While they gave Malachi little power, they were part of his identity. A way of marking his lineage, given to him by his father. Because he'd not scribed them himself, he had no idea if they would ever return.

"It will be as it is meant," Malachi said. "I'm blessed that any have returned at all."

"Ava?"

"She sings to me. She heals me."

Rhys shook his head slowly. "Lucky bastard."

"I am." He lowered his voice again. "Has Max told you—"

"About the Grigora?" His smile fell. "He called everyone to Damien and Sari's as soon as he and Renata got into town. I'm still trying to understand how we could have missed something as big as this."

"They prefer to be called *kareshta*. Silent ones."

"Silent ones?" Rhys asked.

"Those who survived had to be."

Rhys slowly shook his head. "All these years, Malachi. How many have suffered? How many have been killed? They were the Fallen's first victims, and we knew nothing."

"How were we to know?"

"How could we *not*? It seems so obvious now. The Forgiven fathered daughters, why wouldn't the Fallen?"

"The stories only ever speak of male hunters. That's all we were ever taught."

Rhys was incredulous, barely noticing the human waiter who was back with their coffees and two glasses of water, along with a couple of small pastries.

"And we shouldn't have known better?" he asked. "Asked more questions? Our own scrolls speak of the mighty *men* of ancient times. Heroes, not heroines. And yet we know that the Irina were always there." Rhys leaned forward with bright eyes. "And I believe the early singers were with the scribes in battle as well. The Dacia manuscript—"

"This sounds like an academic argument I'm completely unprepared to have with you."

Rhys paused, his mouth likely ready to launch into an explanation of some ancient language interpretation Malachi had no interest in.

"That's… probably true," Rhys admitted. "But it may be relevant to the Irina problem."

"Can we stop calling them a problem?"

The corner of Rhys's mouth turned up. "Oh, I think they rather like being problematic. And you know where Orsala and Sari are going to fall on the Grigora—*kareshta* question, don't you?"

"Probably where Ava is."

"She *is* one, you know."

"She's part *kareshta*. It's…" He hesitated. It wasn't his story to tell. "It's complicated. You need to ask Ava."

Rhys's curiosity had clearly been sparked. "I will. Can I assume she also anticipates a large family reunion? Welcoming the *kareshta* into the arms of their Irin sisters?"

"She's more cautious than that. You have to remember, Ava has been in their place. She had no idea she was anything but human, and she had no control the way our women have. She thought she was insane, and I'm guessing more than one of the Grigori females is in the same situation. She sympathizes with them, but I think she's also more realistic about how damaged or dangerous some of them might be."

Rhys shook his head. "The main question is, can they be trusted? If what Max said is true, then any with living fathers can be tracked by the Fallen who sired them. They have no free will unless their sires are dead. We have to consider them security risks as well as victims."

"All the more reason to shift focus," Malachi said quietly.

Rhys glanced over his shoulder. "Are you saying what I think?"

"We must start going after the Fallen, not just the Grigori."

"A monumentally more difficult task," Rhys said. "And not one that will be popular with the council."

"Rhys." Malachi fought to explain. "The Grigori we met in Sofia—the ones Max has come to a truce with—they're not like the others. They're… more like us. Yes, they are wilder. Untrained. Hungry. But not mindless drones. With their sires dead, they had free will. They were struggling to control themselves, but they were *trying*."

"Not unlike the Irin now."

Malachi frowned. "What do you mean?"

"Surely you can see the parallels," he said, taking a sip of coffee. "We've been without widespread Irina influence for only two hundred years, and where are we as a society? Declining. Touch-hungry. More and more aggressive. We're completely out of balance. We need…" Rhys's voice grew rough. "Our race is dying without the Irina, and not just because so few children are born."

"Then we bring them back. On their terms, not because of some compulsion act dreamed up by old men. And we work to save the women we can, even if that means fighting with the council."

"You're ready for this fight."

"Yes."

Rhys smiled ruefully. "You're almost panting for it."

"And what if I am?"

"Yes." He drained his coffee. "You definitely seem more like yourself."

Chapter Fourteen

"WELCOME TO VIENNA," Ava whispered to her reflection. "Your father is an angelic bastard. Your grandmother was driven insane by the angel who raped her. Your great-grandfather is an archangel who kills things for you as tokens of his twisted affection. And somewhere in the middle of this, you mated a four-hundred-year-old man with amnesia."

She blinked and looked at the cat that had wandered into the apartment when she opened the door to its meow.

"How is this my life?"

The black feline only blinked guileless gold eyes.

"Do you come with the apartment?"

It gave a scratchy growl and jumped down from the dressing table where Ava had been brushing out her hair. It was clean and seemed well fed. She thought it must belong to someone in the building. As long as it didn't trash her stuff, she was fine with him hanging out. She liked cats and dogs; she just couldn't keep one herself because she traveled too much.

Ava sighed as she turned back to the mirror. She needed a haircut badly. And a pedicure. A massage would be a good idea, along with her regular medical checkups. She had a bunch of vaccinations that needed updating, and she felt like she'd put off the regular business of life for way too long.

She checked her phone. No e-mails from her mother or father, but one from Luis, asking how her grandmother was. Ava hoped he didn't feel like he needed to be chatty with her now because she was engaged to the guy who'd threatened his life.

That would be awkward. And frankly a little disturbing.

She shot him back a quick response and checked her calendar, only to realize she had a job coming up. In fact, it was a job she'd booked eighteen months in advance, right before she'd taken the assignment in Cyprus that eventually led her to Istanbul. She remembered it because she felt like the magazine was being overly cautious, booking her so far in advance to cover their summer beach spread for the next year.

Now the shoot was approaching and Ava had some decisions to make. She still had three months before she needed to be on location, but she couldn't cancel any later than six weeks out and not seriously piss them off.

She also realized that she and Malachi had officially been reunited longer than they'd originally been together in Turkey. She didn't know why that seemed significant, but it did.

She heard the key turn in the lock.

"Ava?"

"In the bedroom."

"Why do we have… a cat?"

"He wandered in," she said as Malachi entered the bedroom. "Seemed nice enough. Probably belongs to a neighbor." He leaned down to brush a kiss across her temple and flopped on the bed, only to have the cat jump up and sit on his abdomen.

"I don't think it likes me."

"Well, you are in his bed."

"I'm fairly sure we're the ones renting it."

"That reminds me, I need to get some money transferred to Rhys to pay him back."

He frowned. "Or don't, because the scribe house is covering it."

"Or let me do it, since I'm not worried about my budget? The house resources are probably strapped with the reconstruction."

"Ava, you don't need to do that."

She spun around in her seat. "Is this going to be a macho alpha-male problem for you?"

"Am I a macho alpha-male?"

"Yes. And I'm loaded. It makes more sense to let me—or let's be honest, my asshole of a father—cover the bill for stuff like this. It's a better use of resources. Besides, I'd probably be paying for a hotel and a guide—possibly a bodyguard—if I were traveling on my own."

He propped up on his elbows, his lips twitching. "Are you saying I'm your bodyguard and guide?"

"No." Her face reddened.

"Because I am very fond of your body. So guarding it isn't a problem."

"I'm just trying to help."

Now he was grinning. "You don't have to pay me though."

"Shut up!"

Malachi scooted off the bed and got on his knees, shuffling over to her as she sat at the dressing table. The cat gave an irritated yowl and abandoned the room. The stool she sat on was low enough that Malachi was level with her when he wrapped his arms around her waist from behind. She could see him laughing in the mirror.

"Am I your kept man, *canm?*"

"If you are, I feel like a lot more breakfast in bed should be happening."

"Mmmm." His lips trailed along her neck. "Now I feel this pressure to earn my keep."

"Coffee in bed, at least."

It was getting harder and harder to concentrate. The traitor cat had completely abandoned her. She should probably be getting ready for… something.

But he was playing with her. Teasing her. More and more of his personality was coming back. His humor. His bravado.

Ava fell in love all over again every time she turned around.

"All right, you've convinced me. I will take the job as your kept man. So…" He lifted her in his arms and turned to the bed. "Now it is time for work."

TWO very work-filled hours later, they met the others in the back room of a coffeehouse off Bäckerstraße. It was dark and smoky in the front room, the walls plastered with movie posters and flyers for avant-garde art exhibitions, but the small back room was bright and clean. The smell of coffee, beer, and sausages filled the midday air.

And Ava's friends, both scribes and singers, filled the room.

Suddenly she was fighting back tears.

Orsala sat in quiet conversation with a nodding Rhys. Mala was signing to both Leo and Sari, who was holding Damien's hand as he read from a tablet computer with a frown on his face. Max and Renata were there, even though both were pointedly ignoring the other by checking their phones.

Malachi unwrapped his scarf and hung it with the others tossed over a bench near the door.

"Ava, give me your coat and I'll—what's wrong?"

She turned, smiling. "Nothing is wrong. Sorry. Happy tears, babe." Her hands went to his cheeks. He'd let his beard start to grow, and she was getting used to it. It suited him. "You're coming back to me. And everyone is here. I feel like I've lived with this knot of fear in my stomach for months now, but I just… I know it's going to be okay. Somehow, it's all going to be okay if everyone is here."

He held on to her wrists and squeezed them as she smiled.

"I love you," he whispered, and Ava realized the whole room had gone silent.

She turned, and everyone was smiling at her.

"Hello, Ava." Sari stood and opened her arms. "It's good to see you, sister."

Sister.

Ava would only admit it to herself, but part of her had wondered whether the Irina would treat her differently now that they knew her blood was from the Fallen. She should have known better. Orsala embraced her. Mala pinched her bicep in mock disapproval. And Ava knew without a doubt that Karen would still bake her too many cakes and Astrid would still share a self-deprecating joke to break the tension.

They were her sisters. For the first time, her heart was light enough to enjoy it.

Malachi had his hand on the small of her back, guiding her to a chair near Damien, who looked up, tension plastered over his brow. Sari squeezed his hand, and he lifted her knuckles to his mouth, the easy affection between them another wound healed over in Ava's heart.

They looked like love to Ava. Tested. Broken. Mended. Faithful. Forgiven. She didn't know everything they had lived through, but if Damien and Sari could recover from it, she was certain she and Malachi had a better-than-average chance.

"What's wrong?" Sari asked.

"Anurak has rejected my request for a meeting."

Sari looked shocked. "What? But he's been vocal about the reformation of the Irina council."

"I know. Perhaps he's feeling pressure—"

"If Anurak is the same scribe I once knew," Orsala said, "he's grown tired of *talk*. He's a taciturn man by nature, and I doubt he wants debate. I have a feeling he and many other older scribes simply want the Irina to step forward and claim their role in the Library."

"The Library?" Ava whispered to Malachi.

"The Elder Council meets in the Library. It's symbolic but also practical, as their primary job is interpreting Irin scripture and history and using those interpretations to resolve disputes."

"Where did the singers meet?"

"The same place. There are fourteen desks. Seven have been empty since the Irina elders fled after the Rending."

"A library?"

He shrugged. "It's a very *big* library."

"I thought I heard something about council chambers."

"I believe it is not unlike your court system. All the elders have their own offices and staff, but the actual decisions are made in the Library."

Well, Ava supposed there were worse places to run an entire society.

"But wouldn't meeting in a library favor the scribes?" she asked. "I mean, they're all supposed to be equal, right? Seven scribes and seven singers. But that's kind of a scribe thing, right? Written magic?"

Malachi frowned. "I don't understand."

"I mean, doesn't running the Irin world from a library mean the Irina are at a… tactical disadvantage?"

"No." He was shaking his head. "Irin scribes *must* be in the Library. That is where we draw our strength. But Irina…" Malachi smiled. "Irina singers *are* the library."

Oh. Well, that was cool.

Damien looked up with a rueful expression. "They can be quite superior about it."

Orsala chided him. "Just because you males are forced to rely on books and scrolls doesn't make your magic less powerful, Damien."

The watcher gave her an affectionate smile before he turned his attention to Ava. "It did create a rather major problem when the Irina elders went into hiding, though. While they could take copies of our scriptures with them as references, we had no access to Irina knowledge. It's one of the reasons there's been so much division since the Rending."

"I think Anurak is right," Sari said. "We need to stop debating. Irina elders should just walk in and take their place at their desks. No more debate. No more talk of compulsion. We'd have a voice on the council, and no one would be able to question it."

Mala shook her head and began signing. Sari translated as she signed.

"They would question anything not supported by the wives," Mala signed. "Sari and her supporters are not the only Irina in the city now. Whatever elder singers take their place in the Library must have legitimacy among all the Irina—even if there is dissent—or we lose all rights to challenge the elder scribes."

Max said, "I agree."

"So do I," Orsala said. "The problem is how we can elect our own elders when we're still so scattered."

"How are the elders chosen?" Ava asked. "I know they're chosen by the watchers of the scribe houses, but it's got to be more specific than that. I mean, we're talking about the whole world, right?"

Malachi put an arm around her shoulders. "One from each continent, for the most part. And then one seat that changes depending on population."

"So one from North America and one from South," Rhys said. "One elder from Africa. One from Europe. One from Eurasia—that one is up for debate every single election—and one from Eastern Asia and the Pacific region. That's six, and then when the seventh seat comes up for election every seventy years, it's decided based on population. Right now, there is an additional European elder on the scribe council, but the time before that, there were more scribes in Asia. It changes over time."

Sari said, "And the Irina are basically the same, but we tend to have different population concentrations. Our seventh seat has more often come from Africa or Asia."

"Okay, I get that it's complicated," Ava said. "But Sari, didn't you say the havens are mostly connected online?"

"We all have e-mail, of course."

"So…" She held up her smartphone. "Have elections online. Do it over the Internet."

"Online elections for elders?"

Max leaned forward, smiling. "You know, Ava has a good point. Human revolutions are fueled by social networks now. Don't you think the Irina could organize their own revolution on the Internet?"

Damien and Sari exchanged a look that told Ava they'd be talking more about it later. Yeah, so it kinda made her feel like a kid at the grown-ups table, but she had to remind herself that to these people she *was* a kid.

"Hey," she whispered to Malachi. "When are Irin considered adults?"

He was following what looked to be a quiet argument between Sari and Mala. "Full adults? Around sixty to seventy-five years. When we're finished with our training. Why?"

She flushed. Wow.

"So, you're quite the cradle robber, aren't you?"

Malachi turned to her abruptly. "What? No, I'm not."

"I'm not even thirty. That's like… a teenager to you guys."

She could see the flush crawl up his neck, even behind the beard. "You're human. You mature differently."

"But I'm *not* really human."

His shoulders were stiff and his posture screamed his discomfort. It was really a shame that Ava found teasing him to be so amusing.

"I mean, what would your mom say if she found out you were mated—and I mean well and thoroughly *mated*—to what she would basically consider a kid?"

He wiped a hand over his forehead. "Heaven above, please stop talking."

"So are we going to stop fooling around now?"

He groaned. "Ava."

"I'm just yanking your chain."

"You're going to have to speak up, because the mental lecture my mother's memory is giving me right now is rather loud."

She bit her lip so she didn't burst into laughter. "Malachi?"

"What?"

"Have you ever heard of Irin teenagers finding their mate before they're adults?"

"No."

"So, even though I'm young in your world, I'm thinking the universe decided I was an adult a while back."

He squeezed her hand and said, "I hate you a little right now. You know that, right?"

"The *kareshta*," Damien said after they'd eaten together.

Everyone turned to Ava.

"Hey, I don't have any inside information," she said quietly. She wasn't ready to share her grandmother's story. She'd talked to Malachi about it, and they'd both decided that until it became important, it wasn't something everyone needed to know.

"Did you find your grandmother?" Orsala asked.

"I did."

"And?"

"She's *kareshta*," Ava said as Malachi took her hand. "Jaron is her sire. She's his only daughter."

Renata said, "That's why he's taken an interest in you."

"Yes."

Leo asked, "Can he track you? Like Max said the other Fallen can track their children?"

"Yes," Malachi said. "But I want to point out he has tracked Ava from the beginning, and she's come to no harm from him. In fact, he's protected her more than once. Jaron's motivations are still murky—"

Orsala's eyes narrowed on Ava's mate as if she could sense the lie.

"—but for now, I do not believe he's a threat."

Rhys asked, "When do we tell the elders about them?"

Damien said, "When we know they're protected."

"You don't think the elders would try to harm them?" Rhys said. "Why—"

"We don't know how they'll react," the watcher said.

Max added, "And I told Kostas we would keep his secret. No place is more of a hotbed for gossip than this city. There are spies everywhere. I want to be cautious."

Malachi nodded. "And let's be honest. Not all the elder scribes want the singers to return. They like wielding total control over the council. If the *kareshta* are taken in by the Irina, that could make them more powerful. They're first generation blood. If they were trained—"

"Ava is second generation," Mala signed as Orsala translated. "And we've all seen how powerful she is."

"She's also mated to a scribe," Sari said. "That focuses our power. The *kareshta* have no focus. The Grigori are their brothers; they have no mates."

"But they could," Leo said quietly. He looked around the room. "I'm not the only scribe who will think of this. I don't want to be selfish, but there are so few Irina." He paused and a red flush stained the giant's cheeks. "Ava and Malachi are mated. We know it's possible. To those of us without mates, the existence of these women offers us some hope that our *reshon* could be out there. That we will not always walk alone. Malachi is right. Many Irin may worry. But many will be motivated to help for that reason alone."

Mala put a hand on his shoulder and squeezed.

Damien said, "That's not selfish, Leo. When I look at Ava and Malachi, I see nothing one-sided about their relationship." Damien gave her a small smile. "We all need a place to belong."

"But we have to be cautious," Renata said. "These women have been lost for generations. Many died as infants or were discarded by the fathers who should have protected them. I think we all have the desire to help them, but they could also be a threat."

"I agree," Orsala said. "We need more information. I'm going to look in the archives, but right now Sari should focus on organizing elections and reaching out to the Irina in the city."

"The pro-compulsion sympathizers?" Sari scoffed.

"Yes." Orsala's tone brooked no argument. "Remember, some of those women you ridicule lost their children during the Rending. While you see compulsion, they see protection. Loss is a powerful motivator. Don't dismiss it. Or them."

Ava said, "I can help. I think. At least with the computer part. The organization."

"Thank you, Ava."

"And us?" Malachi asked his watcher.

"I want you to come with me to the Library this week," Damien said. "I know you don't have all your memories, but I need a new perspective. Rhys, I have a different project for you. Can you start looking through the police statistics here in the city?"

"Of course," Rhys said. "What am I looking for?"

"I don't buy that the Grigori have been absent from Vienna for generations," Damien said. "Though it makes the elder scribes look very good if any trace of attacks are silenced. We need to know the truth. Can you look in the human records?"

"Easily."

"Leo and me?" Max asked.

"I want you around the city. Keep your eyes out and tell me what you see. I want to know who has people here. Which elders have more than the average number of staff. Who's traveling lately and where."

"What do you suspect?" Leo asked.

"I'm not sure yet," Damien said with a frown. "For now, we should simply be cautious."

Sari said, "Mala and Renata, you can help with that, along with gathering information on the Irina who have showed up in the city. I want to know who is here and what their connections are. Are they mated? Do they have families? Where do their loyalties lie?"

"Of course," Renata said. "Consider it done."

THE second time Death visited her, Ava wasn't as surprised. She sat up in bed when she heard him, rustling in the shadows of the room. The angel leaned forward, his black cloak falling from his head and his silver eyes piercing the darkness.

"You were talking about my grandmother before, weren't you? When you said you couldn't go to her."

He nodded.

"Why not?"

No answer, but the silver grey of the angel's eyes grew darker, like storm clouds gathering.

"It's not up to you, is it?"

Come with me.

"More secrets?"

Humor lit his face. She glanced down at Malachi, then slid out of bed.

Death embraced her again and she allowed it, sinking into his arms as he covered her with his star-filled cloak. In a heartbeat, they were sitting in a brightly lit hall. Ava couldn't decide if it was a church or a library. The walls were covered in tall bookcases, but the windows were filled with brilliantly colored stained glass. The whole room had a weight of holiness she couldn't dismiss. Church or library?

Both.

Death kept her shrouded as the room coalesced around them. Once again, there were muffled voices that came from a distance, as if she were eavesdropping in a hallway. Shadows became visible and formed in the room. It was Volund again, Ava now had the taste of his power from her grandmother's memories, and she struggled to control her immediate nausea.

"…tell your children to eliminate the threat."

"I am not one to waste my sons on foolish gambles. Didn't Oslo teach you anything?"

"It taught me that any with human blood are expendable."

A long pause.

"Are you sure of that, brother?"

A hissing sound, then a grunt in reply.

"Do not make the mistake of thinking we are equals, Svarog."

"You may be assured I do not."

Ava could tell by the tone of his voice that whoever Svarog was, he didn't think Volund was superior.

"The heretic has spies everywhere," a third voice hissed. "Even among our own people. More and more are listening to him. We must send a message. Once the city falls into our hands, any thought of rebellion will be quashed."

"And Vienna will be yours," Volund said.

"Yes," the one called Svarog replied. "That is our arrangement."

Ava could tell the angel wasn't one hundred percent certain of it, though.

"Grimold, are your children ready?"

"Yes. *All* of them."

"All?" She thought it was Svarog who spoke.

"All. If there are singers with them, they will not be a problem."

She tried to repeat the details to herself, knowing her memory of dreams could be sketchy. Volund and his allies seemed to be in some kind of strategy meeting, and Ava knew the information would be valuable to Malachi and Damien.

But the scene was too hazy. The figures never truly took shape. Ava only had a vague impression of them and their relative power. Two greater powers with a third attached to Volund. The voices faded in and out.

"Will I remember this?" she asked Death.

When you need to.

She sighed. "I love answers like that."

"Eliminate them and make it clear who killed them," Volund said. "It is past time that your allegiance became known. Unless you have something to hide, Svarog."

"Becoming your ally doesn't mean you are privy to my secrets. I do not trust you."

"Nor I you."

A slight pause before Svarog said, "Then we are agreed. I will take care of the heretic. Have you found her yet?"

"It is more than Jaron guarding her. There can be no other explanation."

"Another, then. She is more of a problem than we anticipated."

Ava turned to her angelic shadow and asked, "Are they talking about me or—?"

Before she could finish her sentence, Death enfolded her in his cloak and she was back in her bedroom, sitting next to Malachi who murmured once, then rolled toward her in sleep, pressing his face to her belly and wrapping his arms around her waist.

Death turned his back to Ava and walked back toward the shadows.

"Azril?"

He stopped.

"That's your name, isn't it?"

He slowly turned. Nodded.

"Why?"

His shining eyes moved from Ava to Malachi, then back again.

You are beautiful together. She would want to see such beauty.

When Ava blinked, he was gone.

Chapter Fifteen

THE NEXT MORNING, MALACHI dragged himself out of bed when he heard the sound of carriages clopping down the street nearby.

Ava's sleepy voice stopped him. "Babe?"

"I'm going to the Library, *canim*."

She burrowed farther. "So early. Wanted to talk to you about…"

"Ava?" He smiled when he realized she'd drifted back to sleep.

"I'm awake. Kinda. Funny dream. Why so early?"

"We have to go through the cleansing ritual first."

"Explain later, okay?

"I will." He brushed a kiss over her temple, then started toward the door. "You're with Sari today?"

"Mmhmm. Love you. See you tonight. I'll tell you then, okay?"

"Okay."

Malachi closed the door softly and paused, his palm pressed to the wood.

It was a little thing. The sleepy greeting. The recitation of the day's activities and the kiss good-bye.

Love you. See you tonight.

A simple thing. Infinitely precious.

And precarious.

Even with his memories returning, his world had never felt more uncertain. Fallen angels played with mortal lives as if they were pawns on a chess board, and an insidious threat lived in his mate's own blood.

Volund could find her anywhere.

Malachi hadn't had another dream since Italy. He was half-convinced they'd been nightmares of his own making. He hadn't told Ava. Every time he decided to share it with her, it seemed another problem or revelation came their way.

He leaned his head against the doorway and fervently prayed for the privilege of years. Years he'd be able to kiss her good-bye and come home to her at night. A lifetime of routines they would build. Everyday intimacies they would share.

Please.

Is a thousand years too much to ask?

For now… give me one.

His soul cried the unspeakable name of the one who had returned him to the mortal plane. He felt the yearning pull at his chest as the door opened. Then she was there, pressing a kiss over his heart. She leaned her forehead against his collar, wrapped her arms around his waist. She said nothing, but he knew she'd heard his voice. Her touch bolstered him; he grew taller under her small hands.

"I could hear you," she said. "Woke me up."

"I'm sorry."

"Don't be."

"I love you." He squeezed her tightly. "I'll see you tonight."

"I'll be here."

She stepped away from him and took a deep breath. "Coffee?"

"I'll get some with Damien on our way. I think he's probably waiting."

"Okay." She smiled, then cocked her head toward the door. "Really?"

"What?"

"You can't hear him?" She unlocked the hallway door and cracked it open, only to see the black cat from the other day slip in. He went to the kitchen and hopped up on the window ledge, staring out into the street.

Malachi shook his head. "We're not keeping him."

"That's so weird. Why would his owner even let him out so early? He doesn't look like a stray." She yawned and went to the kettle to heat water.

"Getting a cat through quarantine is a nightmare. If you truly want one, we'll find one when we get home."

"It's fine, babe. I won't get attached."

The "babe" thing she'd started had annoyed him at first, considering he was roughly three hundred and seventy-five years older than she was. Then… it didn't. It was Ava. His human-Irina-Grigora mate who called him ridiculous things like "babe" and said the word "dude" in actual conversation.

Maybe it was a California thing. He didn't care.

Heading toward the door with a smile, he called out, "I'll see you tonight."

"I'll… cook meatloaf or something."

Malachi turned. "Really?"

"No." She snickered. "I have no idea how to cook meatloaf."

"Chinese takeout it is."

"As much as I travel, Chinese takeout is my comfort food."

His eyes fixed on her.

"You have to go," she whispered.

"I don't want to."

A shy smile teased her lips. The cat growled at the window, pawing it before he looked over his shoulder.

"Go," Ava said. "The cat says Damien is here. Call me when you're done at the Library."

"The cat does not know that Damien is here." Still, he kissed her and walked out the door before he lingered any longer, walking down the stairs to find Damien waiting on the street, his breath frosting in the morning air.

He was looking up to the window of their flat. "Did you get a cat?"

"We're not keeping the cat."

"Huh. Coffee?"

"Please."

HE'D sated his craving for coffee, but Malachi's stomach was rumbling. He should have eaten a bigger meal the night before.

Hunger would have to wait. Liquids were permitted before the cleansing ritual but not food. The satchel over his shoulder held the linen wrap he'd wear, along with his ceremonial robe. They had both been in storage in Istanbul. Rhys had retrieved them before he came to the city. While scribe houses were more informal, Vienna was not. If he and Damien were to be permitted entrance to the Library, they would have to visit the cleansing rooms attached and enter in ceremonial garb.

"You've been doing this every day?" he asked his watcher.

Damien nodded as he drained his coffee cup. "Almost. I've managed to be granted audience with Konrad—whom my brother-in-law works for—and Kibwe. But both are already traditionalists in favor of restoring the Irina council. I need to speak with Anurak and Rafael. They're the swing votes. Currently, there are three elders who are openly in favor of compulsion."

The whole concept irritated Malachi. "Do they actually think they can force the Irina into retreats again? They don't have any control over them."

"No, but they have control over their mates. Other than a few deserters, the Irina in hiding are mated to active scribes who owe their own allegiance to the council. For the past two hundred years, the council has asked no questions when a scribe has left his post for a time—even if it's for years—"

"Somebody has to raise children if our race is going to survive. I can count on one hand the number of scribes I've known who've had children in the past two hundred years."

"Exactly. They've ignored it when a scribe has left his post when his mate was with child. Asked no questions. But what will happen to those mates if compulsion becomes law? They can make an issue of scribes leaving their posts if they want to. If the Irina they're mated to is not in a retreat."

"It's madness."

"It's control wearing the mantle of security. And some on the council are obsessed with it."

Malachi walked in silence, entering the maze of the palace complex along with myriad other workers and suited men as they made their way into the tangled streets and the network of passageways that made up the Hofburg Palace.

THE SECRET

Massive buildings of every design—Gothic, Baroque, and Classical—surrounded them as he and Damien moved among the working population of the palace. Over five thousand humans worked in the Hofburg complex, janitors and tour guides, clerks and government officials. It was the perfect hiding place for the Irin Library, and some version of the council had resided here for over five hundred years after having made a secret pact with the Hapsburgs. The empire had been lost, but the Irin had remained hidden with the help of their gold, influence, and magic.

Malachi knew that many of the suited men making their way into the government buildings wore *talesm* under their dress shirts. As a center of commerce, culture, and international intelligence, Vienna was the perfect seat of Irin power.

Damien knocked on an intricately carved wooden door hidden in the corner of a small courtyard. A buzzing sound followed and they pushed it open, only to be met by two scribes who were obviously part of the Library Guard. They wore suits and earpieces Rhys would be jealous of. They nodded to Damien with familiarity but still searched both their bags. Malachi turned in the pair of silver daggers he carried and received a receipt to retrieve them at the end of his business.

Damien was smiling when Malachi finally joined him.

"What?"

"You have caught the Guard's attention. They don't often see scribes carrying weapons here."

The Library Guard was one of the most prestigious postings a warrior could have, but it was also one of the least dangerous.

Malachi grunted. "Then they are complacent."

"Don't underestimate them."

The ground floor housed the cleansing rooms. Malachi breathed deeply of the steam and smoke when they stepped through the door. His heart swelled with longing. It had been too long since he'd been able to truly pray. While the political maneuvering was not how he would wish to spend his day, the ritual of the bath was welcome.

Stripping off his street clothes, he entered the chamber.

The bath's marble walls were carved with centuries of protective spells. Words dark with age. He could hear low prayers chanted from the

181

far room as scribes who had already cleansed their bodies cleared their minds of earthly cares.

Malachi walked into the pool and took a deep breath before he immersed himself. Warmth, light, and love. Held in the water's embrace, he felt another door open in his mind.

"Like this?"

"Evet, oğul. Just like that, Malachi."

Water sluiced over his small body as his father hummed a song his mother had taught him.

"You have taken your first marks. Every year, we will do this now. To give thanks."

"Every year?"

"It is tradition. Tradition is important."

Whispers drifted in the water, and there came a flash of light behind closed eyes.

Malachi floated.

Songs in the air.

A vivid sky cut with beams of gold light. Crystal waters and presence.

Holy and wholly.

His body feels no pain. His soul, no struggle. Body and soul are one. Complete joy. Complete peace.

Love surrounds him. Perfect love.

He cries with joy because he is home.

"Son."

He is there. He is eternal.

This is what they long for.

Who would not long for this?

He is surrounded by love. Complete. Replete.

He needs nothing.

"She calls you," a familiar voice whispers.

He hears.

Longing.

Need.

He chooses.

And like the angels before him, he falls.

Malachi rose with a gasp and lifted his eyes to see the carved marble and stone encasing him.

His body ached, his flesh a prison he'd never felt before.

In the space of a single breath, in the thin line between the present and eternity, Malachi remembered heaven.

He had danced in the presence of the angels. Welcomed as a beloved son.

"Vashama canem, reshon."

He had come back for her.

But until that moment, Malachi hadn't remembered what he'd given up to return.

He didn't sense the tears on his face until Damien reached him.

"Brother?"

"I'm fine." He wiped his eyes and dipped in the water again, brushing the wet hair back from his face and pulling the water from his beard. "I'm fine, Damien."

His watcher held Malachi with his eyes. "Tell me."

Malachi shook his head. How could he explain?

"I was in the heavenly realm for months, brother." He wiped the water from his face and moved to exit the bath. "Some memories I wish I did not recover."

"But why?" Damien followed him, and the men dried themselves with the linen towels provided. Their wraps had been placed on marble benches near the entrance to the ritual room. "You must have seen things—"

"It was perfect beauty. Perfect peace," Malachi said quietly. "And I chose to give it up. It was my choice, and I'm glad of it. But at this moment, it hurts."

He held the towel to his face and sat on the marble bench, staring into the steaming pool where the memory of heaven had been given to him.

Why?

"Choose."

He'd chosen Ava. He would still choose her.

Perhaps this was the answer to his desperate prayer that morning. Perhaps it was only the assurance that, no matter what the future held for him and his beloved in the earthly realm, something even more beautiful waited for them should they fall.

"I think I'd pull down heaven if that's what it took to keep you here with me."

"And I'd abandon it if you weren't there."

The memory snapped into place next to his vision of heaven. He and Ava, lying in bed after they'd made love. A different kind of completion, but no less beautiful. His mate, a daughter of the Fallen. Malachi, the son of the Forgiven.

"We were meant to be like this. Two halves of the same soul. Dark and light together."

Their union was a reflection of the peace he'd seen. Holy and wholly.

And Malachi finally realized what Jaron truly wanted.

Forgiveness.

He wrapped himself in linen and entered the prayer room, kneeling before the sacred fire and giving up the remnants of his pain as thousands of others had done before him. He left his sorrow and regret there. Burned slips of prayers in the fire. He let his soul mourn for what it had given up, while it caught fire with the vision he'd seen.

He'd left the heavenly realm for a reason. He was Mikhael's son, and he'd returned to earth to battle for the soul of his people.

THE Irin Library was a palace of knowledge—every ritual, every rule serving a purpose that had something to do with its preservation. Malachi and Damien wore linen shifts and ceremonial robes that dated back thousands of years. The linen, pure and undyed, was worn because it would not react to the ancient scrolls or manuscripts the scribes preserved. Baths served a spiritual purpose but also cleansed the environment of any pollutants or molds that could harm the books.

The first time his father had brought him here, Malachi had been thirteen years old and on the precipice of starting his training. A child in awe of the ceremony and solemnity, he'd bathed with other boys his age from all over the world under the watchful eyes of their fathers, passing the traditions on to the next generation of scribes. He'd received his family marks only weeks before, the first tattoos that had signaled his passage from childhood to adolescence.

That morning, he'd seen no boys readying themselves in the ritual room with barely concealed excitement. No fathers introducing the next generation to the sacred fire. No awe-filled eyes as they climbed the wooden steps to the scribes' gallery above the Library floor.

His heart hurt.

Malachi and Damien climbed the stairs in silence.

Seven scribes worked diligently below the gallery, assistants fetching them books or pens or ink, depending on what they were doing. Some were copying manuscripts. Others made notes in careful handwriting as they studied manuscripts or scrolls with silk-gloved hands.

Whispers filled the gallery. Quiet negotiations between secretaries and petitioners. While the work the scribes did below was sacred in nature, the Library was a political theater. Damien and Malachi were only two men in dozens who were visiting the Library that morning, hoping for an audience with an elder. They presented their petitions on paper slips passed to the secretaries. Those secretaries examined the petitions and decided which ones would be passed down to the elder on the Library floor.

The singers' gallery, on the opposite side of the room, stood empty but for three silent figures standing at one end, watching the elder scribes working below.

"Who are they?" Malachi asked.

"The mates of three of the elders—Jerome, Edmund, and Rasesh. They're the only Irina I've seen in the Library since I've been here."

His mother had once stood there. Had once sung there, joined by the chorus of her sisters.

Now there were only three.

The women also wore ceremonial clothing. Long linen shifts and robes, high-necked to warm the voices that held their magic. Their hair was freshly washed and tied back in simple plaits or cut short and clean around their faces. One woman stood out to him as the obvious leader.

"Who is she?" Malachi murmured. "The woman with short hair."

"Jerome's mate."

"She's powerful." It wasn't a question. Old magic surrounded her.

"Constance is also the most outspoken Irina proponent of compulsion."

What would lead such a powerful singer to give up so much of her self-determination? And if she was as powerful as she seemed, why wasn't she on the floor of the Library herself? Though Constance's youthful features glowed from the magic of her longevity spells, Malachi could see she was a singer of age and experience simply by the way she carried herself.

"She reminds me of Orsala."

"They are contemporaries, from what I've heard, though she is a daughter of Rafael."

"A healer?"

"A powerful one."

They paused at the counter where the papers and inkwells resided to let Damien compose the petition he'd give to Rafael's secretary. Rafael was the current elder from South America and, according to Damien, one of the swing votes in the council.

Malachi looked down, realizing what seemed off. "Where are the other desks?"

When he'd been a boy, the seven desks of the Irina elders had been in the center of the Library under the magnificent dome painted with scenes from Irin history. Now only the scribes' desks were visible. Skirting the perimeter of the bookcases, the elders worked. But the center of the Library was empty.

"There." Damien pointed his chin to seven empty desks tucked into the corners of the Library. "They were moved when it became clear the Irina council had fled. Stay here." He went to deliver his petition into the soft hands of the bureaucrat standing near the stairs leading down to the floor of the gallery. Unless an audience was granted, no one but the elders and their assistants were allowed on the floor.

Malachi could see two scribes making their way down the stairs already. One headed for Jerome. The North American elder was waiting for him, pale hands resting softly on the polished desk. Malachi couldn't help but see smug self-satisfaction on the scribe's handsome face. He glanced at Constance, who watched her mate from the gallery above with an inscrutable expression.

THE SECRET

The other petitioner headed toward Anurak, the elder from Asia, who stood with a solemn expression and an outstretched hand.

The other elders continued their work, whether research, study, or manuscript transcription. Until their secretaries sent a petitioner to them, they would remain at their tasks. Quiet and solemn as political machinations twisted above.

It all looked so wrong. Malachi remembered thinking as a child that the Library floor looked like a star. The Irina desks in the center, radiating the singers' power out to the edges of the room where the solid desks of the scribes sat. That memory had been a dance of light and song. Had it only been a child's perception?

Damien returned to his side after delivering his petition to Rafael's secretary.

"Brother," Malachi said, "I have an idea."

"Oh?" Damien leaned against the railing and stared at the fresco on the ceiling. "Does it involve anything that will help pass the time? Because I've been staring at Leoc and Ariel's naked asses for more hours than I'd care to count in the past two weeks."

"Is there any way to make a call from here?"

"Of course. There are telephones in the hall outside."

"You want attention directed to the Irina problem, do you not?"

"Yes."

Malachi's eyes scanned the abandoned Irina desks along the edges of the room before they came back to Damien.

"Exactly how much attention would you like to attract?"

Chapter Sixteen

IT HAD BEEN YEARS since Ava had visited Vienna. At the time, she'd been on an assignment covering the numerous historic cemeteries in the city. She hadn't spent much time at the Hofburg other than when she passed through on the way to her hotel.

"What are we doing again?"

Sari flashed a grin at her. "Causing trouble."

"Oh, that sounds like a great idea."

Mala caught Ava's eyes and rolled her own, clearly along for the ride but not as enthusiastic as Sari was.

"Where's Orsala?"

"I believe she is the designated person taking the high road in this scheme. Therefore she's at the archives today."

"You know," Ava said, "this just sounds worse the more you explain it."

"It was your mate's idea."

"I love him like crazy, but you should know that Malachi"—Ava was out of breath trying to keep up with the two taller women—"can be a reckless troublemaker. Assuming Damien hasn't told you that already."

Sari said, "I knew I liked him."

"He got killed once. Just in case you've forgotten that part. Not too interested in repeating that experience, you know?"

"Nothing dangerous today," Sari said as they turned the corner into an empty courtyard. "Just tweaking the noses of some old men with superiority complexes and making a statement."

"Oh." They stopped at a door flanked by two potted hydrangea blooming a brilliant blue despite the winter chill. "Well, that sounds like fun."

Sari paused and turned to Ava. "You're not too American about nudity, are you?"

"Excuse me?"

"Communal baths. Do they bother you?"

"No." She shrugged. "I love the *hamam*, so—"

"This is actually quite similar. You'll be fine."

Mala and Sari rang a discreet bell, waited for the door to buzz, and pushed it open. Ava walked through to see a wide-eyed attendant and a suspicious guard who gave Mala a run for her money in the fierce department. She was tall and blond, carrying a staff that looked well used. She saw the guard eying Mala in particular, and Ava was grateful Sari had convinced her sister to leave her weapon at home.

The attendant stammered, "We were not expecting—"

"We have come for the ritual bath before we enter the gallery," Sari said smoothly. "It is my sister's first time in Vienna."

Ava didn't correct her. The guard eyed them warily before she searched their bags. Back at Sari and Damien's town house, Mala had given Ava a linen shift, strips of cloth to bind her breasts if she wanted them, and a high-necked robe. Ava had tucked all this in her old messenger bag and tried to sneak her camera in, but Mala had caught her and forced her to hand it over.

They left their shoes near the door and entered a marble bathing room that reminded Ava very much of the *hamams* in Istanbul. Grey marble benches lined the circular room. A seven-sided pool was in the center, and steam wafted into the air. It was humid and damp, lit only by oil lamps embedded in the wall. No electric light touched her skin as she undressed and stowed her bag in an intricately woven basket the attendant provided.

Mala and Sari disrobed beside her, obviously at ease with the ceremony of the bath. Ava simply followed their example.

"We bathe here before we pray," Sari said quietly. "The ritual bath is to cleanse your spirit and calm your mind."

Ava heard Mala take a deep breath before she immersed herself in the water. Sari hummed a quiet song as she closed her eyes and floated. Ava let the magic flow through her as she listened. She still didn't understand all the words of the Old Language, but she could sense the power behind them. Almost as one, the three women's mating marks lit on their skin as Sari's chanting grew stronger.

Mala's shone incandescent against her dark skin, no less beautiful for the mourning collar painted thick around her scarred neck. Sari's were a luminous glow against her pale skin. And Ava's shone clearly, the edges seared black against the olive tones of her skin. She looked down.

Her skin tone had always been a bit of a mystery, considering her parents were both fair. But with her father's family history being unknown, she'd never thought about it much.

"My grandmother is Persian," she said quietly.

"Ah." Sari tucked a wet lock of hair behind Ava's ear. "Yes, I can see that."

Mala signed something.

Sari said, "Mala asked if you look like her."

"Maybe a little. But she's much more beautiful."

Mala poured an almond-scented oil over Ava's hair, helping her to work it through the heavy mass while Sari rubbed her shoulders with a soap scented with amber.

"These are beautiful," Sari said, running a finger over Ava's shoulder where her mating marks gleamed. She could feel Mala turning her back to examine the marks there. "Malachi has a steady hand." She grinned as she ran the amber soap over her own skin. "Damien was so nervous on our mating night—I think a few of mine are barely readable."

Mala pointed to a faint mark on her hip as Sari and Ava turned to help her wash.

"Zander completely smudged that one," Mala signed as Sari translated. "He was so impatient. I'm amazed any of them dried properly before he attacked me." Mala smiled. "I was his first woman. His only woman. He was very eager."

Ava had never heard Mala talk about her lost mate, but in the darkness of the bathhouse, no topic seemed off-limits.

"My grandmother is in a mental institution," Ava whispered. "She's pretty much insane."

Mala signed with fierce movements. "She is not insane. She's only lived in the human world too long. We will find a way to help her."

"She is, though," Ava said. "More than me. It's a long story. I'll tell you. I promise. Just not today."

Sari took her hand and led her out of the bath after they'd all dipped in the water to wash the excess oil and soap from their bodies.

"We'll help them all," Sari said. "But to do that, we need standing again. That's partly why we're here. Come to the prayer room. Sing with me."

Ava did. She sat cross legged before a low fire, linking her hands with the two women at her side while Sari chanted a song that made Ava's heart fly. In that moment, she had no question where she belonged. No matter whose blood ran in her veins, these were her sisters. She belonged with them. She was made to sing these songs. Made to wear Malachi's marks on her skin.

She'd wandered for years, and now she was home.

"ARE you ready?" Sari whispered at the door that led to what she called the singers' gallery.

"My hair's wet, I have no bra, and I'm dressed in what feels like a toga. This is not exactly the wardrobe I would have chosen to rock the world in, but I guess it'll have to do."

She felt Mala shaking with laughter behind her. Ava thought Sari and Mala looked like warrior goddesses from some cool sci-fi movie, while she looked like a kid playing dress-up. She needed platform boots, not felt-lined sandals.

"Just follow my lead. Don't feel like you need to say anything."

"Sounds good to me."

Sari pushed open the door, and Ava immediately felt every eye in the gallery swing toward them.

"Holy shit," she murmured.

It was a palace. No, it was a temple. Of books. Three stories of book-cases lined the walls, ladders and balconies built in to access what must have been thousands of shelves. She'd seen the Austrian National Library in this same palace complex, but it was nothing to the Irin Library.

The gallery across from them was crowded with scribes. She searched for Malachi but couldn't make him out among the crowd of men all wearing linen wraps and ceremonial robes similar to theirs but open at the neck.

"I guess everyone's in on the toga party," she whispered.

"Shh," Sari said.

The scribes' chests were bare, black *talesm* on display down the center of their robes, and Ava was relieved that Malachi's had mostly returned where they'd be visible. She had a feeling that more *talesm* equaled greater badass, and she didn't want her mate at a disadvantage.

Every eye was on them as they climbed the stairs to the gallery. Ava had never felt more conspicuous in her life. Just then, she caught her mate's smile. He was standing with Damien at the end of the railing, looking like the cat that had stolen the cream.

"Oh, yeah," she muttered, "this was totally your idea."

Sari ignored the shocked stares and whispers from the floor, heading toward the end of the gallery with Mala and Ava trailing after her.

"Constance," she said to the woman who waited there.

"Sari."

"I see we're once again missing our Irina elders from the floor today."

A slight smile crossed the woman's coldly beautiful features. "We are fortunate, then, that in the face of abandonment by our leadership, we have such excellent care from our mates."

Ava felt Mala tense beside her.

"That's an… interesting perspective," Sari said.

"Why are you here? You've been open in your contempt for the elder scribes before."

"I have no contempt for the office of elder, only for some who sit at their desks and try to 'unburden' me of my own self-determination."

"Don't put words in my mate's mouth," Constance said.

"The words in my own mouth have more than enough power," Sari whispered. "We've waited long enough."

With that parting shot, Sari strode down the steps and onto the floor of the Library.

Constance put out her hand and hissed, "You are no elder!"

Sari shoved it off and continued walking. "I never claimed to be."

Ava could barely breathe as Sari strode to the center of the room and spoke to the galleries on either side. "I am a singer of Ariel's line, and I request an audience with the Irina council."

Silence blanketed the Library.

The whispers from the scribes' gallery ceased. The muttering of the elder scribes stopped. Ava felt as if the entire room was holding its collective breath.

"I am an Irina singer," Sari said again, a little louder. "A daughter of Ariel's line. I request an audience with my representative on the Irina council."

Ava's heart was in her throat as she watched the fierce woman look around the silent room.

"Where is my council?" Sari asked. "Where are the elder singers who speak for me?"

Finally, a lone elder stood.

Mala shoved a small writing pad into her hands.

Konrad. European elder. Pro-Irina.

"Daughter," Konrad said with pain in his eyes. "I'm sorry, but your council has fled."

"No," Sari said. "My council was attacked."

Another elder stood. "Your council is in hiding."

Mala wrote again. *Jerome. North American elder. Pro-compulsion. Constance's mate.*

Sari stepped to Jerome's desk. "My council was protecting itself. Protecting its daughters when the scribes did not."

Furious whispers from the scribes' gallery.

Jerome spread his hands, a tense smile on his face. "And they do not trust us to protect our sisters even now?" Jerome raised his eyes to the scribes' gallery above him. "Does the Irina council not trust us to protect our own mates? Our daughters?" He looked back at Sari. "We *want* to protect them, and yet they hide."

She walked back to the center of the room. "And I *want* to speak to my council."

Jerome said, "I'm sorry, but your council is no more."

Sari raised her hands, standing in the center of the library, and began to whisper. Ava felt magic rise in the air. Dust motes hung frozen in the light that poured through the high windows.

No one breathed.

There was a low rumble, then with a mighty crash the seven desks of the elder singers slid to the center of the room, pulled by Sari's elemental power.

Papers and dust went flying. Furniture shifted as people ran to escape their path.

Sari stood motionless in the center of the floor, eyes traveling to meet the gaze of each elder as the massive wooden desks settled into place in a star-shaped pattern around her.

Ava released the breath she'd been holding.

"It's time." It was all Sari said before she left the floor of the Library and walked up the steps.

At the top of the stairs, Constance grabbed her arm.

"I see you like theater," the woman said. "You will come with me if you ever want to be welcome here again."

Mala stepped forward, but Sari held up a hand and shook her head. "Good. I've been wanting to have a little chat."

Constance and her two companions swept out of the gallery with Mala and Sari following them. Ava threw one more glance over her shoulder to see Malachi standing across from her, wearing a triumphant expression. Damien stood next to him, his face glowing with pride.

Ava gave them both a wide smile and followed her sisters out.

AT least if she was going to have coffee with the most passive-aggressive woman she'd ever met, she had her bra and shoes back on.

Ava sat in the airy sitting room of the town house near city hall. The neo-Gothic spire of the Rathaus was visible through the parlor window as Constance's maid served coffee and delicate cakes to the seven women in the sitting room.

"I'm glad we have this opportunity to talk," Constance said. "Perhaps we can come to an understanding."

"You're from the South," Ava said.

"Virginia." Constance nodded. "And you're American."

"I am. Los Angeles."

"How lovely."

Ava was pretty sure Constance actually meant the complete opposite. The singer turned her attention away from Ava and looked at Sari. Renata had joined them, and she and Mala stood along the back wall while Sari and Ava took the couch.

"Well?" Constance asked.

"Well what? I have every right to demand an audience with my elders." Sari sat, her strong arms spread across the back of the delicate settee decorated in blue silk, which complemented the butter-yellow walls and cream molding of the room. Her hair was wild from the baths, her face ruddy from the winter air. Like the Northern fjords she hailed from, Sari was primal and beautiful at the same time.

Ava thought she looked like a Valkyrie at a tea party.

Constance had her own kind of power, though. She was the kind of woman Americans would call a "steel magnolia." She sat rigid in the chair across from Sari, unbowed by the other singer's presence. Her pixie-cut hair was utterly feminine and showcased high cheekbones and a strong jaw. Beautiful and cold.

"You know perfectly well our elders abandoned us," she said.

"Abandoned us?" Sari said. "Or were driven out of Vienna in fear for their lives?"

"I have been in Vienna for almost two hundred years," Constance said. She held a hand out to the woman at her left. "Helen has been here for one hundred." She nodded to the woman on her right. "Vania has been here for over seventy. There are many Irina living safely in our city."

"Then where are they? Why have none organized? Why have none stepped forward to try to reform the council?"

Tension was evident around Constance's eyes. "Because we believe our mates are correct. The Irina belong in retreats where we're protected. Not out chasing after Grigori like animals."

Renata said, "Did you hear that, Mala? We're like animals." She leaned over the couch and grinned. "Good. I like having teeth."

Constance's eyes narrowed. "Do not mistake bravado for strength. We have our own influence here. We've been working behind the scenes for years, trying to protect our sisters while you've been out throwing tantrums and killing angel spawn."

"What's wrong with killing Grigori?" Ava asked. "If they're attacking human women—"

"War is a scribe's job," Helen said, her voice crisply accented.

Renata stepped forward. "You ignorant little—"

"Enough!" Sari said. "I don't know what my grandmother was thinking. You know *nothing*. You pretty birds sit in your gilded cages and play at politics while a war happens on the other side of the door. I have nothing to say to you when you are blind to reality."

Constance's chin lifted. "We have a good life here. If singers would accept the protection of their scribes, they would have a good life too. A *safe* life."

Childish chatter came from the hallway a moment before the door opened. A small girl, no more than five or six years old, bounced into the room, her honey-brown curls pulled into two pigtails on the sides of her head.

"Mama!" she cried and climbed into Constance's lap.

Ava saw the transformation immediately. All coldness fled from the woman's face.

"Lexi, what are you doing back from the park?"

"I was too cold. And we have visitors!" the little girl said, turning her sparkling eyes to Sari and Ava. "Hello."

Sari's yearning was an aching thing beside her.

"Hello," she said.

"Did you bring any children?" Lexi said.

"I'm sorry," Sari said softly. "I don't have any children."

"Oh." The girl's disappointment was clear. "Miss Helen's son comes to play sometimes, but he's so much older than me. Mama"—she turned in her mother's arms—"I want to see a baby. Does anyone have a baby I can play with?"

Constance ran a hand over her daughter's hair. "I'm sorry, Lexi. No babies are visiting today."

Lexi turned and confided to Ava, "I have lots of dollies, but babies are better, aren't they?"

Ava leaned forward, transfixed. "I suppose so."

"Go with Anna," Constance said. "We need to talk about grown-up things for a little longer."

"Okay." Lexi scrambled to the floor. "But come back if you have babies!" she called out as she left the room.

Silence followed her exit.

"There are still so few," Vania whispered.

"I understand," Sari said.

"I highly doubt that," Helen said.

Sari's voice was hoarse when she spoke again. "I was pregnant when our retreat was attacked," she said. "My mate was hundreds of miles away. I had… I'd lent him my power so he could fight in Paris. When the attack came, I was injured. My body could not—"

"They killed my son in front of my eyes," Constance said in an icy voice. "The Grigori animal sliced his throat in front of me and he bled over my kitchen floor while his friend held me down, choked my voice silent, and raped me. Thomas was seven years old, and the last thing he saw was animals raping his mother. Do you understand that?"

Ava's body was frozen in horror.

Vania reached for her friend's hand.

No one spoke.

"I only survived the Rending because of my mate. And Jerome was near death when he found me. He said the prayers for our son alone because no one else was left, and my voice was so damaged, I could not sing. I said nothing for twenty years. Nothing."

Sari closed her eyes. "Constance—"

"If I can save *any* mother from seeing that—save any child by rebuilding the retreats. Make them stronger. Make them safer—"

"There is no such thing as total safety," Sari said. "We both know that. *We* have to be stronger. *We* have to defend our children. Defend ourselves."

"We aren't capable of it. Are you so proud that you cannot acknowledge the truth? *We are not as strong as the scribes.*"

"Our power is different, not less."

"Don't you understand?" Constance stood. "Nothing can bring them back. No revenge will ever be enough. No blood can repay what we've lost. Don't you think I've wanted to hunt the animals who killed my son?" Her voice rose. "I could stop their hearts in their chests and pull the blood from their veins. I am a singer of Rafael's line. I could do those things and more. But that will not bring Thomas back."

Renata said, "You should be able to hunt them if you want. You have the right."

Constance shook her head. "Alexis is a miracle. We never thought…" She dragged in a breath and put a hand over her belly. "No one thought I'd be able to conceive another child."

Sari stood to face her. "And I may never have the opportunity to be a mother again. But if I do, I don't want my daughter growing up in fear."

"Your mate is a *legend*. Damien of Bohemia was a Templar knight, for heaven's sake! Don't you trust him to protect you?"

"It's not about trust," Renata said from the back of the room. "It's about using our own power. It's our job to protect them too."

Constance shook her head. "We are not meant for such things. We have a greater purpose. It is our job to rebuild our race. There is magic—healing magic—we can use to increase fertility. To build our families again. I've spent the past hundred years—"

"But that's our whole job?" Ava asked. "Having children to rebuild the Irin race?"

Vania narrowed her eyes. "You know nothing. I don't know where you come from, but every *true* Irina in this room would consider it a blessing to be able to bear a child. We're not like the humans."

Ava looked at the other singer. "I'm not saying motherhood isn't amazing, but that's it? That's all you do?"

"You're ignorant," Helen said. "I have heard the rumors. You grew up among humans. Be quiet and let others speak."

Ava rose to her feet. "*I'm* ignorant?"

Sari put her hand on Ava's arm. "We're done here. Orsala was right. I understand your position. I don't agree with it, but I understand. You deserve to have your voice heard too."

Renata's voice was an ice-cold blade. "Even if she's a fool?"

Constance lifted her chin. "Think that if it makes you feel superior. It doesn't matter to me. I'm not the only Irina who believes compulsion is the best way to save our people."

"I know," Sari said. "And as much as I disagree with you, I hope the Irina council speaks for you too."

"We have no council. We need none."

"That," Sari said as she walked to the door, "is truly ignorant. I'll tell you the same thing I told your mate. It's time. The elder singers are returning, whether you want them to or not."

"Then prepare yourself," Constance said. "The Irina of Vienna will not bow to your wishes. If you reform the council, you and your grandmother won't get puppets."

"Good." Sari opened the door. "We don't want them."

IV.

THE MAN WORE AN IMPECCABLE three-piece suit when he entered the church. His dark hair was cut in the current fashion, and his silk tie was knotted firmly against his throat. After setting down his briefcase at the edge of one pew, he sat next to the ash-blond man in an overcoat who stared at the priest starting the evening mass.

"Where is he?" Barak muttered.

"Playing games."

Vasu entered from the back of the church, not dressed as a human businessman as the other two were, but looking more like one of the artists or musicians crowding the pedestrian street outside. His hair was pulled back in a knot, and he wore a rough beard that tangled in the scarf wrapped around his neck. He sat next to Barak, his physical body making audible noise his brothers avoided.

Jaron and Barak both turned their heads to their brother.

"What are you doing?" they asked as one.

Vasu shrugged. An irritating human habit he'd decided to adopt. "It amuses me."

"You did not ask my permission to track the girl."

"I'm not tracking. I'm watching."

"Enough." Barak's voice cut through their quiet argument. "Is he near? I've shielded myself so thoroughly in this city I'm having difficulty hearing at a distance."

"Is it still so important your children think you're dead?" Vasu asked.

"My reappearance at this stage would alter their actions. I want to see where things lead."

"I've shown you," Jaron said.

"Nevertheless." Barak watched a human mother and small child as they made their way up the center aisle. The child was small. He was fussing in the incense-laden air and his eyes were running. "Where is he, brother?"

"Hungary."

"Is Svarog in play?"

"He will be," Jaron said. "He has created too many vulnerabilities. Volund will use it to sway him to his cause."

"We shall see," Vasu said cryptically.

Barak asked, "What do you know?"

"Know? Nothing. But I have my suspicions." Vasu sat up straighter. "Grimold was never a surprise. He has long been Volund's puppet. But the status quo has been beneficial to Svarog."

"It has," Barak said. "But he knows he will not sway Volund from his path. He may decide backing him will serve his long-term interests."

"That makes little sense," Vasu said, "considering the probable actions of the scribes. This city is complacent, but not without strong magic. There are more mature Irin here now than there have ever been, and Mikhael's armory is here, along with their Library. The Irin blend in with the humans now. They control wealth and power. And their magic has been honed since Volund's last attack."

Barak said, "But they are still without their mates. Most of them are only a fraction of who they could be. And if the Grigora secret comes to light, the Irin will be on the offensive again. Their power will multiply with every mating. They will have purpose again, and a scribe with purpose is a dangerous thing. Volund knows he must strike now."

"The Irin council is not the primary problem," Jaron said, "It is no longer just the scribes we must anticipate. That much is easy. Their council is utterly predictable."

"The singers have returned," Barak and Vasu said together.

"And more are coming."

There was a new light in Vasu's eyes. "The songs have returned to Vienna."

Jaron longed for them. Not the echo of beauty in the Irina voices, but the true songs. He could still hear them, carrying across a crystal sea, rising into the endless sky where he had lived. Surrounding the throne. Jaron had once lived with their beauty in his veins. Their words remained embedded in his very skin.

Every moment. Every step he'd taken since the birth of his daughter had been with this purpose in mind.

He'd forgotten once.

But then his daughter sang to him, and Jaron had remembered beauty.

And he would have it back.

Chapter Seventeen

"I FEEL LIKE WE NEED to tell them." Ava was lying beside Malachi, enjoying the low morning light as they lingered in bed. He played with the ends of her hair, which were still scented with almonds and amber from the ritual baths the day before.

Malachi had barely been able to contain himself when he'd seen her enter the library with her sisters. Though she was slight, power had radiated from her. He'd heard the curious whispers in the scribe's gallery where he and Damien had watched Sari's powerful address.

"Who is she?"

"Such golden eyes…"

"Whose line?"

"…already mated? With whom?"

Malachi had wanted to crow, *Mine! She is mine.* Pride swelled from his chest as she held her head up against the curious stares.

Damien had stood solid and fearsome in the gallery as he watched his mate. Watched the elders near her with his hawklike stare. The soft scribes of Vienna had given the old warrior a wide berth when his *talesm* began to glow.

Such strong magic. There were few matings as powerful as Damien and Sari's left among the Irin. Every scribe in the gallery was in awe.

Malachi knew that, as the years passed, he and Ava would become stronger. Trials. Battles. Their power would grow until seeing the magic of one was the same as witnessing both.

He hungered for it. And her.

The echo of the Irina's desks hadn't even died before he was bolting from the gallery, but Damien stopped him on the stairs. Their mates were meeting with the Irina of Vienna, and Malachi would have to wait.

"Tell who about what?" he murmured, still half-asleep. He'd sated his appetite for Ava late into the night, intoxicated by the lingering magic on her skin and the scent of her hair.

"I think we need to tell our friends about my grandmother."

"Are you sure?" It was a sensitive subject, and though Malachi worried about Volund's ability to track Ava, he also had confidence in Jaron's protection.

"I don't feel like it's my story to tell," Ava said. "I feel like I'd be telling her secret. But I think the others need to know."

"How about this?" He rolled to his side and propped himself up on his elbow so he could see her face. "Talk to Orsala. Tell her. She will know if it is something that needs to be shared with the others."

"That's a good idea."

"I'm brimming with them."

She smiled and pushed his shoulder. "That was your idea yesterday, wasn't it? For Sari to create a scene."

"I think Sari likes creating scenes. And all the quiet machinations there annoyed me." He rolled to his back and pulled her onto his chest. "Where is the passion in our race?" he asked. "Where is the purpose? We have lost the fire of our mission. Become consumed with ancient lines and intricate interpretations. That is not what we were meant for."

"I thought the scribes' purpose was to preserve knowledge."

"It is. But I felt no love for it in that room. It was all routine and ceremony. No heart. No heat. And we are supposed to use that knowledge to fight the Fallen To protect humanity. To help them. We cannot protect them if we can't see past our own walls."

"And the singers—"

"The moment the singers withdrew their magic from the human race, we put up walls. We let the fear of loss consume us. And in letting that fear rule us, we abandoned our purpose. We must change."

"Look at you." She smiled down at him. "A visionary."

"I came back for a reason, Ava. The two of us… we are meant for a purpose."

"The *kareshta*?"

"Part of breaking down walls is finding these women you've seen in Jaron's vision. We find them, we kill the Fallen who fathered them, and they will be free."

An odd expression crossed her face.

"What?" he asked.

"I think I'd better cancel that beach shoot in Spain. I don't think taking pictures of girls in bikinis is quite as important as saving the world."

He threw his head back and laughed.

"And we need to complete the mating ritual. I'll talk to Orsala about that too."

Malachi stopped laughing. "No."

SHE was angry with him, but he could live with that. What he couldn't live with was Ava with even a fraction less power. Eventually, yes. When the current battle was past. When they'd gone back to Istanbul and were able to rest. Then she could complete her half of the ritual.

"I cannot believe you're being so stubborn about this." She railed at him as they entered Damien and Sari's home. "Why do you even get a vote? This is *my* magic."

"Well, since I'm the one who has to tattoo the mark for it to be permanent," he said flippantly, "then I suppose you have no choice."

"I can always start singing when you're asleep. I'd be halfway through by the time you woke up, and you know you'd go along with it."

He stopped so abruptly she ran into his back. Malachi spun and gripped her shoulders.

"Don't try to manipulate me. If you did that—if you denied me even a moment of hearing your mating song—I don't know if I could forgive you, Ava."

She flushed. "Malachi—"

"Don't make threats about something that important. I would never do that to you."

He could see angry tears in the corner of her eyes, but she blinked them back. "But you'd deny me taking that step? Deny my own promise to you?"

"You know why."

"Because it's not safe? News flash: We're in a millennia-long war that shows no signs of dying down. There will never be a time when it's totally safe."

"She's right, you know," Rhys said from the doorway of the library.

Malachi said, "Shut up, Rhys."

"You're the ones making a racket in the hallway when I'm just trying to work." He shot a charming smile at Malachi's mate. "Hello, Ava, you smell amazing. The ritual baths suit you."

She smiled back. "Thank you."

He put a hand over his heart. "I would never deny your mark. Malachi is an idiot."

Malachi leaned against the wall. "I have now detailed fifty-seven specific and effective ways of killing you, Rhys. Would you like me to start listing them?"

"No need. I'm fairly sure your mate is thinking up a comparable list for you right now."

Orsala shouted from inside the library. "You're like children! Bicker bicker bicker."

Ava said, "I keep telling them—"

"You're as bad as the rest of them, Ava."

Malachi, Rhys, and Ava wandered into the library where Orsala was reading a scroll.

"Don't threaten your mate," she chided without looking up. "You would be furious if he did that to you. Rhys, stop antagonizing your brother. Malachi, stop being a stubborn know-it-all. I may have liked you better when you didn't remember anything."

Rhys knocked Malachi's skull with a fist. "There's still plenty of patchy spaces up here, Orsala."

Malachi punched him in the shoulder. Hard.

Ava wandered over to the old singer. "I'm sorry. He's driving me a little crazy this morning."

"That's their job, dear. Sari's grandfather was a menace." She looked up with a smile. "And yet we love them. What are you doing this morning?"

Malachi sat next to Ava and threw an arm around her shoulders. "We were hoping to speak with you privately, as a matter of fact."

Orsala's keen eyes grew even sharper. "Does this have something to do with your grandmother?"

Ava nodded.

"I knew it." Orsala said, "Rhys, that trip you were going to make to the archives. Do it now."

"But—"

"Now."

Muttering about bossy women, the other scribe left the room and shut the door.

"Before we start with anything else," Orsala said, "Ava and Rhys are both correct, Malachi. You need to complete the ritual. Now is as safe a time as any. There is little Grigori activity in the city, and Ava has become known to the Irin hierarchy. Rumors about her history are starting to circulate. She is quite obviously mated, but for the two of you to reach your full potential together, you need to be marked. It might also hasten the return of your power, which we need."

He looked down at his chest. "She sings to me. It's helping."

"It's not enough." The old singer leaned forward. "Stop being so stubborn! Let her protect you too. That is what the mating bond was intended it to be."

"I lost everything when I returned to earth. Ava was all I had. She says I help her remain sane against the voices? Her voice is the only reason I didn't lose my mind when I lost my memories." He felt Ava's hand curl into his, and he squeezed it tight. "Do you truly not understand why I don't want to take a chance?"

"You are holding her back if you don't. And holding yourself back as well." She held up a hand when he opened his mouth again. "Just think about it. Don't hold your mate back because you allow your fear to rule you. Now is not the time for defense, but offense."

Orsala's words were a mirror of his own. Only she was challenging Malachi personally, not the Irin race as a whole.

And Malachi had no defense.

Damn.

"YOU already know that my grandmother is Jaron's child." Ava started the story after Orsala had called for coffee. "But… she is also Volund's mate."

Orsala sat back and her mouth fell open. "Heaven above."

Malachi kept his arm around Ava's shoulders.

"It was not by choice," she said. "Volund took her from Jaron's protection. He raped her."

"And he marked her?" Orsala said.

Ava nodded. "He wanted to know if it was possible."

"It is." Orsala blinked. "But there would have been no need for it to be violent. Volund is an archangel. He could have seduced—"

"He didn't," Malachi said. "I didn't see the vision she sent Ava until afterward when she shared it with me, but it was *not* a seduction. Volund wanted to terrorize her, and he did."

"I suppose…" Orsala's face was bleak. "I'll admit I suspected something of that nature, though I never imagined rape."

"What do you mean?" Ava asked.

"Your blood." She shook her head. "It never made sense for you to have so much magic with so little of your blood angelic. The Grigori sire children with human women, and they are not magical. Geniuses, yes. Great artists who are often unstable. Not like you. But you're not a normal Grigori—or Grigora in this case—child. You don't have one angel in your line, but two. Your great-grandfather and your grandfather. And both are archangels. It changes things."

"How?" Malachi asked.

Orsala looked at Malachi. "Do you remember when I had Rhys get the copy of *Gabriel's Old Tales* for me?"

"Back in Istanbul. Yes."

"The fairy tales?" Ava asked.

"They're not fairy tales in the human sense," Orsala said. "These are more like... legends. Folk tales, I suppose."

The story popped into his mind immediately, coming from the childhood memories he'd already recovered. "Of course," Malachi said. "'Adelina's Son.'"

"Who's Adelina?" Ava's eyes darted between them.

"'Adelina's Son' is a cautionary tale," Orsala said. "In *Gabriel's Old Tales*, Adelina is a beautiful and gifted singer—the most treasured daughter of her village and a notable healer of Rafael's line. She appears in many of the tales and is always a very powerful character. But Adelina is also so beautiful that one of the Fallen—some translations imply Bozidar, others imply a lesser angel—fell in love with her and mated with her."

Ava asked, "And that can't happen?"

Malachi shook his head. "Not love. You heard Jaron. The angels are not truly capable of love. Emotion comes from our human blood, not the angelic."

"But it is a story, of course," Orsala said. "Not reality. The story says that Adelina was seduced by this angel and fell in love with him. They lay together and she became pregnant. At first, she was very happy. She sang that her child would be blessed above all others and would be a gift to the world. A child of heaven who would finally reconcile the Irin and the Fallen so we could live in peace."

"This is fiction, right?"

"Is it?" Malachi asked. "In the story, Adelina gives birth to a monster who consumes her as soon as it's born; his father has to kill it before it goes on to terrorize the world."

"Hey." Ava punched his arm. "My father is three-quarters angelic, and he's not violent or scary. Irresponsible and unstable, yes. But he's never hurt anyone but himself. And did they seriously read shit like that to you when you were kids?" She looked horrified. "I mean, that's just wrong."

Orsala patted Ava's hand. "It is a story. It's intended to frighten. And I think in this case it's intended to frighten young Irina away from ever being seduced by one of the Fallen. It's a taboo in our race for a reason."

"And no Irina has ever mated with a Fallen?" Ava asked.

Malachi and Orsala both shuddered.

"No," he said. "I can't even imagine the most rebellious Irina doing something so dangerous. We are taught to run screaming from the Fallen from the time we can walk."

"With stories about monster-babies, I'm not surprised. According to Jaron, it's never happened to one of the *kareshta* either. Just my grandmother."

"The Fallen are possessive of their offspring. Not loving, of course. But proprietary. For one of them to violate Jaron's child would be considered an aggressive act in any case. I'm guessing that for Volund to not only violate Jaron's daughter but then mark her as his own would be an act of war. He essentially stole her and tied her to himself."

"She dream-walks with him."

Orsala was at a loss for words for a moment. "That is… a torture I cannot imagine. And Jaron can do nothing to shield her?"

"When he's physically present with her, she's safe. Other than that? Volund can touch her mind any time she sleeps."

"Can Volund reach you?"

"Yes," Malachi said, "but not when Jaron is shielding her. And as far as we know, he's never lifted his protection."

"No…" Orsala's eyes went blurry. "He won't, of course. Not until he's ready."

"Orsala?"

She blinked and her eyes widened. "Jaron wants Volund."

"Of course." Malachi and Ava exchanged looks. "We've already told you—"

"Jaron wants Volund," she said again, rising to her feet and starting to pace. "He doesn't care about our war with the Fallen. He is at war with *Volund*. But Jaron's forces are depleted. According to rumors, his children are few. Jaron may be more powerful than Volund personally, but his army is not."

Ava frowned. "Yes, but what—"

"Malachi," Orsala said, spinning around. "In a battle, what is the most important step you can take to ensure victory before the fighting even starts?"

"Claim your ground," he answered immediately. "The combatant with a greater position can defeat an enemy more powerful than himself if he picks the right location." Malachi stood when the realization hit. "He's using Ava as bait."

"Jaron has picked his location," Orsala said, staring at Ava. "His and Volund's only blood tie is mated to an Irin scribe and currently residing in the most Irin-powerful city in the world. She's part of us now. A Grigori female mated within our race. Jaron knows we will fight for her."

The soldier in Malachi saw the brilliance of Jaron's move immediately.

"He's shielding Ava as he gathers his allies. And when he's ready…"

Ava's face was pale. "He's using me as bait to draw Volund here so the Irin will be forced to protect me and kill his enemy."

He could see the wheels begin to turn in her head.

Malachi said, "Don't even think about it."

She looked away from him.

"You're not leaving," he said. "That's not even an option, Ava."

Ava glared at him. "I'm putting an entire city at risk. It's stupid for me to stay."

"Where would you go that Volund and Jaron could not find you?" Orsala asked. "At least here we can protect you."

"And risk a battle in the middle of a major metropolitan area?"

Orsala frowned. "He will have thought of that. The Fallen have no desire to attract attention. In any case, Jaron's goals align with our own. Volund needs to die. He masterminded the Rending. He raped your grandmother. He has targeted females of both races for centuries. This is a battle we must fight."

"I agree, but I don't think the entire city of Vienna needs to be part of the carnage."

"So what are you going to do?" Malachi asked. "Run away?"

"Why should I stick around to be a pawn in their game?"

"Jaron is a powerful ally," Orsala said. "We've never worked with one of the Fallen before. Nor have they attempted to work with us. And yet it appears he wishes to do so. We should not dismiss him. Whatever plan he has will work to our advantage. If you leave, that could complicate things."

"And might possibly save thousands of lives," Ava said. "I should be in the middle of nowhere, where no one else can get hurt."

Malachi blurted out, "If you stay without arguing, I'll let you complete the mating ritual."

Ava's jaw dropped. "Unbelievable."

Without another word, she turned and left the room.

Malachi turned to Orsala. She was shaking her head. Her eyes pressed closed. His mother's mental voice had started to lecture him again.

"I can't help you with that one," Orsala said.

"Bad timing?"

Chapter Eighteen

"AVA, WAIT!"

She heard his voice, but she didn't stop. She'd grown comfortable on the streets here. There was no scent of Grigori in the air, and she'd learned to find her way around. She headed back to the apartment and didn't turn, even when she heard him getting closer.

"Ava, stop!"

He caught up with her a few blocks from the apartment.

"I'm sorry," he said, clutching her shoulders. "*Canim*, I—"

She shook him off. "And you accused *me* of being manipulative?"

"I know."

"No." She walked away, burying her hands in the pockets of her coat. "You really, really don't."

They were starting to attract attention, so they kept walking. Malachi fell in step beside her but didn't try to touch her again.

"Would it help if I told you I'd decided on it before you threatened to leave?"

She nodded. "Oh, so you were just holding that one in reserve for a moment when you needed to get your way."

"No. Not… exactly."

"Got it."

"I'd only just decided! Why are you trying to start a fight with me?"

"Nope. This isn't starting a fight. This is *fighting*. This is the two of us fighting over you being a controlling asshole."

It irritated her that she was walking as fast as she could, and yet he kept up with her effortlessly.

"Ava." He sighed.

She reached the front door and opened it with the key, ignoring how his hand reached out to hold the door for her. How he stopped to make sure it closed securely behind them. How he brushed a drift of snow from her shoulder.

Ava started up the stairs. The black cat was waiting at the door. It slipped in when she opened it and ran to the window to watch the street. Malachi followed behind her.

"What do I do to fix this?"

She was angry. Frustrated. Mostly, she was hurt. "I don't know. I honestly don't. It's supposed to be special. I've been memorizing all the songs for weeks now, so worried that I wouldn't be able to do things right. That I'd mess things up and embarrass myself. And you! And then… you don't want it. Do you know how that makes me feel?"

Rejected.

She didn't want to say it, because she knew he loved her. Knew he was proud to be her mate. But a lifetime of rejection from her father—from every man in her life—wouldn't disappear just by Malachi loving her. She wished it would.

Ava stripped off her coat and scarf, turned up the thermostat, and went to start the kettle for tea. She'd drunk so much coffee in the past few days she thought her stomach lining might start a revolt.

She felt his hands on her shoulders. Felt the roughness of his beard against her neck. "I want it."

"Maybe you're right. It's probably not a good idea. Not when Jaron is using me as bait. We don't understand Volund's connection with me. It might make you vulnerable too."

He wrapped his arms around her waist. "Please don't do this. It was stupid for me to say it then, but it doesn't mean I wasn't sincere."

"So you'll go through the rest of the mating ritual with me, but only if I agree to stay in Vienna?"

"You're not truly thinking of leaving, are you?"

She didn't say anything. She *was* thinking about it. Orsala and Malachi could scheme all they wanted, but the fact of the matter was if Ava stayed in the city and people were killed in some massive angelic battle, she'd never be able to live with herself.

His arms tightened. "You can't be serious."

"If I leave, then who do they have to kill but each other? No Irin would be forced into battle—"

"And you'd be caught in the middle." He stepped back.

She turned slowly. "I am one person. We're talking about thousands—"

"We're talking about you! My mate. Do you honestly think I'd leave you unprotected?"

Ava said nothing. If she left, Malachi would have a hard time finding her, even with Rhys's help. She could go to her mother and Carl. If she asked Carl to make her disappear somewhere, he'd do it. He'd probably be grateful.

He put his hands on her cheeks. "Stop it."

"I'm not doing anything."

"You're leaving me in your mind," he whispered. "Don't do it. Don't you know I'd rather die than lose you?"

She shook her head. "I need to think."

"Enough!" He cut his hand through the air. "You're not going anywhere. I forbid it."

"Oh really?" She balled up the power welling in her chest and said, "*Ya fasham.*"

Malachi's eyes widened in shock as the unbalancing spell hit him full force. He reeled to the side and fell over. Ava stepped to the door and grabbed her coat and scarf. Then she threw another spell at him that Sari had taught her, and Ava knew Malachi's legs were going to be immobilized long enough for her to leave.

"Ava!"

Okay, his mouth could move.

"I'm going out for a walk."

"What did you do?"

"You're a smart guy, I'm sure you'll figure it out."

The cat had come to sit on his chest.

"Ava!"

She ran down the stairs and flagged down the first taxi she could find. "Zentralfriedhof," she told the driver. "Gate two."

AVA didn't know why she was so attracted to cemeteries. Maybe it was the quiet. For as long as she'd been alive, she'd found them soothing. She could walk among others, never feeling alone, but not plagued by the voices of the living. No matter what city she visited, she sought them out, content to linger among the dead while the living only tormented her.

The Central Cemetery in Vienna was one of the largest in Europe, containing the graves of many of Austria's most famous composers. Knowing what she did now about Irin history there and the Irina tie to music, the city's musical history made even more sense.

She walked the barren pathways toward the church, surrounded by grey headstones and the rare passing tourist. Some spaces were over-grown, but most on the central walkway were trimmed and many had freshly cut flowers, even in the dead of winter. It was one of her favorite cemeteries, a veritable city of the dead. Carefully tended, trimmed with lush gardens and populated by the marble figures of angels, poets, and mourners.

And Ava was freezing.

She tucked her scarf closer around her neck and wondered just how mad Malachi was going to be. Probably pretty mad.

It was the "I forbid it" that had been the last straw.

No. Just no.

He might have been hundreds of years older than her, but she wasn't a child to order around.

She turned left past the graves of famous composers, leaving Strauss, Beethoven, and Schubert behind as she searched for the gravestone that had become her first magazine cover.

It was a darkly sensual embrace emerging from stone. The male fig-ure's hands possessive. Commanding. An odd sculpture to find on the grave of an obscure nineteenth-century writer. But it had spoken to her, the woman's face tilted up to her lover in surrender.

Ava remembered how she'd felt when she photographed it.

Longing. For possession. To belong to another utterly. To be precious. Needed.

She heard a hoarse chirp by her leg. She looked down to see the black cat from her apartment building sitting by her leg.

"What the—"

Before her eyes, the cat grew, stretching in the shadows of the evergreen trees that surrounded the old graves. He became a man with gold eyes, his dark hair streaked with amber. His lips were lush, the angles of his face and eyes speaking Eastern heat. Silk and spices. Hooded eyes lined with black stared down at her.

"Your lover holds you that way."

"Holy shit," she breathed out.

"No, Vasu."

"Who are you?"

He cocked his head, as if it should have been obvious. "Vasu."

Ava blinked. "Okay then, Vasu. *What* are you?"

"Isn't it obvious?"

Awe turned to irritation. "First Jaron, then Death, now you—"

"Azril? Has he visited you?" Vasu cocked his head. "How interesting."

"I'm really just wondering if I should run screaming at this point, or if you're a friend of Jaron's."

"I would not call your sire a friend, but he is my brother. And screaming would do you no good. If I wanted to kill you, I would have already."

Ava turned to look around. All the humans that had been in the vicinity—groundskeepers, carriage drivers, a few tourists—were gone. She was alone with the fallen angel in the long black overcoat who called Jaron his brother.

She narrowed her eyes. "Why were you pretending to be a cat?"

"Why not? Cats are very unobtrusive. I often pretend to be a cat."

"That's…"

"Ingenious?"

"Weird."

A smile lifted the corner of his lips. "You are amusing. I can see why Jaron and Azril are interested in you."

"Does Jaron know you're here? How did you find me?"

217

"I followed your taxi after I left the scribe. He is very angry with you."

"I bet." Ava took a deep breath, reassured that the angel didn't seem to be trying to kill her. "You must run really fast as a cat."

"No, I took the shape of a bird when you entered the automobile."

"Of course you did."

Ava started walking toward the church. Vasu fell in step beside her.

"You're not really going to leave Vienna, are you?" He sounded as irritated as Malachi had. "It will ruin everything. And I don't like being here."

"Vienna?"

"It's very cold."

"What am I ruining? Jaron's plans to use me as bait to draw Volund here and use the Irin to help kill his enemy?"

"I believe Jaron has every intention of killing Volund himself. The Irin are only useful to take care of the Grigori and lesser angels. You would be no match for Volund."

"There aren't any Grigori in Vienna."

Vasu's mouth ticked up at the corner, and he looked past her. "Are you sure?"

She smelled it when the wind kicked up. A hint of sandalwood on the air.

"What have you done?" she hissed. "Did you lead them to me?"

"Don't be ridiculous. Grimold's sons have been trailing you for days." Vasu opened his jacket and Ava saw a row of silver daggers. "Come, Singer. Choose your weapon. Or have you learned to fight with magic alone?"

She ripped two daggers from his coat and turned to scan her surroundings. The cemetery was still utterly empty except for the two men who stood at the end of the row, black against the limestone path. Ava turned and saw two more.

"They're tracking me?" she asked.

"There are two more by the gate where you entered. How fast can you run?"

"Not fast enough." She began whispering a spell of protection around her mind. She was mostly immune to Grigori seduction, but she didn't want to take any chances. "If they're just tracking me—"

"No." Vasu cocked his head. "They want you. For what, I don't know."

Ava started running. There would be few taxis this far out of the city center. But the tram line ran near the main road. If she could get out of the gate…

"What are you doing?" Vasu ran beside her. Or did he? The Fallen didn't even look like he was moving, but… he was.

"Trying to escape. I'm not stupid; it's six against one. Are you going to help me or what?"

"I can't really do anything to them unless they attack me. And they won't attack me. It wouldn't be courteous."

"Must be nice!" She could hear their steps coming closer. "Listen," she panted. "Really nice to meet you, but I'm kind of fighting for my life here, so if you're not going to help—"

"If you promise to stay in Vienna, I will help."

"What?" she rasped out a breath. "You too?"

She cursed the immortal lives of stubborn men everywhere.

"I want this to be over. I want to go back to Chittorgarh."

"I don't know where that is, but… fine. I'll stay here."

"You vow this?"

"Yes!"

"Excellent."

Then Vasu grinned—actually grinned—and it was brilliant, beautiful, and utterly cruel. Her body came to a halt and Vasu came behind her.

"Turn."

Ava spun and the two Grigori soldiers were right on top of her. The spell came to her mind immediately.

"*Shanda vash,*" Ava whispered, and she felt and heard the whisper of Vasu's voice overlaying hers.

The Grigori soldiers didn't just stop, they flew back as if thrown by an invisible hand.

"*Man.*"

"Good," he whispered in her ear. "Now sing with me."

He whispered again, and she moved, racing toward the Grigori, both blades in her hands. She could feel Vasu like a shadow at her back.

Magic hummed in her veins as she whispered the next spell. "*Ba dahaa.*"

Both men screamed, clutching their temples in agony as she leapt on them.

"Now," Vasu whispered, and she kicked one in the side, her body reacting as if she were a trained soldier. The thought was in the back of her mind that she wasn't entirely in control of her body, but when she heard the shouts of the other Grigori and the approaching footsteps, she ignored it.

"Now, Ava!"

She twisted the head of one Grigori to the side, plunging the silver dagger into his neck. He began to dissolve beneath her, even as his friend tried to roll away.

Vasu pushed her toward him, whispering another spell in her ear.

"*Zi yada,*" she hissed and the soldier froze.

These weren't Irina spells. Had nothing to do with what she'd been taught, but Vasu whispered them in her ear, the formless mass of him at her back, and she repeated his words, the dark power in her rising to the surface.

Not Irina magic. Fallen magic.

It came as easy as breathing.

"*Kareshta,*" Vasu murmured as she plunged the dagger into the neck of the second Grigori. "Beautiful."

He rose as she did, turning and stripping off her coat so she could move. Her black shirt clung to her body like a second skin, and Ava ran toward the men who would pursue her, gold eyes flashing in rage, with Vasu pressing against her back.

They killed my son in front of my eyes… the last thing he saw was animals raping his mother.

Constance's pain was all she could hear as she threw her remaining knife, catching a Grigori in the eye.

"*Zi yada!*"

The Grigori collapsed to the ground and froze.

Another knife was in her hand, pressed there by Vasu's hand.

"Again."

Another dagger flung. Another bleeding Grigori on the ground.

He writhed as Ava ran to him, Vasu her shadow and the dust of the first two Grigori coating her lips.

The rage took her, spurred by the angel's voice in her ear.

"Kill him."

Ava didn't kill him cleanly. She stabbed the soldier in the gut twice, slicing up to his throat, slashing it as his blood spurted over her and tears ran down her face. Vasu's voice still whispered in her ear.

"They killed your sisters. Take your revenge. You deserve it and more."

She felt her gorge rise as she flipped the man over and stabbed him in the back of the neck.

"No more," Ava groaned.

"Finish it."

She plunged the blade into the neck of the fourth Grigori and waited, her hand frozen as the gold dust began to rise around her.

Vasu was in front of her, crouching down with fire in his eyes.

"The other two fled."

"Okay," she sobbed.

"That was beautiful, Ava."

Then Vasu leaned forward and gently kissed her on the lips.

The magic left in the space of a heartbeat, and Ava crawled to the bushes near an overgrown grave and threw up everything in her stomach. Vasu watched her with a curious expression.

"What do you feel? Guilt?"

"I don't know what I feel. I want to go home."

"Hmm." He stretched out next to her on the gravel path, ignoring the grit that must have embedded in his palms. He didn't move like Jaron did. This creature was at home in his body. "Where is home to you, I wonder? Not America."

Malachi.

Malachi was home. Wherever he was. However angry he was with her or she with him, Malachi was home, and she needed him.

"Tinc," Vasu murmured. "I'll take you to the scribe."

A tug in her belly, and then they were in the entryway of Ava and Malachi's apartment. She'd lost her coat. Her hair was tangled around her face, and she was covered in blood.

"Ava!" Malachi ran toward her, eyes on the angel who held her.

Vasu winked out of sight, and Ava collapsed.

"What happened?"

He picked her up and carried her to the bedroom, but Ava put her hand on the doorjamb.

"Shower. I have to get it off."

"Is this your blood?" His voice was panicked.

"Their blood. Their dust."

She licked her lips and tried to spit out the grit that had collected there.

"Who was that?"

"Vasu. Jaron's brother."

"Did the Fallen do this to you?"

"Grigori," she whispered as he opened the shower door and started stripping the bloody clothes off her. "They're here."

SHE curled into his chest, trying to crawl into as much of his heat as possible. Malachi had already called Damien and told him about the attack at the cemetery and Vasu's appearance. Rhys was digging into anything he could find on the archangel from the Indian subcontinent who was supposed to be dead.

"He wasn't dead," she whispered into his chest. "He… helped me. It was like he was in my body."

"*In* your body?"

"No, that's not right. More like he was… behind me maybe. Pushing me. I felt him with me the whole time. I moved so fast, Malachi. I've never moved that fast on my own. And he whispered spells to me. Magic I've never heard before, but it worked. Using those spells was as easy as breathing."

Malachi was silent for a minute, but his arms never left her. He'd wrapped himself around her and was holding her as if she might fall apart.

When Ava closed her eyes and remembered the blood spurting from the Grigori's throat, she felt like she might.

"But this Vasu didn't hurt you?"

"No, he helped. And the minute I thought about you, he brought me back here."

"So he could have taken you from there at any time?"

She nodded.

"Why?"

"What do you mean?"

"If he wanted to help you, why didn't he just take you away immediately? Bear in mind, I've never heard of a Fallen who can transport others, only themselves, so this might be unique to him. I don't know his power."

"I don't think he wanted to take me away. I think he was curious."

"Curious?"

"He made me promise to stay in Vienna, because he didn't like the cold. I have a feeling whoever Vasu is, Jaron is still the one in charge."

"He made you promise to stay in Vienna because he doesn't like the cold?"

"Yep. Whatever Jaron's plan is, this Vasu guy wants to get it over with."

"This sounds like a very odd angel."

She nodded. "He was the cat."

Malachi pulled away. "What?"

"The black cat who wandered in here? That was him."

Malachi cursed long and low.

"Hey, at least he got me to promise to stay in Vienna, right? You should be happy."

He squeezed her more tightly. "I don't care where we are. I only want you safe."

Ava's love for him was an ache in her heart. She kissed his chest, over his heart. Up his neck. Trailing her lips across his jaw.

"Kiss me," she whispered.

"Ava—"

"Please. I need you."

He met her mouth, his arms everything warm and real and safe. She was back at the cemetery, looking at the statue of the lovers, but it was Malachi who held her. Malachi who needed her. Malachi who was everything…

Everything.

She pushed him to his back, and his fingers dug into the small of her back as she crawled over him. When she sat up, he followed her, rocking up to take her mouth as Ava straddled his lap. She could feel him, hard and real beneath her, not a lover made of stone, but a man burning for her.

"Malachi."

"Want you," he breathed out, burying his hands in the waves of her hair, still damp from the shower. Her skin felt clean, but she hadn't felt whole again until he touched her. She dug her fingers into his shoulders as she felt the magic rise. Her mating marks began to glow in the dark room. His *talesm* shone with a silver light.

"*Reshon*," she whispered. "My *reshon*."

"Ava."

She threw her head back and felt the magic take over. The song hung in her throat, ready to be released.

Malachi put both hands on her cheeks, turning her face to meet his kiss. He drew back with a groan, the dark fire burning in his eyes.

"I'm ready," she whispered. "So ready. Please, let me sing to you. It's time."

Her mate wrapped his arms around her waist and nodded.

"Sing."

Chapter Nineteen

VOLUND LIFTED HIS HEAD and raged against the heavens, shattering the frozen valley where he rested. A chasm split the earth, raining water, ice, and mud into the rift that formed beneath his feet.

"NO!"

The blood boundaries were falling. He could feel the power of his old rival's blood twine within the blessings of the Forgiven.

Jaron was winning.

In his mind's eye, he saw the black sun rise as light and dark magic melded together. And as the moon's shadow covered the sun, the light from the stars hidden for a thousand years blinked to life.

"Do not fear the darkness."

His scream reached the heavens.

MALACHI lay in thrall to his mate. Rising above him, Ava was a vision in the dim room. Her hair damp against her shoulders, her skin dewy from the warmth of the shower and their shared heat. He braced himself, not knowing what to expect. Though he knew some of the traditions—the songs and litanies she had learned—the mating ritual happened only once in a scribe's lifetime. In this moment, he was as innocent as Ava.

He felt rather than heard when she started to sing.

"My beloved comes to me as the ground beneath my feet
Steadfast and faithful
The heavens direct our path…"

The words of the Old Language rose from her throat, her lips carefully forming the angelic tongue. Halting at first, then clearer as the magic took control of them both. Ancient instinct took over. He pushed the shirt she was wearing up and over her head, desperate to see his own vow written on her skin.

I am for Ava.

He released a breath when he saw it. Part of him was still transfixed every time it appeared over her heart. His finger traced the words he'd written. A memory locked in the black vault of his mind.

For her, my hand and voice.
For her, my body and mind.
Her strength in weakness.
Her sword in battle.
Her balm in pain.
I am hers.
Hers to cherish.
Hers to hold.
Hers to command.

The world around him ceased to exist. There was no city. No war. No angels or brothers or elders. Nothing could distract him from the purity of her voice. Her mating marks gleamed in the darkness as she continued to sing.

"My beloved holds me as the sky holds the moon
Vast and eternal
Our union is without end…"

Ava pushed his shirt up and over his head so they were both bare before the other. Her voice rose and fell as she sang the words legend said were given by the Forgiven to their children. The vows that bound them, not only in this life, but the next.

"My beloved warms me as the sun warms the earth
Sweet and rich
Our love mirrors the heavens…"

He felt the magic swell. The small electric lamp by the bedside flickered out and the only illumination was from the small window and the spells that lit their bodies. Tugged from his chest, the power spread over his skin, lighting his *talesm prim*, both old marks and new, before it traveled up and over, like a thread of quicksilver under his skin.

Malachi burned for her.

"My beloved is my own
First before others.
Before the bond of kin
Before mother or father
Brother or sister
Before the angelic host…"

He could feel her voice swell, reach a crescendo.

"This day I make my vow
I pledge my soul's magic to my beloved
In time of joy
In time of grief
In darkness and light
In life and death
This day I promise…"

And Malachi waited to hear the words she would give him, the words he would carve into his own skin in the ritual room, marking his body and heart as hers for all time. The words he would wear for the world to see that his mate had claimed him as her own.

"I promise," Ava whispered as she wrapped her arms around his neck, "to love you and protect you in every way I can. I will not let fear rule me. I will trust you with my heart and my song." He heard her choke back tears, and he pressed her cheek to his as she continued. "Because I called you in the darkest night of my soul. You heard me and you returned." She brushed a kiss across his temple. "You are my home."

She sat back and framed his face with her hands, looking into his eyes as she whispered, *"Da livkara bavatara ma."*

This scribe belongs to me.

The force of the mating spell drew a groan from his throat as it hit him, powerful and sweet. Ava's magic was blinding light edged in darkness. He closed his eyes as his back arched and the fire burned beneath his skin.

"Ava!"

"Stay still." She braced her hands on his shoulders as he leaned back and let the power of it wash over him. "Don't move. I can see them."

"I can *feel* them."

Pleasure and pain roiled in one intoxicating wave as the burning grew. He felt the knife dip into the fire and ink. The doors of memory slamming open in his mind.

Through the searing pain, he felt her. Through the flood, she held him. Her magic lifted him, turning his mind in circles as the invisible knife carved the ancient runes. Over his shoulders and chest. Down his arm and across his back.

"Touch me, Ava," he groaned. "Please."

"I don't want to hurt you."

"You won't."

He needed her to anchor him, because the flood of magic began to take him under. He could feel his power rushing back. It was like waking up after a vivid dream. Days and weeks and years tumbled in his mind, like the strands of an intricate tapestry tangling, unraveling, then forming something new. But the pattern was familiar. These were his years. His moments. His words.

They fell into his mind until their weight threatened madness.

Then…

One piece locked into place.

I heard you!

A hiss of steel and the bite against his skin.

Another piece locked.

"Do you have a name?"

A name?

"My name is Malachi."

Another and another and another.

Colored threads twisting in a hedgerow. Pine needles on the forest floor. Salt and cedar and wind in the pines.

In the crash of memory he became hers again.

"You make the voices go away."

A kiss.

One touch that had changed the world.

"You're not crazy, Ava. You're a miracle."

A miracle.

He didn't know what was real except for her.

She was real. The single voice in his mind.

"Come back to me."

So he did.

"MALACHI."

He heard her. Smelled the magic in the room like the lingering bite of ozone after a storm.

"Malachi?"

He blinked his eyes open and saw… everything.

Ava's hair hung around her face, a dark halo surrounding radiant gold eyes. Her mating marks still lit the room, and a sheen of silver reflected on her breasts. He looked down, then looked back at Ava. Her smile trembled on her lips.

"They're back."

He nodded. He could feel every inch, even the aching scars on his back where he knew his family marks had returned. But he couldn't take his eyes from her face. She must have given him new eyes, because his mate's skin was luminous.

"Does it hurt?"

Malachi paused. He knew that it must hurt. His brain registered the pain in his arms. But it was nothing to the pure jolt of power her mating song had given him.

"Will you say something?"

"No."

He sat up, wrapped his arms around her waist, and tackled her to the bed.

Ava gasped as he covered her. His mouth fell on hers in a ravenous kiss. He felt her breasts crushed against his chest. His hands tangled in her hair. Heat and magic and hunger swirled together in a vicious cocktail of need.

Malachi kissed her mouth, opening her lips with his tongue to taste her. Stroking along the lips that had worked such painful, beautiful magic. He bit her lower lip, sucked it into his mouth, and released it before he did the same to her upper.

ELIZABETH HUNTER

One of her hands clutched his hair, the other dug into his neck, pulling him closer as her legs wrapped around his waist.

Jaw. Neck. Throat.

He let his lips linger at the rapid pulse in her neck as she gasped for breath.

Then his lips and tongue went lower, tasting the golden skin of her breasts, teasing frantic cries of pleasure from her. He bit the inner curve that tempted him, marking her with his teeth as he pressed up at the small of her back. He lifted her soft belly to his lips. He could feel his aching skin stretch and heal around the black ink that had reappeared, but the silver glow of the magic she'd given him was a pure current running through his body.

He pressed forward, taking her mouth again.

She was his. Every inch of her. Every breath. Every cry.

"Malachi, I need you."

His to cherish. His to hold.

He ran a hand down the curve of her waist to her hip, stroking back and squeezing the tight round muscle in the palm of his hand. He pressed up and in, holding her there as the scent of her arousal filled the room.

"Please," she whispered. "Please."

He released her mouth only long enough to tear away the loose pants she wore. Then he shoved down his own and he was over her, poised at her entrance.

"Ava," he commanded. "Look at me."

Gold eyes met grey.

"You are mine."

"Yes."

Malachi drove into his mate with one thrust, sinking to the hilt and allowing his face to fall into her neck on a groan.

He closed his eyes and saw it again, a gold sky streaked with light.

Holy and wholly.

Their union a perfect mirror of eternity as their magic met and twined together. Light and dark spun in an endless whorl.

FAST. Then slow. Fast again.

"You're going to kill me," she panted after the second time they'd come together, and Malachi showed no sign of slowing down.

"Never."

Malachi teased her for hours, the potent cocktail of magic and endorphins forming a perfect storm of sexual energy. Ava was wrung out. Exhausted.

But he could also feel her happiness.

Her contentment was a balm over his soul. He could feel the magic she'd sacrificed to bond herself to him, but he refused to let fear spoil her gift.

"I love your vow." He stretched his arms over his head as she rode him.

She bent down, ran her lips over the flat, sensitive nipple surrounded by spells. Let her lips trail over the skin where he'd put her words.

"I will be proud to wear it," he said.

"I'm glad."

"I promise to always be a good home, Ava."

She paused and looked at him, her eyes stripped of every defense.

Malachi whispered, "A safe home. Always."

"I know."

"No matter where we go," he continued. "No matter what happens as the years pass, I promise."

He sat up, held her cheeks with both hands and watched her smile spread.

"I love you."

"I came back to you," he said. "I remember. It was a choice, and I chose you."

Ava's jaw dropped when she realized what he was talking about. "Was it beautiful?"

"Very."

"I'm so sorry."

"Don't. I told you," he said, rubbing his thumb over her trembling lip. "I'd abandon heaven if you weren't there."

"How can I repay that?" she said. "There's nothing—"

"There is no debt. Love is not a debt. It's a promise. And I promised you once that I'd be back. Don't you remember?"

"In the cistern," she said. "Before—"

"I promised." He smiled when he pinched her chin. "You only had to call me, *canim*. You may not have noticed this, but sometimes your mate is forgetful."

She laughed and laughed, and that too was a balm on his soul. Because though Malachi had left her, he hadn't known to miss her in heaven. Not until she called.

Ava pressed a delicate kiss to his lips. "I'm glad you're back," she said against his mouth.

"I don't plan on leaving again." He rolled so she was under him. "And now I have a powerful singer as my mate."

She arched her back and ran her hands over his shoulders, along his biceps, and over the spells on his forearms until she could wrap her fingers around his wrists. "And I have a magnificent scribe who has claimed me."

He flexed his hips against hers and hummed in satisfaction when she moaned.
"You do."

"Make me yours again."

He leaned down, bracing an arm near her shoulder as he took her mouth.

"Always."

Chapter Twenty

SHE WATCHED HIM AS HE left for the Library. He'd woken before dawn to go and tattoo the mating vow on his chest. And though he
would only be walking through the city center, he was strapping silver
daggers to his body, taking every precaution before he left her.

"You're staring," he whispered. "You should go back to sleep."

"I'm not tired. And you're too beautiful not to stare at."

He smiled. It might have been just a little smug. But then, they'd both
been voracious the night before. Ava guessed it was only the magic making
her restless.

"Damien will be here in a minute," he said, sitting on the edge of the
bed. "How do you feel?"

"I don't feel weaker or anything like that."

He tucked a piece of her hair behind her ear. "With Grigori in the
city, I don't want you going anywhere alone. Normally we would have
performed our mating away from everything. Taken time apart to give our
bond time to mature so we would both be at full strength. We probably
should have done it at my grandparents' house when we were there."

"We weren't ready then."

"No."

She took a deep breath and traced the line of a tattoo that peeked
over his collar. "Do you really remember everything?"

"Yes. Including how stubborn you've always been. You pulled a gun
on me once," he said with a grin.

"I thought you were a nefarious kidnapper. Bent on seducing me and
stealing me away."

"That sounds like an excellent plan."

"Yes, let's do that."

He grabbed her hand and kissed it. "Until we can, I want you to be careful."

"The spells Vasu told me, they were pretty effective."

"Hmm."

She'd written down what they had sounded like to her, but he hadn't recognized the words. She's told him the instant effect—both the excruciating mental pain and the paralysis they'd caused—and he'd been impressed.

"What are you thinking?"

"I'm thinking that the Fallen and Forgiven might have very different magic."

Ava frowned. "Isn't it all basically the same thing?"

Malachi shrugged. "Yes? I don't really know, to be honest. The Old Language is the angelic tongue, but you have to remember we only have what our ancestors were taught. We're talking about thousands of years of oral and written tradition following that. Irin magic has changed over time. I'm sure of it. It could be the spells Vasu taught you are words that have been forgotten. Or were never given to us at all."

"Well, I'm not forgetting them. If I can use those against Grigori—"

"I still want you to be careful. The Grigori advantage has always been numbers. In Vienna, that threat is mitigated because of the larger Irin population. At the same time, it's a city of bureaucrats and politicians, not active soldiers."

"I'll be careful."

He pressed a hard kiss to her lips. "Thank you, *canm*. That puts my mind at ease. I'm going to the ritual room with Rhys, but we'll be back as soon as I'm done."

She spread her hand over his heart. "So it's going here, huh?"

He nodded.

"Do I need to write it down for you?"

He shook his head. "I remember every word."

"Good."

Malachi stood and stretched his shoulders. "It doesn't hurt, but I feel them. I don't know how to describe it."

"You really remember everything?" She didn't know why she was having a hard time believing it, but she was. "Really?"

His smile turned wicked. "Yes. Even that thing you told me you like when—"

A quiet knock came at the door.

"Oh look." She jumped up and threw on her robe. "Sounds like Damien. You better go."

His low chuckle followed her out the bedroom door.

Yes, her mate was definitely back.

Malachi waited at the door until he heard Damien's quiet voice, then he cracked it open and greeted his brother with a solid embrace. Damien started in surprise until he pulled back and looked into his brother's eyes.

"You're back?" he asked. Damien's warm eyes turned to Ava. "He's back. Sister?"

Ava shrugged. "We completed our mating ritual. And when I gave him my magic, it just…"

Damien clapped Malachi on the shoulder. "And your *talesm*?"

"Complete." He patted his left chest. "Except for one very important one here."

"This is a beautiful day," Damien said. "I'll call Sari after you've left. She'll want to plan a mating feast for you."

Ava said, "That's really not necessary. I mean—"

"It is," Damien said. "Part of rebuilding our people is recovering our traditions. Sari and I have already claimed you as a sister. Please let us, Ava."

Ava threw her arms around the big man. "Thank you."

Damien kissed the top of her head. "I hadn't planned to let you go, you know. Just because he came back. You're our family now."

"Give me my mate," Malachi pulled her away from Damien. "A kiss before I go."

It was sweet, lingering, and long. Malachi paid no mind to his audience, even if that audience was his watcher and the man who'd claimed Ava as a younger sister.

He only pulled away when Damien started laughing.

"Go," he said. "Put her brand on your chest before you see her again. I'll keep her safe."

"Stay with Damien," he said, his hand on her cheek. "I'll be back soon."

She nodded and he slipped out the door.

Then Ava took a deep breath and turned to Damien. "Coffee?"

"Please. And you need to tell me about this angel you met. Malachi called, but I want to hear it from you."

"Fine." She started the water. "But I want to know about this rumor I heard about the Templar Knights."

"Damn gossiping Irina," he muttered.

HE was silent for a long time after she described the fight she'd had with the four Grigori at the cemetery.

"All the humans disappeared?"

She nodded. "Jaron did the same thing once. He said something about them being in a dream."

"We know the Fallen can manipulate time and human perception. It must have something to do with that."

"Whatever his reasons, Vasu did protect me. I didn't even know the Grigori had followed me, and I'm usually pretty good at spotting a tail after years of having bodyguards when I travel. I'd let down my guard."

Damien shrugged. "Or he led them to you to see what you'd do. We have no idea what his motives could be."

"He was… oddly honest. I think he's an ally of Jaron's. He could have hurt me anytime he wanted. I'd let him in the apartment when he was a cat."

"A cat? Malachi left that part out."

Ava explained as she downed another cup of coffee and devoured the breakfast pastry Damien had brought. If it weren't for the typical voracious Irina metabolism, she'd blow up like a whale. The sweets in Vienna were out of this world.

"I've never heard of one shifting to an animal before, but that could be something unique to this Vasu. Perhaps the same talent that allows him to transport you over distances."

"Aren't angels basically the same?"

"No." Damien stood to get himself another coffee. "They were created to perform different duties, therefore they have different talents. That's why a daughter of Leoc has visions, but a daughter of Ariel has an affinity for the elements, like Sari." He lifted an eyebrow. "Can you move rocks and wood?"

Ava grinned. "That was pretty cool at the Library, huh?"

Damien's mouth lifted in the corner. "She was a vision. I was the envy of every scribe in that room."

"I love that you're not intimidated by her power. By how outspoken she is."

"Why would I be? It only makes me stronger." He sighed. "You lived in the human world for too long."

"I'm better now."

"I remember when I first met you."

"You were so suspicious."

"You were so jumpy."

They both smiled, and Ava was glad—as painful as Malachi's loss had been—that she'd found Damien.

She put a hand over his. "It's good to have a brother."

THE mating feast at Damien and Sari's house wasn't quite the grand event that Ava had imagined. It was more like a really fun, really long dinner party with lots of speeches and blessings. Everyone stood up to say something really eloquent or really funny. All the scribes from the Istanbul house were there, along with Renata and Mala. Orsala, Sari, and Damien were the hosts. Sari and Damien's brother-in-law had also been invited. Gabriel was the mate of Sari's sister, who had died during the Rending. Ava could see the tension between him and Damien, but she didn't ask questions.

She was too happy.

Malachi was at her side. The passionate, intense man who had slowly been returning to her was back completely. He joked with his brothers. Held her close to his side all night. Teased her shamelessly and was quick to open his shirt and show off the new mating mark to anyone who asked.

He also watched every door and window like commandos might crash through at any time.

"Relax," she whispered to him when she'd gone to stand by the window and watch the moon. He'd drawn her away from the window without a word, distracting her with a kiss.

"What are you talking about?"

"You. You've been like... poised for action all night."

He slid his hand down to cup her bottom. "Well, if you'd like to leave now—"

"That's not what I'm talking about," she said with a laugh as she wiggled away. "You and Max and Leo looked all over the city today. And I know you've got some of your buddies outside right now. We're not going to be invaded by enemy forces."

His smile wavered. "We don't know that."

"What did Orsala find out about Vasu?"

"That he was supposedly killed by the archangel Galal over two centuries ago. But before then, he'd been an ally of Jaron's in Central Asia. He was also known as one of the more... human of the angels."

"How—"

"The legends say that Vasu was young—the equivalent of an angelic child—when the angels fell. He interacted with humanity more than the other Fallen. Humans in his area considered him a kind of god because he came among the population so much."

"Interesting. Well, he was different from Jaron. He, um..." She cleared her throat. "He kissed me."

"What?"

"It wasn't sexual." She put a hand on his chest. "It was after the fighting. I was in shock. And he was... curious, I think."

Malachi's face was stormy. "He kissed you?"

"I didn't kiss him back!"

"What did you do?"

"Well…" She paused, trying to remember the tumult in the cemetery. "I think right after that I crawled over to the bushes and puked. Probably not the reaction he was going for."

Malachi burst into laughter. "Probably not."

"Just relax," she said. "How many mating feasts are we going to have after all?"

"My mother had seven."

Ava blinked. "What?"

"Yes, one with her immediate family and new mate. One with my father's. Then the extended families host one. And of course, my father's family was in Turkey, so—"

"Wow, so…" She looked around the room. "Are we going to have to do a lot of these?"

"Not if you don't want to," he said. "We're not exactly the traditional Irin couple."

"No." She smiled. "We're just… us."

Rhys wandered over. "I feel privileged. The first mating of an Irin scribe and one of the *kareshta*. Doesn't this feel historic?"

Ava could see the scholarly excitement, but she had a hard time thinking of her own life as historic in any sense.

"Historic may be stretching things, Rhys."

"I don't think so," he said. "I want to know when Damien plans to reveal the existence of the Grigori women. We should all be in the Library for that."

Malachi seemed hesitant. "Do we need to? We promised Kostas our discretion. He has women and children he's protecting. Revealing anything to the elders could be dangerous at this point."

"But we must," Rhys said. "Not only could this change everything about how our race views the Grigori, but we may have trouble getting a mandate from the elders unless they know there is something to be gained."

Ava asked, "What exactly do you mean by mandate? In Irin terms."

Rhys said, "Think of it as… a rule of engagement. Officially, our mandate as scribes now includes protecting humans, killing Grigori, and hunting angels if they hunt us first. A watcher who deviates from that can be disciplined. His scribes could receive censure."

"So, officially, Damien and you guys have been breaking all kinds of rules."

"Yes," Malachi said. "But Damien is old and powerful enough that no one is going to question him too much."

"Did you know he was a Templar Knight?"

Both the men blinked.

"What?" Malachi said.

"This is awesome," she said. "I love knowing stuff you guys don't."

"Whether that's true or not," Rhys continued, "one of the reasons Damien has been petitioning the elders is to change the mandate of the scribe houses to include more offense against the Fallen—specifically Volund—based on the attacks in Istanbul and Oslo."

Malachi nodded. "He's not having much success."

"But the knowledge that there are Grigori women being victimized would be another motivation for taking action."

"Yes," Rhys said. "Leo was right. There are thousands of scribes without mates because there are so few women left after the Rending. The elders would not be able to ignore that. The Watchers' Council would force them to expand the mandate. They would see the *kareshta* as potential mates, as you and Ava are mates."

Malachi tensed. "You're saying that not only should we reveal the existence of the *kareshta*, but we should also reveal that Ava is of their blood?"

"Why wouldn't we?"

He squeezed her tighter as one of the scribes she didn't know came up to Rhys.

"We have a situation," he said quietly.

"What is it?" Rhys asked.

"There is a… I don't know what he is. He smelled Grigori, but he didn't attack." The guard sounded confused. "Just handed me a note to give to Maxim and ran."

"What did he look like?" Malachi asked.

The guard shrugged. "Like a Grigori. I would have killed him, but he came and left quickly. He looked to have a dozen men with him. I was prepared to call for help when he mentioned Maxim's name."

"Give me the note," Rhys said. "And wait here."

"Kostas?" Malachi murmured as they walked to a quieter corner.

"Possibly. Or a trap."

"Have you ever heard of a dozen Grigori walking through the middle of Vienna like that? We're only blocks from the Library."

"None would dare."

Except, Ava suspected, a heretic Grigori with nothing to lose. But Kostas had been adamant about secrecy when they'd met him in Sofia. What could have caused him to seek them out now?

"Ava?" Malachi reached for her hand and she took it. So much for reassuring him nothing was going to happen.

Rhys approached Max in the corner, who started and grabbed for the note his brother held out.

"Malachi," he called from across the room. "With me?"

Malachi nodded and tried to let Ava's hand go, but she held on tighter.

"I'm going with you."

"Ava—"

"He didn't hurt me before. He's not likely to do it now. And Kyra might be with him."

After meeting her grandmother, Ava was desperate to talk to the *kareshta* woman again.

Malachi paused, nodded. "Stay close."

"I will."

THE four of them slipped out of the house and down the stairs, turning right when the earlier guard nodded in that direction. In an alley, just off the main road, they caught the muted scent of sandalwood.

"Maxim," someone hissed from the shadows.

"Kostas?"

The man flew from the shadows and grabbed Max by the neck, tackling him to the ground.

Malachi and Rhys immediately flew to their brother's aid.

"Who did you tell?" Kostas shouted. "Who was it?"

"Kostas, I—"

"I trusted you!"

Ava saw the dozen Grigori standing in the shadows, but none went to aid their brother. They were watching. Waiting to see what Malachi and Rhys would do. Ava had the feeling that the minute any knives came out, all bets were off.

She saw Malachi reach for one of his daggers. "Malachi!" she cried.

Her mate pulled away from the fight to go to her, leaving Max, Kostas, and Rhys tumbling on the ground.

"Stop them!" she yelled. "Something's happened. We need to talk, not fight."

One of the Grigori stepped forward just as Rhys tore Kostas from Max's throat and stood between the two men.

"Yes, something happened," the beautiful man's face was twisted in rage. "One of you betrayed us. Betrayed our sisters. The children…"

Ava gasped and Malachi immediately sheathed the knife he'd been about to pull and put his hands down.

"None of us betrayed you," he said. "And we would never put your women in jeopardy. We've been trying to find a way to help."

"The monastery was attacked," Kostas panted out. "Old women. Children. They killed anyone who couldn't flee."

"No." Ava felt her knees give out.

Malachi caught her.

"Kostas," Max panted. "I would never—"

"No one knew where it was. We were so careful. We turned away dozens because we couldn't be sure their sires were dead."

Beyond the anger, Ava could see grief tearing up Kostas's eyes. The sickening rage of a protector who had failed.

"Who was it?" Kostas asked again. "*Who did you tell?*"

Max shook his head. "I don't know, my friend. None of us would put children at risk."

Kostas still glared. "Kyra was in the city with me. Sirius"—he pointed at the Grigori who had spoken up—"was the guard there. Most of his men are dead now. There were too many. Some of the older girls and women were able to escape with some of the smallest. But the oldest *kareshta* and some of the youngest…"

Sirius said, "We lost thirteen of our sisters and a dozen free Grigori. The monastery was compromised. They knew exactly how to attack."

Max said, "You've never taken me there. None of us knew where it was, Kostas. Think. This betrayal did not come from us."

"It was Svarog's men. Assassins from Hungary. We didn't even know they were in our territory." Kostas's shoulders slumped in defeat. "We didn't even know."

"The other women, are they safe?" Ava asked.

"For now," Sirius said.

"How many are left?"

"Eighteen. We need to find them a new place. Right now they're scattered among our brothers in populated areas. They can't stay there for long. It's not good for the little ones."

"I may know a place," Ava said. "But you'll need papers for them. It's not in Bulgaria."

The safe house Karen, Bruno, and Astrid had set up outside Prague was intended for Irina, but it could work for the *kareshta* as well. Ava was certain they wouldn't turn innocents away. She knew it was remote, but she had no idea how hard it would be to get papers for foreign women and children.

"It shouldn't be a problem," Max said. "I've already helped with IDs for them in the past." He turned to Kostas. "How could you think I'd tell?"

Kostas only shook his head.

Sirius said, "Kostas told me you were coming here to petition the elders. Some of them must know about the *kareshta*. We think some in Vienna are in league with the Fallen."

"Conspiracy theories," Malachi said.

"We have said nothing publicly," Rhys said. "Not even to our allies. These women are innocents. Most of the Irin—"

243

"Most of the Irin would kill them on sight, simply because they carry the blood of their enemy," Kostas bit out. "I have no faith in your mercy." He hung his head. "Nor should I expect it."

Ava pushed past Malachi and knelt by him. "I have Grigori blood. The scribes in Istanbul didn't turn me away."

Kostas lifted his eyes. "Did they know?"

"No. But when they found out, my mate didn't turn his back on me. None of them did. It will matter to some Irin, but not all."

Kostas shook his head.

"We're more than our blood," Ava whispered. "More than our pasts. We just have to make them see that. They need to see you and Kyra. See the good that you're doing."

"I'm not dragging my sister into this"— he looked around—"vipers' nest. Vienna would never be safe for her."

"You don't know that. And I think that decision should be left up to Kyra." Ava rose to her feet and held out her hand. "Stand up. Sitting on the ground angry isn't helping anyone. Brooding isn't productive."

Her irritation made the corner of his mouth turn up. "You remind me of her, you know."

"Then you should be able to predict how stubborn I can be. Come on," Ava said. "Come inside and let's figure out a way to fix this."

V.

BARAK SAT IN HIS MOST FAMILIAR human form, watching the groundskeepers trim the bushes in the snow-blanketed cemetery in the middle of the Irin city. A conspiracy of ravens watched him from the bare branches of a lime tree arching over a family crypt where a frost-dusted woman sat with a scroll on her lap, staring into the heavens. Some melancholic mourner had placed a red rose there, and the despairing woman clutched it in her hand.

Vasu appeared behind him, also in his most familiar form.

"What has gotten into you?" Barak asked.

"I have decided this is amusing. Is he here yet?"

"No, but I've put the cemetery into a dream for when he comes."

"Why? I merely—"

His voice was cut off when Jaron appeared beside him in a rage.

Without a word, Jaron launched Vasu across the graveyard, his body hurled through the pillars of a memorial, which crashed with a massive thud, marble shards and ice flying through the frosty air.

Barak sighed. "You should have known."

Vasu countered, his human form disappearing in a blink, then reappearing behind his brother, clutching Jaron's shoulders as the two disappeared, only to reappear at the top of the church dome in the distance. Vasu threw Jaron off the tower, but the more powerful angel blinked out of sight and reappeared next to Vasu, shoving the angel off the blue-green dome and into the air where Vasu transformed into a large raven, one of his favorite forms.

The raven came to light on the tree across from Barak. The conspiracy took flight, leaving him alone and staring at Barak.

"I told you not to play games with her," the other angel said. "He is possessive of his daughters."

The voice that came from the raven's mouth was human, even if its form was not. "She's not his daughter."

Jaron appeared beneath the tree. "She is of my line, and she is mine. That is all you need to know. Play your games with your own blood, brother."

With a spread of wings, Vasu transformed again into the black-haired man with deep gold eyes. His black coat flapping behind him, he walked to Barak and sat down next to the weary angel.

"It was very informative to shadow her."

"You spoke knowledge to her mind," Barak said. "It has entered the world now. Are you aware of the consequences?"

"So our Master has not given us leave to tell our secrets to our children." Vasu rolled his eyes. "This would be important if I cared about staying in His graces. I do not."

Jaron hissed. Even Barak drew away.

"You tempt heaven, brother."

"I tempt nothing but the whims of the Creator. And since I do not aim to leave this realm, it is of no concern to me."

"Someday you will remember," Jaron said. "And you will curse this day."

"I will curse nothing. I am not capable of regret."

Jaron's mouth curled up at the corner. "We are capable of entirely more than what we like to admit, Vasu. For now, stay away from my daughter."

"She has given her magic to the scribe," Barak said. "This has never happened before. Their union is unique."

"It will not be for long. I have seen it."

"Was this your aim?" Vasu asked, his head cocked to the side. "A blending of Irin and Grigori magic? My brother, you have more heretical tendencies than I gave you credit for. My apologies for doubting you."

"I hate to disappoint you, Vasu. But I believe this serves the will of our Master."

Barak asked, "Why?"

"Azril returned the scribe."

Barak and Vasu said at once, "His Will be done."

"He desires unity?" Barak asked.

"If He did not, I would not have seen our triumph over Volund. Would not have seen our return."

"Redemption," Barak whispered, "was never my goal."

"But if it allows us to return," Jaron said, "I am willing to play on the side of the light."

Vasu crouched on the ground and drew his fingers through the snow, writing words that would disappear in moments as the snow began to fall.

"Svarog's children have routed your son," Vasu said, staring at the crystalline flakes. "They will be here in days."

Barak said, "Grimold's get have been here for months, playing quietly while Volund chased the Irina from his territory. Svarog has called his sons. They will drag themselves here—screaming in rebellion, perhaps—but they will come."

Vasu said, "Two armies are aligned against us, Jaron. Are you content to let your sons stay in hiding?"

"My sons have other tasks now. I do not need my army. I will take the Irin as my own."

"The Irina are here," Barak said. "Volund is foolish to underestimate them. They have no authority that constrains them as the scribes do."

"And we will use that to defeat him," Jaron said, brushing drifts of snow from his bare arms. The glyphs that marked his skin glowed with a faint silver light. As his daughter's magic had transformed with her bonding to the scribe, he felt his own powers changing. Melding into something he could not predict. A rush of emotion had reached him the night of their union. Feelings he had not experienced for thousands of years.

He found the experience disconcerting.

And if he had found it disconcerting, he could not predict how Volund would feel when he lowered the shields around Ava. Whatever strange magic their union had worked would hit his enemy full force the moment he could feel her blood.

Volund would be unbalanced, and Jaron would strike.

It would not be long now. The singers had returned. The scent of magic in the city had shifted.

"He knows we're here," Barak said. "How long must we wait? Their numbers grow by the hour."

"Not long," Jaron said. "Soon the council will be complete, and we will reveal ourselves."

Vasu looked up from the snow, a smile on his face. "Then we demons shall play at being heroes, and Death will visit us again."

Chapter Twenty-one

IT WASN'T, MALACHI MUSED, a traditional end to a mating feast. But it seemed oddly appropriate for him and Ava.

Kostas and the Grigori who seemed to be his lieutenant, Sirius, were sitting across the dinner table from Damien and Sari. Orsala was on their right, and Gabriel on their left. Maxim sat next to Kostas, and Ava and Malachi had taken a spot at the end of the table, bridging the gap. Rhys and Leo stood in one corner with Renata and Mala. Both sides eyed the other with distrust, while the rest of the guests had joined the free Grigori soldiers outside.

The scent of sandalwood filled the air, and Malachi knew every scribe in the room struggled to restrain the ingrained instinct to kill the two men.

Gabriel was the first one to speak. "If this gets out, we will both be under censure, no matter what allies we have."

"The world is changing," Damien said.

"Not that much. This is too soon."

"I agree with you," Kostas said. "But this has been forced on us. Svarog's forces are coming to Vienna. Grimold's are already here."

Ava asked, "How do you know?"

"I can spot the signs," Kostas said. "If you look at police reports, there will be a slow build of attacks against indigents and prostitutes. The winter weather helps conceal it. Most will probably be written off by the human authorities because of the cold."

"Are you sure?" Rhys asked.

Sirius answered him. "You can verify it with human authorities if you like, but I agree with Kostas. The Grigori here haven't been attacking Irin targets. They wouldn't dare. But Grimold is Volund's lapdog. His people have been here since Volund lost so many of his children in Oslo."

"We'll look," Sari said. "But that doesn't solve the problem of your women."

"Prague," Ava said. "Can you contact Astrid?"

Sari and Damien exchanged a look.

"It is an acceptable risk," Damien said. "But we must give them the option to refuse."

"They won't," Orsala said. "There are children among them."

"I thank you," Sirius told her graciously. The man's beautiful features were obscured by the obvious stress in the lines of his face. His accent marked him as Russian in origin, and he'd grown his hair and beard long. Malachi guessed it was to detract from the unnatural beauty of his race.

"The failure is mine," Sirius continued. "They are my responsibility. I will accompany them and provide whatever assistance your people require."

"There are scribes there who can watch over them," Damien said. "The location of our safe houses must not be compromised."

Sirius stiffened, and Kostas laid a hand on his second's arm. "Peace. We can work out the details later, and Kyra will be with them."

"We would never harm innocents," Orsala said.

"You would be wrong to think them all innocent," Kostas said. "Not all of our sisters are… well. Some are a danger to themselves and others. Part of Sirius's job is to watch those who are not wholly sane."

Sari said, "The children—"

"Some of the children are the worst," Sirius said quietly.

The silence was tangible as Malachi imagined children driven mad by the voices in their minds and the horrors they might have witnessed at the hands of their own sires.

Orsala asked, "Can they be restrained with magic?"

Sirius and Kostas exchanged a look. "Possibly. We have no magic that can affect them, but we are not Irina."

Orsala nodded. "I will go with the *kareshta*," she said. "That should be sufficient."

"Grandmother—"

"I've decided," she said. "The elder singers will be arriving within the week. I have nothing to offer in battle they do not have."

Kostas said, "The singers are returning?"

Sari paused, then said, "Many of them are already here. We've been in contact with havens around the globe. Of the seven former elders, three are still living and willing to take office. The other regions have sent representatives. The Irina council will be active within a week."

"That's when we should announce it then," Malachi said. "When the Irina council has taken their place in the Library."

"Announce what?" Gabriel asked.

"The existence of the *kareshta*."

Malachi felt Ava's hand tighten on his as the room held its collective breath.

"Who are you to make that decision?" Gabriel asked. "A censured scribe from Istanbul who was rumored to be dead. You show up in Vienna with a mate no one has heard of and suggest revelations that could disrupt the foundations of our race. *Who are you?*"

Malachi leaned forward. "I am the only Irin scribe in history mated to one of the *kareshta*."

No one had any response to that, so Malachi continued. "I am a warrior of Mikhael's line. And I've seen the dark edge of power in my mate. I don't fear it. I claim it. I *did* die. And I was returned from heaven for a reason. We met"—he reached out and took Ava's hand—"for a reason. *That* is who I am, and I will bear witness to it."

"We both will," Ava said.

Gabriel sat back, clearly still perturbed by Malachi's presumption. Malachi didn't care.

"And you may not agree with me." He looked around the table. "Any of you. But I think Kostas *and* Kyra need to be present at the Library when we tell the elders the world as they've known it has changed."

"No," Kostas said immediately. "I will not consent to allow my sister here when there are unknown threats against her."

"I agree with Malachi," Damien said.

"As do I," Sari concurred. "We can protect your sister."

Kostas still looked dubious. Malachi could hardly blame him. He was taking a great risk, making allies of those who'd spent their lives trying to kill those of his blood.

Renata said, "I will guard her as well. Practically speaking, the only threat to her would be other Irina, and we can handle them. No scribe would harm a woman in our company, even if she carried the look of a Grigori."

"But they'd kill me on sight," Kostas said. "You cannot argue with that. There is no possible way I could go to the Library. My scent would give me away in a second."

Everyone fell silent, forced to acknowledge the truth of his words until a lone voice at the end of the room spoke.

"I can mask his scent."

They all turned to see the dark form of an angel, chin propped on his hand as he rested his elbow on the edge of the table.

There were shouts of alarm. Weapons were pulled. Defensive positions taken. Malachi edged in front of his mate, but she sighed and pushed him to the side.

"Vasu," she said. "How long have you been here?"

"Long enough. I can mask the scent of Barak's son."

"Everyone relax," Ava said. "I don't think he's here to cause trouble. At least not the violent kind."

Malachi itched to reach across and plunge a silver blade in the nape of the angel's neck. It wouldn't kill him, but it would be very, very satisfying.

Vasu looked at him and winked. "Meow."

Only Ava's hand on Malachi's shoulder kept him from lunging at the black-haired angel.

"Explain," Ava said. "Why would you do it?"

Vasu sat up. "Obviously so I could see the look on their faces when they saw a Grigori in the middle of their precious Library," he said. "Also because it serves our purposes for our sons to be called into battle at this time. It would be better if they were not killed on sight. My children have already felt my call." He cocked his head and looked at Kostas. "So have Barak's, even if they do not recognize it."

The color drained from Kostas's handsome face. "No."

"Oh yes."

The Grigori stood in a rage, realizing his free will had only been an illusion. "No!"

Sirius stood next to him, his eyes tormented. "Why? We thought he was dead. Why would our father—"

"Calm yourselves." Vasu waved a hand at them. "Your sire has no intention of building his army again. He has other purposes in mind."

"He and Jaron want to return to heaven, don't they?" Ava asked quietly. "Jaron told me. 'I will tear the threads of heaven to return.' That's what he told me in a vision."

"Did he?" Vasu asked, all innocence.

It was a disturbing expression on a fallen angel.

"What is their plan?" Malachi asked. "How is Volund a part of it? What do they aim to do?"

Vasu looked him straight in the eye and said, "I have no idea."

And Malachi knew he was lying.

Rage boiled up. Months of frustration at being used like a pawn. Weeks of uncertainty, knowing his mate was in danger and being forced to rely on one of his mortal enemies to protect her.

Malachi flew out of his seat with a roar, only to find the chair Vasu had occupied completely empty. He spun, but the angel was already standing behind Kostas and Sirius. Bending down, he kissed both their foreheads then, with a wink at Ava, he disappeared.

Everybody in the room was frozen, then the shouts all came at once.

"And *these* are our allies?" Gabriel yelled at Damien.

"What did he mean? Does this mean Barak—"

"—how many Grigori is that? Are we supposed to fight *with* them?"

"—not know Jaron was speaking to Ava. Directly to her?"

"We still have no idea—"

Mala's staff crashed down on middle of the dining room table, and she threw out an angry sign.

Everyone fell silent again.

"That means 'Shut up,'" Ava said. "I know that one."

Orsala stood. "First things first. Damien, you are the oldest scribe in the room. Can you detect any scent of Grigori on our new… friends?"

Damien leaned closer, staring at Sirius and Kostas. Then he closed his eyes, stroked long fingers up his forearm to activate his magic, and inhaled one long breath.

"Nothing," he said, opening his eyes. "Not even with my *talesm*. They smell human."

Gabriel also leaned forward. "Astonishing."

"Well, he is an angel," Ava muttered. "Just kind of a weird one."

Sirius said, "Vasu was always known as a trickster. His sons are moody and unpredictable, but they worship him as a god."

"It's true," Kostas said. "He annoyed my father. His sons are madmen, but if Vasu calls them, they'll come without question."

Orsala said, "He's cloaked you for now. It's possible he's cloaked all his children. He mentioned Barak's children and his own. Can we assume Jaron's Grigori will be joining us as well?"

Everyone looked at Kostas. He shrugged. "Most of my father's children follow me now. I've killed those who wouldn't. Jaron's children are more mixed. The majority fled east after he lost Istanbul. A few tried to seek refuge with us, but we turned them away."

"Why?" Leo asked. "Wouldn't more free Grigori help your cause?"

"They weren't free, because I knew Jaron wasn't dead," Sirius said.

"How?" Ava asked.

Malachi returned to her side.

"Because he's been feeding me power for nearly fifty years," Kostas admitted.

Malachi saw Ava's eyes widen.

"Me as well," Sirius said. "Our father disappeared. Jaron was his closest ally. We had both stopped feeding from human women. We would have died without Jaron's help and the help of our sisters. We don't have longevity spells as you do. We're getting older."

Malachi didn't see it in their faces, but he saw it in their eyes. Both men looked exhausted.

"Jaron also directed *kareshta* to us through a doctor in Istanbul. Most had been living in the human world. They thought they were mad. We took them in if we could or found other safe places for them."

Interesting. Kostas appeared clueless that the "doctor" who'd been sending women to them was Jaron himself.

"Even after Istanbul, we knew Volund hadn't killed him," Sirius said. "He's one of the most powerful archangels in existence. But his children will never be free until he is dead. We could never trust that they were acting of their own will and not their father's."

Malachi felt Ava shiver at his side.

Though they couldn't affect her will, Ava would never be free until both Jaron and Volund were gone from the earthly realm.

Jaron wanted to kill Volund. Jaron wanted to return to heaven. If both those things were accomplished, Malachi's mate would be truly free.

Malachi said, "I don't know about his children, but for now our purposes align with Jaron's. So what can we do to help him?"

"Wait for the Irina council to reform," Sari said. "Then reveal the truth about the *kareshta*. And about Kostas and his brothers."

More silence as they took in Sari's words.

"Many will resist seeing them as allies," Max said. "Some will find it impossible."

Damien said, "Then we deal with that when it occurs. If the armies of three angels are descending on Vienna, then Mikhael's blood will rise. The Irin here are sleeping, not dead. They will take their allies as they come."

"And more Irina will come if they see the opportunity for vengeance," Renata added. "Plus, the opportunity to save sisters more lost than we ever were."

"Call Kyra," Sirius said to Kostas.

Kostas shook his head. "Brother—"

"Call her. You know it's the right thing to do. It should be her choice. And we cannot defend them ourselves. It is time to ask for help."

"IS it just me," Ava asked, "or does it seem quieter outside than inside?"

"It's not just you." Malachi sat next to her in the corner of the library at Damien and Sari's house.

Three days after Kostas's appearance in Vienna, the *kareshta* had been hidden in Prague. Kostas and Max had moved swiftly to hide the women and children left from the attack in Bulgaria, and Sirius handed over their protection to Orsala, Mala, and the remaining singers of Sarihöfn. Kyra refused to stay in the safe house; she had returned to Vienna with her brother.

Now three singers stood in Damien's study, talking with Sari and arguing while Rhys, Leo, Ava, and Malachi looked on.

The seven elder singers had returned to Vienna, but as Sari warned them all, this was no puppet council.

Abigail and Carmina, the two most traditional of the council, were arguing with Sari over her decision to step aside for the European seat, leaving Constance the chosen favorite.

"Why have you withdrawn?" Abigail asked. She was a strong-boned woman from Newfoundland with a powerful voice. "You're one of the most respected singers in Europe. Many of my own people look to you as an authority."

"But I'm not a politician," Sari said. "I have other roles now."

Like the quiet plan Kostas and Damien were already working on to search for more of the lost *kareshta*. Sari, Damien, and Max were sending out inquiries to their allies across Europe, spreading the news and asking scribe houses to be on the lookout for women with Grigori traits, especially in areas where Fallen had been killed and might have left surviving children.

Minor angels killed each other with alarming regularity. And if their daughters were lost in the human population, they could be helped without danger of their sire's influence.

"She's not even European," Carmina protested. "She's American."

Carmina looked delicate, but Malachi had heard the singer carried Mikhael's blood. Her looks were probably deceiving.

"She's lived here longer than many natives," Sari said. "And her mate has family ties in France. She's a valid choice."

Abigail snorted. "She's a ninny. She'd lock every one of us in a retreat and throw away the key."

Daina, a dark-haired former elder from the Caribbean was one of the more moderate singers on the council and the only calm voice in the room. "She represents many of our sisters who carry this same view. Are they not allowed a voice?"

The singer's face was a stunning blend of African, American, and European blood. Malachi could tell she was very old. Her mate, a watcher of immense reputation, had left public life with her after the Rending. Rumor in Vienna was that Daina and Zamir protected one of the largest havens in the Western Hemisphere, somewhere in the southern Caribbean Sea. She'd been coaxed back to her former position in Vienna when South America had been given the seventh seat on the council.

"If you want to object to her seating," Daina continued, "object to the fact that her mate is one of the elder scribes. There is a reason it is avoided. A mated pair can hold too much power if they speak as one."

"Unfortunately"—Rhys decided to risk his input—"they both have political presences that are independent from the other. According to what Damien and I have been able to learn, they're not seen as a single entity here. They've had years to develop their own allies, and they don't agree on everything."

"They agree on compulsion," Carmina said.

Sari said, "Yes, but compulsion is not the only issue of our race. And on many of the others, Constance carries her own view and is admired for it. Further, she's seen as the leading Irina mind in Vienna. She's a medical doctor as well as a healer. Many of the women who've lived here since the Rending—"

"The ones who've lived in hiding?" Abigail asked. "The ones who allowed their mates to shut them up like prisoners in their own homes? Are we expected to take them seriously?"

"This is useless debate," Daina said. "She will be chosen. She will serve. You can debate with her in the Library."

Leo said, "Some of the elder scribes object to the council being re-formed. They say it is not legitimate."

Daina waved him off. "I've heard the objections, but they are ridiculous. The Irin elders have never had a voice in choosing the Irina council, just as we have never had a voice in choosing their ranks. We will take our place in the Library in two days' time."

"They do object to us," Abigail said, her voice holding barely concealed pain. "Some object to our very presence in the city. My mother would be appalled."

"Let them object," Carmina said. "It is as Daina said. They have no standing."

"What do you think they will do?" Sari said with a wry laugh. "Bar us from the Library? They could try."

Daina said, "And they would fail."

"And how do you feel about compulsion, Daina?" Carmina lifted her chin. "You have not spoken about it since we've been here."

"I do not agree with compulsion," Daina said. "Nor do I agree with those who would throw our singers into war. That has never been our role. You risk throwing artists and teachers and healers into a war that has torn most of their families apart. Are you prepared to truly hear what those sisters have to say? It might not match your plans."

Sari said, "Some of those healers and artists have chosen different paths because of what happened during the Rending. Are you willing to stifle their desire to join this war?"

"Have they trained?" Daina asked. "Have they spent years in the scribe houses preparing for this as our mates have?"

Malachi leaned forward. "And what if there is a mission for which healers and teachers are the most qualified, Daina? What then?"

Diana cocked her head toward him. "I know of no such mandate. But I will be interested to hear you speak, Malachi of Sakarya."

Malachi leaned back after giving her a respectful nod. Daina was not a singer who liked others to make assumptions about her, and she would keep her own council. She reminded Malachi a great deal of his mother. He had a feeling that revealing the secret of the *kareshta* was the key to investing the more moderate Irina in their battle against the Fallen. After all, would women lost in the human world need warriors or healers?

Glancing over his shoulder at his mate who watched everything with perceptive eyes, he was reminded of who she had been.

Hunted. Tormented. Lonely.

Malachi guessed that most of the *kareshta* were much like Ava had been.

Had she needed a warrior or a healer?

She'd needed both.

Chapter Twenty-two

SHE WALKED THROUGH THE FOREST AGAIN, her feet muffled by the dead leaves on the ground, the bare branches of the trees forming a canopy overhead. She could feel her mate at her side, but she did not hear him. She heard only the sound of her own footsteps on the path.

And his.

Her blood recognized his presence now. Her power tied to his.

"Not only mine now," Jaron said.

"I know."

"You've completed your bond with the scribe."

"Yes."

"Are you… happy?"

Ava stopped and turned to Jaron, not understanding the expression he wore. It was the most human he had ever looked. "I am. He makes me happy. I feel complete with him."

Jaron nodded and continued walking. "I confess," he said as he walked, "I did not understand your connection at first. When you mourned him, it made me curious."

"Why? Don't angels mourn?"

"No." His hands were clasped easily behind his back. "I suppose some of us feel a sense of… longing for what we no longer have. That is a kind of mourning."

She knew he was talking about heaven.

"Do you think the Creator longs for you?"

Jaron paused, as if the idea surprised him. "We are His servants. We long for His presence alone."

"Even the Fallen?"

"Especially the Fallen. But longing, if frustrated for millennia, can easily turn to rage."

She stepped in front of Jaron, no longer afraid. "Why did you fall?"

He cocked his head, his brilliant gold eyes glowing in the darkness. "We were greedy. We were looking for something more."

"What?"

"Connection, I think. The love humans are capable of, it was foreign to us. And fascinating. We were seduced by it, only to find that it was not what we were created for."

"What were you made for?"

"Service."

He moved around her and continued walking in the moonless night. The light from the stars was the only thing illuminating the path.

"That seems harsh."

Jaron turned. "It is not for either of us to question the Creator. We see only the weaving of the tapestry, not its completion."

"So everything has a purpose? Is that what you're trying to say?"

Jaron bent down, pressing her cheeks between palms that were warmer than Ava expected. She lifted her gaze and met ruthless eyes.

"What I have seen, what I have shown you, is only a shadow of His mind. That was my gift. My purpose. To experience glory and show those who were less. I was… an interpreter. No human can know His mind. You would go mad."

"So I'm lesser than you?"

"Less and more, daughter. For you have been given the gift of free will, while I only experience the desire for what I have lost." He released her and stepped back. "I have used you, Ava. And I will continue to do so."

She drew in a shuddering breath. "And my grandmother? How is she?"

"Surviving." Jaron paused. "That has been her life for too long."

"If we kill Volund, will she heal?"

"I do not know. I only know she will be released."

"And if you return to heaven like you want?"

She saw the corner of his mouth lift. "I knew you would see it eventually."

"Is it possible?"

"I have seen it."

"Sometimes I see things because I want them too much," Ava said. "How do you know what is vision and what is real?"

"Why do you draw a line between them? One is the same as the other with enough will." He turned. Looked at her. "And the power to make it so."

"Oh God," she breathed out, stopping in the pathway.

"That is one of His names."

"That's why Malachi came back. Is that what you're saying?" She grabbed for his arm, stopping him from walking ahead. "Is that it? I dreamed it—I wanted it so much—that I made it real? Made my vision a reality?"

Jaron turned. "You are of my blood. And of Volund's."

"What does that mean?"

"Not even I can predict your power." He leaned down and whispered, "Be careful what you dream."

Her body was frozen. She felt her mate at her back as Jaron walked into the fog.

"How will this end?"

It slammed into her. The vision of the two eagles battling. Blood sprayed on her face as one fell, then the other, both pierced in the heart by the other's talons. They fell, but they did not hit the ground. A giant sword rose into the sky, its black shadow clawing the heavens with the teeth of a great beast. And when it pierced their breasts, the eagles turned into giants, and the darkness swallowed them whole.

AVA was still thinking about the vision the next day while she waited for Malachi to return from settling Kostas's men. She was making an effort to think of them as Kostas's men and not Grigori. The instinctive aversion was too strong, and she didn't want to offend Kyra, who was waiting with her.

THE SECRET

The *kareshta* was nervous. She'd gone to Prague with the others to settle her sisters into Astrid and Karen's care, had spent some time with Orsala, forming a rudimentary shield over her mind, but she still looked incredibly ill at ease in Vienna. The vulnerability made her otherworldly features somehow more human.

"Kostas and Sirius should be back soon," Ava said.

She nodded. "I worry about them."

"Malachi says that as long as they cover up and don't look too pretty, they should be all right. Their scent is completely gone."

"Good." She tapped her fingers and looked over her shoulder to where Rhys and Leo were trying very hard not to look at the stunning woman. Kyra had masses of long hair, a rich chestnut color streaked with darker shades of brown. Her skin was olive—a legacy from her human mother, who had been Greek—and her eyes were thick-lashed and gold. Ava felt small and plain beside her, and she could understand why Leo and Rhys had a hard time keeping their eyes to themselves.

She gave them a furious look and they went back to studying their books. "Sorry about them."

Kyra shook her head. Forced a smile. "It's fine. I'm sure I'm strange to their eyes."

"Oh, no. That's not it. You're just really, really gorgeous and—as old as these guys are—they're still getting used to being around girls."

Her eyes widened. "But... the Irina."

"Most that survived the Rending have been out of the public eye for two hundred years or so. If a scribe wasn't already mated, they weren't really welcome in the havens. So... most of these guys haven't seen a non-human girl in about two hundred years. Some of the younger scribes who were children during the Rending haven't *ever* seen one."

"Oh." If anything, that seemed to make her even more nervous. "That might explain the looks."

"Yeah, they can't really touch human women, so"—she leaned closer and whispered—"there are a lot of frustrated scribes out there."

Kyra blushed.

"I try to find the humor in the situation, even though it's not really funny."

"No." Kyra choked out the word. "It's not."

"You too, huh?"

Kyra looked around the library. "Is this appropriate to speak of?"

"Girl talk. Do I need to get some wine?"

Kyra shook her head. "That would not be advisable. I have no experience…" She cleared her throat. "Most *kareshta* are more attuned to the human world. Many have had relationships with human men, because of course, they thought—or continue to think—they are human."

"Like me."

"Yes." Kyra nodded, more comfortable now. "I do not have as much experience being out of… our version of havens. Because of my brother. And of course, most of his men are also Barak's children, so—"

"Oh my gosh, so you've been surrounded by like a thousand super-protective big brothers your whole life?"

She frowned. "A thousand would be hyperbole. But many half brothers, yes. Though I am older than most of them."

"That would pretty much kill any hope of a social life, huh?"

Kyra smiled and laughed a little. Rhys and Leo's eyes flew back to her. Ava pointed at them. "Books. Now. Or I'll take her away."

They both averted their eyes, but she could see them sneaking glances.

"No," Kyra said. "No social life at all. Of course, hearing voices also dampens any urge I've ever had to be with a human."

"Yeah, I remember that part."

Kyra still carried the visible anxiety that Ava remembered so well. Her fingers tapped the arm of the chair and she was fidgeting madly, her foot tapping, her body shifting. Ava realized that though she was learning to shield her mind, the *kareshta* still felt the overwhelming excess of energy she channeled from the human souls in Vienna. Irina did too, but with more developed magic and regular contact with males of their own race, it was manageable.

For Kyra, who'd lived her life in purposefully isolated locations, the crowd of a city must have been a nerve-racking experience. And her brother, whose affectionate contact would help her manage her energy, had been gone for hours.

Going with her instincts, Ava glanced at Leo, then at Rhys. "Kyra?"

"Hmm?" The *kereshta* been distracted, looking out the window.

"Will you trust me on something?"

"About what?"

She leaned forward and grasped the other woman's hand, releasing a burst of static electricity.

"Sorry," Ava whispered. "I know how you feel."

Kara's body grew deliberately still. "Do you?"

Ava nodded. "All these people. And you can still feel them."

"I am practicing the technique Orsala taught me, but being in the city is… difficult. Even here, where minds are more guarded and voices are softer, I hear things. There are just so many."

"And you're around new people, which makes you nervous anyway. Has the headache started?"

The slight tension between her eyes told Ava the truth even before Kyra nodded.

"I want to try something. Will you trust me that I would never do something that would make you more uncomfortable unless I thought it would help?"

Kyra was hesitant, but eventually she nodded.

"Hey, Leo?" Ava called.

The giant scribe was at her side in an instant. "Did you need something, Ava?"

Ava wrapped her arms around his middle, giving him a solid hug. Leo smiled and bent down, wrapping his arms around her and touching his lips to her forehead.

"I missed you," he said. "Malachi has been keeping you to himself since you arrived in the city."

Kyra's eyes widened, so Ava was quick to explain.

"Leo's a friend. When I lost my mate"—she squeezed him again —"he and Malachi's other brothers kept me sane."

Her lips parted in understanding. "You have… affection. Friendship. He is as a brother to you."

"Yep." Ava nodded. "Plus, Leo gives great hugs."

The big man smiled wider. "I do."

Ava laughed and saw that Kyra's face had softened.

"Do you need a hug, Kyra?" Ava asked.

It seemed like such a simple thing to her now, but she knew how hard it would be for Kyra. Human contact only made the voices worse, so Ava had learned to live in isolation before she knew what she was.

"I... I don't think..." The woman shook her head.

Ava stepped back, and Leo held out his hand.

"Give me your hand," he said softly. "If you like, Kyra. Just your hand."

Kyra held up a trembling hand, her fingers tense. Without a word, Leo grasped it and held it between both his hands.

She saw the deep breath he took, saw him close his eyes as her energy released. Malachi had once told her that touching Ava after they'd been apart for some time was like a surge of magical adrenaline.

Ava saw Kyra release a breath, saw the tension leave her forehead. Her restless tapping ceased at once. Her shoulders relaxed.

"You make the voices go away," Kyra whispered, staring at him in wonder.

Leo leaned forward, elbows on his knees and Kyra's hand pressed to his cheek, holding it there as his eyes fixed on her.

"Anytime you need me, Kyra. All you have to do is ask."

Kyra's eyes flew to Ava at his words. She could see the discomfort, so she simply took the *kareshta's* other hand and squeezed it.

"None of us are meant to be alone."

"KOSTAS's men are well trained," Malachi told her as he shed his coat and began to take off the weapons strapped to his torso. "And Sirius is an excellent second, though it was obvious his mind was on the *kareshta* in Prague."

"I called Astrid today. They're doing really well, and Orsala has been a huge help. Bruno called some people, so there's about a dozen scribes at the house now along with some of the singers from Sarihöfn."

"I'll pass the message along tomorrow. It will ease his mind." He took a deep breath and collapsed on the couch, obviously exhausted.

Ava straddled his lap, drew his forehead to her chest, and began massaging his temples.

"*Sağ olun, canım.*"

"You're welcome."

His hands rested at her waist as she continued. She could feel the tension begin to release and he squeezed her hips.

"You spent time with Kyra today?"

"I did."

"Why was Leo's face glowing?"

She laughed. "I think a handshake from a *kareshta* is rather… invigorating."

"He didn't—"

"Just held her hand for a little while. She needed it. Don't you remember?"

He took a deep breath and turned his cheek to her breast. "I do now. You were like a live wire the first time I kissed you. It took all my self-control not to lay you down on that hill, strip you naked, and take you there."

"Yes, but then you got all honorable."

He grunted. "That didn't last long."

"Thank goodness."

She felt his smile against her skin.

"Ava."

"Hmm?" She loved being with him like this. Quiet and easy. The massive power of his body at rest against hers. She felt grounded in the best way.

"If we were not *reshon*, would you love me this way?"

She grabbed his hair pulled him back to meet her eyes. "What kind of question is that?"

He shrugged. "One that plagues me, I suppose."

"Fishing for compliments again?"

"Forget I asked. It is a stupid question."

She tugged him back when he tried to move away. Then she bent and whispered in his ear. "I was fascinated by you," she confessed. "Long before you laid a hand on me. Your humor. The passion I could see in your eyes. Your *lips*. I wanted you to kiss me so bad."

She felt his dimple underneath her hand as he said, "In the Basilica Cistern."

"Yes." Ava pinched his ear. "I wanted to kill you when you stepped away and acted all professional."

"I *wanted* to kiss you. I felt so guilty about it too. I spent that entire night writing a new spell to put on my arm the next morning to help my self-control."

She crushed him to her, pressing her face into his neck. "I'm so glad I have you back."

"I'm glad to be back." His voice was hoarse. "I want this to be over so we can have a life together, Ava. I want a family. I want you to take me to visit your mother. I want to travel with you and show you the places I've been. I want you to be able to take pictures again. I miss your pictures."

"You just want me to stop taking all those nudes of you," she muttered.

Malachi laughed. "Maybe."

"Not gonna happen. You're too hot."

"I'm hoping if I take you someplace more scenic, I can distract you."

"You can try."

"Plus"—he drew back and kissed her lips sweetly—"I really do love watching you work."

"That's a relief. I've been feeling like I'm missing a limb without being able to carry my camera around." Though she could carry it around Vienna, it wasn't allowed in the places she most wanted to capture like the Library or the ritual bathhouse. She knew why, but it still irked her that the only camera she had there was the one in her mind.

"Soon," he said, and she could hear the heaviness in his voice again. "Whatever is coming, I think it will be soon."

"Because of my dream with Jaron?" She'd told him about it when she woke, and he'd agreed the vision of the two eagles was disturbing. Something teased the back of her mind. There was something she'd been meaning to tell him…

"Partly your dream with Jaron," he said, "and partly the activity we're seeing in the city. There are definitely Grigori attacks. Kostas's men have volunteered to start patrolling."

"Grigori fighting their own kind," she said. "What has the world come to?"

"A turning point, hopefully."

"Yes."

The next day, the elder singers would take their desks in the Library. Some in Vienna thought the rumors were only rumors. But as more and more singers flowed into the city, even the most stubborn scribes had been forced to acknowledge that something was in the air. Ava had seen singers in Irin-friendly coffeehouses. Seen more and more of them on the street as she ran her daily errands. Faces from all over the world, women with the distinctive thrum of power were starting to move in Vienna.

The air was so electric she had a hard time wondering how the human population didn't notice.

Ava looked at Malachi. "Are Kostas and Sirius ready?"

"They've decided only Kostas will go the Library with us in the morning. Sirius will stay with his men."

"How are you going to get him past the guards?" she asked. "He doesn't have a single *talesm*. Won't he stand out?"

"Damien has a plan to get Kostas in *and* gain access to Mikhael's armory."

"Is that illegal?"

"Highly. Those weapons are passed out at the will of the council because they're so dangerous. You saw what that weapon did to Leo in Istanbul. Any wound from an angelic weapon can be deadly to a scribe or a singer. But if we're going to be fighting angels, we need them. We don't have the angel of Death on our side, waiting to gather their souls."

The angel of death.

Oh shit.

Now she remembered what she needed to tell her mate. What she'd needed to tell him for *days*.

"Malachi?"

"Yes?"

269

She paused, not certain how to proceed.

He squeezed her hips. "What is it?"

"Did I tell you I've had other dreams?"

"What do you mean? Our dreams?"

"No, they're… different. I'm not sure if they're dreams or not. I think they're more like visions."

"From Jaron?"

"No."

Not visions, someone whispered. *Visits*.

"Visits," she murmured. "I've seen Death. As in, the angel of."

Malachi frowned. "I know, *reshon*. You told me. In Norway—"

"Not in Norway. Here. I've seen him here. He… visited me."

She felt him tense beneath her hands. "What?"

"In dreams. But they weren't dreams. Or not exactly dreams. And I wasn't scared. He showed me things," she said quietly. "I thought it was just to reassure me. They didn't seem important. There was something about my grandmother. We talked a little about you—"

"Ava." His voice was frigid. "You were seeing *Death* in your dreams, and you didn't tell me?"

What could she say?

"It was only twice. And there was so much going on. We were traveling everywhere. Besides, I didn't know if you'd believe me," she muttered. "It hardly seemed real."

"What on earth would make you think that?" His voice creeped past irritation and rose toward anger. "When have I ever not believed you?"

"I don't know. Stop yelling at me."

"I'm not yelling!"

Ava gave him an arched brow, and he set her to the side and leaned forward, bracing his elbows on his knees. She could see his temper in the set of his shoulders.

"I'm allowed to be angry that you hid this from me."

"I didn't hide it. They just didn't… come up. Two dreams. In the weeks we've been traveling and plotting and fighting Grigori and discovering mind-blowing revelations. So much was happening that it didn't seem important when it was just about my grandmother."

"Why wouldn't I want to know about your grandmother?"

"But it's not…" She sighed. "I wasn't scared of him."

"You're making excuses."

She *was* making excuses. Mostly she was embarrassed that she hadn't told him before. She really had forgotten, and it made her feel like an idiot.

"These dreams, they were only about your grandmother? About me?"

She bit her lip, felt her heart race in her chest. Now she was the one whose memory was fuzzy. She had a new respect how Malachi had felt for months while he recovered.

"No. Not just…"

He took a deep breath. "What it is?"

"There was more in the dreams. But I can't remember."

Malachi frowned. "What more? Did you see Jaron again?"

"Not Jaron. I think I might have seen Volund."

Malachi swore and rose to his feet as he began to pace across the room. "Were you in danger? How could you not have told me, Ava?"

"I didn't remember Volund until now!"

He spun. "How could you not remember that?"

Why *didn't* she remember? Ava knew she wouldn't have kept something important from her mate. That was past forgetfulness and into negligence, so why…

"Will I remember?"

When you need to.

She hadn't forgotten. Not completely. Azril had hidden it from her.

"Stupid, know-it-all angels!" Ava leapt to her feet. "He hid it, Malachi. Just like Jaron. Azril hid it for some reason. I don't know why."

Ava heard laughter in the back of her mind and felt the memories push forward, timid creatures peeking from the corners where Azril had tucked them. The smell of incense. Muffled voices. Gold eyes and black energy.

"What do you remember?" Malachi put his hands on her shoulders. "Anything, *reshon*. It could be important."

"They couldn't see me. I saw… there were three of them. The three angels Damien was talking about. I don't remember all their names."

"Svarog, Volund, and Grimold?"

"I'm not sure." She shook her head. "I think so? It's not important."

"It *is* important. What did they say?"

She murmured, "'Eliminating threats. It's still not that clear. Something about the monastery, maybe?" Her heart ached. "If I'd remembered, we might have been able to warn them."

"They could have been talking about any number of things. Maybe Azril wanted… He doesn't have wants. Death only follows the command of the Creator. And if the monastery hadn't been attacked, Kostas and Kyra would never have come to Vienna."

She blinked. "You think Azril wanted them to be here?"

"Who knows what the angels want? Was there anything else?"

Ava searched her memories, wading through a cascade of images and voices. "Svarog," she said. "He and Volund don't like each other."

"That's not surprising."

"They *really* don't like each other. They want to take Vienna."

"It is the center of the Irin race."

A headache lurked as Ava struggled to make sense of the new images. She closed her eyes and thought back to the last dream. An image came to her a moment before the door slammed shut in her mind.

"They're here," she said with a gasp. "They're already in Vienna. They were in the Library."

She felt Malachi shiver.

"They were in the Library? Actually *in* it? What else? If there's anything I can tell Damien—"

"Something about the third one."

Yes.

For a second, she thought she caught the reflection of Death smiling through the mirror in the entryway.

"Is it Grimold? He is an ally of Volund's," Malachi said. "Though Volund is widely understood to be the more powerful."

"Yes. I think they called him Grimold. And there was something about his children, but…"

"Max and Kostas believe Grimold's children are the ones already in the city."

"But there's more. 'All of them,'" he said. "There's something about Grimold's children we don't know. Something we're not expecting."

Chapter Twenty-three

MALACHI TRIED TO CALM HIMSELF and sift through the new information Ava had given him.

It wasn't that he didn't understand how information could get lost in the chaos of travel and fighting. And really, the revelations Azril had given her were not much more than what they knew already. Mostly, he was irritated she'd concealed it. And he was worried by Death's fascination with her.

Ava rubbed circles over her temple. He wondered if a headache was building. She still looked confused, and Malachi was angry for her. To have your mind violated was a terrible thing. He'd never felt as helpless as he had when he'd lost his memories.

Convicted by the guilt in his mate's face, Malachi knew he had to confess his own omission, even though he'd been pushing it to the back of his mind for weeks.

"I'm so sorry, Malachi. I don't… I don't know how I forgot. It's just, my dreams are never clear and there's been so much—"

"Ava."

"What?"

He took a deep breath and spoke quickly. "I may have seen Volund in dreams. I didn't know what to think. Part of me thought they were only nightmares. But now I don't think they were."

Her mouth dropped. "What? How long?"

Malachi shook his head. "Weeks. I haven't seen him since Italy. He told me he couldn't get to you but he could get to me."

He could see her irritation spike.

ELIZABETH HUNTER

"Why didn't you tell me?" she asked, unable to hide the anger in her voice. "You're angry at me, while you—"

"I didn't know if it was real or imagined. Not for sure. Why would I worry you if I wasn't certain? You were dreaming about *Death* and didn't tell me."

"His name is Azril."

"Oh, I'm so glad you're friends now. He's the angel of death, Ava. And I'm not going to apologize for trying to protect you."

"So typical! You try to shield me from worry as if I can't handle it. As if I'm still the grieving widow you found in Oslo—"

"I had no way of knowing they weren't just nightmares."

"You still should have told me. Even if you did think they were nightmares."

"Why, so you could worry too?"

"You really don't get this whole 'sharing the burdens' thing, do you?"

"Am I supposed to ignore my instinct to protect you?"

"No, but you're not supposed to protect me from *you*!"

It stopped him short, because it was exactly what he was doing. Malachi was protecting Ava from his own terror. His own fear. Because he didn't want her to know he felt weak.

"I'm sorry." He went to her and enclosed her in his arms. "I'm sorry, Ava. I didn't think—didn't realize. You're right."

She didn't offer any smart remarks, but she didn't return the hug, either.

"Forgive me?" he asked. "For doubting you."

Her shoulders relaxed and she hugged him back. "Only if you forgive me for being forgetful."

He huffed out a breath. "Why are we fighting about this?"

"I don't know."

"Then enough. I suspect Volund was trying to torment me since he couldn't get to you. But he wasn't able to hurt me in any way."

"And I don't know what Azril wants, but I'm pretty sure he's on our side."

Malachi's mouth opened, then closed. He finally said, "I'm honestly not sure what to do with that."

"Me either." She took a deep breath and stepped back. "Should we tell Damien?"

"Yes. About both of us." He walked toward the kitchen, bracing himself in the doorway. "He might be furious we're just telling him now."

"He's not the boss of me."

Malachi gave her a wry smile over his shoulder. "Well, he is of me. Nevertheless, with the schedule we've been keeping, he can hardly blame us for not remembering every dream we have."

"I'm sorry." Ava wrapped her arms around his waist from behind, pressing her cheek to his back. "I would never keep something from you if I thought it could help."

He put his hands over hers. "I know. And I have to remember, you're a woman who is accustomed to keeping her own secrets. I can't expect you to change that overnight just because you're mated to me. I've been part of a team for centuries. And Azril tampered with your mind. If anyone should have sympathy for that, it's me."

She squeezed his waist. "You're right. You're being such a jerk right now."

The laugh burst out of him. He pulled her around to the front and hugged her. "We're still new at this, aren't we?"

"Yeah."

"Don't worry." He kissed the top of her head before he released her and walked to the phone. "We have hundreds of years to get it right."

Hundreds of years. He had to believe it. The Creator wouldn't have brought them together again just to rip them back apart.

Would He?

MALACHI lingered in bed the next morning as long as he could, knowing that it might be days before he would have Ava to himself again. They made love quietly. Deliberately. He memorized her face in the morning light and whispered promises that he would see her soon.

"Soon," she whispered back.

Then she hid under the covers while Malachi slipped out the door, and he pretended he hadn't seen her tears.

Today was the day he would break all the rules.

He was bringing a Grigori into the sacred house, sneaking him into the halls of knowledge, and stealing ancient weapons from Mikhael's armory.

If his mother were alive, she would kill him. Or congratulate him. He wasn't sure which.

A year and a half ago, Malachi knew who the enemy was. He was his father's son. A scribe of Mikhael's line. Taking vengeance on the sons of the Fallen. He walked alone, with no mate and no family.

And then…

One moment in the market. One glance from a golden eye. Like a small rudder charting the path of a massive ship, the course of his life had turned with a single touch.

Ava.

He had died. He had lived. He held a mate in his arms and in his heart. Everything he knew about his race's history he now questioned. Everything he'd trusted could be a lie. He was fighting alongside his enemies to protect the one person he could no longer live without. He would play the pawn in Jaron's games and play the comrade to a villain, all so he could be a hero for the one woman who called him home.

There was no reason to feel peace as he walked through the snow-dusted streets of Vienna, but he did.

Damien, Rhys, Kostas, and an unknown scribe met him outside the town house.

"Are you ready?" his watcher asked.

"Are you?"

Damien gave him half a smile. "It doesn't matter anymore. It's time."

THE house the stranger took them to was hidden behind a block of new construction on the other side of the river. They walked in silence, the empty scent of Kostas a void to Malachi's senses.

"You've told your brothers?" Damien asked the unknown scribe quietly.

A nod was his only answer.

"Do they know what he is?"

The strange scribe held up a single gloved finger. *One.*

"We thank you both for your help."

Malachi and Kostas exchanged a look, but he could see the Grigori was lost as he was. Rhys walked behind them, texting with someone as they walked. When they reached the house, he remained waiting outside.

"Waiting for a call," was his only explanation.

They entered the warm house and stomped their feet, taking off their boots and coats before the stranger motioned them down a narrow hallway.

He was a big man, dark of hair and face, with features that spoke of the Eastern Mediterranean. Malachi realized that while he'd removed his gloves and overcoat, his hands remained wrapped and his neck was covered in what looked like linen strips. He walked in a shroud, silently motioning them into a room at the end of the hallway.

It was a ritual room, carved wooden panels bearing the spells of hundreds of scribes. Malachi narrowed his eyes and stepped closer.

"Of course," he said when he finally interpreted the passage over the door. "They're Rafaene scribes."

Kostas whispered, "What?"

Damien nodded. "Our guide is our friend Evren's son. He took vows in Spain last year, and his father intervened for us. I believe only he and his watcher know we are here."

"And they agreed to help us?" Malachi asked. "Rafaenes are removed from politics."

"But their mission commands shelter and protection of those in need."

Kostas asked, "What is a Rafaene scribe?"

"You need to take off your clothes," Damien said. "All of them. Every stitch. I'll explain as we wrap you, but the process takes some time and we don't have much of it."

The stranger motioned to Malachi and he went to him, taking bundle after bundle of fine linen clothes that looked like bandages and stacking them in a basket as Damien spoke to Kostas.

"All Irin males have the same schooling beginning at the age of thirteen. We are trained as both warriors and scholars, though after some time, it becomes evident where our particular gifts lie. Scholars tend to retreat to libraries or work in the business world. Warriors go to scribe houses to protect humans and hunt Grigori."

"Yes," Kostas said, "I'm rather familiar with those."

"For some," Damien continued, "particularly those of the angel Rafael's line, the cost of being a warrior comes at great cost. Rafael's line is known for their healing ability. For Rafael's sons, even though they are of great skill, hunting takes a toll. To help with this, the Rafaene order was established hundreds of years ago."

Kostas looked at the man stacking bundles of linen. "He is a warrior?"

"A deadly opponent I would not like to meet in battle, despite his age," Damien said.

Malachi saw the young Rafaene smile, but he did not stop his task, dipping each bundle of linen in the clear water heating over the sacred fire.

"Rafaenes take a vow of silence and eschew any unnecessary contact," Damien explained. "They wrap their bodies in clean linen to deprive the senses and maintain quiet as much as physically possible. The idea is to take those years of silence and sensory isolation to practice meditation so they do not lose their souls in battle."

"A respite," Kostas said, nodding. "I understand this. But why are they helping us?"

"They care for those in need, particularly the injured or mentally distressed. Evren, one of Orsala's peers, spoke to his son's watcher, explaining about your women—do not be afraid he will break confidence, he gave me his word."

Kostas tossed Malachi a grim smile. "I suppose the word of a silent monk is about as secure as it gets, eh?"

"I'd agree," Malachi said. "But they're not monks. Rafaene scribes take vows for seven years only. Then they are required to reenter the world. That is the maximum amount of time the council allows for meditation."

"But while they practice their vows," Damien said, "they live in compounds not unlike monasteries. Quiet, *safe* places where troubled minds might heal."

Kostas stood before them, naked to his skin. Malachi couldn't help but notice that despite the man's inhuman beauty, his body was scarred beneath his clothes. He'd either been damaged by angelic blades or been injured too profoundly to heal without marks. The heavy scars were a jarring counterpart to his otherwise perfect form.

"You're thinking of the *kareshta*," Kostas said, standing naked and yet still defiant. "You think they might find refuge in these places."

Malachi said, "There are Rafaene compounds spread around the world. It is an option."

Kostas looked doubtful as he watched the quiet man who had covered his head with a ceremonial wrap.

"Rafaenes protect those who shelter with them as part of their vows," Malachi said. "These are no soft scholars, but some of the fiercest warriors our race possesses. It is because of their skill and prowess in battle that they are most in need of retreat. They will defend those under their care to the death."

Kostas nodded. "I will speak to my sister. I need to be wrapped? Like him?" He pointed toward the silent scribe, who approached with a basket of linen.

The man nodded.

"They will not stop you at the ritual baths," Damien said. "Rafaenes are not common in the Library, but they do occasionally make an appearance. Because they live silently and in peace, they are not required to ritually bathe unless they have recently experienced battle. If you are dressed as a Rafaene, no one will stop you or question your lack of *talesm*."

Malachi smiled. "It's brilliant. As long as we can vouch for you and you have a letter from this house, no one will think twice. You won't have to speak. Rafaenes are even urged to refrain from eye contact."

Kostas looked at the silent scribe who held up a roll of linen, wordlessly asking to begin wrapping him. The Grigori nodded.

"Thank you, brother," Damien said.

279

The scribe said nothing, crouching to wrap Kostas, starting with his feet and working his way up the man's legs, covering every inch of skin in linen.

"I feel like I'm being prepared for the grave," Kostas grumbled. "How do they live like this?"

Malachi saw the silent one's shoulders shake, and he guessed he was laughing.

"It's not easy," Damien said. "Or healthy for us. At least not in the long term. That is another reason only seven years is allowed. Before the Rending, we were an affectionate people. Irin need touch to remain healthy."

"We are the same," Kostas said quietly. "At least that is what we have learned. My soldiers who care for their sisters—especially the children—are stronger. More stable."

"It is the way it was meant to be," Damien said quietly. "I begin to see that now. How could any race survive with no balance?"

Malachi said, "Far more is at stake today than the fate of the Irin Council."

THEY took a taxi to the Hofburg. Luckily, their heavy winter clothes covered the ritual wrappings, which were already making Kostas squirm.

"So this is what those uncomfortable underthings the women wear feel like," he grumbled. "I think I'd prefer to be naked beneath my clothes."

Malachi stifled a smile. "That's a little more information than we wanted, Kostas."

"Then you wear this next time."

"No need." He puffed out his chest a bit. "My *talesm* are complete."

The spiraling vows that Ava had spoken now decorated his left chest. It was a basic tattoo right now, only the words were finished. Malachi would embellish it at his leisure, but the core of the written spell was complete.

"Gabriel's blood, you're going to be obnoxious about that now, aren't you?" Rhys said.

Damien laughed. "Newly mated male."

"I did not congratulate you or Ava," Kostas said. "My apologies and belated good wishes. I'm sure this is cause for celebration."

"It is."

Rhys asked, "Your kind take no mates, do they?"

Kostas's face closed down. "No."

They arrived at the Library past the morning rush, but many scribes were still in the process of bathing when they entered. Damien had been correct. No one gave Kostas a second glance after he handed over the letter signed by the Rafaene watcher. While Malachi, Rhys, and Damien did their ablutions, Kostas quietly changed into the hooded robe Damien gave him.

As they left the baths, the watcher said, "Try to remain silent in company."

"Do I need to guess what the pockets in this robe are for?"

"You'll see," Damien said. "Follow us and do not speak."

The Irina Council was taking their desks today, and the news had spread. The scribes' gallery was packed. They could barely find room along the edges, and some scribes were forced to stand on the stairs.

"Do you see Ava and Sari?" Malachi asked, craning his neck to see across the room. Unlike their last visit, the singers' gallery was also crowded. Not packed, but Malachi could see many Irina watching as the seven chosen elders assembled at the top of the stairs.

The elder scribes waited below, some with sour expressions and others wearing wide smiles. Gabriel's employer, Konrad, was beaming.

"Do you see Gabriel?" Damien asked.

Malachi scanned the crowd nearest to the top of the stairwell where Gabriel would have his position as Konrad's secretary.

"There," Rhys said. "I see him."

Malachi bent closer. "Is he involved in this?"

"No," Damien said. "I simply hoped he would not miss the ceremony. Tala, his mate, was slated to take a council seat when she was killed. This would be… important to her."

Malachi was still searching for Ava.

"It is important to us all," Rhys said. "Damien, are you sure—?"

"I want you here," the watcher said. "Keep in contact with Malachi."

"Fine, just make sure the Luddite checks his phone."

"I'm not a Luddite."

Rhys rolled his eyes. "A higher score in *Angry Birds* does not make you technologically literate. Just keep your phone on. I'm going to stand with Gabriel."

Malachi glanced at Kostas, whom he could tell was bursting with questions he couldn't ask.

He was about to make Rhys's excuses when he saw a flash of dark curls along the stairwell.

Ava.

Malachi smiled. She was radiant in her robes, her hair not tied back as was traditional, but falling in soft waves down her back.

"There she is," Malachi said.

He saw her pull a thick shank of hair over her shoulder just as she drew something small and black from a fold of her robe. She crossed her arms casually as her hand twisted in the fall of hair. Her fingers…

She was holding something.

As her shoulders slowly angled toward the stairs, he saw it.

A tiny camera, no bigger than her thumb. If he wasn't looking for it, it would have totally escaped his notice.

Malachi sighed. "Damn it. The woman is incorrigible."

Damien turned. "What?"

"I'll tell you later." *Maybe.*

"They're almost ready."

He could see the seven women walking down the stairs. The rustles and murmurs of the crowd had stilled. There was only the sound of shuffling feet and excited breaths as, one by one, the seven elder singers took the desks that Sari had pulled to the center of the room.

Daina, the Caribbean singer, spoke in a resonant voice.

"The songs of the Irina have returned to our city. We greet our brother scribes at their desks." She nodded to Jerome first, who was closest to her desk, no doubt enjoying the grim resignation on his face. Jerome couldn't complain, Malachi decided. His own mate was on the council, a rarity in Irin tradition. It was doubtless a concession in his eyes.

"Clearly," Daina continued, "the dust on our desks is simply an over-sight."

"Sisters," Jerome said. "We wel—"

"The Irina will sing," Abigail interrupted him. "And then we will talk of other matters."

Jerome's face turned an ugly shade of red, but Malachi enjoyed knowing there was nothing—nothing—the old scribe could do about it.

It was Constance who started singing, her clear alto voice piercing the air as she began the traditional greeting song.

As soon as she began, Malachi was thrown back to his childhood, to the gatherings his village had hosted and the songs his mother had led to greet visitors. He felt Constance's magic fill the room. The ancient magic of his mother and grandmothers. Of their sisters and daughters. Songs and verses that stretched back a thousand years to the first daughters of the Forgiven.

"We come," Constance sang.

The other women responded, "*We come.*"

> *"The Irina raise their song*
> *We sing of our Creator and his children*
> *We, the daughters of the Forgiven*
> *We honor them with our words."*

One by one, the seven voices of the elder singers joined their sister, chanting their mandate in the Old Language, calling their power as the chamber filled with magic.

> *"We sing a song of Uriel,*
> *Wisest of heaven's host,*
> *Of Rafael, our healer,*
> *He that searched for the lost,*
> *Gabriel, messenger of heaven,*
> *Gave our songs to us,*
> *Ariel, beloved of the earth,*
> *May our children lift you up.*
> *We shout of the power of Mikhael,*
> *The mighty fist of heaven.*
> *And call to the heart of Chamuel,*
> *As we serve beside our brethren.*
> *Let Leoc open up our eyes*
> *That we might seek our path,*

Bring honor to our Creator,
And glory to his crown."

Kostas could not contain his quiet gasp. The strength of the Irina flowed through the room as the women in the singers' gallery joined in the chorus their elders sang. The scribes around him lit with power as the air of the Library charged. The mated singers across the gallery gleamed in the afternoon sun. Malachi saw Kyra raise her hood and stand back, melting into the crowd behind Ava.

"We sing of our fathers
We call to the heavens
We honor the gifts they have given
In thanks, the Irina sing:
Hear us, oh heavens, answer our song
We call on the power of our fathers
We call to our reshon…"

Malachi searched for Ava, only to see his mate looking right at him, her eyes shining with joy.

I love you, he mouthed to her.

I love you too.

He narrowed his eyes and pointed to his chest, letting her know he'd caught her with the small camera.

She only laughed and shook her head.

Incorrigible woman. He hoped she never changed.

The Irina were still singing when Malachi felt a tug on his sleeve. He turned. Damien nodded.

It was time.

Chapter Twenty-four

AVA WATCHED THE THREE MEN slip out of the chamber while every eye in the scribes' gallery was glued to the Irina singing below. She'd never heard anything like it. Voice after voice, climbing and reaching. The Library soared with the ancient music of heaven.

She couldn't understand everything, but she didn't have to. The tone of their voices said it all.

The Irina had returned. They sang with the voice of the angels. And they would not be ignored.

Searching for reactions, Ava scanned the scribes' gallery. Most of the younger scribes stared in shock, the rumors of the elder singers no match for the reality. A few were openly scornful. Others only looked confused. But it was the oldest scribes, the ones who had allowed themselves to age, who caught her attention the most.

Malachi had explained to her once that most of the aging scribes she saw were men who had lost mates and children in the Rending and had chosen not to extend their lives with more magic. They didn't age as fast as humans, but eventually they would pass to join their families. For many, the time could not pass swiftly enough.

It was those scribes—the ones who had lost the most—who arrested her attention. Their eyes were bright. Their faces full of longing and joy. Heartache and resolve. For a moment, she remembered her own mourning, and she ached for them.

As the voices died down, the elder scribes were already rising to their feet.

Konrad was the first to speak. "We welcome our sisters and give thanks for their return." He walked over to Kanti, the elder singer from Africa, and embraced her. She smiled and spoke quietly to him. Obviously, the two were friends.

Jerome and Constance nodded to each other but did not offer formal greetings, and Ava wondered if the two were already fighting about something. Oddly enough, that was reassuring.

Sari, who was standing next to her, explained more to Kyra, whose hood was raised. The *kareshta* was trying to remain inconspicuous, though she'd garnered more than her fair share of looks among the singers gathered. No one, after seeing she was attached to Sari, stopped to question her.

"Konrad and Kibwe are traditionalists. They have been staunch Irina supporters and do not favor forcing us into retreats. Rafael usually votes with them but has been hesitant to expand Irina participation in the scribe houses. Like Daina, he questions whether Irina are suited for battle."

"And the others?" Kyra asked.

"Jerome is the leader of those who favor compulsion. He would vote to censure any scribe whose mate did not enter a retreat and register herself like an animal," Sari said with a growl. "Edmund and Rasesh vote with him, and they can usually gain Anurak's support. Though he has shown more independence lately. It is believed his mate lives quietly in Thailand and does not favor compulsion. That may be part of the reason he hesitates."

"Can the elder scribes really do anything now? The Irina Council is back." Ava smiled. "I mean… game over for them, right?"

"They can still force compulsion if they want to be nasty. They still run the scribe houses. If they invoke censure for noncompliance…" Sari shook her head. "It would be bad." She looked across the gallery. "They're gone. And now we wait."

MALACHI followed Damien down the hall, his heart racing even if his body could not.

"Do you know where we're going?" he murmured.

"Yes."

Farther and farther they traveled into the labyrinth of the Irin headquarters. They passed quiet study rooms and meditation chambers. Offices and guard rooms. Most people didn't seem to take any notice of two scribes and a Rafaene wandering around the hallways. If a guard did catch Damien's eye, all they did was offer him a respectful nod.

Malachi wondered just how much more there was to know about his watcher. "Were you really a Templar Knight?"

Kostas's head came up. "Really?"

"That was a long time ago," Damien said. "We need to go down these stairs. Kostas, shut up."

The look the man gave Damien was priceless. Malachi wondered when the last time was that anyone had told the Grigori commander to shut up.

"That wasn't a 'no,'" Malachi said.

"You really do have a death wish," the watcher said.

"My mate would say, 'Been there. Done that.'" He couldn't stop the grin. He'd forgotten how fun it was to irritate the man.

They climbed down wood-paneled stairwells and into the belly of the Library. The hallways became narrower and the wood paneling ceased. What was left was stone and plaster chilled from the winter temperatures. One long hallway speared into the darkness, smaller passages running off either side. Every single passage looked identical, and every single door looked the same.

Old wood with intricate spellwork written in blood-ink. These were dangerous rooms.

"Here's where things get complicated," Damien said, turning left down one empty corridor and huffing out a frozen breath. "I have a theory. It will either work or bring down the whole of the Library Guard on us."

"That sounds promising."

Kostas said, "Can I speak now?"

"Yes. And to answer what you're probably wondering, no, there are no guards in this section. They would be redundant. Magic protects each of these doors. This corridor"—he spread his arms out—"leads to Mikhael's armory. The armory holds all the heaven-forged weapons the Irin have collected over the years. It has seven doors that correspond to the seven cardinal archangels. Malachi and I would go through Mikhael's door, except it is guarded against any Irin who does not have the password."

"What happens if you just try to break it down?" Kostas asked. "Could we get out fast enough?"

"It wouldn't matter if we flew. If we attempt to breach it without the password, these blood-spells would turn my own magic against me. The more powerful the scribe, the more dangerous the attempt. For someone my age, it would probably be deadly. For someone of Malachi's power, it would be debilitating. Even a child with his mother's magic would be harmed."

Malachi looked at Kostas and suddenly realized Damien's plan. It was ingenious. Or insane.

Kostas said, "I have no written magic. That's what you're thinking, isn't it?"

"You have natural magic, so it's not going to be painless," Damien said. "But it shouldn't kill you. The trick is finding out which door to enter. These spells were written specific to the Forgiven. Though our blood is mixed after so many generations, we all draw our magic from one cardinal in our background."

Malachi frowned. "And those with no cardinal in their blood?"

"It's rare, but if you found an Irin with no cardinal blood, he wouldn't be able to open a door."

"So it might just kick Kostas out?"

"Possibly. Or... kill him. I'm honestly not sure what will happen." Damien gave him a helpless shrug. "There is no way to break the magic. We can only hope to step around it somehow."

"And if I don't try it?" Kostas asked.

"Then we don't have any heaven-forged weapons. We will never kill an angel without a heaven-forged blade."

"Fine," Kostas said. "I will try this on two conditions. I claim one of these weapons for myself."

"Fine."

"And I will hear your vow—either of you, I don't care—that you will kill my father."

Damien and Malachi were both silent.

"Why?" Malachi finally asked. "Your father appears to be acting with us. As an ally."

"I don't care," Kostas said. "I cannot kill him. And until he is dead, I will not be free. Nor will my sister."

"But Kostas—"

"You have never lived as another's slave," the Grigori said with terror and rage battling in his eyes. "You do not know. I will have Kyra free of him, or I will walk out of here, find my sister, and you will never see us again."

"Done," Damien said. "Though I will pick the time. We cannot afford to lose an ally before we win the battle."

Kostas paused. "Fine. But I am not willing to wait years."

"You will not have to."

"Damien!"

"It is done, brother." Damien put his hand on Malachi's shoulder. "I will kill Barak, or I will die in the effort. Would you do less to kill Volund and free your woman from his power?"

No. Malachi knew that while Jaron might leave Ava alone for sentimental reasons he could not fathom, Volund would only use her.

"So," Malachi said. "We don't have three angels to kill, we have five. Lovely."

AVA'S eyes were starting to cross from the tangle of voices on the floor. Debates were already happening as elders fought over the issue of compulsion. It was the only thing anyone wanted to talk about, even though Rafael, the elder from South America, had tried to bring up the growing violence in Vienna and the rest of Europe.

"I cannot condone this council's disregard for the evidence of violence growing daily against humans in our own city," he finally shouted, rising to his feet. "I had hoped—"

"You had hoped the elder singers would rush to support your concern for the humans," Konrad said, "though they have as little interest in it as the rest of us."

"Humans have always been violent toward each other," Edmund, the elder from England, said. "We protect them from the Grigori, but that is the extent of our mandate. It is not our job to hunt human predators."

"These are Grigori attacks," Rafael said.

Anurak, the Asian elder, said, "The evidence from the watcher in Oslo and Barcelona is compelling. But I see no evidence of Grigori here. There has been no Grigori attack in Vienna for a hundred years at least."

Ava leaned over to Sari. "How much longer do we keep our mouths shut?"

"Wait."

Abigail spoke up. "I have seen evidence of Grigori attacks. Even in Vienna, I have seen this. Those of you living too long in the city forget how devious our enemies can be. Do you think the sons of the Fallen will be so obvious?"

"Do not look to the headlines," Daina said. "Look to the stories the humans do not tell. It is the humans no newspaper will note that the Grigori target. And those people are missing in our city."

Silence fell over the Library. No one could discount an Irina elder of Daina's age and experience, and no one wanted to disagree with Abigail, either.

"If this is true," Jerome said carefully, "these attacks are even more evidence that the best place to protect our families is *within guarded retreats*."

The Library floor erupted in groans.

"This is not about compulsion," Abigail shouted. "You force your agenda—"

"We no longer have the luxury of debate," Rasesh said. "If the Grigori are upon us, we must take action to protect our most vulnerable."

"Who is vulnerable?" Gita, the central Asian singer, asked. "Me? Because it has been the *singers* of my region who stabilized the human population there after the Grigori erupted in violence over the death of their sire. The singers, not the scribes."

Rasesh stood. "You speak of an isolated incident—"

"The singers in Africa have been active for at least fifty years," Kanti said with a shrug. "The Grigori are on the decline because of it."

"Exactly." Konrad sounded bored. "Where are they? I see no Grigori. No Fallen. Our city is safe."

Ava frowned when the cacophony started to die.

Konrad stood up, emboldened by the sudden quiet. "With the return of the Irina Council, our enemies must know we are stronger than ever. We draw from the power of both halves of our race now. We can begin to rebuild our society. Why would the Grigori…"

He died off when he heard a low clapping sound.

Ava looked up to see where everyone's heads were pointing.

Vasu.

The angel was sitting on the railing of the balcony just below the organ pipes, slowly clapping with a wide grin on his face.

When he saw everyone's attention on him, he spread his hands. "Why do you stop? This is very entertaining."

DAMIEN, Kostas, and Malachi stared at the row of blood-stained doors.

"The Fallen have cardinals too," Kostas said. "Though only six were believed to be living, we know that's not true now. My father is one of them. Jaron and Volund are as well. Many of them have the same gifts as the Forgiven, and I am of Barak's blood."

Malachi nodded. "His purpose in heaven?"

"Barak was a guardian of the realm before he fell. He listened for unspoken threats. His gift is hearing."

Damien's eyes were sharp. "And you hear as he does?"

"Some." Kostas shrugged. "In bits and pieces. I have no control over the ability, but the magic is there."

"Hearing…," Damien murmured. "Malachi?"

"I say Gabriel's door," he said. "Irin in Gabriel's line have unusual skill in reading, but *Irina* of Gabriel's line can hear beyond the normal range. I'd guess Barak's magic is most closely associated with Gabriel."

"I'd guess the same."

Kostas said, "And I dislike the word *guess*. But I suppose it's worth a shot. Which door is Gabriel's?"

Malachi pointed to the second closest to the main passageway. The spellwork was complex. Layer upon layer of it, written in the black-red that marked them as blood-spells. For the Irin, blood mixed with ash from a sacred fire produced an ink of unmatched power. Indeed, it was the mix of blood and ash in their *talesm* that made the spells written on their body most potent. For written spellwork, you couldn't get more dangerous than a blood-spell.

And this blood-spell would turn a scribe's own magic against him. The more powerful, the more deadly.

Kostas stood in front of the door and took a deep breath. "What do I do?"

"Open it," Damien said quietly. "Just turn the knob."

The brass doorknob sparked when Kostas put his linen-covered hand on it. Malachi could almost see the slither of magic crawl up his arm, twining and testing the creature who dared touch it. Kostas's jaw tensed, but he did not break contact or cry out.

"It feels like a snake tearing through my innards," he forced out the words through gritted teeth. "How long?"

"I don't know," Damien said, carefully keeping his distance from the Grigori.

"What is it doing?" Kostas cast them a sidelong glance.

"It's testing you. I think. Trying to find where you belong."

"Good luck then," the man groaned out. "I don't belong anywhere."

He wasn't sure if the other man heard when Damien whispered, "I'm counting on it."

Malachi saw Kostas's knees buckle, so he stepped forward, only to have his watcher's arm throw him back.

"Don't touch him."

"He's falling."

"But he's not letting go."

It was true. Though Kostas was on his knees, his hand had not dropped from the doorknob. The brass glowed red-hot, and the spells on the doorway slithered over each other, ancient blood rising to life to take its turn testing the strange creature attempting to breach the passageway. The spells moved like living creatures, sliding closer to the doorknob and then slipping away after Kostas's body gave another jerk. Over and over, hundreds of years of blood-spells attacked the foreign intruder.

After more minutes than Malachi wanted to count, the crawling spells slowed. Kostas's body was still jerking, but he hadn't let go. His eyes were glazed over, and sweat soaked through his linen wrappings.

"How much longer?" he whispered.

Damien knelt down next to him. "Hold on, brother. When I tell you, you will give the command to open."

"Command…?"

"*Luoh*," Damian said quietly. "Say it now, Kostas. *Luoh*."

"*Luoh*," Malachi whispered along as Kostas groaned the old command.

With a heavy sigh, the reluctant door to the armory swung open.

THE whole Library stared at Vasu for silent seconds before the guards stationed at the foot of the stairs cried out and threw silver daggers at the angel.

Vasu simply disappeared and reappeared, now hanging on the tallest organ pipe. "That's not going to work," he said. "But do keep trying if you like."

Scribes across the gallery began leaping to the ground, some rushing toward the balcony, others running toward the singers' gallery where Irina had begun to chant over Vasu's laughter. Ava felt the terror in the air.

"What do we do?" she shouted at Sari while trying to shield Kyra from the wave of panic taking over the room.

"I don't know!" Sari looked across the Library, probably searching for Damien, but Ava had just looked and neither Malachi nor Damien were anywhere to be found.

"I think we need to—"

"Stop."

A single word froze the crowd, the room, and everything in it. Knives hung suspended in the afternoon sun. Papers rested in midair. Two scribes froze, their leap from the gallery halted by a single command from the one being Ava had never expected to see in the heart of the Irin Council chambers.

Jaron stood before the crowd, not hovering over them as Vasu did, but standing among them, a creature of such frightening glory that Ava heard some begin to weep. He made no attempt to veil himself. He had become giant. A creature of majesty and power, terrifying and beautiful at the same time.

"I am Jaron," he said, and though his voice was quiet, it filled every corner of the Library. "You will cease."

Silver daggers frozen in the air dropped to the ground. Papers fell, as did the scribes. But though Ava saw them moving, the violence had halted.

In the space of a heartbeat, another angel appeared. If Jaron's harsh features reminded Ava of a bird of prey, this being was a wolf. Silver-black hair hung thick around his face, and though his eyes were a glowing gold, his face reminded Ava of a winter lake. Calm and frozen.

Kyra let out a breath. "Father."

So this was Barak. He angled his head up to the singers' gallery. Kyra stepped forward, and Barak held up his hand.

But it wasn't only Barak who spoke.

With one voice, the two angels said, "Daughter, come."

It wasn't even a question. Jaron spoke, and Ava moved toward him. She and Kyra walked toward the top of the stairs, as the Irina around them whispered furiously and parted the crowd.

"No!" Sari shouted, trying to grab both of their arms.

"He lied," Ava whispered. Jaron had told her he couldn't command her, but she couldn't stop. She kept walking while Kyra wept, and Ava realized for the first time what the compulsion of the Grigori felt like.

Such exquisite torture.

Because nothing in this world, not the love of her mate or the strength of her will, could stop Ava from following Kyra down the stairs. Part of her didn't want to, but the other part wanted nothing else. Her eyes locked with Jaron's, and he was the most beautiful thing she had ever seen. She would do anything for him.

"No," Jaron said. "You will not."

She couldn't turn her head to look at Kyra, but she could hear the *kareshta* weeping, even as Barak made soothing noises to his child.

"I'm sorry," Kyra kept saying. "Forgive me, Father. I'm sorry."

"I do not want your sorrow," a tired voice came. "I never did, child."

When Ava reached Jaron, he turned her to face the crowd.

"This," he began, his solemn voice filling the room, "is the daughter of my blood." He put his hands on Ava's shoulders, and her mating marks lit under his power. "Wholly mated to a son of the Forgiven."

Ava felt every eye in the Library focus on her. She wanted to shrink, but there was nowhere to go. She wanted to hide, but Jaron would never let her. Whatever his purpose had been in keeping her safe, she knew it was for this moment.

"For thousands of years, we have hidden them," Barak said. "But no more. Your enemies gather while you argue over petty human concerns."

Jaron said, "Our sons took your daughters, so this day, we give you ours."

Ava saw the singers around the room flinch.

"Thousands of years they have lingered in hiding. Some killed by the hands of their brothers or fathers. Some mad with the voices you have managed to conquer." Jaron spoke to the gathered elder singers. "Find them and protect them. Add the strength of their blood to the wisdom of yours. Do this, and we will enact vengeance for the crimes against you."

Daina bravely took a step forward. "Why?"

"Volund approaches. He has made allies, even within your own ranks. If you are to wipe this enemy from the earth, you must stop fighting. You have been given the wisdom of the Forgiven. Use it for more than your own interests. Protect these vulnerable, and you will be our allies."

Jerome said, "We want no help from the Fallen."

Anurak stood. "Do not speak for those who have been silent, brother. What do you propose, Angel?"

"An alliance for now. Volund's sons linger at your gates. Grimold's get already walk among you. Walk outside and see what your city has become."

Ava looked at Sari, who rushed from the gallery along with several of the scribes from the opposite sides of the room.

Muttering and whispers filled the Library as Ava felt the eyes of the Irin fix on her and Kyra. She reached out for the other woman's hand, feeling her panic.

"Ava," Jaron said, leaning down till his mouth was at her ear. "It is time to show them."

"Show them what?"

"I show you what was has been, what will be, and what could be. Do not fear the darkness. Sing."

The vision rushed into her mind so quickly Ava knew she was only a conduit between the angel and the audience. Her mouth opened and song poured out. It was not the deliberate poetry she had studied, but a raw rush of tone and emotion. She didn't even recognize the words she spoke. In an instant, she saw the whole of Jaron's vision, and the scales fell from her eyes.

Two dark-haired children with golden eyes. A girl, laughing as butterflies swirled around her. A boy staring back at her with his father's petulance. An ink-black jaguar curled around the children protectively as a wolf and a tiger paced behind. The tiger bent to the girl, opening his mouth. The great beast closed his jaw around her nape as she continued to smile and pet its cheek.

Behind the delicate tableau, a great circle rose in the sky. A sun twisted with gold and silver. Higher and higher it rose until the moon covered its brilliance. In the sudden flash of darkness, a million scattered points of light became visible in the heavens, dancing tremulously in concert to a gathering song.

A bird of prey called as the darkness passed, its scream shattering the song of the stars. The jaguar leapt. It reached into the sky until its arms became the wings of an eagle that crashed into the attacking bird in the light of a blood-red eclipse. They battled, tearing each other's flesh as ash and blood rained down on a city of stones. Turning and twisting, the two battled higher as the wolf below howled and the tiger leapt on the jackals that were laughing in the barren streets.

Then both birds dropped, twisting into men of impossible beauty, and a jagged sword rose from the city of stone, piercing the angels as they fell.

As the last note carried over the assembly, Ava's breath left her and everything went black.

VI.

THE THREE ANGELS KNELT beside her, Vasu brushing the hair from her forehead as delicately as a mother with a child.

"Will she survive?"

"Yes." Jaron's eyes swept the Library, but the assembly had shifted, a slight twist in dimension allowing him a last moment alone with her.

Though Ava still slept, he gathered the girl into his arms and rocked her as he had seen her mother do when she was a child.

Thirty years of watching over her at a distance. A blink of an eye. A sudden gasp of breath.

And yet.

Within her blood lay the secret.

"I know." Jaron bent to her ear, uncaring of his brothers, who listened in. "I understand why now."

Ava's eyes fluttered open. "Me too."

"What have you done to me, daughter?"

"The only worthy sacrifice is the one that hurts. How much do you want forgiveness?"

A drop fell on her cheek, and Jaron realized he was weeping.

"Will you tell her?" he asked his daughter's daughter.

"I'll tell her you loved her, and you wished you could say good-bye."

"I called her Ava because she was the voice of heaven to me. She called me *Bâbâ* when she was a child."

Ava put her hand on his cheek, and for the first time in thousands of years, Jaron felt it. He had been hollow before. Ava's union with the scribe—their impossible, unpredictable love—had altered his reality forever.

For the first time in his eons of existence, Jaron felt. "Now that I must leave, I find that I do not want to go."

"*Bâbâ*," Ava whispered, her voice thick with emotion. "Free her. Free them all. And return."

"Ava," he said. "Daughter of my blood." Jaron bent down and kissed her forehead, then he whispered in her ear.

She closed her eyes and nodded.

Then Jaron blinked, and Ava was gone. He stood and faced his chosen brothers: Barak, who would be with him until the end, and Vasu, who had chosen to stay behind.

"Do you understand what you lose, brother?" he asked Barak.

"Unlike you"—the angel's eyes held what Jaron now recognized as torment—"my magic mixed with the Forgiven's long ago. I am ready."

Jaron narrowed his eyes but asked no more questions.

"And you?" he asked Vasu.

"Someone has to stay behind and watch," Vasu said with a casual shrug.

"Do it," Barak said. "She is one of them now. Power surrounds her. Lower the shields and call him."

Jaron looked at Vasu. "Are you ready?"

The dark angel grinned a predatory smile. "Go."

Chapter Twenty-five

MALACHI HELD ANOTHER KNIFE out to Kostas, who tucked it into the cleverly sewn pockets in his robe. Damien was searching the armory for one specific weapon, but Malachi didn't know what it was. The chamber held case after case of blades of various eras and styles. Knives were most common, with throwing daggers a close second. Spears and swords hung on the stone walls. There were even a few crossbows and an ax or two. Malachi and Kostas were looking through the knives and hiding those they would smuggle out of the Library.

After a few more minutes, Damien came back bearing an intricately cut dagger. "Thought you might like to use this one."

"Why?"

He looked confused. "It's the one Brage used in Istanbul when he killed you. Too morbid?"

Malachi looked at the dagger, remembering the pitch-black blade the Grigori had balanced on his finger on the roof of the building in Oslo, then he looked back at Damien. "This isn't Brage's dagger. He carried it in Oslo. Ava gave it to Jaron when I killed Brage."

Damien's eyes went hard. "Are you saying this isn't a heaven-forged blade?"

Malachi shrugged. "I have no idea. But I know that's not the dagger that killed me."

"Dammit." Damien looked around the armory. "I wonder—"

"How many of these are actually heaven forged?" Kostas asked, picking through the rows of weapons. "Not all of them. Maybe half. Some of these are far too new."

"What do you know about angel blades?" Malachi asked.

"We all have our hobbies," Kostas said, picking up a rusted weapon that looked far from useful.

The Grigori brought it up to his face and breathed on it. Taking the edge of his own knife, he cut a long gash in his forearm, wetting the edge of one of his linen wrappings with blood before he took it and carefully wiped the blade. After a few minutes, he held it up again. The blade was a dull pewter in color, but the edge was sharp again, the blade now clearly lethal.

"Angel blades are best cleaned with blood. It restores them. If you're not sure if a blade is genuine, try that. A good rule of thumb is that anything forged in the past thousand years is probably a fake or simply something confiscated from an angel but isn't a heaven-forged blade."

"I thought all angels carried them," Malachi said.

"They're rare," Kostas told them, "even among the Fallen. Lesser angels usually can't keep them, so any blade taken from one of the lesser Fallen is probably just a sword. And of course, some of them don't need them. Guardians of heaven carry swords within their bodies."

Malachi and Damien both gawked.

"Unlike you," Kostas said with a grim smile, "my father is an angel. I do know a few things."

"I'll keep looking," Malachi said, turning back to the racks.

"Wait." Damien held up a hand. "I hear…"

Without warning, the doors to the armory groaned and swung open. Library guards rushed in, only to halt with wide eyes when they saw the two scribes and the man dressed as a Rafaene in the process of stealing weapons.

"Well," Kostas muttered, "this is awkward."

Damien stepped forward. "Brothers, we are—"

"Out of time." The captain of the Library Guard stepped forward. "I know who you are, Damien of Bohemia. The enemy is here. There are Fallen in the Library as we speak."

"Is it Jaron?"

"How did you know that?" the captain asked.

"Jaron is an ally. For now," Malachi said. "But there are others who are not."

The captain did not question him but nodded briskly and spoke to his men. "Distribute the weapons. Take one for yourself and others for the men under you, then head back to the Library and join those protecting the council."

Malachi saw Kostas swipe another blade. He must have had almost a dozen hidden in his robe. He tugged on the heavy wool and nodded toward the doors just as the captain of the guard turned back to them.

"I recognize you too, Malachi of Sakarya. I fought with your father. I will trust the son of Ilyas and Hanna would not betray his brothers."

"You trust rightly."

"Then go. We need all the able warriors we can spare," the captain growled. "This city has been soft for too long. Politicians and financiers are not warriors. They forget what it means to fear."

Damien, Kostas, and Malachi ran down the hallway as more guards flooded in. They ran up the stairs and out the main entrance, which was completely unguarded.

"Damien?" Someone shouted across the empty courtyard.

Malachi turned his head. It was Sari.

She came to her mate, completely out of breath. "The humans. They're gone."

"What do you mean, they're gone?"

Malachi walked toward one of the larger courtyards in the Hofburg, searching for the bustle of tourists or the honking of taxis.

There was nothing.

Cars sat empty on the small side streets. Horses snuffled and shuffled, waiting for empty carriages to roll.

"Heaven above," he whispered.

Who had done it? Jaron or Volund? More importantly, where was his mate?

He walked back to Kostas, Damien, and Sari, who were all frozen in the center of the courtyard.

"This is Jaron's doing," Malachi said. "Or one of the other angels."

"It's a city of ghosts," Sari said. "What have they done with them?"

"I don't think any of the humans will be harmed. They're just… away. More importantly, where is Ava? Which angels were in the library?"

Sari said, "It was Vasu first, then Jaron and Barak. I've just called Renata and told her, Rhys, Max, and Leo to meet us here. She checked the elder singers' homes this morning, and every one had been ransacked. The Grigori have been watching."

"They know the singers have returned," Damien said. "And your men, Kostas?"

"I'll call." The Grigori pulled his mobile phone from a pocket in his robe before he handed a gold blade to Sari with a wink. "That's for you. Matches your hair."

Sari frowned at Damien but took the blade. "Is this—"

"We'll explain later," Malachi said. "For now, let's head into the library. If the enemy has finally reached Vienna, we need a plan. And I want to see my mate."

AVA'S eyes were closed, but she heard the whispered command.

"Go."

For a moment, she was still in her dream, then her eyes blinked open and three angels stood over her. Jaron and Barak she knew. The third was a frighteningly pale figure with icy gold eyes and face cut from pale marble.

"Yes," he whispered, and with his voice she knew.

Volund.

But Ava didn't have time to be frightened before Vasu was there. He wrapped his arms around Volund from the back, then with a wink, both angels were gone.

Jaron held out a hand. "Come and stand with your people."

"What just happened?"

"You are no longer under my shields," Jaron said. "Be wary. Vasu will keep Volund occupied for a time. You have no defenses against him except the words my brother spoke to you. Do you remember them?"

Ava nodded.

"Good. Use them if he comes near."

He began to walk from the room. Barak followed.

"Where are you going?" she asked. "And can't you just… blink away or something?"

Jaron smiled, and for once, it appeared to be a true smile. "Only Vasu can do that without cost, as it is in his nature. For us, transporting takes power I would rather save for now. I am not, after all, a god."

"Oh."

Jaron looked around to the crowd of still-staring Irin. "These women and their kind are precious. Will you protect them?"

Daina stepped forward. "I give them my protection."

Jerome joined her. "As do I."

"Ava!"

She heard her name from down the hall. Jaron spared her a single look before he melted into the facade of her old doctor from Istanbul, then he and an older man with a beard slipped out of the hall as if no one had seen them transform.

Malachi stormed into the room, Damien, Sari, and Kostas on his heels. He ran down the stairs and caught her in an embrace.

"You're here," he breathed out in relief. "You're safe."

The elders around them were silent, but Ava could feel their eyes.

"So you are the scribe," Abigail said, "who mated with the daughter of the Fallen."

It was a little more complicated than that, but Ava didn't feel like explaining.

Malachi simply said, "I am. We are *reshon*."

She heard the concerned muttering around the room.

"What is your name, brother?"

"Malachi of Sakarya. Right now, we must—"

His words were cut off when a dozen solemn men marched into the library. The remaining scribes parted as they headed for the stairs and sped down, surrounding the Irin and Irina elders.

"Elders," the captain said, "we must make you safe."

"No," Carmina said. "We are the strongest singers in the city. We need to face this threat and defend our people."

"No, sister," Daina counseled, "we must make the council safe. For the Irina council to be wiped out now—just when we've finally reformed—would be devastating to our people. We will let the captain guard us and trust our sisters to play their part in the battle."

Several of the elder singers glared, but none contradicted Daina. They knew the woman was right.

Sari stepped forward. "We believe that Grimold's children are in the city. The human population appears to be gone. They have come for us."

"What do you mean 'gone?'" Konrad asked.

"Just that," Damien said. "They are not here. One of the archangels appears to have put the city in stasis."

"The whole city?" Jerome asked. "But—"

"It doesn't work on any with angelic blood," Ava said. "Jaron told us. So there may be humans with Grigori blood roaming around really, really confused. Other than that, yes, they can do it. I've seen Jaron do it before, and it may be something that other angels can do too. The humans aren't gone, they're just… elsewhere right now."

"Vienna is under attack," Malachi said. "The elder singers' homes have been invaded. We need to get guards checking any Irina safe houses in the city."

Constance stepped forward and said, "I will tell the captain where they are, but I only trust the Library guards."

Jerome sighed. "Constance—"

"The Library Guard or we stay in hiding," the singer said with an ironclad will. "These are not warriors. These are teachers and healers. And I will not trust these women to any but our strongest."

"How many?" Damien asked. "How many of your Irina are in the city right now?"

Constance glared at him, but then looked between him and Sari and relented. "No more than forty. Some are capable of defending themselves. But if we are overrun—"

"There is a Rafaene house in the second district near the Carmelite Church. Your sisters could take refuge there. The scribes would be bound to protect them."

Constance nodded. "They are mostly in the first district. That could work."

"Let the Library Guard protect you and the other elders," Damien said. "When my men get here, I will give them the task of helping your sisters to the Rafaene scribe house. No one will be able to touch them there."

"Very well," Constance said. "And the rest of us?"

The fourteen elders stood solemnly, watching the captain of the Library Guard.

"Come with me," he said. "We have defenses set up to protect the Council." He held out a hand when the secretaries and other assistants stepped forward. "Only the council."

A pale scribe asked, "But what should we do?"

"Fight," Malachi said. "Or stay out of the way of those who will."

VASU materialized in midair, tossing Volund's body into the sculpture rising from the stones of the Graben. The normally bustling pedestrian mall was empty, thanks to Jaron's manipulations, and no one was there to hear the archangel scream.

"Did that hurt?" Vasu taunted. "Surely not. Surely an archangel has more fortitude than to be hurt by the petty constructions of man."

"You?" Volund roared and flung himself across the street, tackling the younger angel from his perch near the column of a nearby building. The stone cracked as they rolled into it, and the towering structure groaned. "Galal killed you!"

"Obviously not." Vasu laughed and blinked away, appearing to perch on top of the marble and gold angels of the plague column, the grand Baroque sculpture in the heart of Old Vienna some human ruler had commissioned to thank their god for mercy.

"Why do the humans make angels look like babies?" he mused. "It's insulting."

He ducked to the side as Volund leapt for him, his hands and feet crumbling the marble like so much dust as he crawled up the column.

"You do like to hear yourself talk, don't you?" Volund sneered.

"Yes." Vasu stood balanced on one foot at the very top of the twenty-one- meter column. "I'm very clever."

"You're very irritating. I'm going to kill you now, whelp. Then I will deal with Galal."

"You can try. But don't worry." His voice lost its humor. "I have my own plans for Galal."

From his perch, Vasu could see the shadows of Grigori slipping into the city. But he couldn't look long because Volund grabbed his foot, flinging him from the sculpture and slamming him into the stones below.

He'd forgotten how much impact could hurt in this form. How irritating. Still, it was better to be able to shift quickly.

Volund's lip curled. He stopped playing and drew a flaming sword from his side. "Do you remember this?"

Vasu's eyes gleamed. "Oh yes."

"I will slay you with it and feed your body to your children."

He ignored Volund but not the sword. "A Guardian's sword. Oh Volund, I should be afraid, shouldn't I?" He paused, looked his enemy in the eye. "And yet… I wonder."

"You won't have to wonder for long," Volund growled.

"Would Jaron trust me with her location?"

Volund froze.

"I could be there in a heartbeat." Vasu smiled. "Did you think your secret was safe?"

The other angel bared his teeth.

"I've always wondered what would happen if one of us killed her. Killed your *mate*." Vasu sneered.

Volund roared and swung his sword at Vasu. He flipped and spun, an expert with the angelic blade. And yet Vasu had been created to be a messenger of the heavens. His speed exceeded even the most dangerous of the Creator's guard.

"Would it hurt, Volund?" Vasu appeared behind Volund. "Would you bleed if she died?"

Volund turned and flung the blade at Vasu, only to have it come spinning back when its mark dissolved seconds before it hit.

"Is that why you hate her *so much*?" he whispered in Volund's ear.

And he was gone.

"Where is Jaron?" Volund spun in a rage, kicking the stone as shattered pieces of the old buildings rained down on the gracious streets below.

"You'd like to know, wouldn't you?" Vasu was perched on the plague column again, sitting on the head of a fat cherub, leaning his dark head against the gold. "You won't find him until he wants you. Just like you won't find your *mate.*" He sneered the word. "But I can. Jaron hasn't hidden her from *me*, has he?"

Volund moved with lightning speed, leaping from the corner of his building and climbing up the sculpture. But it was not fast enough for Vasu, who blinked away again.

And appeared at the top of a building one hundred meters down the Graben. "Of course, maybe I already know where she is!" Vasu shouted. "Is that why you let Jaron hide her from the world? To protect yourself?"

With a roar, Volund jumped over the rooftops, raining stone and glass down on the street below. Just as he swung his body over the last one, Vasu grinned and blinked away.

Then he was at Volund's back, a heaven-forged blade pressed to the angel's throat. "I have no love for Jaron's blood. And your very soul would split in two if your mate died, wouldn't it? What a brilliant idea." He kissed the angel's cheek. "I think I'll go pay her a visit."

Volund grabbed Vasu's arm and swung him overhead. The younger angel grimaced. His eyes swam and his body made a sickening crack into the building. The ground shook below them as Volund began to bring the blade down.

Vasu only smiled and disappeared.

"WHAT is that crashing sound?" Ava asked.

"I don't know, but I want you to listen to me." Malachi pulled Ava away from Damien and the others, who were shouting orders to the scribes who had joined them. The whole group had run out of the Hofburg and behind the riding school, taking the smaller side streets as they made their way toward St. Stephen's Cathedral, drawing attention away from the Library and toward a position they would be able to secure.

"Narrow streets and tall buildings," Malachi said as they jogged, "are not your friends. The plaza will be better. At least we'll be able to see them coming."

As they ran, Ava saw nothing but a few flickering shadows that quickly disappeared. More and more scribes joined them until their number included at least fifty. Also among their number was a collection of singers, most in groups of two or three. They whispered spells to surround the company, short staffs in hand, while the scribes surrounded them instinctively.

"Where is everyone?" she asked. "There are hundreds of Irin scribes in Vienna you told me. Where are they?"

"Politicians and financiers," Malachi said. "Most of these scribes have forgotten how to fight. Or they simply don't have the stomach for it."

When they reached the plaza, Malachi pulled her over to an isolated corner in the window of a pharmacy.

"When Leo arrives," he said. "I'm sending you and Kyra with him."

"What?" Her jaw dropped. "No, I'm not leaving you."

"You are. You and Kyra are too important. And you're not strong enough for this fight. I can't protect you and face this at the same time."

"Malachi, no."

"Listen—"

"Vasu gave the words to me. Spells I can use against the angels and the Grigori. I can protect—"

"Ava, we're not only facing soldiers." Malachi's voice dropped.

He turned them to face across the plaza and toward the Graben where the violent crashes and skittering footsteps had grown progressively louder. It was only then she saw them.

"I know you can kill Grigori," he said. "But can you kill *all* of them?"

Ava turned and saw Grimold's secret.

Slipping between shadows and jumping from balcony to balcony, the sons of the Fallen trickled into the square from streets and alleys and even from above. No longer distracted by the presence of humans, they focused on the scribes. There were hundreds of them, blending into the shadows and curling from the darkest corners of the street. They didn't come as an army but as thieves, their shadowed eyes watching the gathering of scribes in utter silence. They crouched in small groups or slipped from side streets as the Irin gathered at the foot of St. Stephen's Cathedral.

Especially the children.

Round-cheeked and slim. Fair-haired and dark. They crept like cats along the corners, trailing after their older kin with vicious smiles and hungry eyes.

"No."

His hands tightened on her shoulders. "Grimold is a monster. But so are these children."

"They're babies, Malachi."

"Babies"—his voice broke—"who would feed on you until you died. Babies you would have to kill to survive. Please, Ava. I do not want you here."

She could hear the agony in his voice, and she knew her mate had no love for this battle. Not when defeating their enemy meant the deaths of children. The Fallen's secret weapon was effective. She looked over the clutch of singers with Sari in the middle, holding Kyra close to her as the women around them chanted louder and louder. The barren, agonized expression on the singer's face and the terror in Kyra's eyes made her decision.

"I'll go with Leo," she whispered, then she threw her arms around his neck. "Please come back to me."

"I will."

Ava blinked away tears. "I won't be far. I want to be close enough that I can use my magic if I need to."

"I can live with that. Leo will find some place secure and out of the way of the worst of it."

A child watched them embrace, head cocked as a dog watches something curious. His feral gaze fixed on Ava, and she knew that Malachi was telling the truth. Though he wore the face of a child, Grimold's son was a monster.

"Where are Kostas's men?"

"They are hunting Grimold with Barak. If Kostas and his men can kill Grimold, his children—"

"Some of the youngest could be saved."

Malachi nodded. "That's what he's hoping."

Ava watched the street as more and more Grigori gathered. "Why aren't they attacking?"

"The Irina are holding them off. But we can't attack them in the middle of their protection, and the minute we leave the circle of their magic…"

She pulled away and pressed her forehead into his chest, kissing over his heart where her vow to him lay.

"Are you strong?" she whispered.

"Stronger than I have ever been, *canim*." He cupped her face, bringing her lips to his in a kiss that broke her heart. "I have your power in me," he whispered. "Your magic along with my own. Nothing will defeat me."

Ava saw Leo from the corner of her eye, so she squeezed them shut and gave Malachi one more kiss.

"I'm counting on it," she whispered. "Leo's here."

Malachi left her and walked to Leo, speaking low into the tall man's ear. Leo looked for Kyra, still frozen in the center of the singers' circle, obviously terrified. He nodded solemnly, then narrowed his eyes. She saw him shake his head once, but Malachi kept talking, putting his hand on Leo's shoulder, obviously trying to convince him. Ava was guessing Leo didn't want to miss the action any more than she did.

Though the singers' magic held, Ava saw the numbers of Grigori growing. If she and Kyra were going to hide, they needed to leave when their enemies were distracted. She saw Malachi walking over as Leo went to speak with Sari.

"When we break through, they will be confused," Malachi said. "Stay with Leo and use your magic to help him clear a path for Kyra. She has no defenses, Ava. You must help Leo get her away."

"I will."

She saw them walking over and knew she only had a few more seconds alone with her mate.

"I love you," she said. "At the end of the day, no matter what happens, I will never be sorry I was given the time to love you."

Malachi lifted her in his arms, crushing her to his chest. She felt the rapid beat of his heart as his body prepared for battle. Felt the pulse of magic over his skin as he kissed the breath from her lungs. His hand gripped the back of her head, holding her with painful possession for one precious moment before he made himself break away. Then he met her eyes and Ava saw the battle lust begin to rise.

"I love you," he said. "Stay safe."

Leo came, holding Kyra's hand and watching her. "Are you ready?"

She nodded. "Do what you have to do," Ava said. "Then come back to me."

He smiled and drew his knives. "Always."

Chapter Twenty-six

MALACHI WATCHED LEO LEAD the two women to the edge of the Irin defenses. The attack would begin soon, but it was too dangerous for the females to run far. They'd be targeted immediately. Malachi and Leo's plan was to make a quick run to one of the nearby buildings in the initial rush of confusion. If they could hide in one of the upper floors, it would be the safest place. The majority of the Grigori were focused with preternatural concentration on the circle of singers in the middle of the plaza. Between Ava and Leo, Malachi hoped they'd be able to fend off any random attackers in the right position.

There were few scribes he trusted as much as Leo. Despite the man's affable demeanor, he was a fierce protector and a skilled warrior. His soft heart never blinded him to the realities of a fight.

But he was young. If Malachi could keep the man from the necessity of slaughtering children, he would.

He watched the small ones with dread in his heart, their perverse excitement more visible than their elders'. Grimold's children jumped and shouted, eager for the fight.

"A monster," Damien said as he came to stand with Malachi. "Not even Volund sends children to fight his wars."

"No."

"Be strong, brother. We'll try to disable as many as we can in hopes that Kostas's men will find Grimold in time, but do not let their faces fool you."

"I know," Malachi said. "Some will die."

It was inevitable.

Malachi saw Leo, Ava, and Kyra reach the edge of the Irin lines. With only a little push, the scribes in front of them would be the first into the battle. He saw some of the Oslo scribes there, along with others from Sofia and Berlin. The warriors had come to Vienna, and just in time.

Rhys, Max, and Gabriel were part of the core of scribes circling the Irina, guarding the women who sang out a circle of magic. Malachi could feel it move through the air around him but knew they must move out of it to kill their enemy.

"It's coming," Damien said. "They're pushing out and then we must go."

Malachi nodded.

"Do you have your blade ready?"

"Yes, Watcher."

"Be strong," Damien said. "And return to your mate."

Malachi touched his *talesm prim*, felt the power of his magic grow and swell, covering his body like armor. His marks glowed silver and his skin heated with excitement and power.

Sari let loose a loud cry, shouting a command into the sky, and Malachi felt the circle of magic pulse up and out. Grigori cowered before it, some falling from their perches on balconies and others covering their ears as they let out a wail.

Malachi charged.

He rushed past Leo and the women, throwing his knives at two Grigori who had spotted what they thought was easy prey. They fell down with knives in their throats as Malachi ran and threw an elbow in the face of another.

He felt the first knife slash across his arm, but his skin healed within seconds. With a loud grunt, he head-butted the soldier who had attacked him, sending him to the ground. From the corner of his eye, he saw Leo and Ava making their way toward a red-fronted building with Kyra between them, soldiers falling and writhing around them as he saw his mate's lips move. For a second, he saw the knife headed toward her throat, then Leo batted it away, pulling the arm of the Grigori who wielded it in one smooth motion, grabbing his head and twisting his neck until it snapped. The Grigori dropped to the ground and the three kept running.

Malachi lost sight of them in the fighting.

He let the power flow through him as he moved in instinctive rhythm. Punch, slash, kick, slash. His knife pierced the spine of so many Grigori soldiers he felt their dust coat his skin.

The crowd thinned, then thickened again, becoming more erratic. A knife pierced his groin, digging into the inside of his thigh as it reached for the artery there. He tugged the tiny attacker away. It was a child, no more than seven or eight, who wielded the silver knife that had struck him. The boy bit his arm and screamed, trying to scramble away, but Malachi shook him once, and he fell still. Then he clocked the child on the side of the head, sending him to the ground unconscious before he laid him on the side of the street, hoping he would not rise before Grimold was dead. Already too many small bodies had fallen, their diminutive outlines of dust staining the wet cobblestones in the shadow of Stephansdom.

And still they came, pouring down the streets and over the buildings. Hundreds of Grimold's children battled to take the city the Irin claimed as the scribes and a remnant of singers protected their home.

"YOU!" Volund stalked across the brilliantly tiled roof of the Stephansdom, headed toward Jaron. "Where is she?"

Jaron watched him coming, leaning against the base of one spire. "I don't know who you mean. My child? Your granddaughter? Which female do you fear today, brother?"

"But you would give her to Vasu?"

Jaron had long suspected that Vasu knew about Ava and Volund, but clearly the thought of another having access to his mate had pushed Volund into madness. His eyes were wide and raging. His form had lost all semblance of humanity.

He had to die, and Jaron had to kill him before his rage passed and he remembered his granddaughter.

Volund had already drawn the flaming sword from his body, so Jaron knew he would be weakened. Still, it was no easy thing to kill an angel of Volund's age. Jaron was depleted from shifting so many humans in the city. He was the only one of his brothers able to hold a dream for so long, and he had no weapon to match a guardian's sword. Only a consecrated blade would work.

All Jaron had was knives.

"I will kill you," Volund said. "I will kill you and your children. Take what is mine and—"

"She was never yours!" Jaron flew at him, felt Volund's blade pierce his shoulder, but he did not stop. "She is my child. She was *never* yours, thief." He and Volund rolled across the bright roof of the cathedral, then Jaron pushed back until the sword left his body, knowing he would not heal from the wound.

"I claimed her," Volund said, panting. "And she is mine. And when you are dead, I will find her and she will *torment me no more*!"

"If you want her," Jaron said, "then follow me."

He pushed off the building and launched his angelic form into the air, knowing that Volund would follow.

Ava watched from a window across from the Stephansdom, the great gothic spire of the cathedral knifing into the grey sky as the Irin and Grigori battled beneath it. Dark clouds hung over the normally bright roof, hiding it from human eyes. Thunder rumbled, though no lightning struck. And like a dark fog, the Grigori spread over the square, lurking as the shadows fell.

"There's no end to them," she whispered. Kyra was huddled in a corner, eyes closed, clearly in agony over the violence below. Ava had tried to enhance the woman's shields, but panic was her enemy. The only relief Kyra seemed to find was clutching Leo's hand with grim determination. Of course, when Leo had to let go…

"There is an end," he said, stepping beside Ava to look down. "And Malachi will survive."

His face was set, his eyes fixed on his brothers fighting below.

"You don't know that."

"Look." He pointed to one small clearing. "There he is."

Ava squinted. "Are you sure? How can you see?"

"I can't see his face. I know how he fights, though…" Leo's eyes shuttered. "The children are unexpected."

Ava turned her eyes away. "Am I a coward?"

"No." Leo placed a hand on her shoulder. "He needs you to be here, away from the blood. So that when he returns he'll remember what it is to be clean. Some memories you carry until you die. There is no reason you need to carry them as well."

"Leo—"

"I need you to stay with Kyra while I check this floor," he said. "Can you do that, Ava?"

She nodded. "Find me something I can use as a staff."

He grinned. "I'm sure there's a janitor's closet somewhere."

Ava gave one last glance to the fighting below the building, then she turned back to Kyra, opening the door in her mind to listen and keep watch as thunder sounded over the city.

"THEY'RE attacking the Irina," Damien said, running up to him. "Fall back and protect the singers or we will have no shield."

Malachi looked over his shoulder, and he could see Sari and the others wielding their short staffs, batting back the children who had managed to sneak past their circle of magic. That must have been why Grimold had sent them. For some reason, the smallest of the Grigori seemed immune to the singers' power.

Children. His watcher was ordering him to kill the children.

"Damien—"

"We *must* protect the Irina. The small ones are immune to their magic."

Children.

He saw one holding two daggers, rushing at the legs of a singer who tried to kick him away. Blood bloomed above her knees, and Malachi ran toward them just as the child tried to plunge a blade into the Irina's abdomen.

Sari's staff lifted and struck, tossing the child away.

"Sari!"

Her tortured eyes met his. "We can't hold them back. I have no spells that work on them."

"Then defend yourself," Damien said. "*Míla*, you know you have no choice."

She nodded, even though tears filled her eyes.

There was no time to mourn. The Grigori children were unrelenting.

Damien glanced at the sky. "I do not see any sign of Volund."

"I think Jaron might be taking care of that problem. Grimold is directing his sons. We just need to hold them off until Kostas and his men find him."

Malachi was hoping it would be soon. And he really hoped they hadn't overestimated the skills of their free Grigori allies.

He hazarded a glance at the building where Ava hid before he fell back to his grim task.

"DON'T look at me," Ava whispered as she watched him as he retreated to defend the circle of Irina. "Pay attention."

Ava was sick to her stomach as she watched the vicious children with beautiful faces assault the Irin below.

"Why doesn't the magic hold them off?" Kyra asked, coming to stand next to Ava, her face pale and her eyes sunken.

"Maybe the magic is designed that way," Ava said. "Irina wouldn't want to hurt children."

"*I* want to hurt those children," she said. "Grigori children are more vicious than the adults."

Ava gave her a look.

Kyra said, "Harbor no illusions, sister. The female children can be just as frightening. There is a reason I was glad your friend Mala stayed with the group in Prague."

"He will hate himself. If only there was a way…" Ava blinked before she grabbed the Kyra's arms.

Kyra looked at her like Ava had lost it. "What's wrong?"

"Their sires can control them, can't they?"

"The angels? Of course. But I don't know how."

317

"I know," Ava said with a smile. "I just have to get close enough."

"What are you talking about?"

Ava was trying to pry open a window. There was a balcony out there, and if she could get near enough…

"Vasu gave me spells. Words that knocked the Grigori on their ass when they came after me in the cemetery. I know the Irina probably created spells with safeguards to protect children, but I'm betting Vasu didn't."

Kyra nodded. "Try."

Ava finally stopped trying to pry open the window and just grabbed a chair.

"Stand back."

She threw the wooden chair at the window and it bounced off.

"Well… shit."

She heard Leo approaching and turned to—

"Not Leo!" Kyra shouted.

Three Grigori smiled, hungry eyes on Ava and Kyra.

"What do we have here?" one said. "Humans?"

"Humans with angel blood," said another. "Even better."

BARAK was relieved to admit he had underestimated his sons. What he had seen as cowardice had clearly been something else. They had retreated, yes, but then they had regrouped. Grown stronger. More stable. A better-trained group of Grigori he had never seen. Kostas wielded authority like a true child of the Fallen. Violence was his currency. Praise rare. Discipline expected.

"It helps them," Kostas said quietly as they walked the rail yards in Simmering.

Snow blanketed the grey tracks. The bustle of humans was eerily silent. Though trains smoked in the station, no one boarded them. Nothing moved but the drifts of dirty snow that fell from the clouds above.

"Oh?" Barak said, mind on the strange swirling movement of the sky overhead.

"The discipline," Kostas said. "It helps the hunger."

Yes, that made sense. It had never occurred to Barak to teach his sons discipline. They were… incidental. Though he had ruled much of Northern Europe for thousands of years, he didn't have the patience for strategy. He'd held his enemies at bay with strength, and that had been reflected in his Grigori. Most were brutally handsome children with more power than brains in his opinion.

When Volund had outmaneuvered him, he hadn't been surprised. He'd been… resigned.

"They control everything better if they're disciplined," his son said. "Bodies and minds. Your death gave them hope. Their sisters gave them purpose."

"I do not wish to steal that."

"Oh?" Kostas asked. "So if we walk away now, you'll do nothing to call us back?"

"No. I'll just kill Grimold myself."

"Why are we here then?"

"Because he'll have his sons with him. The strongest—though none of his children are particularly that strong—he'll keep close by. I imagine with your newly grown goodwill, you don't want to set them loose upon the humans."

As if by signal, a clutch of Grimold's children leapt down on some of his men. They were quickly surrounded and killed. Their dust rose to the sky within seconds, and Kostas's men barely slowed down.

"No," Kostas said. "We do not want them loose."

Barak watched him from the corner of his eye. "I did not teach you conscience."

"No, I acquired it when I saw what killing humans did to my sister."

"Oh?"

His son was quiet for a long while. "She heard their terror. Even worse, their love."

"Ah." Barak shrugged, beginning to like the human gestures Vasu imitated. "And your brothers?"

"I have bent them to my way of thinking whether they like it or not."

Barak smiled as his son walked forward, surveying his men as they searched the train yard, exterminating any of the stray Grigori that were starting to creep out to meet them.

"We're getting closer."

"Yes."

"There are many," Kostas said.

"He finds them useful," Barak said. "Grimold has never been powerful. Only… prolific."

"Most of the Fallen have adopted that strategy. You did not."

"You and your sister are some of the last children I sired. I grew tired of human attention after that."

"Why?"

"The earth has little appeal for me anymore." The image of two small children drifted across his tired mind. He had thought they were brothers. Twins. They wouldn't remember him any longer. It had been too long. But the image of their small, blood-covered bodies held in his arms would remain with him through eternity. "This realm is so very brutal."

"And whose fault is that?"

"Humans," Barak said. "It has always been so. Be careful. Free will is a dangerous thing."

He was only looking a little. Sight had never been his strength. The Creator had given him the gift of hearing, so he used it now. Throughout the rail yard and the industrial neighborhoods of the district, he could hear the humans dreaming. Soft and soothing, their voices melded together in a murmur he'd become accustomed to over his thousands of years on the earth.

There were so many more now.

Perhaps that was another part of it. And another reason he wanted the daughters of the Fallen to find relief.

"Do you hear anything?" Kostas asked.

"Not yet, but I know Grimold is here."

"How?"

"His children are growing bolder." He nodded toward another small group of Kostas's men who surrounded two men twitching on the ground. "And because of what I do not hear."

THE SECRET

"What is that?"

"Birds." Barak lifted an eyebrow and returned his son's incredulous expression. "They don't like Grimold. I have no idea why."

AVA didn't hesitate when she saw the three Grigori soldiers.

"*Zi yada*," she hissed the spell Vasu had whispered in her mind.

The first froze just as Leo burst into the room. He halted for only a second, then drove the point of his silver blade into the spine of the frozen Grigori.

"*Zi yada!*" Ava said again, louder. Another stopped. The third lunged at her, but Ava grabbed Kyra and threw herself out of his path. Within seconds, Leo had killed the two remaining attackers. One still twitched while the others stood frozen. Ava watched as they dissolved like statues melting into the sky.

"What did you do?" Leo asked.

"Fallen magic," Ava said. "Can you get a window open for me?"

Leo kicked the chair out of the way. "Will it work at this distance?"

"Hopefully?"

"It's worth a try." Then he stopped and turned. "But will it affect the Irin?"

Ava paused. "I don't know."

Kyra said, "It only worked one at a time on the Grigori. Maybe you have to direct it at each person."

Ava looked at Leo. "Should I try it?"

"If it freezes the Irin down there, they're dead."

"Especially since I have no idea how to undo it."

Kyra stepped forward. "Try with us."

"What?"

Leo nodded. "I'm Irin. She's Grigori."

"But—"

"If you knock me out and Leo's still moving," Kyra said, "you'll know it's safe. And if you knock both me and Leo out... just do your best. It can't last forever."

Ava eyed the open door.

"We'll barricade the door," Leo said, tossing her the short staff that looked more like a sawed-off broom handle. "You can protect us, Ava. But we need to try."

"Okay."

They pushed as much furniture in front of the door as they could. It was an older office, dusty from disuse and isolated about halfway up the building.

"What if I can't reach them?" she said, eyes darting to the fighting below.

"We try. That's all we can do," Leo said. "Now, Ava."

"Aim the spell at me," Kyra said. "Leo, stay close. They're fighting close to each other."

Leo stood behind Kyra, one arm around her waist. "Now."

Ava took a deep breath and focused on Kyra. She stared at her, felt the power grow in her belly.

"*Zi yada.*"

Leo caught Kyra when she fell.

"Did you feel it?"

"I felt it, but it didn't hit me. I just… felt it." Leo carefully placed Kyra on the floor, then ran to the window.

He yanked the drapes down, and Ava saw his thumb circle his left wrist. The power coursed over his skin as his *talesm* glowed for a moment. He held the drape up to the window, then with one powerful punch, the glass blew outward.

"Try now, Ava. The children are getting closer. You have to try."

Chapter Twenty-seven

MALACHI HEARD SARI SHOUT as he cut through another small body. He'd already vomited everything in his stomach as he defended the Irina from the children's attacks. The Grigori boys darted around and under the blades of the scribes, and none of the Irina spells seemed to work.

He had slain hundreds in his long life. Felt his enemies' blood stain his face. Felt their death rattles under his hands and watched the life drain from their eyes before their bodies turned to dust.

But Malachi had never faced a fight like this.

His enemy carried the face of the innocent. He had to battle every instinct to protect as he beat them back. One singer lay unconscious in the arms of a scribe, her leg hacked off by one of the children. Other singers had wrapped their robes around their throats, trying to guard their voices from the relentless assault. He felt the blood drip where they'd jabbed their knives at his face and chest. Malachi was certain he'd lost part of an ear, trying to disable them without killing.

He'd knocked as many unconscious as he could, but there had been some who'd left him no option. The beautiful children knew their advantage and took it as their elder brothers attacked the Irin front line.

Struggling through the attack on the Irina, the scribes had been pushed to the gates of the cathedral, their focus now on keeping the Grigori back as long as possible, hoping that more Irin would come. Hoping that Kostas's men would be able to kill Grimold. Without the angel's direction, the Grigori soldiers would lose their focus.

"Sari?" he called over his right shoulder. "What do you see?"

He threw two unconscious Grigori children away from the circle of Irina and turned. Sari was standing, her hands held up and her mouth hanging open. Two Grigori children lay at her feet, eyes open and bodies frozen.

"What is this?" she asked, pushing them with her foot. "They're not dead, but…"

"I don't know."

He looked up. Ava was hanging out a window, Leo holding her as she stared at the gates of Stephansdom. Her eyes were narrowed and he could see her lips moving. He felt their magic rise.

Another child dropped at his feet.

"Ava," he said. "She's using Fallen magic."

"It works on the children?" Sari said. "Do you know how—"

"I know the word, but not how to write it!" he said, flinging a child from his waist. "I can't write it, Sari, not even with my blood."

"Tell me!"

Tears were running down Malachi's face as he struck the arm of a Grigori boy who'd latched on to the singer at his left.

Mercy.

He was so small.

The boy's warm blood spurted on Malachi's face, but he would not let go of the Irina's throat. Another scribe's blade reached the child's neck as he bared his teeth. The Grigori froze; his eyes went wide. His mouth, soft with youth, hung open as Malachi fell to his knees, catching the child's body before it hit the ground. It shouldn't hit the dirty cobblestones. It wasn't right. None of this was right.

The child's unearthly gaze met Malachi's as he caught him. They stared for a moment, Irin and Grigori. Then the bright life drained out of his eyes just before the small body dissolved to dust.

"I can't," he groaned. "Ava, forgive me. I can't."

Mercy.

"Malachi!" Sari was at his shoulder. "Tell me the spell!"

The spell?

"*Zi yada*," he whispered. "Make it stop."

Make them stop.

THE SECRET

Sari rose and flung her staff to the side. "*Zi yada!*"

A child froze mid-jump, then fell to the cobblestones at their feet. He did not move.

Other Irina heard and took up the spell, and the air rang with the shouts of Fallen magic as the Grigori children froze in their attacks.

Malachi looked up, searching for her, his cheeks wet with blood and tears. She hung over the window, her attention directed at the Grigori fighting the Irin scribes.

One by one, they began to fall, writhing in pain as their dust filled the air.

The scribes in the square rallied as their enemy began to fall back. Some of the children looked confused. A few followed their elders, though most continued trying for the Irina, even as their small bodies fell.

Malachi began to pick up the bodies of the fallen children, carrying them to the side of the cathedral so they wouldn't be trampled. He heard a shout and looked up. Walking down the Rotenturmstraße from the direction of the river and running behind the cathedral came a large group of the Irin. Led by a scribe in Rafaene robes, they walked with grim purpose and more than a few frightened expressions. Some of the men wore business suits that covered their *talesm*. Some wore scholar's robes. All carried weapons.

He heard the Grigori hiss and fall back from the edges of the plaza.

The Irin had awoken.

BARAK and Kostas followed the rail tracks north from the Zentralfriedhof, fanning out as the tracks spread west of the freeway.

"He's here," Barak said.

Kostas motioned to Sirius, then the commander and six of his men spread their Grigori out in teams of three to five men, searching the rail yard which was empty of humans but teeming with Grigori assassins.

"Where?" Kostas asked.

"Quiet."

He let the profound noise fill him. Thousands of souls, tormented and peaceful, full of joy or sorrow. They surrounded him. Spread over him.

Filled his mind and body until he could not separate himself from the voices of heaven. Then he reached out, looking for a single thread among many.

Gravel scraped along his senses.

There.

His eyes still closed, he drifted toward it, calling his children with him.

"Father, no."

A plea tugged at the edges of his mind. He opened his eyes to see Kostas before him, holding a black, heaven-forged blade to his throat. "Where did you get that?"

"Do not command us," he said through gritted teeth. "We will follow you, but do not take our will."

The fine blood vessels in Kostas's eyes had burst, and the Grigori's gaze was red and angry.

"Put it down, child—"

"Father—"

"—and follow me."

Barak strode over the rail yard, his form growing with each step. He reached into his body, pulling out the flaming sword of the guardians.

He had once been a protector of heaven, his purest joy in guarding the Creator and those who dwelt at his side. Then he fell into darkness, and the darkness had overcome him.

Do not fear the darkness.

He felt the sword draw from his flesh and gasped with the agony and ecstasy of it, for no angel carried a guardian's sword without pain. It fed on the blood of heaven's sons. Mortal hands could not touch it. And no angel would survive its strike.

"Grimold," he whispered. "It is time."

The angel met Barak with a hail of bullets shot from the hands of his children. Kostas's men sprang forward, attacking them as the angel fell on the archangel, his face flaming with rage.

"You will not do this!" Grimold screamed. "He has seen our victory!"

"He lied."

THE SECRET

JARON landed on the roof of the opera house, the building rattling under his feet as chips of stone went flying. Volund crashed into him, his blade arching through the air and glancing off Jaron's shoulder before he spun away.

"Where is she?"

"Grimold's sons are dying," Jaron said, ignoring Volund's question. "You are going to lose."

Volund laughed. "Svarog's men have not even arrived to join the fun! This battle is not over."

"No," Jaron said with a slow smile. "Svarog's children have not arrived. How curious."

Volund's smile fell, then he sneered again, rushing Jaron in a rage.

Jaron accepted the slashing blow to his arm, reveling in the pain as he felt his right hand turn to dust under the guardian's blade.

"What do you see now, you fool?" Volund shouted. "What vision did our Master send you? Did you see this, Jaron? Did you see your brother take you apart, piece by piece?"

He felt. For the first time in his millennia of existence, Jaron reveled in anguish. He fell to his knees laughing and shouting. Volund cocked his head, no doubt wondering where the solemn advisor of heaven had gone.

But Jaron saw.

He had seen the truth in his daughter's eyes, and it had made him yearn. Made him want.

Made him rage.

He had planned for decades, only to have his own machinations turned upside down by something as simple—as profound—as love.

Do not fear the darkness—his Creator had whispered to him once—*for it is only a shadow of the sun.*

Then Jaron, son of heaven, raised his eyes as his Master showed him the blade that would bring him home.

He jumped to his feet and ran at Volund, grinning when the guardian's sword pierced his belly. He wrapped his good arm around Volund's waist and jumped from the top of the Opera house, leaping into the storm as icy rain began to fall on empty streets.

"AVA, come back inside."

"I can't." She could hear them, curling on the ground in utter pain. She could hear their screams.

And she loved it.

Ba dahaa.

She felt their suffering in her bones, but she would not relent. Ava fed the black void and felt her power grow. The hollow Malachi had drawn from was full, not with his own bright magic, but the black power that grew and flourished in her.

"Ava, come back."

"No."

She felt the glass cutting into her stomach, felt the sharp, icy rain at her back, and the tearing pain in her abdomen and legs.

Ava didn't care.

Ba dahaa.

Zi yada.

She could taste it. The sweet satisfaction of her enemies' cries. They screamed, their voices echoing down the city streets as the Irin cut them back.

"Ava!" Leo pulled her into the building and she spun, tearing at his face with clawed hands.

"Let me go!"

"They're winning!" He pointed to the streets below where Irin scribes and even a few singers had flooded the plaza, overwhelming the Grigori forces, many of whom were in retreat. "They're beating them back. You have to stop."

"I don't want to."

"You must!"

"No!"

"You are hurting Kyra," he shouted. "You have to stop."

She turned to the corner where the *kareshta* lay, no longer frozen but curled in agonized silence, her body twitching in the wake of Ava's magic.

Ava took a deep breath and pulled her power in. "No."

Leo knelt next to her. "I don't know what happened. But every time you hit one of the Grigori outside, she feels it."

"She can't filter them out," Ava said. "She's not strong enough yet. Hold her, Leo."

"I need to protect you too!"

"I've got it!" She glanced out the window. "And I think they have it too. Something is happening to the Grigori."

BARAK and Grimold wrestled, and the ground shook below them. Iron tracks buckled and popped, tossing railcars into the air as the sky let loose the hail that had gathered in the clouds. A great rumbling shook the earth as the train cars cracked together, drawn to Grimold's elemental power.

Barak felt his sons fighting around him, and for the first time in millennium he felt... pride. His child had resisted his draw. Once Barak was gone, they would be strong. Safe. They would not bring shame to his line. He wanted to pretend it did not matter, but he was a creature of brutal honesty, if nothing else.

He cared.

Grimold had no such pride. He drew his children to his side, throwing them at Barak like so much fodder. The guardian's sword sprayed dust as it slew them.

"Stop, Grimold. You kill them for nothing."

"I will kill you," the angel screamed. "Traitor!"

Barak stood, sword pulsing in the darkness. "That is the point."

Grimold stopped, his eyes narrowed.

Barak saw the twin railings coming from either side. His eyes met Kostas's for a second before his son ran toward his sire.

"Father!"

"I knew you would kill me," Barak said.

Grimold smiled.

So did Barak. "I always planned to take you with me."

Laughing, Grimold pulled the iron railings into his hands, the metal phosphorescent with angelic power. He brought them together, tearing

Barak's head from his shoulders, and as he did, he looked down to see the guardian's sword sunk deep and glowing in the center of his chest.

He lifted his head to scream, but Grimold's voice was drowned by thunder as the two angels were sucked into the clouds.

JARON'S breath stopped for a moment.

Barak was gone.

He landed on the green dome of Peterskirche, but he knew it wasn't high enough, and he was growing weaker.

Volund struggled, trying to get away, but Jaron's grip was like iron. He had no will to fight back, so he trapped his brother to his chest and ignored the spreading burn of the sword in his gut as Volund twisted and laughed.

He closed his eyes and, with the last of his strength, imagined the blade of heaven below him.

Father, let me fall.

AVA raised her eyes when the thunder crashed. She saw the shadows of giants rolling in the clouds.

MALACHI looked up as lightning struck the spire.

"Impossible," Rhys whispered at his side.

JARON opened his eyes to the heavens and laughed as the stars danced over Volund's back. He felt his body falling and wondered what the humans below thought of his true form.

"No!" Volund screamed, though his blade bound them together. "NO!"

"The angel came upon them," Jaron whispered as the ground rushed up, "and they were sore afraid."

Then his back arched and he clutched Volund closer as the consecrated spire of the Stephansdom split them both in two.

Chapter Twenty-eight

FIFTEEN HUNDRED KILOMETERS AWAY, she screamed, beating her fists against the painted walls until her hands were bloody and broken. The humans rushed in to contain her, but she kept screaming. Then, as abruptly as it started, it stopped.

The woman known as Ava Rezai fell unconscious to the floor.

Vasu stared at her from the corner of the room as the humans raced in and tried to revive her.

Then he looked at Azril, standing by his side.

"She will live?"

Death nodded slowly and returned to Vienna.

AVA saw the shadows, then lightning touched the top of the spire, illuminating it for a fraction of a second before the vision was gone.

No thunder rolled through the air.

No rain fell.

She knew Jaron was dead.

Everything was quiet. The biting sleet that had fallen on the street below had stilled, and the air was almost balmy. Bodies, fallen bloody to the cobblestones, began to dissolve. Dust rose, so thick it resembled a golden fog rising from the street.

No bells rang. No birds flew.

Ava looked down to see Death walking among them. He stood over her mate and her heart stopped. Then Death looked up and met her eyes.

Not for many years, daughter.

Azril knelt and lifted an Irina from the ground, holding her up to heaven as her body dissolved and rose.

Another scribe. And another.

He ignored the bodies of the Grigori, except for the children. Gentle hands lifted them to the heavens, and their shadows passed by her as they rose.

So many.

Then the bodies were gone, and Death was too.

QUIET groans and sobbing rose from the street below as humans began to reappear in the plaza, walking as if nothing had happened. They ducked into brightly lit restaurants and bars, laughing with friends as street musicians played night music in the square.

Ava watched in a panic as dozens of scribes and singers scattered, whispering spells and touching *talesm* to hide themselves and the wounded from human eyes. The few Grigori who had survived scurried into the shadows, melting into alleys and side streets. Children woke and looked around in confusion, some of them dragged off by their brethren, others scattering to the streets to fend for themselves.

The dust of the dead still wafted on the breeze as the clouds cleared; stars shone in a pitch-black sky.

And the humans saw nothing.

"Ava, away from the window," Leo said.

"They don't see," she whispered, unable to tear her eyes from the busy, unthinking populace below.

"They never see," Kyra murmured, rubbing her temples. "My father is dead."

Leo looked at Ava. "Jaron?"

"Yes." She didn't know how she knew, but it was there. An inexplicable lightness in her mind. A weight off her shoulders. "Volund too."

"Are you sure?"

Ava looked at the street below. Scribes and singers had fallen in battle. Children of the Fallen were slain before her eyes. But the rain washed the blood away, and the bodies had dissolved into dust.

Within moments, the battle was a memory. Her own mate had disappeared.

"I'm not sure of anything anymore," she said. "I just want to go home."

She knew he was alive. The threads of magic connecting them had not broken. All Ava felt was an unspeakable sorrow deep in her chest.

"He's not answering messages." Leo was texting madly on his cell phone. "Damien and Rhys are going to the Library to check on the council. They think Sari is with Malachi, but they lost them after the battle. I'm trying to find out what happened to your brother, Kyra."

"Text Sirius," Kyra murmured in a daze. "Kostas is horrible about keeping his phone on. Just horrible."

Ava turned and leaned against the wall, sliding down until she was sitting on the ground.

"I don't hear any humans outside."

"This is an office building," Leo said, still texting. "It's nighttime, Ava."

Oh, of course it was. The moon was already in the sky, peeking through the clouds that had cleared away. Ava realized that none of the lights were on in the room. When they had entered, it had been daylight. How long had the battle raged? She couldn't grasp it. Hours? It hadn't seemed like hours.

Leo let out a relieved breath. "The council is safe."

Ava didn't care about the council anymore.

"Sari called Damien. She's taking Malachi back to their house, then home."

"Okay." She got to her feet and started to move the furniture from in front of the door.

"Ava," Leo said. "What are you doing?"

"I want to go home."

"There may still be Grigori—"

"Then I'm taking my broom handle"—she picked up the stick that was lying on the ground—"and I'm going home, Leo."

She could feel it building. Ava didn't want to break down in front of Kyra or Leo. She wanted solitude and Malachi.

"Okay, okay." Leo jumped to his feet. He started to help her clear the door. "Let's get you home."

WHEN they reached the flat in Judenplatz, Malachi was waiting on the steps of their building with hollow eyes and a black cat sitting near his feet. Rhys stood over him, haggard but wearing a smile.

"Go," Leo said. "I'll get Kyra back to Damien and Sari's."

Ava looked at Kyra, who nodded swiftly.

"Go," she said. "I'll be fine."

"Call me when you get back so I know everyone's safe."

Ava walked over and Rhys gave her a quick hug.

"All right?" he asked quietly.

"I will be."

"I'll leave him to you." He bent down. "He was protecting the Irina. And… the children. You know—"

"I know."

Her mate hadn't only killed soldiers.

Then Rhys, Leo, and Kyra ambled into the night and Ava held out her hand.

Malachi took it but didn't stand. He didn't look at her or embrace her.

"Go away, Vasu," Ava said.

So ungrateful.

The cat sauntered off, then turned.

They're dead, you know. You're safe now. Jaron made sure of it.

"Really?"

Truly.

"Thanks. I guess… thank you."

You're welcome. I'd forgotten how entertaining humans can be. I'll see you again, Ava.

She said nothing more to Vasu. Ava pulled Malachi to his feet and led him up to their apartment. When they got inside, she removed his clothes. He was wearing jeans; someone had thrown a jacket over him and pushed boots on his feet. The shirt under it was stained with blood.

Ava tore it off, searching for wounds.

"Not my blood," he said quietly. "It's not my blood."

She broke.

Pressing her face into his chest, she sobbed. Great, wracking, painful cries of relief and agony over the lives lost. For what she had done. For what he had been forced to do. He put tentative hands on her shoulders, but he did not embrace her.

"Ava." His voice sounded more fragile than she'd ever heard before. "I need to get clean."

She led him to the bathroom and stripped the clothes off them both. She would throw them away in the morning. Maybe she would burn them. Ava stood with Malachi under blistering hot water until it ran cold. She washed his hair for him and cleaned the dust from every inch of his skin. Then she led him to bed and crawled under the covers.

Neither one of them slept, but they held each other until dawn. And when the night had passed and Rhys had called to check on them both, Ava returned to him. Sometime after she heard the humans rouse in the streets below, she slept.

"I'M sorry," he whispered, clutching her in the forest as night birds sang overhead. "I'm sorry."

"You did nothing wrong."

"I'm sorry," he whispered into her neck as she held him.

The forest was darker than it had ever been, though the oppressive fog around them had lifted. No moon shone in the sky above. The earth they rested on was bleak and cold.

"It's so dark," he said, his powerful body curled into her, shivering. "Why is it so dark?"

"It won't always be dark," she told him, running her fingers through his hair and down his neck, feeling the strength of him more powerfully for the way he bared himself to her. "I promise. The moon will come out again."

He said nothing, but allowed her to hold him.

"It's okay," she said, over and over again. "It will be okay."

She held him in the night, comforting him when she felt his shoulders shaking.

"You found me once," she said. "Do you remember? I was broken. You picked me up and you carried me."

"Yes."

"And you told me you would never leave me again."

"I'm tired, *reshon*."

"Rest then. I'll hold you."

He relaxed into her arms.

"Remember," she whispered, "it's only when the night is darkest that you can see the light of the stars."

He stretched her out and there was a soft blanket beneath them. The forest became a refuge, and she saw some of the sorrow leave his eyes.

"Sing to me," he asked her.

So she did.

VII.

"THERE YOU ARE."

Svarog turned when he heard Vasu's voice. The house in Wieden was empty. Had been empty for years, though Vasu had heard that the angel had kept a home and a mistress in the city at one time. He'd enjoyed tweaking the noses of the Irin Council—even if the council hadn't known it—only a few blocks from the famous Naschmarkt of Vienna.

Vasu wore his most comfortable human guise, a lean form native to the Indian subcontinent he called home. He was ready, so ready, to return to the warm climes of his home in Chittorgarh. He was ready to come out of hiding.

"And there *you* are, old friend," Svarog said. He'd taken on the appearance of an urban gentleman. His suit cut was immaculate. But then, Svarog had always liked his luxuries. "I knew rumors of your death must be exaggerated."

"Aren't they always?"

"It appears so. Both you and Barak were a surprise." His voice dropped when they spoke of the fallen archangel. "Jaron kept his allies close."

Vasu smiled. "Volund could have learned a lesson from him."

"Volund," Svarog growled, "was too proud to learn from anyone."

Vasu leaned against the banister in the spacious entryway. "And where are your children, my friend? I did not see Svarog's sons in the midst of battle."

The angel turned. "Where were Volund's?"

"Dead in Oslo."

Svarog raised a steel-grey eyebrow. "Exactly."

Vasu was delighted by the angel's trickery. Svarog wasn't an archangel. Like Vasu, he'd been quite young when he fell. And unlike many of his brethren, he still enjoyed the pleasures of human women. His progeny were widespread among Central and Eastern Europe.

"You double-crossed him. I'm delighted."

"I knew Jaron would kill Volund," Svarog said, looking out the window. "I never doubted that. And when he did, I was not going to lie among his sacrifices. My sons herded Barak's heretic children here. Then they returned to their homes. I would not waste my men for Volund's mad quest."

"And"—Vasu crept to Svarog's back, leaning his chin on the other angel's shoulder—"now that he is gone, it does leave such a delicious vacuum of power."

Svarog stared out the window into the cold grey Viennese morning. "So it does."

"And what will you do with it?"

"Nothing." Svarog paused. "For now… nothing."

Vasu stepped back and smiled as he shifted away.

"Liar."

Chapter Twenty-nine

AVA AND MALACHI SAT in Damien's study three days later with Damien and Sari. Renata, Max, Rhys, Leo, and Gabriel were also there. Orsala and Mala were still on the way from Prague.

Kostas was nowhere to be found.

"Where is he?" Rhys asked.

Max said, "He's taken his sisters and the women who were in Prague. They disappeared the night after the battle. I don't know where they went. He left Sirius and some of his other men here in the city to try to round up as many of the Grigori children as they could."

"They just left?" Leo asked.

Malachi wondered if Leo was more concerned with Kostas or his lovely sister.

Gabriel cleared his throat. "Trust does not come overnight."

"And what does the council say," Damien asked, "about the battle of Vienna?"

"We won one battle, but some act as if we won the war."

Malachi shook his head but said nothing. He shouldn't have expected miracles, even when they'd appeared in the sky over a major European city.

"And the *kareshta*?" Ava asked.

"They are drafting a mandate," Gabriel said. "It's still being debated, but it looks as though the scribe houses will be joining the hunt to find as many *kareshta* as they can. The elder scribes are not all in agreement, but the elder singers are unanimous. By next week, the daughters of the Fallen will be under the protection of the Irin race."

At least there was that. Malachi knew that ambitious watchers could use that mandate to go after the Fallen, interpreting the "protection of the *kareshta*" to mean freedom from the tyranny of their sires. He exchanged a quick glance with Damien and knew his watcher was thinking the same thing.

"And the free Grigori?" Max asked.

Gabriel's mouth firmed. "Like I said. Trust takes time."

"And us?" Sari asked, reaching for Damien's hand.

Gabriel smiled. "You know politicians. I expect any resolution will be months—if not years—away now that the Irina have their voice in the Library. Until then, our sisters will do as they want."

Max smiled. "Just as they always have."

"Good," Renata said. "I for one have things to do." She looked around the room. "I can't say that it's been fun. But… I'll see you when I see you." Then with one lingering glance at Maxim, Renata left the room.

Max bit his lower lip but said nothing.

Finally Damien spoke. "Are my scribes ready to return to their house?" he asked. "The brothers from Cappadocia have kept our fire burning, but Svarog's sons still live, and we have work to do."

Malachi was ready. So ready. Ready to hide away with Ava. Ready to rid his mind of the nightmares that met him every time he closed his eyes. For the first time since he'd returned, Malachi wanted to forget. But he knew the memories of the tiny lives he'd snuffed out would live with him for the rest of his days. He wanted to flee the city and never return, but he wasn't the only one who mattered. He looked at Ava, and she nodded.

"Ready, Watcher," Rhys said.

"Ready." Leo and Max joined him.

Damien looked at Malachi. He took Ava's hand and nodded.

"We're ready," Ava said. "Very ready to go home."

"And my mate?" Damien asked Sari with a smile.

"I can't leave Ava all alone with you males, can I?" Sari said. "Let's go home, Watcher. As you said, we have work to do."

Ava pressed her face into Malachi's shoulder, and he brought his hand up to cup her head, holding her close.

He wanted to return to Istanbul. But no matter where they were, with Ava, he was home.

Chapter Thirty

"HOPE AND PURPOSE," he said quietly as they lay in bed.

It was early and the first call of the *muezzin* snuck in through the open window. Winter had passed. Istanbul hovered on the edge of summer. They woke every morning together, and Malachi never failed to ask Ava her plans for the day.

She had never been in Istanbul in the spring. It was beautiful. It felt like home.

He brushed the hair from her face, and Ava forced herself to open her eyes. She was lying nestled in the crook of his arm, one hand resting on his chest. She could feel his stubble catch in her hair and the warm, solid beat of his heart under her hand.

"What about hope and purpose?"

"It's what we were missing. What we got back when the Irina returned. And what will make us better as we look for the *kareshta*."

Things were changing. Maybe not as fast as Ava liked, but change was coming. Damien and Sari were regularly in Vienna, though Malachi refused to go back. The watcher and his singer had returned the night before with more news about debates in the council and a new air of vitality in a city that had once lost its passion for anything more than the status quo. Irina were visible again.

There were even a few reports of what Rhys called the Irin baby boom. Families were reuniting. Young scribes and singers meeting and mating. With all the changes, a new generation had begun. Ava hoped it was a safer and healthier generation that what had passed.

For Malachi, the ghosts still lingered. She saw the slight flinch when he spotted a group of children in the street. The shadows when he remembered what he'd been forced to do. The well of grief he carried seemed endless some nights. It pained her far more than any scar he wore on his body.

"The Irin needed hope," she said.

"Everyone needs hope."

Ava said, "And purpose? Protecting humans—"

"Is important. But empty. The Irin lived for a race we could never be a part of."

"Do you have hope?" She would battle an angel for this man. Walk through the darkest forest of grief. Give up her own life if she had to.

But she could not force his eyes to see the hope she kept wrapped in her heart if he didn't want to see.

"Talk to me," she said. "Please."

"I have hope, *reshon*."

"I'm scared sometimes," she confessed. "You scare me."

She pressed on even when she felt his body tense. "Not because of what you might do to others. I trust you more than anything. But what you might do to punish yourself for things you couldn't prevent."

"Ava—"

"It wasn't your fault, Malachi."

"I know that."

"Do you?"

He paused and in the silence, she felt his body begin to relax.

"You told me once that a wound doesn't heal just because it stops bleeding." She lifted her head and propped her chin on his chest. "And you gave me time."

"You needed it."

"And you need it now."

Malachi nodded.

"Okay," she said. "But here's the rule. Only one of us gets to be messed up at a time. Otherwise, we're seriously screwed."

The slow smile she loved spread across his face.

"Deal."

THE SECRET

"STOP it."

"No." She grinned when she said it, clicking the camera when she snapped the picture.

Malachi had on his sunglasses, his face grim. He was in full body-guard mode, every inch the overprotective mate, and he was trying hard not to smile.

"You're supposed to be working, Mrs. Sakarya."

"I told you, you're too handsome to pass by."

She laughed as they followed the crew farther into the village. Dogs ran around their feet, and curious Chinese tourists watched them as the models and makeup artists arranged a small studio in the square.

The fashion shoot was not the kind of job she would normally take, but it was a favor for one of the few editors who'd continued to give Ava work after the eighteen-month break in her schedule. Conveniently, she was from LA. An explanation like "nervous breakdown followed by rehab" was hardly the strangest thing anyone had heard.

She and Malachi had been married in Malibu the month before, with her father and mother in attendance. Lena had been excited, thrilled to inform her friends about her daughter's exotic new husband and home in Istanbul. Jasper had seemed... better. Slightly more stable, but still a giant mess. He'd also lost about ten years to his face, Jaron's glamour dying with him. Luckily, he was in entertainment. Plastic surgery was almost expected.

That would work for now, but Malachi knew a serious conversation was inevitable.

Ava, by virtue of living in Turkey, was now on call for a lot more shoots in Asia, which kept her out of Los Angeles and away from curious eyes. Malachi was pleased. Ava... didn't really care. She still enjoyed her job, but she could take pictures anywhere.

And though they kept the mansion in Southern California, they lived in Istanbul, sharing a house with his four brothers and Damien's mate. It was crowded, but Ava was growing used to it. And when they periodically left for his grandparents' house in Germany or a random photography job, Malachi's people said nothing.

He watched her work, enjoying the sun on his face and the balmy air of Southern China. They were in the hills around Lijiang, and the weather was mild. The people were friendly, but he still kept an eye on the crowd. More were looking at the trio of American models posing with the old man in tribal costume, but a few had their eyes on his mate.

Because she was electric.

The anxiety, worry, and stress of living in danger had drained away, leaving Ava the woman she was born to be. Vibrant and curious. Funny and strong.

She had drawn him back from the edge of darkness more times than he could count. He still avoided children. Still flinched when he heard them laughing. The guilt assaulted him at the most unexpected times. He hated his weakness. Adored her strength.

"It will get better," she told him, over and over again. "We have time."

If Malachi wasn't quite healed yet from the mental anguish of the battle in Vienna, someday he knew he would be.

His mate—his wife—had told him so.

She spun as if she'd known he was thinking about her and captured the smile he couldn't hold back.

"Gotcha, handsome."

HE rolled her to her back and moved down the bed.

"Yes," she panted.

"Yes?"

"Mmmm." Ava arched back, unable to say another word because the thing Malachi was doing should have been illegal. It probably was illegal in some countries.

He smiled against the inside of her thigh. "You have to be quiet."

"When you say you want to take a break from work, you really mean a break."

"I was feeling tense."

"Oh yeah? How's that going?"

"Better." Malachi's tongue circled her belly button and she groaned. "Much better now."

"I live to help work out your tension."

"Such a supportive mate."

He laughed quietly and bit her thigh before he lowered his head again. Then his arm wrapped around her leg and his hand pressed down on her belly and Ava wanted to move, but she couldn't and he—

The door crashed open. "Malachi, did you borrow the—*Gabriel's bloody fist!*"

Ava screamed, and Rhys spun around to face the open doorway as Malachi roared and came off the bed, throwing a blanket over Ava's body as she curled into a ball.

"What are you doing?" he shouted.

"Haven't you heard of locks? Locks, Malachi!"

"Try knocking, you bloody—"

"Get out of our room and close the door!" Ava yelled.

Malachi shoved his brother out of the room and slammed the door shut. Then he locked it and leaned against it for good measure.

She pulled the covers over her head again and tried to get the image of Rhys's face out of her mind. She pulled a pillow over her head too. It didn't help much.

Malachi sat on the edge of the bed. "I'm sorry."

She burst from under the covers and battered him with the pillow. "You. Forgot. To. Lock. The. Door!"

"I'm sorry!" She could tell he was trying not to laugh. "I'm so sorry. I was just… distracted. And there were a couple hundred years when privacy wasn't an issue."

She fell back on the bed and covered herself with the blanket again. "I live in a supernatural fraternity house."

"It's not that bad." He peeled the covers away and spooned her from behind. Ava tried to hide her head under a pillow, but he stole it. "*Canim?*"

"What?"

He kissed the back of her neck. "Does this mean you don't want to —"

"Go back to work before I stun you."

Chapter Thirty-one

Germany

HE WOKE WITH A START, the face of the child in the front of his mind. He sat up and put his head in his hands. This time when Malachi had caught the small body, the boy hadn't dissolved. Instead, his eyes had opened and he'd lunged toward Ava, leaping on her and tearing into her throat before Malachi could catch him.

"Babe?" her sleepy voice asked at his side.

"I'm fine."

"Come here."

"I'm fine."

"Come here anyway."

He lay down next to her and gathered her into his arms.

Maybe it was the winter wind that echoed outside the house, reminding him how it had shrieked through the Stephansplatz. Maybe it was the way the snow fell outside. He hadn't had a dream of the boy in months.

"Kiss me," she whispered.

"*Canim—*"

"It'll make the bad dreams go away. Promise."

Ava smiled up at him, so he kissed her, sinking into her mouth in relief.

She was here. She was alive. No one was after her, and Volund was gone.

His hands ran down her sides, cupping her hips as he brought her closer. And while the cold waves crashed outside, he made love to her.

Long and slow with deliberate strokes that drew her pleasure out and forced his mind back to the beauty that was Ava and their union.

"I love you," she gasped as she came. "I love you so much."

Her mating marks shone on her skin and he read the words he'd written there.

I am for Ava.

Not for nightmares and death. Not for guilt and recrimination.

"For you," he said into her mouth. "I love you."

She held him after the pleasure wracked his body. Wrapped her arms around him and held on.

For Ava.

He was for Ava.

Chapter Thirty-two

"YOU'RE BETTER," AVA SAID, smiling at her grandmother.

The woman looked more like her sister than her grandmother. The staff didn't ask questions, but she could see their inquisitive looks.

"A little more every day," Maheen said.

She'd asked Ava to call her by her new name the first time she'd visited after Jaron's death.

Why Maheen?

Someone called me that once. I liked it.

Ava didn't ask more. If her grandmother had chosen a new name for a new life, it was more than understandable.

She still lived in the hospital. Ava guessed she would live there for some time.

"You don't look like me," Maheen said.

"No. The eyes. I think that's the only thing."

"Grigora are more beautiful than human women," she said, her eyes drifting. "It's good you look human."

Maheen was not an easy person to talk with. Brittle pain leached into the air around her, though Ava could occasionally see echoes of the woman she might have been before her rape and binding to Volund. She hated Malachi's presence, and it had taken more than a little persuading to let her visit Maheen alone.

Malachi didn't trust her. Neither, if Ava were completely honest, did she.

The hospital said she hadn't been violent since the night almost a year ago when she'd started screaming and collapsed. She'd beaten her hands so badly they'd required surgery. She still struggled to hold one of the paintbrushes she was now allowed, but she was healing.

Ava hoped it was more than her hands.

"Is the scribe with you?" she asked.

"Yep. Waiting in the living room downstairs."

She nodded, rocking back and forth a little in her seat.

"He won't come up."

"They were the monsters in the night, you know?"

"Who?"

"Irin scribes. My brothers would tell me stories. If I saw one in the market, I had to run. They never let me go anywhere alone." She laughed. "Except…"

Ava waited for a long while, but Maheen had drifted again. It was a pretty common occurrence.

"Grandmother?"

"You shouldn't call me that." Her head jerked toward the door. "You know they watch me."

Did they? Ava made a mental note to check. She couldn't see any cameras, but you never knew. Maheen was highly paranoid.

"Is he here again?" Maheen asked. "Did you bring him?"

"Jasper?" Ava hesitated to say. Maheen had refused to see Jasper the other two times they'd brought him. Ava kept convincing her father to give his mother another chance, but she could see him spiral each time his mother rejected his attempts to speak with her. According to Maheen's doctor, Jasper paid the bills, but he hadn't visited since Ava—*Maheen* had attacked him three years before.

"Yeah," Ava finally said. "He… He's waiting with Malachi. If you want—"

"Not today."

Not *today*.

Not *no*. Not *never*.

Not today. Which, in Ava's mind, meant there was still hope. Maybe it was a small hope, but that was better than nothing.

"Do you know anything about gemstones?" Maheen asked.

"Gemstones?" Ava frowned. "Not much."

"I studied history. I couldn't go to the university, but my father brought me books. Gemstones have fascinating history. Mythology…"

Her eyes drifted to the wall over Ava's head. They were sitting at a table having lunch in her room. Though her grandmother was allowed to walk throughout the estate now that her rages and seizures had calmed down, Maheen still preferred to live in isolation.

Her mind was a raw wound.

She resisted any attempts to learn shielding, explaining to Ava that she was used to the voices and it let her know when someone was approaching. The shield Jaron had forced over her at times had been stifling. She said it felt like a prison, and she didn't want another.

"Do you think you'll ever want to leave here?" Ava asked.

"I'll have to someday." She took a deep breath. "I've been preparing myself for months now. I've been here five years. I can only be somewhere for six or seven before they start to notice.

"You have time."

"It might be better…"

Ava waited, but Maheen was staring out the window now.

"No one's going to force you out," Ava said. "And there are places you can go if you want to leave."

Ava was thinking of the various scribe houses and libraries that had begun to open to Irina who wanted to rejoin Irin society, and a few *kareshta* who had found their way to them. She didn't know if her grandmother would be open to it, but she could try.

Maheen shook her head. "Not now. Not yet."

"Okay."

Their eyes met over the pot of honey-sweetened tea Maheen had requested.

"Thank you," her grandmother told her. "I know I'm not the easiest person to visit. I didn't even bake cookies."

Ava saw one of those rare glimpses in that moment. Fire and intelligence and humor. The spark of life that had woken an archangel and drawn the lethal attention of a predator.

"I know," Ava said. "You're really falling down on the grandmother thing."

Maheen barked out a short laugh. "I was a horrible mother too."

Her smile fell.

She didn't talk about Jasper.

"What do you do," Ava asked, "when you don't have visitors? Do you paint a lot? I like your canvases."

Maheen waved to a row of them stacked against a wall. "Take them. As many as you like. I run out of room."

"Thanks."

"I paint." Maheen nodded. "I read. I can enjoy music again. But mostly…"

She took a deep breath and closed her eyes, an expression of utter peace falling across her face.

"I sleep."

JASPER took a deep drag from another cigarette as they sat at the cafe in Toulouse. His coffee cup was empty. Ava was just glad it wasn't a wineglass. After all, it was only ten in the morning. Spring had come early, so they were enjoying the morning sun as Malachi talked on his phone in the small park nearby. Talked and paced. Paced and scanned the streets.

"That guy ever calm down?" Jasper asked.

"Kinda." She sipped her café au lait. "Not really."

"I'm starting to think he's more paranoid than Carl."

"Old habits are hard to break."

Jasper grunted. "I'm not complaining if it keeps you safe."

"It does." She nudged the ashtray with her own cup. "Is this all you're doing lately?"

"It's… ah, hell." He looked sheepish. "I'm trying. Whatever your man said to Luis sent him on some kind of crusade, but you know me, baby girl. I ain't ever gonna be father of the year."

"I just want you healthy."

He was. He would be for a long, long time, as far as any of them knew. Orsala had said nothing in Irina oral tradition spoke of humans with as much angelic blood as Jasper carried, and Rhys couldn't find anything in the archives either. The glamour Jaron had placed over Jasper had disappeared, leaving him looking more like her brother than her father.

He didn't ask questions. Mostly, Ava thought, because he didn't want to know the answers.

"How was she this time?" He scratched at the stubble on his chin.

"She's better," Ava said. "Thanks for coming. Again. I keep hoping—"

"It's cool, Ava." He nodded. "Yeah, you never know. I'm glad she's better. Is the uh…?" His finger lifted to tap at his temple. "That any better?"

"Not for her. Not yet. But I'm better." She glanced at Malachi. "A lot better."

Jasper could pretend they were normal. For now. But that wouldn't and didn't stop Ava from speaking the truth.

Words, she'd learned through experience, had immense power.

He'd have to learn eventually.

For now, they could drink their coffee and watch the flowers break open on the trees. Watch new life starting again and ignore the quickly passing years.

"I love you, baby girl." Jasper slid an open hand across the table. "Best thing I ever did in my life."

Ava put her palm in his. "Love you too, Jasper."

He wasn't much of a father, but he was hers. And Ava had realized he was the only part of her old life that would last into the new.

Malachi. Jasper. Maheen.

They would be her family.

She saw the car pull up and Luis step out, eyes flicking nervously between Jasper and Malachi.

"Do not know why your guy makes him so nervous." Jasper stubbed out his cigarette and patted his pockets. "I've seen Luis scare dudes twice Malachi's size, and yet that guy…" He shook his head. "No idea."

"Oh, you know," Ava said, trying to suppress the nervous smile. "It's probably the tattoos."

Jasper stood. "Ava, he's in the music business. Tattoos are like cardigans to us."

Ava threw her head back and laughed. Jasper took the opportunity to haul her to her feet to he could wrap his arms around her and squeeze. She hugged him back and relished the small kiss he planted on her head.

"Okay." His voice was rough when he let go. "Back to the studio."

"I'll see you in a couple of months."

"You better."

He was patting his pockets again. "I know I put it in here…"

"What?"

"Ah." He plucked a small USB drive out of the pocket on his chest. "There it is."

He handed it to her, bent down and kissed her cheek before he walked toward the car.

"Jasper?" She looked at the drive and took a few steps toward him. "Dad!"

He turned, grinning. Mischief lit his eyes. "What?"

"What is this?"

The smile turned wistful. "I finally got it right."

"Got what right?"

"It's for you, Ava." He slipped on his sunglasses. "It's your song."

Ava gripped the precious piece of plastic in her hand and watched him drive away.

"CANIM?" Malachi peeked his head through the door of their room in Istanbul. Ava pulled off the earphones and set them to the side of the desk where she had her books spread out.

"Hey," she said. "What's up?"

He watched her, his heart shining out of his eyes. "Your song again?"

"It's beautiful."

"It is." He walked over and sat on the bed. "It's the best thing he's ever written."

"Yeah." She smiled and spread her hand over the history book she'd been reading. "It is."

She fell silent and he watched her.

"You have a secret," he whispered. "I can see it in your eyes."

"You must be magic."

"You have no idea."

She didn't say anything for a moment. Malachi just waited for her to speak.

"Do you know anything about gemstones?"

"Not much," he said. "Is this a hint?"

"No, I don't need a ring from you." She closed the book and went to him, straddling his lap so they were face-to-face. "Jasper is an ancient stone," she said, stroking her fingers along the close-cropped hair near his neck. "It's used for protection."

"Is that so?" he whispered.

"Yes." She laid her head on his shoulder as his arms came around her. "It's supposed to keep away evil spirits."

His hands tightened on her hips.

"She gave him the name Jasper to protect him." Ava closed her eyes and released a sigh. "She did it to protect her child."

Chapter Thirty-three

MALACHI LAY ON THE PICNIC blanket in Yıldız Park, his face soaking in the afternoon sun as Ava combed her hand through his hair and took pictures with her phone. A group of children shrieked nearby, the laughter almost piercing his eardrums.

"What are they doing?" he murmured.

"I think there's a squirrel." She laughed. "Uh-oh. And now there's a dog."

"*Özel dilerim!*" Malachi heard one mother call, apologizing for the racket.

"*Bir şey değil!*" Ava reassured the harried mother with a laugh. *It's nothing.*

She had picked up the language quickly after they'd moved to Istanbul. After living there over a year, she chatted with the vendor at the market and ordered from her favorite cafe with ease. Ava was still fascinated by languages, but most of her study was now focused on learning everything she could about the Old Language, particularly spells—like those Vasu had given her—that might have been lost.

She and Sari also corresponded regularly with Kyra, though the *kareshta* still lived in hiding.

He kept his eyes closed and imagined the scene as the dog barked and the children ran laughing into the trees. Their shouts and laughter had finally become a comfort. He loved his city, and human families were a part of it. A tumble of accents and languages flowed along the paths, though most of the visitors in the middle of the week were local. He heard a teacher instructing a drawing class several meters away, but no one came close enough to bother them.

Damien and Sari were away from the scribe house, visiting Orsala, who had taken residence in Cappadocia with Mala. The quiet scholars in Göreme didn't quite know what to do with the fierce Irina warrior, but Mala would not leave Orsala, so they learned to stay out of her way.

Officially, Malachi was in charge. But since Rhys was at the house, cranky because the air-conditioning was out again, Malachi was more than happy to escape. He and Ava had snuck out with a picnic basket, Leo giving them rude hand gestures as he waited on the phone with the repair company.

"Malachi?"

"Hmm?"

"There's something…"

He heard the catch in her voice and opened his eyes. She looked upset. "What is it?"

Ava shook her head. "I don't know how to tell you. I didn't expect…"

"Ava, what's wrong?"

Her cheeks were flushed. "Everyone said it wasn't likely, so—"

"What are you talking about?"

"I'm pregnant."

His heart skipped a beat.

"I know," she whispered, "with everything, it's not the best time. You still have concerns. I know that. And the dreams still… I need you to be happy."

"Ava." His heart was so full he thought it would pound out of his chest.

"I need you to be okay with this because I'm scared to death."

He wanted to reassure her. Wanted to tell her what a gift she'd given him, but the words wouldn't come.

So Malachi turned his face to her belly, wrapped his arms around her waist, and kissed the tiny life that grew inside.

Impossible, improbable life.

A miracle.

She bent down and leaned her head on his. "You're happy?"

He nodded. Then Malachi rose and took her in his arms, forcing himself to take deep breaths. It wasn't enough. He could feel tears in the corners of his eyes, but he could not be ashamed of them. He held Ava in his arms and let himself smile.

"You're happy," she said on a sigh, wrapping her arms tight around his neck.

He pulled away and kissed her face until she was laughing. Then he wrapped his arms around her and held her close, the wonder of what they had become a vibrant song in his heart.

"Sometimes, *canum*, words are not enough."

End of Book Three.

February 20, 2015

To my readers,

I hope you enjoyed *The Secret*.

Sometimes it's very difficult to pinpoint where an idea comes from or when inspiration strikes.

For the *Irin Chronicles*, it is not.

This series grew from a single dream on a winter afternoon. It was fed by music and the intoxicating sights, sounds, and smells of Turkey and Israel and Austria. It grew as I explored my love of language and history and myth, along with the intricacies of love and family and faith.

I love this series. (Which is not to say that I haven't hated it a few times too.)

While the *Irin Chronicles* was originally envisioned as a trilogy featuring Ava and Malachi, it grew into a world that I can't quite leave behind yet. There are too many stories left to tell. So while Ava and Malachi's journey has come to an end, the Irin world will continue.

I hope you look forward to visiting again.

Thank you so much for reading,
Elizabeth

For more information about my work, to join my mailing list for new releases, or access bonus content, please visit:
ElizabethHunterWrites.com

ACKNOWLEDGEMENTS

Many thanks to my family, who had to suffer through the rather grouchy version of me who wrote these books. Writing magic is hard, readers. Thank goodness the people who love me put up with my mood swings. Special thanks to Genevieve and Kelli, who bear the brunt. (A round or two at Bourbon & Branch is on me.)

Thanks to extraordinary beta readers like Sarah and Sandra and Iriet, who give me such important feedback from a reader perspective. What sounds right in my head doesn't always make sense on the page. Thank you for not letting me get away with anything. Thank you to writer friends like Grace Draven, Colleen Vanderlinden, and Michele Scott, who understand and also put up with a lot of my whining.

A special thanks to the ever-talented Killian McRae for being my go-to expert on all things Turkish and an enthusiastic fan of Malachi and Ava. Your help was invaluable, and we need to plan a trip to Istanbul when we're actually in the city together.

Thanks to the city of Vienna for its coffee, its hospitality, and its truly excellent airport. A special thanks to the wonderful staff of the Guesthouse Vienna, which was my home away from home while researching this book. To the cooks at Haas & Haas, thank you for one great breakfast after another. To that cute guy outside the Albertina on Thursday afternoon, thanks for wearing those socks with your very conservative suit. It was kind of a glum day and you gave me a smile. And I'm just going to mention the coffee again, because it really is amazing and wonderful.

To my agents, Jane Dystel and Lauren Abramo, thank you for all your hard work on my behalf. Thanks to the talented Zachary Webber, the voice of the *Irin Chronicles* who makes my words come alive for all my audiobook listeners. Thanks to the folks at Damonza, who put up with me being very, *very* picky about this cover. And a hearty and well-deserved thank-you to my editor Anne Victory, a true professional in a sea of… less than professionals. You make me look *good*.

To all my publishing partners who make this business possible and help bring my words to readers, thank you so much. To the retailers, to the magazine editors and reviewers, to the bloggers and forum administrators, thank you all.

We live in an extraordinary time for writers. I'm very blessed and proud to be a part of this business. Let us never forget that it's about the stories.

"He has made everything beautiful in its time. He has also set eternity in the hearts of men; yet no one can fathom what God has done from beginning to end." —Ecclesiastes 3:11

ELIZABETH HUNTER is a contemporary fantasy, paranormal romance, and contemporary romance writer. She is a graduate of the University of Houston Honors College and a former English teacher. She once substitute taught a kindergarten class but decided that middle school was far less frightening. Thankfully, people now pay her to write books and eighth graders everywhere rejoice.

She currently lives in Central California with her son, two dogs, many plants, and a sadly empty fish tank. She is the author of the Elemental Mysteries and Elemental World series, the Cambio Springs series, the Irin Chronicles, and other works of fiction.

Website: ElizabethHunterWrites.com

E-mail: elizabethhunterwrites@gmail.com.

Twitter: @E__Hunter

Printed in Great Britain
by Amazon